Engaged or Estranged?

"Do you want this ring back?"

"Certainly not," he replied, forcibly, with a dark flush spreading over his face.

"Then—you love me?" she whispered.

"Yes—I love you," he returned, deliberately. "And in spite of all you say—very probably more than you love me ... But you, like all women, make love and its expression the sole object of life. Carley, I have been concerned with keeping my body from the grave and my soul from hell."

"But—dear—you're well now?" she returned, with trembling lips.

"Yes, I've almost pulled out."

"Then what is wrong?"

"Wrong? With me or you?" he queried.

"What is wrong between us? There is something."

"Carley, a man who has been on the verge—as I have been—seldom or never comes back to happiness. But perhaps ..."

HarperPaperbacks by Zane Grey

THE DUDE RANGER
THE LOST WAGON TRAIN
THE MAN OF THE FOREST
THE RAINBOW TRAIL
WILDFIRE
THE BORDER LEGION
SUNSET PASS
30,000 ON THE HOOF
WANDERER OF THE WASTELAND
TWIN SOMBREROS
BOULDER DAM
THE MYSTERIOUS RIDER
THE DEER STALKER
THE TRAIL DRIVER
THE DESERT OF WHEAT
THE U. P. TRAIL
TO THE LAST MAN
WESTERN UNION
THUNDER MOUNTAIN
CODE OF THE WEST
ARIZONA AMES
THE THUNDERING HERD
HORSE HEAVEN HILL
VALLEY OF WILD HORSES
ROGUE RIVER FEUD
WILDERNESS TREK
BLACK MESA
THE VANISHING AMERICAN
CAPTIVES OF THE DESERT
THE SPIRIT OF THE BORDER
ROBBERS' ROOST
UNDER THE TONTO RIM

WILD HORSE MESA
THE MAVERICK QUEEN
THE LIGHT OF WESTERN STARS
MAJESTY'S RANCHO
WYOMING
THE CALL OF THE CANYON
FORLORN RIVER
RAIDERS OF SPANISH PEAKS
THE DAY OF THE BEAST
THE REEF GIRL
THE SHEPHERD OF GUADALOUPE
LOST PUEBLO
STRANGER FROM THE TONTO
KNIGHTS OF THE RANGE
WEST OF THE PECOS
SHADOW ON THE TRAIL
RIDERS OF THE PURPLE SAGE
STAIRS OF SAND
BETTY ZANE
THE ARIZONA CLAN
THE HASH KNIFE OUTFIT
THE HERITAGE OF THE DESERT
THE DRIFT FENCE
FIGHTING CARAVANS
THE LONE STAR RANGER
TAPPAN'S BURRO
THE FUGITIVE TRAIL
THE RANGER AND OTHER STORIES
BLUE FEATHER AND OTHER
    STORIES
DESERT GOLD
NEVADA

ZANE GREY

THE CALL OF THE CANYON

HarperPaperbacks
A Division of HarperCollins*Publishers*

HarperPaperbacks   *A Division of* HarperCollins*Publishers*
10 East 53rd Street, New York, N.Y. 10022

THE CALL OF THE CANYON. Copyright © 1921, 1922, 1924 by Zane Grey. Copyright renewed 1949, 1950, 1952 by Lina Elise Grey.

THE MYSTERIOUS RIDER. Copyright © 1921 by Harper & Brothers. Copyright renewed 1949 by Lina Elise Grey.

THE CALL OF THE CANYON/THE MYSTERIOUS RIDER. Copyright © 1995 by Lina Elise Grey.

Cover art courtesy of H. Armstrong Roberts, Inc. and the Bettman Archive

First HarperPaperbacks Zane Grey double western printing: May 1995

The Call of the Canyon was published by HarperPaperbacks in March 1992. *The Mysterious Rider* was published by HarperPaperbacks in January 1991.

Printed in the United States of America

HarperPaperbacks and colophon are trademarks of HarperCollins*Publishers*

10 9 8 7 6 5 4 3 2 1

CHAPTER

1

WHAT subtle strange message had come to her out of the West? Carley Burch laid the letter in her lap and gazed dreamily through the window.

It was a day typical of early April in New York, rather cold and gray, with steely sunlight. Spring breathed in the air, but the women passing along Fifty-seventh Street wore furs and wraps. She heard the distant clatter of an L train and then the hum of a motor car. A hurdy-gurdy jarred into the interval of quiet.

"Glenn has been gone over a year," she mused, "three months over a year—and of all his strange letters this seems the strangest yet."

She lived again, for the thousandth time, the last moments she had spent with him. It had been on New Year's Eve, 1918. They had called upon friends who were staying at the McAlpin, in a suite on the twenty-first floor overlooking Broadway. And when the last quarter hour of that eventful and tragic year began slowly to pass with the low swell of whistles and bells, Carley's friends had discreetly left her alone with her lover, at the open window, to watch and hear the old year out, the new year in.

Glenn Kilbourne had returned from France early that fall, shell-shocked and gassed, and otherwise incapacitated for service in the army—a wreck of his former sterling self and in many unaccountable ways a stranger to her. Cold, silent, haunted by something, he had made her miserable with his aloofness. But as the bells began to ring out the year that had been his ruin Glenn had drawn her close, tenderly, passionately, and yet strangely, too.

"Carley, look and listen!" he had whispered.

Under them stretched the great long white flare of Broadway, with its snow-covered length glittering under a myriad of electric lights. Sixth Avenue swerved away to the right, a less brilliant lane of blanched snow. The L trains crept along like huge fire-eyed serpents. The hum of the ceaseless moving line of motor cars drifted upward faintly, almost drowned in the rising clamor of the street. Broadway's gay and thoughtless crowds surged to and fro, from that height merely a thick stream of black figures, like contending columns of ants on the march. And everywhere the monstrous electric signs flared up vivid in white and red and green, and dimmed and paled, only to flash up again.

Ring out the Old! Ring in the New! Carley had poignantly felt the sadness of the one, the promise of the other. As one by one the siren factory whistles opened up with deep, hoarse bellows, the clamor of the street and the ringing of the bells were lost in a volume of continuous sound that swelled on high into a magnificent roar. It was the voice of a city—

of a nation. It was the voice of a people crying out the strife and the agony of the year—pealing forth a prayer for the future.

Glenn had put his lips to her ear: "It's like the voice in my soul!" Never would she forget the shock of that. And how she had stood spellbound, enveloped in the mighty volume of sound no longer discordant, but full of great, pregnant melody, until the white ball burst upon the tower of the Times Building, showing the bright figures 1919.

The new year had not been many minutes old when Glenn Kilbourne had told her he was going west to try to recover his health.

Carley roused out of her memories to take up the letter that had so perplexed her. It bore the postmark, Flagstaff, Arizona. She reread it with slow pondering thoughtfulness.

West Fork,
March 25.

Dear Carley:

It does seem my neglect in writing you is unpardonable. I used to be a pretty fair correspondent, but in that as in other things I have changed.

One reason I have not answered sooner is because your letter was so sweet and loving that it made me feel an ungrateful and unappreciative wretch. Another is that this life I now lead does not induce writing. I am outdoors all day, and when I get back to this cabin at night I am too tired for anything but bed.

Your imperious questions I must answer— and that *must,* of course, is a third reason why I have delayed my reply. First, you ask, "Don't you love me any more as you used to?" . . . Frankly, I do not. I am sure my old love for you, before I went to France, was selfish, thoughtless, sentimental, and boyish. I am a man now. And my love for you is different. Let me assure you that it has been about all left to me of what is noble and beautiful. Whatever the changes in me for the worse, my love for you, at least, has grown better, finer, purer.

And now for your second question, "Are you coming home as soon as you are well again?" . . . Carley, I *am* well. I have delayed telling you this because I knew you would expect me to rush back East with the telling. But—the fact is, Carley, I am not coming—just yet. I wish it were possible for me to make you understand. For a long time I seem to have been frozen within. You know when I came back from France I couldn't talk. It's almost as bad as that now. Yet all that I was then seems to have changed again. It is only fair to you to tell you that, as I feel now, I hate the city, I hate people, and particularly I hate that dancing, drinking, lounging set you chase with. I don't want to come East until I am over that, you know. . . . Suppose I never get over it?—Well, Carley, you can free yourself from me by one word that I could never utter. I could never break our engagement. During the hell I went through in the war my attachment to you saved me from moral ruin, if it did not from perfect honor and fidelity. This is another thing I despair of making you understand. And in the chaos I've wandered through *since* the war my love for you was my only anchor. You never guessed, did you, that I lived on your letters until I got well. And now the fact that I might get along without them is no discredit to their charm or to you.

It is all so hard to put in words, Carley. To lie down with death and get up with death was nothing. To face one's degradation was nothing. But to come home—an incomprehensibly changed man—and to see my old life as strange as if it were the new life of another planet—to try to slip into the old groove—well, no words of mine can tell you how utterly impossible it was.

My old job was not open to me, even if I had been able to work. The government that I fought for left me to starve, or to die of my maladies like a dog, for all it cared. I could not live on your money, Carley. My people are poor, as you know. So there was nothing for me to do but to borrow a little money from my friends and to come West. I'm glad I had the courage to come. What this West is I'll never try to tell you, because, loving the luxury and excitement and glitter of the city as you do, you'd think I was crazy.

Getting on here, in my condition, was as hard as trench life. But now, Carley—something has come to me out of the West. That, too, I am unable to put into words. Maybe I can give you an inkling of it. I'm strong enough to chop wood all day. No man or woman passes my cabin in a month. But I am never lonely. I love these vast red canyon walls towering above me. And the silence is so sweet. Think of the hellish din that filled my ears. Even now—sometimes, the brook here changes its babbling murmur to the roar of war. I never understood anything of the meaning of nature until I lived under these looming stone walls and whispering pines.

So, Carley, try to understand me, or at least be kind. You know they came very near writing, "Gone west!" after my name, and considering *that*, this "Out West" signifies for me a very fortunate difference. A tremendous difference! For the present I'll let well enough alone.

Adios. Write soon. Love from

Glenn.

Carley's second reaction to the letter was a sudden upflashing desire to see her lover—to go out West and find him. Impulses with her were rather rare and inhibited, but this one made her tremble. If Glenn was well again he must have vastly changed from the moody, stone-faced, and haunted-eyed man who had so worried and distressed her. He had embarrassed her, too, for sometimes, in her home, meeting young men there who had not gone into the service, he had seemed to retreat into himself, singularly aloof, as if his world was not theirs.

Again, with eager eyes and quivering lips, she read the letter. It contained words that lifted her heart. Her starved love greedily absorbed them. In them she had excuse for any resolve that might bring Glenn closer to her. And she pondered over this longing to go to him.

Carley had the means to come and go and live as she liked. She did not remember her father, who had died when she was a child. Her mother had left her in the care of a sister, and before the war they had divided their time between New York and Europe, the Adirondacks and Florida. Carley had gone in for Red Cross and relief work with more of sincerity than most of her set. But she was really not used to making any decision as definite and important as that of going out West alone. She had never been farther west than Jersey City; and her conception of the West was a hazy one of vast plains and rough mountains, squalid towns, cattle herds, and uncouth ill-clad men.

So she carried the letter to her aunt, a rather slight woman with a kindly face and shrewd eyes, and who appeared somewhat given to old-fashioned garments.

"Aunt Mary, here's a letter from Glenn," said Carley. "It's more of a stumper than usual. Please read it."

"Dear me! you look upset," replied the aunt, mildly, and, adjusting her spectacles, she took the letter.

Carley waited impatiently for the perusal, conscious of inward forces coming more and more to the aid of her impulse to go West. Her aunt paused once to murmur how glad she was that Glenn had gotten well. Then she read on to the close.

"Carley, that's a fine letter," she said, fervently. "Do you see through it?"

"No, I don't," replied Carley. "That's why I asked you to read it."

"Do you still love Glenn as you used to— before—"

"Why, Aunt Mary!" exclaimed Carley, in surprise.

"Excuse me, Carley, if I'm blunt. But the fact is young women of modern times are very different from my kind when I was a girl. You haven't acted as though you pined for Glenn. You gad around almost the same as ever."

"What's a girl to do?" protested Carley.

"You are twenty-six years old, Carley," retorted Aunt Mary.

"Suppose I am. I'm as young—as I ever was."

"Well, let's not argue about modern girls and modern times. We never get anywhere," returned her aunt, kindly. "But I can tell you something of what Glenn Kilbourne means in that letter—if you want to hear it."

"I do—indeed."

"The war did something horrible to Glenn aside from wrecking his health. Shell-shock, they said! I don't understand that. Out of his mind, they said! But that never was true. Glenn was as sane as I am, and, my dear, that's pretty sane, I'll have you remember. But he must have suffered some terrible blight to his spirit—some blunting of his soul. For months after he returned he walked as one in a trance. Then came a change. He grew restless. Perhaps that change was for the better. At least it showed he'd roused. Glenn saw you and your friends and the life you lead, and all the present, with eyes from which the scales had dropped. He saw what was *wrong*. He never said so to me, but I knew it. It wasn't only to get well that he went West. It was to get *away*. . . and, Carley Burch, if your happiness depends on him you had better be up and doing—or you'll *lose* him!"

"Aunt Mary!" gasped Carley.

"I mean it. That letter shows how near he came to the Valley of the Shadow—and how he has become a man. . . . If I were you I'd go out West. Surely there must be a place where it would be all right for you to stay."

"Oh, yes," replied Carley, eagerly. "Glenn wrote me there was a lodge where people went in nice weather—right down in the canyon not far from his place. Then, of course, the town—Flagstaff— isn't far. . . . Aunt Mary, I think I'll go."

"I would. You're certainly wasting your time here."

"But I could only go for a visit," rejoined Carley, thoughtfully. "A month, perhaps six weeks, if I could stand it."

"Seems to me if you can stand New York you could stand that place," said Aunt Mary, dryly.

"The idea of staying away from New York—any length of time—why, I couldn't do it! But I can stay out there long enough to bring Glenn back with me."

"That may take you longer than you think," replied her aunt, with a gleam in her shrewd eyes. "If you want my advice you will surprise Glenn. Don't write him—don't give him a chance to—well—to suggest courteously that you'd better not come just yet. I don't like his words 'just yet.' "

"Auntie, you're—rather—more than blunt," said Carley, divided between resentment and amaze. "Glenn would be simply wild to have me come."

"Maybe he would. Has he ever asked you?"

"No-o—come to think of it, he hasn't," replied Carley, reluctantly. "Aunt Mary, you hurt my feelings."

"Well, child, I'm glad to learn your feelings are hurt," returned the aunt. "I'm sure, Carley, that underneath all this—this blasé ultra something you've acquired, there's a real heart. Only you must hurry and listen to it—or—"

"Or what?" queried Carley.

Aunt Mary shook her gray head sagely. "Never mind what. Carley, I'd like your idea of the most significant thing in Glenn's letter."

"Why, his love for me, of course!" replied Carley.

"Naturally you think that. But I don't. What struck me most were his words, 'out of the West.' . . . Carley, you'd do well to ponder over them."

"I will," rejoined Carley, positively. "I'll do more. I'll go out to his wonderful West and see what he meant by them."

Carley Burch possessed in full degree the prevailing modern craze for speed. She loved a motor car ride at sixty miles an hour along a smooth, straight road, or, better, on the level seashore of Ormond, where on moonlit nights the white blanched sand seemed to flash toward her. Therefore quite to her taste was the Twentieth Century Limited which was hurtling her on the way to Chicago. The unceasingly smooth and even rush of the train satisfied something in her. An old lady sitting in an adjoining seat with a companion amused Carley by the remark: "I wish we didn't go so fast. People nowadays haven't time to draw a comfortable breath. Suppose we should run off the track!"

Carley had no fear of express trains, or motor cars, or transatlantic liners; in fact, she prided herself in not being afraid of anything. But she wondered if this was not the false courage of association with a crowd. Before this enterprise at hand she could not remember anything she had undertaken alone. Her thrills seemed to be in abeyance to the end of her journey. That night her sleep was permeated with the steady low whirring of the wheels. Once, roused by a jerk, she lay awake in the darkness while the thought came to her that she and all her fellow passengers were really at the mercy of the engineer. Who was he, and did he stand at his throttle keen and vigilant, thinking of the lives entrusted to him? Such thoughts vaguely annoyed Carley, and she dismissed them.

A long half-day wait in Chicago was a tedious preliminary to the second part of her journey. But at last she found herself aboard the California Limited, and went to bed with a relief quite a stranger to her. The glare of the sun under the curtain awakened her. Propped up on her pillows, she looked out at apparently endless green fields or pastures, dotted now and then with little farmhouses and tree-skirted villages. This country, she thought, must be the prairie land she remembered lay west of the Mississippi.

Later, in the dining car, the steward smilingly answered her question: "This is Kansas, and those green fields out there are the wheat that feeds the nation."

Carley was not impressed. The color of the short wheat appeared soft and rich, and the boundless fields stretched away monotonously. She had not known there was so much flat land in the world, and she imagined it might be a fine country for automobile roads. When she got back to her seat she drew the blinds down and read her magazines. Then tiring of that, she went back to the observation car. Carley was accustomed to attracting attention, and did not resent it, unless she was annoyed. The train evidently had a full complement of passengers, who, as far as Carley could see, were people not of her station in life. The glare from the many windows, and the rather crass interest of several men, drove her back to her own section. There she discovered that some one had drawn up her window shades. Carley promptly pulled them down and settled herself comfortably. Then she heard a woman speak, not particularly low: "I thought people traveled west to see the country." And a man replied, rather dryly. "Wal, not always." His companion went on: "If that girl was mine I'd let down her skirt." The man laughed and replied: "Martha, you're shore behind the times. Look at the pictures in the magazines."

Such remarks amused Carley, and later she took advantage of an opportunity to notice her neighbors. They appeared a rather quaint old couple, reminding her of the natives of country towns in the Adirondacks. She was not amused, however, when another of her woman neighbors, speaking low, referred to her as a "lunger." Carley appreciated the fact that she was pale, but she assured herself that there ended any possible resemblance she might have to a consumptive. And she was somewhat pleased to hear this woman's male companion forcibly voice her own convictions. In fact, he was nothing if not admiring.

Kansas was interminably long to Carley, and she went to sleep before riding out of it. Next morning she found herself looking out at the rough gray and black land of New Mexico. She searched the horizon for mountains, but there did not appear to be any. She received a vague, slow-dawning impression that was hard to define. She did not like the country, though that was not the impression which eluded her. Bare gray flats, low scrub-fringed hills, bleak cliffs, jumble after jumble of rocks, and occasionally a long vista down a valley, somehow compelling— these passed before her gaze until she tired of them. Where was the West Glenn had written about? One thing seemed sure, and it was that every mile of this crude country brought her nearer to him. This recurring thought gave Carley all the pleasure she had felt so far in this endless ride. It struck her that England or France could be dropped down into New Mexico and scarcely noticed.

By and by the sun grew hot, the train wound slowly and creakingly upgrade, the car became full of dust, all of which was disagreeable to Carley. She dozed on her pillow for hours, until she was stirred by a passenger crying out, delightedly: "Look! Indians!"

Carley looked, not without interest. As a child she had read about Indians, and memory returned images both colorful and romantic. From the car window she espied dusty flat barrens, low squat mud houses, and queer-looking little people, children naked or extremely ragged and dirty, women in loose garments with flares of red, and men in white man's garb, slovenly and motley. All these strange individuals stared apathetically as the train slowly passed.

"Indians," muttered Carley, incredulously. "Well, if they are the noble red people, my illusions are dispelled." She did not look out of the window again, not even when the brakeman called out the remarkable name of Albuquerque.

Next day Carley's languid attention quickened to the name of Arizona, and to the frowning red walls of rock, and to the vast rolling stretches of cedar-dotted land. Nevertheless, it affronted her. This was no country for people to live in, and so far as she could see it was indeed uninhabited. Her sensations were not, however, limited to sight. She became aware of unfamiliar disturbing little shocks or vibrations in her ear drums, and after that a disagreeable bleeding of the nose. The porter told her this was owing to the altitude. Thus, one thing and another kept Carley most of the time away from the window, so that she really saw very little of the country. From what she had seen she drew the conviction that she had not missed much. At sunset she deliberately gazed out to discover what an Arizona sunset was like. Just a pale yellow flare! She had seen better than that above the Palisades. Not until reaching Winslow did she realize how near she was to her journey's end and that she would arrive at Flagstaff after dark. She grew conscious of nervousness. Suppose Flagstaff was like these other queer little towns!

Not only once, but several times before the train slowed down for her destination did Carley wish she had sent Glenn word to meet her. And when, presently, she found herself standing out in the dark, cold, windy night before a dim-lit railroad station she more than regretted her decision to surprise Glenn. But that was too late and she must make the best of her poor judgment.

Men were passing to and fro on the platform, some of whom appeared to be very dark of skin and eye, and were probably Mexicans. At length an expressman approached Carley, soliciting patronage. He took her bags and, depositing them in a wagon, he pointed up the wide street: "One block up an' turn. Hotel Wetherford." Then he drove off. Carley followed, carrying her small satchel. A cold wind, driving the dust, stung her face as she crossed the street to a high sidewalk that extended along the block. There were lights in the stores and on the corners, yet she seemed impressed by a dark, cold, windy bigness. Many people, mostly men, were passing up and down, and there were motor cars everywhere. No one paid any attention to her. Gaining the corner of the block, she turned, and was relieved to see the hotel sign. As she entered the lobby a clicking of pool balls and the discordant rasp of a phonograph assailed her ears. The expressman set down her bags and left Carley standing there. The clerk or proprietor was talking from behind his desk to several men, and there were loungers in the lobby. The air was thick with tobacco smoke. No one paid any attention to Carley until at length she stepped up to the desk and interrupted the conversation there.

"Is this a hotel?" she queried, brusquely.

The shirt-sleeved individual leisurely turned and replied, "Yes, ma'am."

And Carley said: "No one would recognize it by the courtesy shown. I have been standing here waiting to register."

With the same leisurely ease and a cool, laconic stare the clerk turned the book toward her. "Reckon people round here ask for what they want."

Carley made no further comment. She assuredly recognized that what she had been accustomed to could not be expected out here. What she most wished to do at the moment was to get close to the big open grate where a cheery red-and-gold fire cracked. It was necessary, however, to follow the clerk. He assigned her to a small drab room which contained a bed, a bureau, and a stationary washstand with one spigot. There was also a chair. While Carley removed her coat and hat the clerk went downstairs for the rest of her luggage. Upon his return Carley learned that a stage left the hotel for Oak Creek Canyon at nine o'clock next morning. And this cheered her so much that she faced the strange sense of loneliness and discomfort with something of fortitude. There was no heat in the room, and no hot water. When Carley squeezed the spigot handle there burst forth a torrent of water that spouted up out of the washbasin to deluge her. It was colder than any ice water she had ever felt. It was piercingly cold. Hard upon the surprise and shock Carley suffered a flash of temper. But then the humor of it struck her and she had to laugh.

"Serves you right—you spoiled doll of luxury!" she mocked. "This is out West. Shiver and wait on yourself!"

Never before had she undressed so swiftly nor felt grateful for thick woollen blankets on a hard bed. Gradually she grew warm. The blackness, too, seemed rather comforting.

"I'm only twenty miles from Glenn," she whispered. "How strange! I wonder will he be glad." She felt a sweet, glowing assurance of that. Sleep did not come readily. Excitement had laid hold of her nerves, and for a long time she lay awake. After a while the chug of motor cars, the click of pool balls, the murmur of low voices all ceased. Then she heard a sound of wind outside, an intermittent, low moaning, new to her ears, and somehow pleasant. Another sound greeted her—the musical clanging of a clock that struck the quarters of the hour. Some time late sleep claimed her.

Upon awakening she found she had overslept, necessitating haste upon her part. As to that, the temperature of the room did not admit of leisurely dressing. She had no adequate name for the feeling of the water. And her fingers grew so numb that she made what she considered a disgraceful matter of her attire.

Downstairs in the lobby another cheerful red fire burned in the grate. How perfectly satisfying was an open fireplace! She thrust her numb hands almost into the blaze, and simply shook with the tingling pain that slowly warmed out of them. The lobby was deserted. A sign directed her to a dining room in the basement, where of the ham and eggs and strong coffee she managed to partake a little. Then she went upstairs into the lobby and out into the street.

A cold, piercing air seemed to blow right through her. Walking to the near corner, she paused to look around. Down the main street flowed a leisurely stream of pedestrians, horses, cars, extending between two blocks of low buildings. Across from where she stood lay a vacant lot, beyond which began a line of neat, oddly constructed houses, evidently residences of the town. And then lifting her gaze, instinctively drawn by something obstructing the sky line, she was suddenly struck with surprise and delight.

"Oh! how perfectly splendid!" she burst out.

Two magnificent mountains loomed right over her, sloping up with a majestic sweep of green and black timber, to a ragged tree-fringed snow area that swept up cleaner and whiter, at last to lift pure glistening peaks, noble and sharp, and sunrise-flushed against the blue.

Carley had climbed Mont Blanc and she had seen the Matterhorn, but they had never struck such amaze and admiration from her as these twin peaks of her native land.

"What mountains are those?" she asked a passerby.

"San Francisco Peaks, ma'am," replied the man.

"Why, they can't be over a mile away!" she said.

"Eighteen miles, ma'am," he returned, with a grin. "Shore this Arizonie air is deceivin'."

"How strange," murmured Carley. "It's not that way in the Adirondacks."

She was still gazing upward when a man approached her and said the stage for Oak Creek Canyon would soon be ready to start, and he wanted to know if her baggage was ready. Carley hurried back to her room to pack.

She had expected the stage would be a motor bus, or at least a large touring car, but it turned out to be a two-seated vehicle drawn by a team of ragged horses. The driver was a little wizen-faced man of doubtful years, and he did not appear obviously susceptible to the importance of his passenger. There was considerable freight to be hauled, besides Carley's luggage, but evidently she was the only passenger.

"Reckon it's goin' to be a bad day," said the driver. "These April days high up on the desert are windy an' cold. Mebbe it'll snow, too. Them clouds hangin' around the peaks ain't very promisin'. Now, miss, haven't you a heavier coat or somethin'?"

"No, I have not," replied Carley. "I'll have to stand it. Did you say this was desert?"

"I shore did. Wal, there's a hoss blanket under the seat, an' you can have that," he replied, and, climbing to the seat in front of Carley, he took up the reins and started the horses off at a trot.

At the first turning Carley became specifically acquainted with the driver's meaning of a bad day. A gust of wind, raw and penetrating, laden with dust and stinging sand, swept full in her face. It came so suddenly that she was scarcely quick enough to close her eyes. It took considerable clumsy effort on her part with a handkerchief, aided by relieving tears, to clear her sight again. Thus uncomfortably Carley found herself launched on the last lap of her journey.

All before her and alongside lay the squalid environs of the town. Looked back at, with the peaks rising behind, it was not unpicturesque. But the hard road with its sheets of flying dust, the bleak railroad yards, the round pens she took for cattle corrals, and the sordid debris littering the approach to a huge sawmill,—these were offensive in Carley's sight. From a tall domelike stack rose a yellowish smoke that spread overhead, adding to the lowering aspect of the sky. Beyond the sawmill extended the open country sloping somewhat roughly, and evidently once a forest, but now a hideous bare slash, with ghastly burned stems of trees still standing, and myriads of stumps attesting to denudation.

The bleak road wound away to the southwest, and from this direction came the gusty wind. It did not blow regularly so that Carley could be on her guard. It lulled now and then, permitting her to look about, and then suddenly again whipping dust into her face. The smell of the dust was as unpleasant as the sting. It made her nostrils smart. It was penetrating, and a little more of it would have been suffocating. And as a leaden gray bank of broken clouds rolled up the wind grew stronger and the air colder. Chilled before, Carley now became thoroughly cold. There appeared to be no end to the devastated forest land, and the farther she rode the more barren and sordid grew the landscape. Carley forgot about the impressive mountains behind her. And as the ride wore into hours, such was her discomfort and disillusion that she forgot about Glenn Kilbourne. She did not reach the point of regretting her adventure, but she grew mightily unhappy. Now and then she espied dilapidated log cabins and surroundings even more squalid than the ruined forest. What wretched abodes! Could it be possible that people had lived in them? She imagined men had but hardly women and children. Somewhere she had gotten an idea that women and children were extremely scarce in the West.

Straggling bits of forest—yellow pines, the driver called the trees—began to encroach upon the burned-over and arid barren land. To Carley these groves, by reason of contrast and proof of what once was, only rendered the landscape more forlorn and dreary. Why had these miles and miles of forest been cut? By money grubbers, she supposed, the same as were devastating the Adirondacks. Presently, when the driver had to halt to repair or adjust something wrong with the harness, Carley was grateful for a respite from cold inaction. She got out and walked. Sleet began to fall, and when she resumed her seat in the vehicle she asked the driver for the blanket to cover her. The smell of this horse blanket was less endurable than the cold. Carley huddled down into a state of apathetic misery. Already she had enough of the West.

But the sleet storm passed, the clouds broke, the sun shone through, greatly mitigating her discomfort. By and by the road led into a section of real forest, unspoiled in any degree. Carley saw large gray squirrels with tufted ears and white bushy tails. Presently the driver pointed out a flock of huge birds, which Carley, on second glance, recognized as turkeys, only these were sleek and glossy, with flecks of bronze and black and white, quite different from turkeys back East. "There must be a farm near," said Carley, gazing about.

"No, ma'am. Them's wild turkeys," replied the driver, "an' shore the best eatin' you ever had in your life."

A little while afterwards, as they were emerging from the woodland into more denuded country, he pointed out to Carley a herd of gray white-rumped animals that she took to be sheep.

"An' them's antelope," he said. "Once this desert was overrun by antelope. Then they nearly disappeared. An' now they're increasin' again."

More barren country, more bad weather, and especially an exceedingly rough road reduced Carley to her former state of dejection. The jolting over roots and rocks and ruts was worse than uncomfortable. She had to hold on to the seat to keep from being thrown out. The horses did not appreciably change their gait for rough sections of the road. Then a more severe jolt brought Carley's knee in violent

contact with an iron bolt on the forward seat, and
it hurt her so acutely that she had to bite her lips
to keep from screaming. A smoother stretch of road
did not come any too soon for her.

It led into forest again. And Carley soon became
aware that they had at last left the cut and burned-
over district of timberland behind. A cold wind
moaned through the treetops and set the drops
of water pattering down upon her. It lashed her
wet face. Carley closed her eyes and sagged in her
seat, mostly oblivious to the passing scenery. "The
girls will never believe this of me," she soliloquized.
And indeed she was amazed at herself. Then thought
of Glenn strengthened her. It did not really matter
what she suffered on the way to him. Only she was
disgusted at her lack of stamina, and her appalling
sensitiveness to discomfort.

"Wal, hyar's Oak Creek Canyon," called the driver.

Carley, rousing out of her weary preoccupation,
opened her eyes to see that the driver had halted at
a turn of the road, where apparently it descended a
fearful declivity.

The very forest-fringed earth seemed to have
opened into a deep abyss, ribbed by red rock
walls and choked by steep mats of green timber.
The chasm was a V-shaped split and so deep that
looking downward sent at once a chill and a shudder
over Carley. At that point it appeared narrow and
ended in a box. In the other direction, it widened and
deepened, and stretched farther on between tremendous walls of red, and split its winding floor of green
with glimpses of a gleaming creek, bowlder-strewn
and ridged by white rapids. A low mellow roar of

rushing waters floated up to Carley's ears. What a wild, lonely, terrible place! Could Glenn possibly live down there in that ragged rent in the earth? It frightened her—the sheer sudden plunge of it from the heights. Far down the gorge a purple light shone on the forested floor. And on the moment the sun burst through the clouds and sent a golden blaze down into the depths, transforming them incalculably. The great cliffs turned gold, the creek changed to glancing silver, the green of trees vividly freshened, and in the clefts rays of sunlight burned into the blue shadows. Carley had never gazed upon a scene like this. Hostile and prejudiced, she yet felt wrung from her an acknowledgment of beauty and grandeur. But wild, violent, savage! Not livable! This insulated rift in the crust of the earth was a gigantic burrow for beasts, perhaps for outlawed men—not for a civilized person—not for Glenn Kilbourne.

"Don't be scart, ma'am," spoke up the driver. "It's safe if you're careful. An' I've druv this manys the time."

Carley's heartbeats thumped at her side, rather denying her taunted assurance of fearlessness. Then the rickety vehicle started down at an angle that forced her to cling to her seat.

CHAPTER 2

*C*ARLEY, clutching her support, with abated
breath and prickling skin, gazed in fascinated
suspense over the rim of the gorge. Sometimes
the wheels on that side of the vehicle passed within
a few inches of the edge. The brakes squeaked, the
wheels slid; and she could hear the scrape of the
iron-shod hoofs of the horses as they held back stiff
legged, obedient to the wary call of the driver.

The first hundred yards of that steep road cut
out of the cliff appeared to be the worst. It began
to widen, with descents less precipitous. Tips of
trees rose level with her gaze, obstructing sight
of the blue depths. Then brush appeared on each
side of the road. Gradually Carley's strain relaxed,
and also the muscular contraction by which she had
braced herself in the seat. The horses began to trot
again. The wheels rattled. The road wound around
abrupt corners, and soon the green and red wall of
the opposite side of the canyon loomed close. Low
roar of running water rose to Carley's ears. When at
length she looked out instead of down she could see

nothing but a mass of green foliage crossed by tree trunks and branches of brown and gray. Then the vehicle bowled under dark cool shade, into a tunnel with a mossy wet cliff on one side, and close-standing trees on the other.

"Reckon we're all right now, unless we meet somebody comin' up," declared the driver.

Carley relaxed. She drew a deep breath of relief. She had her first faint intimation that perhaps her extensive experience of motor cars, express trains, transatlantic liners, and even a little of airplanes, did not range over the whole of adventurous life. She was likely to meet something entirely new and striking out here in the West.

The murmur of falling water sounded closer. Presently Carley saw that the road turned at the notch in the canyon, and crossed a clear swift stream. Here were huge mossy bowlders, and red walls covered by lichens, and the air appeared dim and moist, and full of mellow, hollow roar. Beyond this crossing the road descended the west side of the canyon, drawing away and higher from the creek. Huge trees, the like of which Carley had never seen, began to stand majestically up out of the gorge, dwarfing the maples and white-spotted sycamores. The driver called these great trees yellow pines.

At last the road led down from the steep slope to the floor of the canyon. What from far above had appeared only a green timber-choked cleft proved from close relation to be a wide winding valley, up and down, densely forested for the most part, yet having open glades and bisected from wall to wall by the creek. Every quarter of a mile or so the road crossed the stream; and at these fords Carley again held on desperately and gazed out dubiously, for the creek was deep, swift, and full of bowlders. Neither driver nor horses appeared to mind obstacles. Carley was splashed and jolted not inconsiderably. They passed through groves of oak trees, from which the creek manifestly derived its name; and under gleaming walls, cold, wet, gloomy, and silent; and between lines of solemn wide-spreading pines. Carley saw deep, still green pools eddying under a huge massed jumble of cliffs, and stretches of white water, and then, high above the treetops, a wild line of canyon rim, cold against the sky. She felt shut in from the world, lost in an unscalable rut of the earth. Again the sunlight had failed, and the gray gloom of the canyon oppressed her. It struck Carley as singular that she could not help being affected by mere weather, mere heights and depths, mere rock walls and pine trees, and rushing water. For really, what had these to do with her? These were only physical things that she was passing. Nevertheless, although she resisted sensation, she was more and more shot through and through with the wildness and savageness of this canyon.

A sharp turn of the road to the right disclosed a slope down the creek, across which showed orchards and fields, and a cottage nestling at the base of the wall. The ford at this crossing gave Carley more concern than any that had been passed, for there was greater volume and depth of water. One of the horses slipped on the rocks, plunged up and on with a great splash. They crossed, however, without more mishap to Carley than further acquaintance with this iciest of waters. From this point the driver turned back along the creek, passed between orchards and fields, and drove along the base of the red wall to come suddenly upon a large rustic house that had been hidden from Carley's sight. It sat almost against the stone cliff, from which poured a white foamy sheet of water. The house was built of slabs with the bark on, and it had a lower and upper porch running all around, at least as far as the cliff. Green growths from the rock wall over-hung the upper porch. A column of blue smoke curled lazily upward from a stone chimney. On one of the porch posts hung a sign with rude lettering: "Lolomi Lodge."

"Hey, Josh, did you fetch the flour?" called a woman's voice from inside.

"Hullo! Reckon I didn't forgit nothin'," replied the man, as he got down. "An' say, Mrs. Hutter, hyar's a young lady from Noo Yorrk."

That latter speech of the driver's brought Mrs. Hutter out on the porch. "Flo, come here," she called to some one evidently near at hand. And then she smilingly greeted Carley.

"Get down an' come in, miss," she said. "I'm sure glad to see you."

Carley, being stiff and cold, did not very gracefully disengage herself from the high muddy wheel and step. When she mounted to the porch she saw that Mrs. Hutter was a woman of middle age, rather stout, with a strong face full of fine wavy lines, and kind dark eyes.

"I'm Miss Burch," said Carley.

"You're the girl whose picture Glenn Kilbourne has over his fireplace," declared the woman, heartily. "I'm sure glad to meet you, an' my daughter Flo will be, too."

That about her picture pleased and warmed
Carley. "Yes, I'm Glenn Kilbourne's fiancée. I've come
West to surprise him. Is he here . . . Is—is he well?"

"Fine. I saw him yesterday. He's changed a great
deal from what he was at first. Most all the last few
months. I reckon you won't know him . . . But you're
wet an' cold an' you look fagged. Come right in to
the fire."

"Thank you; I'm all right," returned Carley.

At the doorway they encountered a girl of lithe
and robust figure, quick in her movements. Carley
was swift to see the youth and grace of her; and
then a face that struck Carley as neither pretty nor
beautiful, but still wonderfully attractive.

"Flo, here's Miss Burch," burst out Mrs. Hutter,
with cheerful importance. "Glenn Kilbourne's girl
come all the way from New York to surprise him!"

"Oh, Carley, I'm shore happy to meet you!" said
the girl, in a voice of slow drawling richness. "I know
you. Glenn has told me all about you."

If this greeting, sweet and warm as it seemed,
was a shock to Carley, she gave no sign. But as she
murmured something in reply she looked with all a
woman's keenness into the face before her. Flo Hutter
had a fair skin generously freckled; a mouth and chin
too firmly cut to suggest a softer feminine beauty; and
eyes of clear light hazel, penetrating, frank, fearless.
Her hair was very abundant, almost silver-gold in
color, and it was either rebellious or showed lack
of care. Carley liked the girl's looks and liked the
sincerity of her greeting; but instinctively she reacted
antagonistically because of the frank suggestion of
intimacy with Glenn. But for that she would have been
spontaneous and friendly rather than restrained.

They ushered Carley into a big living room and up to a fire of blazing logs, where they helped divest her of the wet wraps. And all the time they talked in the solicitous way natural to women who were kind and unused to many visitors. Then Mrs. Hutter bustled off to make a cup of hot coffee while Flo talked.

"We'll shore give you the nicest room—with a sleeping porch right under the cliff where the water falls. It'll sing you to sleep. Of course you needn't use the bed outdoors until it's warmer. Spring is late here, you know, and we'll have nasty weather yet. You really happened on Oak Creek at its least attractive season. But then it's always—well, just Oak Creek. You'll come to know."

"I dare say I'll remember my first sight of it— and the ride down that cliff road," said Carley, with a wan smile.

"Oh, that's nothing to what you'll see and do," returned Flo, knowingly. "We've had Eastern tender-feet here before. And never was there a one of them who didn't come to love Arizona."

"Tenderfoot! It hadn't occurred to me. But of course—" murmured Carley.

Then Mrs. Hutter returned, carrying a tray, which she set upon a chair, and drew to Carley's side. "Eat an' drink," she said, as if these actions were the cardinally important ones of life. "Flo, you carry her bags up to that west room we always give to some particular person we want to love Lolomi." Next she threw sticks of wood upon the fire, making it crackle and blaze; then seated herself near Carley and beamed upon her.

"You'll not mind if we call you Carley?" she asked, eagerly.

"Oh, indeed no! I—I'd like it," returned Carley, made to feel friendly and at home in spite of herself.

"You see it's not as if you were just a stranger," went on Mrs. Hutter. "Tom—that's Flo's father—took a likin' to Glenn Kilbourne when he first came to Oak Creek over a year ago. I wonder if you all know how sick that soldier boy was. . . . Well, he lay on his back for two solid weeks—in the room we're givin' you. An' I for one didn't think he'd ever get up. But he did. An' he got better. An' after a while he went to work for Tom. Then six months an' more ago he invested in the sheep business with Tom. He lived with us until he built his cabin up West Fork. He an' Flo have run together a good deal, an' naturally he told her about you. So you see you're not a stranger. An' we want you to feel you're with friends."

"I thank you, Mrs. Hutter," replied Carley, feelingly. "I never could thank you enough for being good to Glenn. I did not know he was so—so sick. At first he wrote but seldom."

"Reckon he never wrote you or told you what he did in the war," declared Mrs. Hutter.

"Indeed he never did!"

"Well, I'll tell you some day. For Tom found out all about him. Got some of it from a soldier who came to Flagstaff for lung trouble. He'd been in the same company with Glenn. We didn't know this boy's name while he was in Flagstaff. But later Tom found out. John Henderson. He was only twenty-two, a fine lad. An' he died in Phoenix. We tried to get him out here. But the boy wouldn't live on charity. He was always expectin' money—a war bonus, whatever that was. It didn't come. He was a clerk at the El Tovar for a

while. Then he came to Flagstaff. But it was too cold
an' he stayed there too long."

"Too bad," rejoined Carley, thoughtfully. This
information as to the suffering of American soldiers had augmented during the last few months,
and seemed to possess strange, poignant power to
depress Carley. Always she had turned away from
the unpleasant. And the misery of unfortunates was
as disturbing almost as direct contact with disease
and squalor. But it had begun to dawn upon Carley
that there might occur circumstances of life, in every
way affronting her comfort and happiness, which it
would be impossible to turn her back upon.

At this juncture Flo returned to the room, and
again Carley was struck with the girl's singular freedom of movement and the sense of sure poise and
joy that seemed to emanate from her presence.

"I've made a fire in your little stove," she said.
"There's water heating. Now won't you come up and
change those traveling clothes. You'll want to fix up
for Glenn, won't you?"

Carley had to smile at that. This girl indeed was
frank and unsophisticated, and somehow refreshing.
Carley rose.

"You are both very good to receive me as a
friend," she said. "I hope I shall not disappoint
you. . . . Yes, I do want to improve my appearance
before Glenn sees me. . . . Is there any way I can send
word to him—by some one who has not seen me?"

"There shore is. I'll send Charley, one of our hired
boys."

"Thank you. Then tell him to say there is a lady
here from New York to see him, and it is very
important."

Flo Hutter clapped her hands and laughed with glee. Her gladness gave Carley a little twinge of conscience. Jealousy was an unjust and stifling thing.

Carley was conducted up a broad stairway and along a boarded hallway to a room that opened out on the porch. A steady low murmur of falling water assailed her ears. Through the open door she saw across the porch to a white tumbling lacy veil of water falling, leaping, changing, so close that it seemed to touch the heavy pole railing of the porch.

This room resembled a tent. The sides were of canvas. It had no ceiling. But the rough-hewn shingles of the roof of the house sloped down closely. The furniture was home made. An Indian rug covered the floor. The bed with its woolly clean blankets and the white pillows looked inviting.

"Is this where Glenn lay—when he was sick?" queried Carley.

"Yes," replied Flo, gravely, and a shadow darkened her eyes. "I ought to tell you all about it. I will some day. But you must not be made unhappy now. . . . Glenn nearly died here. Mother or I never left his side—for a while there—when he was so bad."

She showed Carley how to open the little stove and put the short billets of wood inside and work the damper; and cautioning her to keep an eye on it so that it would not get too hot, she left Carley to herself.

Carley found herself in unfamiliar mood. There came a leap of her heart every time she thought of the meeting with Glenn, so soon now to be, but it was not that which was unfamiliar. She seemed to have difficult approach to undefined and unusual thoughts. All this was so different from her regular life. Besides she was tired. But these explanations did not suffice. There was a pang in her breast which must owe its origin to the fact that Glenn Kilbourne had been ill in this little room and some other girl than Carley Burch had nursed him. "Am I jealous?" she whispered. "No!" But she knew in her heart that she lied. A woman could no more help being jealous, under such circumstances, than she could help the beat and throb of her blood. Nevertheless, Carley was glad Flo Hutter had been there, and always she would be grateful to her for that kindness.

Carley disrobed and, donning her dressing gown, she unpacked her bags and hung her things upon pegs under the curtained shelves. Then she lay down to rest, with no intention of slumber. But there was a strange magic in the fragrance of the room, like the piny tang outdoors, and in the feel of the bed, and especially in the low, dreamy hum and murmur of the waterfall. She fell asleep. When she awakened it was five o'clock. The fire in the stove was out, but the water was still warm. She bathed and dressed, not without care, yet as swiftly as was her habit at home; and she wore white because Glenn had always liked her best in white. But it was assuredly not a gown to wear in a country house where draughts of cold air filled the unheated rooms and halls. So she threw round her a warm sweater-shawl, with colorful bars becoming to her dark eyes and hair.

All the time that she dressed and thought, her very being seemed to be permeated by that soft murmuring sound of falling water. No moment of waking life there at Lolomi Lodge, or perhaps of slumber hours, could be wholly free of that sound. It vaguely tormented Carley, yet was not uncomfortable. She went out upon the porch. The small alcove space held a bed and a rustic chair. Above her the peeled poles of the roof descended to within a few feet of her head. She had to lean over the rail of the porch to look up. The green and red rock wall sheered ponderously near. The waterfall showed first at the notch of a fissure, where the cliff split; and down over smooth places the water gleamed, to narrow in a crack with little drops, and suddenly to leap into a thin white sheet.

Out from the porch the view was restricted to glimpses between the pines, and beyond to the opposite wall of the canyon. How shut-in, how walled in this home!

"In summer it might be good to spend a couple of weeks here," soliloquized Carley. "But to *live* here? Heavens! A person might as well be buried."

Heavy footsteps upon the porch below accompanied by a man's voice quickened Carley's pulse. Did they belong to Glenn? After a strained second she decided not. Nevertheless, the acceleration of her blood and an unwonted glow of excitement, long a stranger to her, persisted as she left the porch and entered the boarded hall. How gray and barnlike this upper part of the house! From the head of the stairway, however, the big living room presented a cheerful contrast. There were warm colors, some comfortable rockers, a lamp that shed a bright light, and an open fire which alone would have dispelled the raw gloom of the day.

A large man in corduroys and top boots advanced to meet Carley. He had a clean-shaven face that might have been hard and stern but for his smile, and one look into his eyes revealed their resemblance to Flo's.

"I'm Tom Hutter, an' I'm shore glad to welcome you to Lolomi, Miss Carley," he said. His voice was deep and slow. There were ease and force in his presence, and the grip he gave Carley's hand was that of a man who made no distinction in hand-shaking. Carley, quick in her perceptions, instantly liked him and sensed in him a strong personality. She greeted him in turn and expressed her thanks for his goodness to Glenn. Naturally Carley expected him to say something about her fiancé, but he did not.

"Well, Miss Carley, if you don't mind, I'll say you're prettier than your picture," said Hutter. "An' that is shore sayin' a lot. All the sheep herders in the country have taken a peep at your picture. Without permission, you understand."

"I'm greatly flattered," laughed Carley.

"We're glad you've come," replied Hutter, simply. "I just got back from the East myself. Chicago an' Kansas City. I came to Arizona from Illinois over thirty years ago. An' this was my first trip since. Reckon I've not got back my breath yet. Times have changed, Miss Carley. Times an' people!"

Mrs. Hutter bustled in from the kitchen, where manifestly she had been importantly engaged. "For the land's sakes!" she exclaimed, fervently, as she threw up her hands at sight of Carley. Her expression was indeed a compliment, but there was a suggestion of shock in it. Then Flo came in. She wore a simple gray gown that reached the top of her high shoes.

"Carley, don't mind mother," said Flo. "She means your dress is lovely. Which is my say, too. . . . But, listen. I just saw Glenn comin' up the road."

Carley ran to the open door with more haste than dignity. She saw a tall man striding along. Something about him appeared familiar. It was his walk—an erect swift carriage, with a swing of the march still visible. She recognized Glenn. And all within her seemed to become unstable. She watched him cross the road, face the house. How changed! No—this was not Glenn Kilbourne. This was a bronzed man, wide of shoulder, roughly garbed, heavy limbed, quite different from the Glenn she remembered. He mounted the porch steps. And Carley, still unseen herself, saw his face. Yes— Glenn! Hot blood seemed to be tingling liberated in her veins. Wheeling away, she backed against the wall behind the door and held up a warning finger to Flo, who stood nearest. Strange and disturbing then, to see something in Flo Hutter's eyes that could be read by a woman in only one way!

A tall form darkened the doorway. It strode in and halted.

"Flo!—who—where?" he began, breathlessly.

His voice, so well remembered, yet deeper, huski- er, fell upon Carley's ears as something unconsciously longed for. His frame had so filled out that she did not recognize it. His face, too, had unbelievably changed—not in the regularity of feature that had been its chief charm, but in contour of cheek and vanishing of pallid hue and tragic line. Carley's heart swelled with joy. Beyond all else she had hoped to see the sad fixed hopelessness, the havoc, gone from his face. Therefore the restraint and nonchalance upon which Carley prided herself sustained eclipse.

"Glenn! Look—who's—here!" she called, in voice she could not have steadied to save her life. This meeting was more than she had anticipated.

Glenn whirled with an inarticulate cry. He saw Carley. Then—no matter how unreasonable or exacting had been Carley's longings, they were satisfied.

"You!" he cried, and leaped at her with radiant face.

Carley not only did not care about the spectators of this meeting, but forgot them utterly. More than the joy of seeing Glenn, more than the all-satisfying assurance to her woman's heart that she was still beloved, welled up a deep, strange, profound something that shook her to her depths. It was beyond selfishness. It was gratitude to God and to the West that had restored him.

"Carley! I couldn't believe it was you," he declared, releasing her from his close embrace, yet still holding her.

"Yes, Glenn—it's I—all you've left of me," she replied, tremulously, and she sought with unsteady hands to put up her dishevelled hair. "You—you big sheep herder! You Goliath!"

"I never was so knocked off my pins," he said. "A lady to see me—from New York! . . . Of course it had to be you. But I couldn't believe. Carley, you were good to come."

Somehow the soft, warm look of his dark eyes hurt her. New and strange indeed it was to her, as were other things about him. Why had she not come West sooner? She disengaged herself from his hold and moved away, striving for the composure habitual with her. Flo Hutter was standing before the fire, looking down. Mrs. Hutter beamed upon Carley.

"Now let's have supper," she said.

"Reckon Miss Carley can't eat now, after that hug Glenn gave her," drawled Tom Hutter. "I was some worried. You see Glenn has gained seventy pounds in six months. An' he doesn't know his strength."

"Seventy pounds!" exclaimed Carley, gayly. "I thought it was more."

"Carley, you must excuse my violence," said Glenn. "I've been hugging sheep. That is, when I shear a sheep I have to hold him."

They all laughed, and so the moment of readjustment passed. Presently Carley found herself sitting at the table, directly across from Flo. A pearly whiteness was slowly warming out of the girl's face. Her frank clear eyes met Carley's and they had nothing to hide. Carley's first requisite for character in a woman was that she be a thoroughbred. She lacked it often enough herself to admire it greatly in another woman. And that moment saw a birth of respect and sincere liking in her for this Western girl. If Flo Hutter ever was a rival she would be an honest one.

Not long after supper Tom Hutter winked at Carley and said he "reckoned on general principles it was his hunch to go to bed." Mrs. Hutter suddenly discovered tasks to perform elsewhere. And Flo said in her cool sweet drawl, somehow audacious and tantalizing, "Shore you two will want to spoon."

"Now, Flo, Eastern girls are no longer old-fashioned enough for that," declared Glenn.

"Too bad! Reckon I can't see how love could ever be old-fashioned. . . . Good night, Glenn. Good night, Carley."

Flo stood an instant at the foot of the dark stairway where the light from the lamp fell upon her face. It seemed sweet and earnest to Carley. It expressed unconscious longing, but no envy. Then she ran up the stairs to disappear.

"Glenn, is that girl in love with you?" asked Carley, bluntly.

To her amaze, Glenn laughed. When had she heard him laugh? It thrilled her, yet nettled her a little.

"If that isn't like you!" he ejaculated. "Your very first words after we are left alone! It brings back the East, Carley."

"Probably recall to memory will be good for you," returned Carley. "But tell me. Is she in love with you?"

"Why, no, certainly not!" replied Glenn. "Anyway, how could I answer such a question? It just made me laugh, that's all."

"Humph! I can remember when you were not above making love to a pretty girl. You certainly had me worn to a frazzle—before we became engaged," said Carley.

"Old times! How long ago they seem! Carley, it's sure wonderful to see you."

"How do you like my gown?" asked Carley, pirouetting for his benefit.

"Well, what little there is of it is beautiful," he replied, with a slow smile. "I always liked you best in white. Did you remember?"

"Yes. I got the gown for you. And I'll never wear it except for you."

"Same old coquette—same old eternal feminine," he said, half sadly. "You know when you look stunning. . . . But, Carley, the cut of that—or rather the abbreviation of it—inclines me to think that style for women's clothes has not changed for the better. In fact, it's worse than two years ago in Paris and later in New York. Where will you women draw the line?"

"Women are slaves to the prevailing mode," rejoined Carley. "I don't imagine women who dress would ever draw a line, if fashion went on dictating."

"But would they care so much—if they had to work—plenty of work—and children?" inquired Glenn, wistfully.

"Glenn! Work and children for modern women? Why, you are dreaming!" said Carley, with a laugh.

She saw him gaze thoughtfully into the glowing embers of the fire, and as she watched him her quick intuition grasped a subtle change in his mood. It brought a sternness to his face. She could hardly realize she was looking at the Glenn Kilbourne of old.

"Come close to the fire," he said, and pulled up a chair for her. Then he threw more wood upon the red coals. "You must be careful not to catch cold out here. The altitude makes a cold dangerous. And that gown is no protection."

"Glenn, one chair used to be enough for us," she said, archly, standing beside him.

But he did not respond to her hint, and, a little affronted, she accepted the proffered chair. Then he began to ask questions rapidly. He was eager for news from home—from his people—from old friends. However he did not inquire of Carley about her friends. She talked unremittingly for an hour, before she satisfied his hunger. But when her turn came to ask questions she found him reticent.

He had fallen upon rather hard days at first out here in the West; then his health had begun to improve; and as soon as he was able to work his condition rapidly changed for the better; and now he was getting along pretty well. Carley felt hurt at his apparent disinclination to confide in her. The strong cast of his face, as if it had been chiseled in bronze; the stern set of his lips and the jaw that protruded lean and square cut; the quiet masked light of his eyes; the coarse roughness of his brown hands, mute evidence of strenuous labors—these all gave a different impression from his brief remarks about himself. Lastly there was a little gray in the light-brown hair over his temples. Glenn was only twenty-seven, yet he looked ten years older. Studying him so, with the memory of earlier years in her mind, she was forced to admit that she liked him infinitely more as he was now. He seemed proven. Something had made him a man. Had it been his love for her, or the army service, or the war in France, or the struggle for life and health afterwards? Or had it been this rugged, uncouth West? Carley felt insidious jealousy of this last possibility. She feared this West. She was going to hate it. She had womanly intuition enough to see in Flo Hutter a girl somehow to be reckoned with. Still, Carley would not acknowledge to herself that this simple, unsophisticated Western girl could possibly be a rival. Carley did not need to consider the fact that she had been spoiled by the attention of men. It was not her vanity that precluded Flo Hutter as a rival.

Gradually the conversation drew to a lapse, and it suited Carley to let it be so. She watched Glenn as he gazed thoughtfully into the amber depths of the fire. What was going on in his mind? Carley's old perplexity suddenly had rebirth. And with it came an unfamiliar fear which she could not smother. Every moment that she sat there beside Glenn she was realizing more and more a yearning, passionate love for him. The unmistakable manifestation of his joy at the sight of her, the strong, almost rude expression of his love, had called to some responsive, but hitherto unplumbed deeps of her. If it had not been for these undeniable facts Carley would have been panic-stricken. They reassured her, yet only made her state of mind more dissatisfied.

"Carley, do you still go in for dancing?" Glenn asked, presently, with his thoughtful eyes turning to her.

"Of course. I like dancing, and it's about all the exercise I get," she replied.

"Have the dances changed—again?"

"It's the music, perhaps, that changes the dancing. Jazz is becoming popular. And about all the crowd dances now is an infinite variation of fox-trot."

"No waltzing?"

"I don't believe I waltzed once this winter."

"Jazz? That's a sort of tinpanning, jiggly stuff, isn't it?"

"Glenn, it's the fever of the public pulse," replied Carley. "The graceful waltz, like the stately minuet, flourished back in the days when people rested rather than raced."

"More's the pity," said Glenn. Then after a moment, in which his gaze returned to the fire, he inquired rather too casually, "Does Morrison still chase after you?"

"Glenn, I'm neither old—nor married," she replied, laughing.

"No, that's true. But if you were married it wouldn't make any difference to Morrison."

Carley could not detect bitterness or jealousy in his voice. She would not have been averse to hearing either. She gathered from his remark, however, that he was going to be harder than ever to understand. What had she said or done to make him retreat within himself, aloof, impersonal, unfamiliar? He did not impress her as loverlike. What irony of fate was this that held her there yearning for his kisses and caresses as never before, while he watched the fire, and talked as to a mere acquaintance, and seemed sad and far away? Or did she merely imagine that? Only one thing could she be sure of at the moment, and it was that pride would never be her ally.

"Glenn, look here," she said, sliding her chair close to his and holding out her left hand, slim and white, with its glittering diamond on the third finger.

He took her hand in his and pressed it, and smiled at her. "Yes, Carley, it's a beautiful, soft little hand. But I think I'd like it better if it were strong and brown, and coarse on the inside—from useful work."

"Like Flo Hutter's?" queried Carley.

"Yes."

Carley looked proudly into his eyes. "People are born in different stations. I respect your little Western friend, Glenn, but could I wash and sweep, milk cows and chop wood, and all that sort of thing?"

"I suppose you couldn't," he admitted, with a blunt little laugh.

"Would you want me to?" she asked.

"Well, that's hard to say," he replied, knitting his brows. "I hardly know. I think it depends on you. . . . But if you did do such work wouldn't you be happier?"

"Happier! Why Glenn, I'd be miserable! But listen. It wasn't my beautiful and useless hand I wanted you to see. It was my engagement ring."

"Oh!—Well?" he went on, slowly.

"I've never had it off since you left New York," she said, softly. "You gave it to me four years ago. Do you remember? It was on my twenty-second birthday. You said it would take two months' salary to pay the bill."

"It sure did," he retorted, with a hint of humor.

"Glenn, during the war it was not so—so very hard to wear this ring as an engagement ring should be worn," said Carley, growing more earnest. "But after the war—especially after your departure West— it was terribly hard to be true to the significance of this betrothal ring. There was a let-down in all women. Oh, no one need tell *me!* There was. And men were affected by that and the chaotic condition of the times. New York was wild during the year of your absence. Prohibition was a joke.—Well, I gadded, danced, dressed, drank, smoked, motored, just the same as the other women in our crowd. Something drove me to. I never rested. Excitement seemed to be happiness.—Glenn, I am not making any plea to excuse all that. But I want you to know—how under trying circumstances—I was absolutely true to you. Understand me. I mean true as regards love. Through it all I loved you just the same. And now I'm with you, it seems, oh, so much more! . . . Your last letter hurt me. I don't know just how. But I came West to see you— to tell you this—and to ask you. . . . Do you want this ring back?"

"Certainly not," he replied, forcibly, with a dark flush spreading over his face.

"Then—you love me?" she whispered.

"Yes—I love you," he returned, deliberately. "And in spite of all you say—very probably more than you love me. . . . But you, like all women, make love and its expression the sole object of life. Carley, I have been concerned with keeping my body from the grave and my soul from hell."

"But—dear—you're well now?" she returned, with trembling lips.

"Yes, I've almost pulled out."

"Then what is wrong?"

"Wrong?—With me or you?" he queried, with keen, enigmatical glance upon her.

"What is wrong between us? There is something."

"Carley, a man who has been on the verge—as I have been—seldom or never comes back to happiness. But perhaps—"

"You frighten me," cried Carley, and, rising, she sat upon the arm of his chair and encircled his neck with her arms. "How can I help if I do not understand? Am I so miserably little? Glenn, *must* I tell you? No woman can live without love. I need to be loved. That's all that's wrong with *me*."

"Carley, you are still an imperious, mushy girl," replied Glenn, taking her into his arms. "I need to be loved, too. But that's not what is wrong with me. You'll have to find it out yourself."

"You're a dear old Sphinx," she retorted.

"Listen, Carley," he said, earnestly. "About this love-making stuff. Please don't misunderstand me. I love you. I'm starved for your kisses. But—is it right to ask them?"

"Right! Aren't we engaged? And don't I want to give them?"

"If I were only *sure* we'd be married!" he said, in low, tense voice, as if speaking more to himself.

"Married!" cried Carley, convulsively clasping him. "Of course we'll be married. Glenn, you wouldn't jilt me?"

"Carley, what I mean is that you might never really marry me," he answered, seriously.

"Oh, if that's all you need be sure of, Glenn Kilbourne, you may begin to make love to me now."

It was late when Carley went up to her room. And she was in such a softened mood, so happy and excited and yet disturbed in mind, that the coldness and the darkness did not matter in the least. She undressed in pitchy blackness, stumbling over chair and bed, feeling for what she needed. And in her mood this unusual proceeding was fun. When ready for bed she opened the door to take a peep out. Through the dense blackness the waterfall showed dimly opaque. Carley felt a soft mist wet her face. The low roar of the falling water seemed to envelop her. Under the cliff wall brooded impenetrable gloom. But out above the treetops shone great stars, wonderfully white and radiant and cold, with a piercing contrast to the deep clear blue of sky. The waterfall hummed into an absolutely dead silence. It emphasized the silence. Not only cold was it that made Carley shudder. How lonely, how lost, how hidden this canyon!

Then she hurried to bed, grateful for the warm woolly blankets. Relaxation and thought brought consciousness of the heat of her blood, the beat and throb and swell of her heart, of the tumult within her. In the lonely darkness of her room she might have faced the truth of her strangely renewed and augmented love for Glenn Kilbourne. But she was more concerned with her happiness. She had won him back. Her presence, her love had overcome his restraint. She thrilled in the sweet consciousness of her woman's conquest. How splendid he was! To hold back physical tenderness, the simple expressions of love, because he had feared they might unduly influence her! He had grown in many ways. She must be careful to reach up to his ideals. That about Flo Hutter's toil-hardened hands! Was that significance somehow connected with the rift in the lute? For Carley admitted to herself that there was something amiss, something incomprehensible, something intangible that obtruded its menace into her dream of future happiness. Still, what had she to fear, so long as she could be with Glenn?

And yet there were forced upon her, insistent and perplexing, the questions—was her love selfish? Was she considering him? Was she blind to something he could see? Tomorrow and the next day and the days to come held promise of joyous companionship with Glenn, yet likewise they seemed full of a portent of trouble for her, of fight and ordeal, of lessons that would make life significant for her.

CHAPTER
3

*C*ARLEY was awakened by rattling sounds in her room. The raising of sleepy eyelids disclosed Flo on her knees before the little stove, in the act of lighting a fire.

"Mawnin', Carley," she drawled. "It's shore cold. Reckon it'll snow to-day, worse luck, just because you're here. Take my hunch and stay in bed till the fire burns up."

"I shall do no such thing," declared Carley, heroically.

"We're afraid you'll take cold," said Flo. "This is desert country with high altitude. Spring is here when the sun shines. But it's only shinin' in streaks these days. That means winter, really. Please be good."

"Well, it doesn't require much self-denial to stay here awhile longer," replied Carley, lazily.

Flo left with a parting admonition not to let the stove get red-hot. And Carley lay snuggled in the warm blankets, dreading the ordeal of getting out into that cold bare room. Her nose was cold. When her nose grew cold, it being a faithful barometer as to temperature, Carley knew there was frost in the air. She preferred summer. Steam-heated rooms with hothouse flowers lending their perfume had certainly not trained Carley for primitive conditions. She had a spirit, however, that was waxing a little rebellious to all this intimation as to her susceptibility to colds and her probable weakness under privation. Carley got up. Her bare feet landed upon the board floor instead of the Navajo rug, and she thought she had encountered cold stone. Stove and hot water notwithstanding, by the time she was half dressed she was also half frozen. "Some actor fellow once said w-when you w-went West you were c-camping out," chattered Carley. "Believe me, he said something."

The fact was Carley had never camped out. Her set played golf, rode horseback, motored and houseboated, but they had never gone in for uncomfortable trips. The camps and hotels in the Adirondacks were as warm and luxurious as Carley's own home. Carley now missed many things. And assuredly her flesh was weak. It cost her effort of will and real pain to finish lacing her boots. As she had made an engagement with Glenn to visit his cabin, she had donned an outdoor suit. She wondered if the cold had anything to do with the perceptible diminishing of the sound of the waterfall. Perhaps some of the water had frozen, like her fingers.

Carley went downstairs to the living room, and made no effort to resist a rush to the open fire. Flo and her mother were amused at Carley's impetuosity. "You'll like that stingin' of the air after you get used to it," said Mrs. Hutter. Carley had her doubts. When she was thoroughly thawed out she discovered an appetite quite unusual for her, and she enjoyed her breakfast. Then it was time to sally forth to meet Glenn.

"It's pretty sharp this mawnin'," said Flo. "You'll need gloves and sweater."

Having fortified herself with these, Carley asked how to find West Fork Canyon.

"It's down the road a little way," replied Flo. "A great narrow canyon opening on the right side. You can't miss it."

Flo accompanied her as far as the porch steps. A queer-looking individual was slouching along with an ax over his shoulder.

"There's Charley," said Flo. "He'll show you." Then she whispered: "He's sort of dotty sometimes. A horse kicked him once. But mostly he's sensible."

At Flo's call the fellow halted with a grin. He was long, lean, loose jointed, dressed in blue overalls stuck into the tops of muddy boots, and his face was clear olive without beard or line. His brow bulged a little, and from under it peered out a pair of wistful brown eyes that reminded Carley of those of a dog she had once owned.

"Wal, it ain't a-goin' to be a nice day," remarked Charley, as he tried to accommodate his strides to Carley's steps.

"How can you tell?" asked Carley. "It looks clear and bright."

"Naw, this is a dark mawnin'. Thet's a cloudy sun. We'll hev snow on an' off."

"Do you mind bad weather?"

"Me? All the same to me. Reckon, though, I like it cold so I can loaf round a big fire at night."

"I like a big fire, too."

"Ever camped out?" he asked.

"Not what you'd call the real thing," replied Carley.

"Wal, thet's too bad. Reckon it'll be tough fer you," he went on, kindly. "There was a gurl tenderfoot heah two years ago an' she had a hell of a time. They all joked her, 'cept me, an' played tricks on her. An' on her side she was always puttin' her foot in it. I was shore sorry fer her."

"You were very kind to be an exception," murmured Carley.

"You look out fer Tom Hutter, an' I reckon Flo ain't so darn above layin' traps fer you. 'Specially as she's sweet on your beau. I seen them together a lot."

"Yes?" interrogated Carley, encouragingly.

"Kilbourne is the best fellar thet ever happened along Oak Creek. I helped him build his cabin. We've hunted some together. Did you ever hunt?"

"No."

"Wal, you've shore missed a lot of fun," he said. "Turkey huntin'. Thet's what fetches the gurls. I reckon because turkeys are so good to eat. The old gobblers hev begun to gobble now. I'll take you gobbler huntin' if you'd like to go."

"I'm sure I would."

"There's good trout fishin' along heah a little later," he said, pointing to the stream. "Crick's too high now. I like West Fork best. I've ketched some lammin' big ones up there."

Carley was amused and interested. She could not say that Charley had shown any indication of his mental peculiarity to her. It took considerable restraint not to lead him to talk more about Flo and Glenn. Presently they reached the turn in the road,

opposite the cottage Carley had noticed yesterday,
and here her loquacious escort halted.

"You take the trail heah," he said, pointing it out,
"an' foller it into West Fork. So long, an' don't forget
we're goin' huntin' turkeys."

Carley smiled her thanks, and, taking to the trail,
she stepped out briskly, now giving attention to her
surroundings. The canyon had widened, and the creek
with its deep thicket of green and white had sheered
to the left. On her right the canyon wall appeared
to be lifting higher and higher. She could not see
it well, owing to intervening treetops. The trail led
her through a grove of maples and sycamores, out
into an open parklike bench that turned to the right
toward the cliff. Suddenly Carley saw a break in the
red wall. It was the intersecting canyon, West Fork.
What a narrow red-walled gateway! Huge pine trees
spread wide gnarled branches over her head. The
wind made soft rush in their tops, sending the brown
needles lightly on the air. Carley turned the bulging
corner, to be halted by a magnificent spectacle. It
seemed a mountain wall loomed over her. It was the
western side of this canyon, so lofty that Carley had
to tip back her head to see the top. She swept her
astonished gaze down the face of this tremendous
red mountain wall and then slowly swept it upward
again. This phenomenon of a cliff seemed beyond the
comprehension of her sight. It looked a mile high.
The few trees along its bold rampart resembled short
spear-pointed bushes outlined against the steel gray
of sky. Ledges, caves, seams, cracks, fissures, beetling
red brows, yellow crumbling crags, benches of green
growths and niches choked with brush, and bold
points where single lonely pine trees grew perilously,

and blank walls a thousand feet across their shadowed faces—these features gradually took shape in Carley's confused sight, until the colossal mountain front stood up before her in all its strange, wild, magnificent ruggedness and beauty.

"Arizona! Perhaps this is what he meant," murmured Carley. "I never dreamed of anything like this. . . . But, oh! it overshadows me—bears me down! I could never have a moment's peace under it."

It fascinated her. There were inaccessible ledges that haunted her with their remote fastnesses. How wonderful would it be to get there, rest there, if that were possible! But only eagles could reach them. There were places, then, that the desecrating hands of man could not touch. The dark caves were mystically potent in their vacant staring out at the world beneath them. The crumbling crags, the toppling ledges, the leaning rocks all threatened to come thundering down at the breath of wind. How deep and soft the red color in contrast with the green! How splendid the sheer bold uplift of gigantic steps! Carley found herself marveling at the forces that had so rudely, violently, and grandly left this monument to nature.

"Well, old Fifth Avenue gadder!" called a gay voice. "If the back wall of my yard so halts you— what will you ever do when you see the Painted Desert, or climb Sunset Peak, or look down into the Grand Canyon?"

"Oh, Glenn, where are you?" cried Carley, gazing everywhere near at hand. But he was farther away. The clearness of his voice had deceived her. Presently she espied him a little distance away, across a creek she had not before noticed.

"Come on," he called. "I want to see you cross the stepping stones."

Carley ran ahead, down a little slope of clean red rock, to the shore of the green water. It was clear, swift, deep in some places and shallow in others, with white wreaths or ripples around the rocks evidently placed there as a means to cross. Carley drew back aghast.

"Glenn, I could never make it," she called.

"Come on, my Alpine climber," he taunted. "Will you let Arizona daunt you?"

"Do you want me to fall in and catch cold?" she cried, desperately.

"Carley, big women might even cross the bad places of modern life on stepping stones of their dead selves!" he went on, with something of mockery. "Surely a few physical steps are not beyond you."

"Say, are you mangling *Tennyson* or just kidding me?" she demanded slangily.

"My love, Flo could cross here with her eyes shut."

That thrust spurred Carley to action. His words were jest, yet they held a hint of earnest. With her heart at her throat Carley stepped on the first rock, and, poising, she calculated on a running leap from stone to stone. Once launched, she felt she was falling downhill. She swayed, she splashed, she slipped; and clearing the longest leap from the last stone to shore she lost her balance and fell into Glenn's arms. His kisses drove away both her panic and her resentment.

"By Jove! I didn't think you'd even attempt it!" he declared, manifestly pleased. "I made sure I'd have to pack you over—in fact, rather liked the idea."

"I wouldn't advise you to employ any such means again—to dare me," she retorted.

"That's a nifty outdoor suit you've on," he said, admiringly. "I was wondering what you'd wear. I like short outing skirts for women, rather than trousers. The service sort of made the fair sex dippy about pants."

"It made them dippy about more than that," she replied. "You and I will never live to see the day that women recover their balance."

"I agree with you," replied Glenn.

Carley locked her arm in his. "Honey, I want to have a good time to-day. Cut out all the *other* women stuff. . . . Take me to see your little gray home in the West. Or is it gray?"

He laughed. "Why, yes, it's gray, just about. The logs have bleached some."

Glenn led her away up a trail that climbed between bowlders, and meandered on over piny mats of needles under great, silent, spreading pines; and closer to the impondering mountain wall, where at the base of the red rock the creek murmured strangely with hollow gurgle, where the sun had no chance to affect the cold damp gloom; and on through sweet-smelling woods, out into the sunlight again, and across a wider breadth of stream; and up a slow slope covered with stately pines, to a little cabin that faced the west.

"Here we are, sweetheart," said Glenn. "Now we shall see what you are made of."

Carley was noncommittal as to that. Her intense interest precluded any humor at this moment. Not until she actually saw the log cabin Glenn had erected with his own hands had she been conscious of any great interest. But sight of it awoke something unaccustomed in Carley. As she stepped into the cabin her heart was not acting normally for a young woman who had no illusions about love in a cottage.

Glenn's cabin contained one room about fifteen feet wide by twenty long. Between the peeled logs were lines of red mud, dried hard. There was a small window opposite the door. In one corner was a couch of poles, with green tips of pine boughs peeping from under the blankets. The floor consisted of flat rocks laid irregularly, with many spaces of earth showing between. The open fireplace appeared too large for the room, but the very bigness of it, as well as the blazing sticks and glowing embers, appealed strongly to Carley. A rough-hewn log formed the mantel, and on it Carley's picture held the place of honor. Above this a rifle lay across deer antlers. Carley paused here in her survey long enough to kiss Glenn and point to her photograph.

"You couldn't have pleased me more."

To the left of the fireplace was a rude cupboard of shelves, packed with boxes, cans, bags, and utensils. Below the cupboard, hung upon pegs, were blackened pots and pans, a long-handled skillet, and a bucket. Glenn's table was a masterpiece. There was no danger of knocking it over. It consisted of four poles driven into the ground, upon which had been nailed two wide slabs. This table showed considerable evidence of having been scrubbed scrupulously clean. There were two low stools, made out of boughs, and the seats had been covered with woolly sheep hide. In the right-hand corner stood a neat pile of firewood, cut with an ax, and beyond this hung saddle and saddle blanket, bridle and spurs. An old sombrero was hooked upon the pommel of the saddle. Upon the wall, higher up, hung a lantern, resting in a coil of rope that Carley took to be a lasso. Under a shelf upon which lay a suit case hung some rough wearing apparel.

Carley noted that her picture and the suit case were absolutely the only physical evidences of Glenn's connection with his Eastern life. That had an unaccountable effect upon Carley. What had she expected? Then, after another survey of the room, she began to pester Glenn with questions. He had to show her the spring outside and the little bench with basin and soap. Sight of his soiled towel made her throw up her hands. She sat on the stools. She lay on the couch. She rummaged into the contents of the cupboard. She threw wood on the fire. Then, finally, having exhausted her search and inquiry, she flopped down on one of the stools to gaze at Glenn in awe and admiration and incredulity.

"Glenn—you've actually lived here!" she ejaculated.

"Since last fall before the snow came," he said, smiling.

"Snow! Did it snow?" she inquired.

"Well, I guess. I was snowed in for a week."

"Why did you choose this lonely place—way off from the Lodge?" she asked, slowly.

"I wanted to be by myself," he replied, briefly.

"You mean this is a sort of camp-out place?"

"Carley, I call it my home," he replied, and there was a low, strong sweetness in his voice she had never heard before.

That silenced her for a while. She went to the door and gazed up at the towering wall, more wonderful

than ever, and more fearful, too, in her sight. Presently
tears dimmed her eyes. She did not understand her
feeling; she was ashamed of it; she hid it from Glenn.
Indeed, there was something terribly wrong between
her and Glenn, and it was not in him. This cabin he
called home gave her a shock which would take time
to analyze. At length she turned to him with gay utterance upon her lips. She tried to put out of her mind a
dawning sense that this close-to-the-earth habitation,
this primitive dwelling, held strange inscrutable power over a self she had never divined she possessed.
The very stones in the hearth seemed to call out from
some remote past, and the strong sweet smell of burnt
wood thrilled her to the marrow of her bones. How
little she knew of herself! But she had intelligence
enough to understand that there was a woman in her,
the female of the species; and through that the sensations from logs and stones and earth and fire had
strange power to call up the emotions handed down
to her from the ages. The thrill, the queer heart-
beat, the vague, haunting memory of something, as
of a dim childhood adventure, the strange prickling
sense of dread—these abided with her and augmented while she tried to show Glenn her pride in him and
also how funny his cabin seemed to her.

Once or twice he hesitatingly, and somewhat
appealingly, she imagined, tried to broach the subject of his work there in the West. But Carley wanted
a little while with him free of disagreeable argument.
It was a foregone conclusion that she would not like
his work. Her intention at first had been to begin
at once to use all persuasion in her power toward
having him go back East with her, or at the latest
some time this year. But the rude log cabin had

checked her impulse. She felt that haste would be unwise.

"Glenn Kilbourne, I told you why I came West to see you," she said, spiritedly. "Well, since you still swear allegiance to your girl from the East, you might entertain her a little bit before getting down to business talk."

"All right, Carley," he replied, laughing. "What do you want to do? The day is at your disposal. I wish it were June. Then if you didn't fall in love with West Fork you'd be no good."

"Glenn, I love people, not places," she returned.

"So I remember. And that's one thing I don't like. But let's not quarrel. What 'll we do?"

"Suppose you tramp with me all around, until I'm good and hungry. Then we'll come back here—and you can cook dinner for me."

"Fine! Oh, I know you're just bursting with curiosity to see how I'll do it. Well, you may be surprised, miss."

"Let's go," she urged.

"Shall I take my gun or fishing rod?"

"You shall take nothing but *me,*" retorted Carley. "What chance has a girl with a man, if he can hunt or fish?"

So they went out hand in hand. Half of the belt of sky above was obscured by swiftly moving gray clouds. The other half was blue and was being slowly encroached upon by the dark stormlike pall. How cold the air! Carley had already learned that when the sun was hidden the atmosphere was cold. Glenn led her down a trail to the brook, where he calmly picked her up in his arms, quite easily, it appeared, and leisurely packed her across, kissing her half a dozen times before he deposited her on her feet.

"Glenn, you do this sort of thing so well that it makes me imagine you have practice now and then," she said.

"No. But you are pretty and sweet, and like the girl you were four years ago. That takes me back to those days."

"Thank you. That's dear of you. I think I am something of a cat. . . . I'll be glad if this walk leads us often to the creek."

Spring might have been fresh and keen in the air, but it had not yet brought much green to the brown earth or to the trees. The cotton-woods showed a light feathery verdure. The long grass was a bleached white, and low down close to the sod fresh tiny green blades showed. The great fern leaves were sear and ragged, and they rustled in the breeze. Small gray sheath-barked trees with clumpy foliage and snags of dead branches, Glenn called cedars; and, grotesque as these were, Carley rather liked them. They were approachable, not majestic and lofty like the pines, and they smelled sweetly wild, and best of all they afforded some protection from the bitter wind. Carley rested better than she walked. The huge sections of red rock that had tumbled from above also interested Carley, especially when the sun happened to come out for a few moments and brought out their color. She enjoyed walking on the fallen pines, with Glenn below, keeping pace with her and holding her hand. Carley looked in vain for flowers and birds. The only living things she saw were rainbow trout that Glenn pointed out to her in the beautiful clear pools. The way the great gray bowlders trooped down to the brook as if they were cattle going to drink; the dark caverns under the shelving cliffs, where the water murmured with such hollow mockery; the low spear-pointed gray plants, resembling century plants, and which Glenn called mescal cactus, each with its single straight dead stalk standing on high with fluted head; the narrow gorges, perpendicularly walled in red, where the constricted brook plunged in amber and white cascades over fall after fall, tumbling, rushing, singing its water melody—these all held singular appeal for Carley as aspects of the wild land, fascinating for the moment, symbolic of the lonely red man and his forbears, and by their raw contrast making more necessary and desirable and elevating the comforts and conventions of civilization. The cave man theory interested Carley only as mythology.

Lonelier, wilder, grander grew Glenn's canyon. Carley was finally forced to shift her attention from the intimate objects of the canyon floor to the aloof and unattainable heights. Singular to feel the difference! That which she could see close at hand, touch if she willed, seemed to become part of her knowledge, could be observed and so possessed and passed by. But the gold-red ramparts against the sky, the crannied cliffs, the crags of the eagles, the lofty, distant blank walls, where the winds of the gods had written their wars—these haunted because they could never be possessed. Carley had often gazed at the Alps as at celebrated pictures. She admired, she appreciated— then she forgot. But the canyon heights did not affect her that way. They vaguely dissatisfied, and as she could not be sure of what they dissatisfied, she had to conclude that it was in herself. To see, to watch, to dream, to seek, to strive, to endure, to find! Was that what they meant? They might make her thoughtful of the vast earth, and its endless age, and its staggering mystery. But what more!

The storm that had threatened blackened the sky, and gray scudding clouds buried the canyon rims, and long veils of rain and sleet began to descend. The wind roared through the pines, drowning the roar of the brook. Quite suddenly the air grew piercingly cold. Carley had forgotten her gloves, and her pockets had not been constructed to protect hands. Glenn drew her into a sheltered nook where a rock jutted out from overhead and a thicket of young pines helped break the onslaught of the wind. There Carley sat on a cold rock, huddled up close to Glenn, and wearing to a state she knew would be misery. Glenn not only seemed content; he was happy. "This is great," he said. His coat was open, his hands uncovered, and he watched the storm and listened with manifest delight. Carley hated to betray what a weakling she was, so she resigned herself to her fate, and imagined she felt her fingers numbing into ice, and her sensitive nose slowly and painfully freezing.

The storm passed, however, before Carley sank into abject and open wretchedness. She managed to keep pace with Glenn until exercise warmed her blood. At every little ascent in the trail she found herself laboring to get her breath. There was assuredly evidence of abundance of air in this canyon, but somehow she could not get enough of it. Glenn detected this and said it was owing to the altitude. When they reached the cabin Carley was wet, stiff, cold, exhausted. How welcome the shelter, the open fireplace! Seeing the cabin in a new light, Carley had the grace to acknowledge to herself that, after all, it was not so bad.

"Now for a good fire and then dinner," announced Glenn, with the air of one who knew his ground.

"Can I help?" queried Carley.

"Not to-day. I do not want you to spring any domestic science on me now."

Carley was not averse to withholding her ignorance. She watched Glenn with surpassing curiosity and interest. First he threw a quantity of wood upon the smoldering fire.

"I have ham and mutton of my own raising," announced Glenn, with importance. "Which would you prefer?"

"Of your own raising. What do you mean?" queried Carley.

"My dear, you've been so steeped in the fog of the crowd that you are blind to the homely and necessary things of living. I mean I have here meat of both sheep and hog that I raised myself. That is to say, mutton and ham. Which do you like?"

"Ham!" cried Carley, incredulously.

Without more ado Glenn settled to brisk action, every move of which Carley watched with keen eyes. The usurping of a woman's province by a man was always an amusing thing. But for Glenn Kilbourne—what more would it be? He evidently knew what he wanted, for every movement was quick, decisive. One after another he placed bags, cans, sacks, pans, utensils on the table. Then he kicked at the roaring fire, settling some of the sticks. He strode outside to return with a bucket of water, a basin, towel, and soap. Then he took down two queer little iron pots with heavy lids. To each pot was attached a wire handle. He removed the lids, then set both the pots right on the fire or in it. Pouring water into the basin, he proceeded to wash his hands. Next he took a large pan, and from a sack he filled it half full of flour. To this he added baking powder and salt. It was instructive for Carley to see him run his skillful fingers all through that flour, as if searching for lumps. After this he knelt before the fire and, lifting off one of the iron pots with a forked stick, he proceeded to wipe out the inside of the pot and grease it with a piece of fat. His next move was to rake out a pile of the red coals, a feat he performed with the stick, and upon these he placed the pot. Also he removed the other pot from the fire, leaving it, however, quite close.

"Well, all eyes?" he bantered, suddenly staring at her. "Didn't I say I'd surprise you?"

"Don't mind me. This is about the happiest—and most bewildered moment—of my life," replied Carley.

Returning to the table, Glenn dug at something in a large red can. He paused a moment to eye Carley.

"Girl, do you know how to make biscuits?" he queried.

"I might have known in my school days, but I've forgotten," she replied.

"Can you make apple pie?" he demanded, imperiously.

"No," rejoined Carley.

"How do you expect to please your husband?"

"Why—by marrying him, I suppose," answered Carley, as if weighing a problem.

"That has been the universal feminine point of view for a good many years," replied Glenn, flourishing a flour-whitened hand. "But it never served the women of the Revolution or the pioneers. And they were the builders of the nation. It will never serve the wives of the future, if we are to survive."

"Glenn, you rave!" ejaculated Carley, not knowing whether to laugh or be grave. "You were talking of humble housewifely things."

"Precisely. The humble things that were the foundation of the great nation of Americans. I meant work and children."

Carley could only stare at him. The look he flashed at her, the sudden intensity and passion of his ringing words, were as if he gave her a glimpse into the very depths of him. He might have begun in fun, but he had finished otherwise. She felt that she really did not know this man. Had he arraigned her in judgment? A flush, seemingly hot and cold, passed over her. Then it relieved her to see that he had returned to his task.

He mixed the shortening with the flour, and, adding water, he began a thorough kneading. When the consistency of the mixture appeared to satisfy him he took a handful of it, rolled it into a ball, patted and flattened it into a biscuit, and dropped it into the oven he had set aside on the hot coals. Swiftly he shaped eight or ten other biscuits and dropped them as the first. Then he put the heavy iron lid on the pot, and with a rude shovel, improvised from a flattened tin can, he shoveled red coals out of the fire, and covered the lid with them. His next move was to pare and slice potatoes, placing these aside in a pan. A small black coffee-pot half full of water, was set on a glowing part of the fire. Then he brought into use a huge, heavy knife, a murderous-looking implement it appeared to Carley, with which he cut slices of ham. These he dropped into the second pot, which he left uncovered. Next he removed the flour sack and other inpedimenta from the table, and proceeded to set places for two—blue-enamel plate and cup, with plain, substantial-looking knives, forks, and spoons. He went outside, to return presently carrying a small crock of butter. Evidently he had kept the butter in or near the spring. It looked dewy and cold and hard. After that he peeped under the lid of the pot which contained the biscuits. The other pot was sizzling and smoking, giving forth a delicious savory odor that affected Carley most agreeably. The coffee-pot had begun to steam. With a long fork Glenn turned the slices of ham and stood a moment watching them. Next he placed cans of three sizes upon the table; and these Carley conjectured contained sugar, salt, and pepper. Carley might not have been present, for all the attention he paid to her. Again he peeped at the biscuits. At the edge of the hot embers he placed a tin plate, upon which he carefully deposited the slices of ham. Carley had not needed sight of them to know she was hungry; they made her simply ravenous. That done, he poured the pan of sliced potatoes into the pot. Carley judged the heat of that pot to be extreme. Next he removed the lid from the other pot, exposing biscuits slightly browned; and evidently satisfied with these, he removed them from the coals. He stirred the slices of potatoes round and round; he emptied two heaping tablespoonfuls of coffee into the coffee-pot.

"Carley," he said, at last turning to her with a warm smile, "out here in the West the cook usually yells, 'Come and get it!' Draw up your stool."

And presently Carley found herself seated across the crude table from Glenn, with the background of chinked logs in her sight, and the smart of wood smoke in her eyes. In years past she had sat with him in the soft, subdued, gold-green shadows of the Astor, or in the sumptuous atmosphere of the St. Regis. But this event was so different, so striking, that she felt it would have limitless significance. For one thing, the look of Glenn! When had he ever seemed like this, wonderfully happy to have her there, consciously proud of this dinner he had prepared in half an hour, strangely studying her as one on trial? This might have had its effect upon Carley's reaction to the situation, making it sweet, trenchant with meaning, but she was hungry enough and the dinner was good enough to make this hour memorable on that score alone. She ate until she was actually ashamed of herself. She laughed heartily, she talked, she made love to Glenn. Then suddenly an idea flashed into her quick mind.

"Glenn, did this girl Flo teach you to cook?" she queried, sharply.

"No. I always was handy in camp. Then out here I had the luck to fall in with an old fellow who was a wonderful cook. He lived with me for a while. . . . Why, what difference would it have made—had Flo taught me?"

Carley felt the heat of blood in her face. "I don't know that it would have made a difference. Only—I'm glad she didn't teach you. I'd rather no girl could teach you what I couldn't."

"You think I'm a pretty good cook, then?" he asked.

"I've enjoyed this dinner more than any I've ever eaten."

"Thanks, Carley. That'll help a lot," he said, gayly, but his eyes shone with earnest, glad light. "I hoped I'd surprise you. I've found out here that I want to do things well. The West stirs something in a man.

It must be an unwritten law. You stand or fall by your own hands. Back East you know meals are just occasions—to hurry through—to dress for—to meet somebody—to eat because you have to eat. But out here they are different. I don't know how. In the city, producers, merchants, waiters serve you for money. The meal is a transaction. It has no significance. It is money that keeps you from starvation. But in the West money doesn't mean much. You must work to live."

Carley leaned her elbows on the table and gazed at him curiously and admiringly. "Old fellow, you're a wonder. I can't tell you how proud I am of you. That you could come West weak and sick, and fight your way to health, and learn to be self-sufficient! It is a splendid achievement. It amazes me. I don't grasp it. I want to think. Nevertheless I—"

"What?" he queried, as she hesitated.

"Oh, never mind now," she replied, hastily, averting her eyes.

The day was far spent when Carley returned to the lodge—and in spite of the discomfort of cold and sleet, and the bitter wind that beat in her face as she struggled up the trail—it was a day never to be forgotten. Nothing had been wanting in Glenn's attention or affection. He had been comrade, lover, all she craved for. And but for his few singular words about work and children there had been no serious talk. Only a play day in his canyon and his cabin! Yet had she appeared at her best? Something vague and perplexing knocked at the gate of her consciousness.

CHAPTER

4

TWO warm sunny days in early May inclined Mr. Hutter to the opinion that pleasant spring weather was at hand and that it would be a propitious time to climb up on the desert to look after his sheep interests. Glenn, of course, would accompany him.

"Carley and I will go too," asserted Flo.

"Reckon that'll be good," said Hutter, with an approving nod.

His wife also agreed that it would be fine for Carley to see the beautiful desert country round Sunset Peak. But Glenn looked dubious.

"Carley, it'll be rather hard," he said. "You're soft, and riding and lying out will stove you up. You ought to break in gradually."

"I rode ten miles to-day," rejoined Carley. "And didn't mind it—much." This was a little deviation from stern veracity.

"Shore Carley's well and strong," protested Flo. "She'll get sore, but that won't kill her."

Glenn eyed Flo with a rather penetrating glance. "I might drive Carley round about in the car," he said.

"But you can't drive over those lava flats, or go round, either. We'd have to send horses in some cases miles to meet you. It's horseback if you go at all."

"Shore we'll go horseback," spoke up Flo. "Carley has got it all over that Spencer girl who was here last summer."

"I think so, too. I am sure I hope so. Because you remember what the ride to Long Valley did to Miss Spencer," rejoined Glenn.

"What?" inquired Carley.

"Bad cold, peeled nose, skinned shin, saddle sores. She was in bed two days. She didn't show much pep the rest of her stay here, and she never got on another horse."

"Oh, is that all, Glenn?" returned Carley, in feigned surprise. "Why, I imagined from your tone that Miss Spencer's ride must have occasioned her discomfort. . . . See here, Glenn. I may be a tenderfoot, but I'm no mollycoddle."

"My dear, I surrender," replied Glenn, with a laugh. "Really, I'm delighted. But if anything happens—don't you blame me. I'm quite sure that a long horseback ride, in spring, on the desert, will show you a good many things about yourself."

That was how Carley came to find herself, the afternoon of the next day, astride a self-willed and unmanageable little mustang, riding in the rear of her friends, on the way through a cedar forest toward a place called Deep Lake.

Carley had not been able yet, during the several hours of their journey, to take any pleasure in the scenery or in her mount. For in the first place there was nothing to see but scrubby little gnarled cedars and drab-looking rocks; and in the second this Indian pony she rode had discovered she was not an adept horsewoman and had proceeded to take advantage of the fact. It did not help Carley's predicament to remember that Glenn had decidedly advised her against riding this particular mustang. To be sure, Flo had approved of Carley's choice, and Mr. Hutter, with a hearty laugh, had fallen in line: "Shore. Let her ride one of the broncs, if she wants." So this animal she bestrode must have been a bronc, for it did not take him long to elicit from Carley a muttered, "I don't know what bronc means, but it sounds like this pony acts."

Carley had inquired the animal's name from the young herder who had saddled him for her.

"Wal, I reckon he ain't got much of a name," replied the lad, with a grin, as he scratched his head. "For us boys always called him Spillbeans."

"Humph! What a beautiful cognomen!" ejaculated Carley. "But according to Shakespeare any name will serve. I'll ride him or—or—"

So far there had not really been any necessity for the completion of that sentence. But five miles of riding up into the cedar forest had convinced Carley that she might not have much farther to go. Spillbeans had ambled along well enough until he reached level ground where a long bleached grass waved in the wind. Here he manifested hunger, then a contrary nature, next insubordination, and finally direct hostility. Carley had urged, pulled, and commanded in vain. Then when she gave Spillbeans a kick in the flank he jumped stiff legged, propelling her up out of the saddle, and while she was descending he made the queer jump again, coming up to meet her. The jolt she got seemed to dislocate every bone in her body. Likewise it hurt. Moreover, along with her idea of what a spectacle she must have presented, it quickly decided Carley that Spillbeans was a horse that was not to be opposed. Whenever he wanted a mouthful of grass he stopped to get it. Therefore Carley was always in the rear, a fact which in itself did not displease her. Despite his contrariness, however, Spillbeans had apparently no intention of allowing the other horses to get completely out of sight.

Several times Flo waited for Carley to catch up. "He's loafing on you, Carley. You ought to have on a spur. Break off a switch and beat him some." Then she whipped the mustang across the flank with her bridle rein, which punishment caused Spillbeans meekly to trot on with alacrity. Carley had a positive belief that he would not do it for her. And after Flo's repeated efforts, assisted by chastisement from Glenn, had kept Spillbeans in a trot for a couple of miles Carley began to discover that the trotting of a horse was the most uncomfortable motion possible to imagine. It grew worse. It became painful. It gradually got unendurable. But pride made Carley endure it until suddenly she thought she had been stabbed in the side. This strange piercing pain must be what Glenn had called a "stitch" in the side, something common to novices on horseback. Carley could have screamed. She pulled the mustang to a walk and sagged in her saddle until the pain subsided. What a blessed relief! Carley had keen sense of the difference between riding in Central Park and in Arizona. She regretted her choice of horses. Spillbeans was attractive to look at, but the pleasure of riding him was a delusion. Flo had said his gait resembled the motion of a rocking chair. This Western girl, according to Charley, the sheep herder, was not above playing Arizona jokes. Be that as it might, Spillbeans now manifested a desire to remain with the other horses, and he broke out of a walk into a trot. Carley could not keep him from trotting. Hence her state soon wore into acute distress.

Her left ankle seemed broken. The stirrup was heavy, and as soon as she was tired she could no longer keep its weight from drawing her foot in. The inside of her right knee was as sore as a boil. Besides, she had other pains, just as severe, and she stood momentarily in mortal dread of that terrible stitch in her side. If it returned she knew she would fall off. But, fortunately, just when she was growing weak and dizzy, the horses ahead slowed to a walk on a descent. The road wound down into a wide deep canyon. Carley had a respite from her severest pains. Never before had she known what it meant to be so grateful for relief from anything.

The afternoon grew far advanced and the sunset was hazily shrouded in gray. Hutter did not like the looks of those clouds. "Reckon we're in for weather," he said. Carley did not care what happened. Weather or anything else that might make it possible to get off her horse! Glenn rode beside her, inquiring solicitously as to her pleasure. "Ride of my life!" she lied heroically. And it helped some to see that she both fooled and pleased him.

Beyond the canyon the cedared desert heaved higher and changed its aspect. The trees grew larger, bushier, greener, and closer together, with patches of bleached grass between, and russet-lichened rocks everywhere. Small cactus plants bristled sparsely in open places; and here and there bright red flowers—Indian paintbrush, Flo called them—added a touch of color to the gray. Glenn pointed to where dark banks of cloud had massed around the mountain peaks. The scene to the west was somber and compelling.

At last the men and the pack-horses ahead came to a halt in a level green forestland with no high trees. Far ahead a chain of soft gray round hills led up to the dark heaved mass of mountains. Carley saw the gleam of water through the trees. Probably her mustang saw or scented it, because he started to trot. Carley had reached a limit of strength, endurance, and patience. She hauled him up short. When Spillbeans evinced a stubborn intention to go on Carley gave him a kick. Then it happened.

She felt the reins jerked out of her hands and the saddle propel her upward. When she descended it was to meet that before-experienced jolt.

"Look!" cried Flo. "That bronc is going to pitch."

"Hold on, Carley!" yelled Glenn.

Desperately Carley essayed to do just that. But Spillbeans jolted her out of the saddle. She came down on his rump and began to slide back and down. Frightened and furious, Carley tried to hang to the saddle with her hands and to squeeze the mustang with her knees. But another jolt broke her hold, and then, helpless and bewildered, with her heart in her throat and a terrible sensation of weakness, she slid back at each upheave of the muscular rump until she slid off and to the ground in a heap. Whereupon Spillbeans trotted off toward the water.

Carley sat up before Glenn and Flo reached her. Manifestly they were concerned about her, but both were ready to burst with laughter. Carley knew she was not hurt and she was so glad to be off the mustang that, on the moment, she could almost have laughed herself.

"That beast is well named," she said. "He spilled me, all right. And I presume I resembled a sack of beans."

"Carley—you're—not hurt?" asked Glenn, choking, as he helped her up.

"Not physically. But my feelings are."

Then Glenn let out a hearty howl of mirth, which was seconded by a loud guffaw from Hutter. Flo, however, appeared to be able to restrain whatever she felt. To Carley she looked queer.

"Pitch! You called it that," said Carley.

"Oh, he didn't really pitch. He just humped up a few times," replied Flo, and then when she saw how Carley was going to take it she burst into a merry peal of laughter. Charley, the sheep herder was grinning, and some of the other men turned away with shaking shoulders.

"Laugh, you wild and woolly Westerners!" ejaculated Carley. "It must have been funny. I hope I can be a good sport. . . . But I bet you I ride him to-morrow."

"Shore—you—will," replied Flo.

Evidently the little incident drew the party closer together. Carley felt a warmth of good nature that overcame her first feeling of humiliation. They expected such things from her, and she should expect them, too, and take them, if not fearlessly or painlessly, at least without resentment.

Carley walked about to ease her swollen and sore joints, and while doing so she took stock of the camp ground and what was going on. At second glance the place had a certain attraction difficult for her to define. She could see far, and the view north toward those strange gray-colored symmetrical hills was one that fascinated while it repelled her. Near at hand the ground sloped down to a large rock-bound lake, perhaps a mile in circumference. In the distance, along the shore she saw a white conical tent, and blue smoke, and moving gray objects she took for sheep.

The men unpacked and unsaddled the horses, and, hobbling their forefeet together, turned them loose. Twilight had fallen and each man appeared to be briskly set upon his own task. Glenn was cutting around the foot of a thickly branched cedar where, he told Carley, he would make a bed for her and Flo. All that Carley could see that could be used for such purpose was a canvas-covered roll. Presently Glenn untied a rope from round this, unrolled it, and dragged it under the cedar. Then he spread down the outer layer of canvas, disclosing a considerable thickness of blankets. From under the top of these he pulled out two flat little pillows. These he placed in position, and turned back some of the blankets.

"Carley, you crawl in here, pile the blankets up, and the tarp over them," directed Glenn. "If it rains pull the tarp up over your head—and let it rain."

This direction sounded in Glenn's cheery voice a good deal more pleasurable than the possibilities suggested. Surely that cedar tree could not keep off rain or snow.

"Glenn, how about—about animals—and crawling things, you know?" queried Carley.

"Oh, there are a few tarantulas and centipedes, and sometimes a scorpion. But these don't crawl around much at night. The only thing to worry about are the hydrophobia skunks."

"What on earth are they?" asked Carley, quite aghast.

"Skunks are polecats, you know," replied Glenn, cheerfully. "Sometimes one gets bitten by a coyote that has rabies, and then he's a dangerous customer. He has no fear and he may run across you and bite you in the face. Queer how they generally bite your nose. Two men have been bitten since I've been here. One of them died, and the other had to go to the Pasteur Institute with a well-developed case of hydrophobia."

"Good heavens!" cried Carley, horrified.

"You needn't be afraid," said Glenn. "I'll tie one of the dogs near your bed."

Carley wondered whether Glenn's casual, easy tone had been adopted for her benefit or was merely an assimilation from this Western life. Not improbably Glenn himself might be capable of playing a trick on her. Carley endeavored to fortify herself against disaster, so that when it befell she might not be wholly ludicrous.

With the coming of twilight a cold, keen wind moaned through the cedars. Carley would have hovered close to the fire even if she had not been too tired to exert herself. Despite her aches, she did justice to the supper. It amazed her that appetite consumed her to the extent of overcoming a distaste for this strong, coarse cooking. Before the meal ended darkness had fallen, a windy raw darkness that enveloped heavily like a blanket. Presently Carley edged closer to the fire, and there she stayed, alternately turning back and front to the welcome heat. She seemingly roasted hands, face, and knees while her back froze. The wind blew the smoke in all directions. When she groped around with blurred, smarting eyes to escape the hot smoke, it followed her. The other members of the party sat comfortably on sacks or rocks, without much notice of the smoke that so exasperated Carley. Twice Glenn insisted that she take a seat he had fixed for her, but she preferred to stand and move around a little.

By and by the camp tasks of the men appeared to be ended, and all gathered near the fire to lounge and smoke and talk. Glenn and Hutter engaged in interested conversation with two Mexicans, evidently sheep herders. If the wind and cold had not made Carley so uncomfortable she might have found the scene picturesque. How black the night! She could scarcely distinguish the sky at all. The cedar branches swished in the wind, and from the gloom came a low sound of waves lapping a rocky shore. Presently Glenn held up a hand.

"Listen, Carley!" he said.

Then she heard strange wild yelps, staccato, piercing, somehow infinitely lonely. They made her shudder.

"Coyotes," said Glenn. "You'll come to love that chorus. Hear the dogs bark back."

Carley listened with interest, but she was inclined to doubt that she would ever become enamoured of such wild cries.

"Do coyotes come near camp?" she queried.

"Shore. Sometimes they pull your pillow out from under your head," replied Flo, laconically.

Carley did not ask any more questions. Natural history was not her favorite study and she was sure she could dispense with any first-hand knowledge of desert beasts. She thought, however, she heard one of the men say, "Big varmint prowlin' round the sheep." To which Hutter replied, "Reckon it was a bear." And Glenn said, "I saw his fresh track by the lake. Some bear!"

The heat from the fire made Carley so drowsy that she could scarcely hold up her head. She longed for bed even if it was out there in the open. Presently Flo called her: "Come. Let's walk a little before turning in."

So Carley permitted herself to be led to and fro down an open aisle between some cedars. The far end of that aisle, dark, gloomy, with the bushy secretive cedars all around, caused Carley apprehension she was ashamed to admit. Flo talked eloquently about the joys of camp life, and how the harder any outdoor task was and the more endurance and pain it required, the more pride and pleasure one had in remembering it. Carley was weighing the import of these words when suddenly Flo clutched her arm. "What's that?" she whispered, tensely.

Carley stood stock-still. They had reached the furthermost end of that aisle, but had turned to go back. The flare of the camp fire threw a wan light into the shadows before them. There came a rustling in the brush, a snapping of twigs. Cold tremors chased up and down Carley's back.

"Shore it's a varmint, all right. Let's hurry," whispered Flo.

Carley needed no urging. It appeared that Flo was not going to run. She walked fast, peering back over her shoulder, and, hanging to Carley's arm, she rounded a large cedar that had obstructed some of the firelight. The gloom was not so thick here. And on the instant Carley espied a low, moving object, somehow furry, and gray in color. She gasped. She could not speak. Her heart gave a mighty throb and seemed to stop.

"What do you see?" cried Flo, sharply, peering ahead. "Oh! . . . come, Carley. *Run!*"

Flo's cry showed she must nearly be strangled with terror. But Carley was frozen in her tracks. Her eyes were riveted upon the gray furry object. It stopped. Then it came faster. It magnified. It was a huge beast. Carley had no control over mind, heart, voice, or muscle. Her legs gave way. She was sinking. A terrible panic, icy, sickening, rending, possessed her whole body.

The huge gray thing came at her. Into the rushing of her ears broke thudding sounds. The thing leaped up. A horrible petrifaction suddenly made stone of Carley. Then she saw a gray mantlelike object cast aside to disclose the dark form of a man. Glenn!

"Carley, dog-gone it! You don't scare worth a cent," he laughingly complained.

She collapsed into his arms. The liberating shock was as great as had been her terror. She began to tremble violently. Her hands got back a sense of strength to clutch. Heart and blood seemed released from that ice-banded vise.

"Say, I believe you were scared," went on Glenn, bending over her.

"Scar-ed!" she gasped. "Oh—there's no word— to tell—what I was!"

Flo came running back, giggling with joy. "Glenn, she shore took you for a bear. Why, I felt her go stiff as a post! . . . Ha! Ha! Ha! Carley, now how do you like the wild and woolly?"

"Oh! You put up—a trick on me!" ejaculated Carley. "Glenn, how could you? . . . Such a terrible trick! I wouldn't have minded—something reasonable. But that! Oh, I'll never forgive you!"

Glenn showed remorse, and kissed her before Flo in a way that made some little amends. "Maybe I overdid it," he said. "But I thought you'd have a momentary start, you know, enough to make you yell, and then you'd see through it. I only had a sheepskin over my shoulders as I crawled on hands and knees."

"Glenn, for me you were a prehistoric monster— a dinosaur, or something," replied Carley.

It developed, upon their return to the camp-fire circle, that everybody had been in the joke; and they all derived hearty enjoyment from it.

"Reckon that makes you one of us," said Hutter, genially. "We've all had our scares."

Carley wondered if she were not so constituted that such trickery alienated her. Deep in her heart she resented being made to show her cowardice. But then she realized that no one had really seen any evidence of her state. It was fun to them.

Soon after this incident Hutter sounded what he called the roll-call for bed. Following Flo's instructions, Carley sat on their bed, pulled off her boots, folded coat and sweater at her head, and slid down under the blankets. How strange and hard a bed! Yet Carley had the most delicious sense of relief and rest she had ever experienced. She straightened out on her back with a feeling that she had never before appreciated the luxury of lying down.

Flo cuddled up to her in quite sisterly fashion, saying: "Now don't cover your head. If it rains I'll wake and pull up the tarp. Good night, Carley." And almost immediately she seemed to fall asleep.

For Carley, however, sleep did not soon come. She had too many aches; the aftermath of her shock of fright abided with her; and the blackness of night, the cold whip of wind over her face, and the unprotected helplessness she felt in this novel bed, were too entirely new and disturbing to be overcome at once. So she lay wide eyed, staring at the dense gray shadow, at the flickering lights upon the cedar. At length her mind formed a conclusion that this sort of thing might be worth the hardship once in a lifetime, anyway. What a concession to Glenn's West! In the secret seclusion of her mind she had to confess that if her vanity had not been so assaulted and humiliated she might have enjoyed herself more. It seemed impossible, however, to have thrills and pleasures and exaltations in the face of discomfort, privation, and an uneasy half-acknowledged fear. No woman could have either a good or a profitable time when she was at her worst. Carley thought she would not be averse to getting Flo Hutter to New York, into an atmosphere wholly strange and difficult, and see how she met situation after situation unfamiliar to her. And so Carley's mind drifted on until at last she succumbed to drowsiness.

A voice pierced her dreams of home, of warmth and comfort. Something sharp, cold, and fragrant was scratching her eyes. She opened them. Glenn stood over her, pushing a sprig of cedar into her face.

"Carley, the day is far spent," he said, gayly. "We want to roll up your bedding. Will you get out of it?"

"Hello, Glenn! What time is it?" she replied.

"It's nearly six."

"What! . . . Do you expect me to get up at that ungodly hour?"

"We're all up. Flo's eating breakfast. It's going to be a bad day, I'm afraid. And we want to get packed and moving before it starts to rain."

"Why do girls leave home?" she asked, tragically.

"To make poor devils happy, of course," he replied, smiling down upon her.

That smile made up to Carley for all the clamoring sensations of stiff, sore muscles. It made her ashamed that she could not fling herself into this adventure with all her heart. Carley essayed to sit up. "Oh, I'm afraid my anatomy has become disconnected! . . . Glenn, do I look a sight?" She never would have asked him that if she had not known she could bear inspection at such an inopportune moment.

"You look great," he asserted, heartily. "You've got color. And as for your hair—I like to see it mussed that way. You were always one to have it dressed—just so. . . . Come, Carley, rustle now."

Thus adjured, Carley did her best under adverse circumstances. And she was gritting her teeth and complimenting herself when she arrived at the task of pulling on her boots. They were damp and her feet appeared to have swollen. Moreover, her ankles were sore. But she accomplished getting into them at the expense of much pain and sundry utterances more forcible than elegant. Glenn brought her warm water, a mitigating circumstance. The morning was cold and thought of that biting desert water had been trying.

"Shore you're doing fine," was Flo's greeting. "Come and get it before we throw it out."

Carley made haste to comply with the Western mandate, and was once again confronted with the singular fact that appetite did not wait upon the troubles of a tenderfoot. Glenn remarked that at least she would not starve to death on the trip.

"Come, climb the ridge with me," he invited. "I want you to take a look to the north and east."

He led her off through the cedars, up a slow red-earth slope, away from the lake. A green moundlike eminence topped with flat red rock appeared near at hand and not at all a hard climb. Nevertheless, her eyes deceived her, as she found to the cost of her breath. It was both far away and high.

"I like this location," said Glenn. "If I had the money I'd buy this section of land—six hundred and forty acres—and make a ranch of it. Just under this bluff is a fine open flat bench for a cabin. You could see away across the desert clear to Sunset Peak. There's a good spring of granite water. I'd run water from the lake down into the lower flats, and I'd sure raise some stock."

"What do you call this place?" asked Carley, curiously.

"Deep Lake. It's only a watering place for sheep and cattle. But there's fine grazing, and it's a wonder to me no one has ever settled here."

Looking down, Carley appreciated his wish to own the place; and immediately there followed in her a desire to get possession of this tract of land before anyone else discovered its advantages, and to hold it for Glenn. But this would surely conflict with her intention of persuading Glenn to go back East. As quickly as her impulse had been born it died.

Suddenly the scene gripped Carley. She looked from near to far, trying to grasp the illusive something. Wild lonely Arizona land! She saw ragged dumpy cedars of gray and green, lines of red earth, and a round space of water, gleaming pale under the lowering clouds; and in the distance isolated hills, strangely curved, wandering away to a black uplift of earth obscured in the sky.

These appeared to be mere steps leading her sight farther and higher to the cloud-navigated sky, where rosy and golden effulgence betokened the sun and the east. Carley held her breath. A transformation was going on before her eyes.

"Carley, it's a stormy sunrise," said Glenn.

His words explained, but they did not convince. Was this sudden-bursting glory only the sun rising behind storm clouds? She could see the clouds moving while they were being colored. The universal gray surrendered under some magic paint brush. The rifts widened, and the gloom of the pale-gray world seemed to vanish. Beyond the billowy, rolling, creamy edges of clouds, white and pink, shone the soft exquisite fresh blue sky. And a blaze of fire, a burst of molten gold, sheered up from behind the rim of cloud and suddenly poured a sea of sunlight from east to west. It transfigured the round foothills. They seemed bathed in ethereal light, and the silver mists that overhung them faded while Carley gazed, and a rosy flush crowned the symmetrical domes. Southward along the horizon line, down-dropping veils of rain, just touched with the sunrise tint, streamed in drifting slow movement from cloud to earth. To the north the range of foothills lifted toward the majestic dome of Sunset Peak, a volcanic upheaval of red and purple cinders, bare as rock, round as the lower hills, and wonderful in its color. Full in the blaze of the rising sun it flaunted an unchangeable front. Carley understood now what had been told her about this peak. Volcanic fires had thrown up a colossal mound of cinders burned forever to the hues of the setting sun. In every light and shade of day it held true to its name. Farther north rose the bold bulk of the San Francisco Peaks, that, half lost in the clouds, still dominated the desert scene. Then as Carley gazed the rifts began to close. Another transformation began, the reverse of what she watched. The golden radiance of sunrise vanished, and under a gray, lowering, coalescing pall of cloud the round hills returned to their bleak somberness, and the green desert took again its cold sheen.

"Wasn't it fine, Carley?" asked Glenn. "But nothing to what you will experience. I hope you stay till the weather gets warm. I want you to see a summer dawn on the Painted Desert, and a noon with the great white clouds rolling up from the horizon, and a sunset of massed purple and gold. If *they* do not get you then I'll give up."

Carley murmured something of her appreciation of what she had just seen. Part of his remark hung on her ear, thought-provoking and disturbing. He hoped she would stay until summer! That was kind of him. But her visit must be short and she now intended it to end with his return East with her. If she did not persuade him to go he might not want to go for a while, as he had written—"just yet." Carley grew troubled in mind. Such mental disturbance, however, lasted no longer than her return with Glenn to camp, where the mustang Spillbeans stood ready for her to mount. He appeared to put one ear up, the other down, and to look at her with mild surprise, as if to say: "What— hello—tenderfoot! Are you going to ride me again?"

Carley recalled that she had avowed she would ride him. There was no alternative, and her misgivings only made matters worse. Nevertheless, once in the saddle, she imagined she had the hallucination that to ride off so, with the long open miles ahead, was really thrilling. This remarkable state of mind lasted until Spillbeans began to trot, and then another day of misery beckoned to Carley with gray stretches of distance.

She was to learn that misery, as well as bliss, can swallow up the hours. She saw the monotony of cedar trees, but with blurred eyes; she saw the ground clearly enough, for she was always looking down, hoping for sandy places or rocky places where her mustang could not trot.

At noon the cavalcade ahead halted near a cabin and corral, which turned out to be a sheep ranch belonging to Hutter. Here Glenn was so busy that he had no time to devote to Carley. And Flo, who was more at home on a horse than on the ground, rode around everywhere with the men. Most assuredly Carley could not pass by the chance to get off Spillbeans and to walk a little. She found, however, that what she wanted most was to rest. The cabin was deserted, a dark, damp place with a rank odor. She did not stay long inside.

Rain and snow began to fall, adding to what Carley felt to be a disagreeable prospect. The immediate present, however, was cheered by a cup of hot soup and some bread and butter which the herder Charley brought her. By and by Glenn and Hutter returned with Flo, and all partook of some lunch.

All too soon Carley found herself astride the mustang again. Glenn helped her don the slicker, an abominable sticky rubber coat that bundled her up and tangled her feet round the stirrups. She was glad to find, though, that it served well indeed to protect her from raw wind and rain.

"Where do we go from here?" Carley inquired, ironically.

Glenn laughed in a way which proved to Carley that he knew perfectly well how she felt. Again his smile caused her self-reproach. Plain indeed was it that he had really expected more of her in the way of complaint and less of fortitude. Carley bit her lips.

Thus began the afternoon ride. As it advanced the sky grew more threatening, the wind rawer, the cold keener, and the rain cut like little bits of sharp ice. It blew in Carley's face. Enough snow fell to whiten the open patches of ground. In an hour Carley realized that she had the hardest task of her life to ride to the end of the day's journey. No one could have guessed her plight. Glenn complimented her upon her adaptation to such unpleasant conditions. Flo evidently was on the lookout for the tenderfoot's troubles. But as Spillbeans had taken to lagging at a walk, Carley was enabled to conceal all outward sign of her woes. It rained, hailed, sleeted, snowed, and grew colder all the time. Carley's feet became lumps of ice. Every step the mustang took sent acute pains ramifying from bruised and raw places all over her body.

Once, finding herself behind the others and out of sight in the cedars, she got off to walk awhile, leading the mustang. This would not do, however, because she fell too far in the rear. Mounting again, she rode on, beginning to feel that nothing mattered, that this trip would be the end of Carley Burch. How she hated that dreary, cold, flat land the road bisected without end. It felt as if she rode hours to cover a mile. In open stretches she saw the whole party straggling along, separated from one another, and each for himself. They certainly could not be enjoying themselves. Carley shut her eyes, clutched the pommel of the saddle, trying to support her weight. How could she endure another mile? Alas! there might be many miles. Suddenly a terrible shock seemed to rack her. But it was only that Spillbeans had once again taken to a trot. Frantically she pulled on the bridle. He was not to be thwarted. Opening her eyes, she saw a cabin far ahead which probably was the destination for the night. Carley knew she would never reach it, yet she clung on desperately. What she dreaded was the return of that stablike pain in her side. It came, and life seemed something abject and monstrous. She rode stiff legged, with her hands propping her stiffly above the pommel, but the stabbing pain went right on, and in deeper. When the mustang halted his trot beside the other horses, Carley was in the last extremity. Yet as Glenn came to her, offering a hand, she still hid her agony. Then Flo called out gayly: "Carley, you've done twenty-five miles on as rotten a day as I remember. Shore we all hand it to you. And I'm confessing I didn't think you'd ever stay the ride out. Spillbeans is the meanest nag we've got and he has the hardest gait."

*L*ATER Carley leaned back in a comfortable seat, before a blazing fire that happily sent its acrid smoke up the chimney, pondering ideas in her mind.

There could be a relation to familiar things that was astounding in its revelation. To get off a horse that had tortured her, to discover an almost insatiable appetite, to rest weary, aching body before the genial warmth of a beautiful fire—these were experiences which Carley found to have been hitherto unknown delights. It struck her suddenly and strangely that to know the real truth about anything in life might require infinite experience and understanding. How could one feel immense gratitude and relief, or the delight of satisfying acute hunger, or the sweet comfort of rest, unless there had been circumstances of extreme contrast? She had been compelled to suffer cruelly on horseback in order to make her appreciate how good it was to get down on the ground. Otherwise she never would have known. She wondered, then, how true that principle might be in all experience. It gave strong food for thought. There were things in the world never before dreamed of in her philosophy.

Carley was wondering if she were narrow and dense to circumstances of life differing from her own when a remark of Flo's gave pause to her reflections.

"Shore the worst is yet to come." Flo had drawled.

Carley wondered if this distressing statement had to do in some way with the rest of the trip. She stifled her curiosity. Painful knowledge of that sort would come quickly enough.

"Flo, are you girls going to sleep here in the cabin?" inquired Glenn.

"Shore. It's cold and wet outside," replied Flo.

"Well, Felix, the Mexican herder, told me some Navajos had been bunking here."

"Navajos? You mean Indians?" interposed Carley, with interest.

"Shore do," said Flo. "I knew that. But don't mind Glenn. He's full of tricks, Carley. He'd give us a hunch to lie out in the wet."

Hutter burst into his hearty laugh. "Wal, I'd rather get some things anyday than a bad cold."

"Shore I've had both," replied Flo, in her easy drawl, "and I'd prefer the cold. But for Carley's sake—"

"Pray don't consider me," said Carley. The rather crude drift of the conversation affronted her.

"Well, my dear," put in Glenn, "it's a bad night outside. We'll all make our beds here."

"Glenn, you shore are a nervy fellow," drawled Flo.

Long after everybody was in bed Carley lay awake in the blackness of the cabin, sensitively fidgeting and quivering over imaginative contact with creeping things. The fire had died out. A cold air passed through the room. On the roof pattered gusts of rain. Carley heard a rustling of mice. It did not seem possible that she could keep awake, yet she strove to do so. But her pangs of body, her extreme fatigue soon yielded to the quiet and rest of her bed, engendering a drowsiness that proved irresistible.

Morning brought fair weather and sunshine, which helped to sustain Carley in her effort to brave out her pains and woes. Another disagreeable day would have forced her to humiliating defeat. Fortunately for her, the business of the men was concerned with the immediate neighborhood, in which they expected to stay all morning.

"Flo, after a while persuade Carley to ride with you to the top of this first foothill," said Glenn. "It's not far, and it's worth a good deal to see the Painted Desert from there. The day is clear and the air free from dust."

"Shore. Leave it to me. I want to get out of camp, anyhow. That conceited *hombre,* Lee Stanton, will be riding in here," answered Flo, laconically.

The slight knowing smile on Glenn's face and the grinning disbelief on Mr. Hutter's were facts not lost upon Carley. And when Charley, the herder, deliberately winked at Carley, she conceived the idea that Flo, like many women, only ran off to be pursued. In some manner Carley did not seek to analyze, the purported advent of this Lee Stanton pleased her. But she did admit to her consciousness that women, herself included, were both as deep and mysterious as the sea, yet as transparent as an inch of crystal water.

It happened that the expected newcomer rode into camp before anyone left. Before he dismounted he made a good impression on Carley, and as he stepped down in lazy, graceful action, a tall lithe figure, she thought him singularly handsome. He wore a black sombrero, a flannel shirt, blue jeans stuffed into high boots, and long, big-roweled spurs.

"How are you-all?" was his greeting.

From the talk that ensued between him and the men, Carley concluded that he must be overseer of the sheep hands. Carley knew that Hutter and Glenn were not interested in cattle raising. And in fact they were, especially Hutter, somewhat inimical to the dominance of the range land by cattle barons of Flagstaff.

"When's Ryan goin' to dip?" asked Hutter.

"To-day or to-morrow," replied Stanton.

"Reckon we ought to ride over," went on Hutter. "Say, Glenn, do you reckon Miss Carley could stand a sheep-dip?"

This was spoken in a low tone, scarcely intended for Carley, but she had keen ears and heard distinctly. Not improbably this sheep-dip was what Flo meant as the worst to come. Carley adopted a listless posture to hide her keen desire to hear what Glenn would reply to Hutter.

"I should say not!" whispered Glenn, fiercely.

"Cut out that talk. She'll hear you and want to go."

Whereupon Carley felt mount in her breast an intense and rebellious determination to see a sheep-dip. She would astonish Glenn. What did he want, anyway? Had she not withstood the torturing trot of the hardest-gaited horse on the range? Carley realized she was going to place considerable store upon that feat. It grew on her.

When the consultation of the men ended, Lee Stanton turned to Flo. And Carley did not need to see the young man look twice to divine what ailed him. He was caught in the toils of love. But seeing through Flo Hutter was entirely another matter.

"Howdy, Lee!" she said, coolly, with her clear eyes on him. A tiny frown knitted her brow. She did not, at the moment, entirely approve of him.

"Shore am glad to see you, Flo," he said, with rather a heavy expulsion of breath. He wore a cheerful grin that in no wise deceived Flo, or Carley either. The young man had a furtive expression of eye.

"Ahuh!" returned Flo.

"I was shore sorry about—about that—" he floundered, in low voice.

"About what?"

"Aw, you know, Flo."

Carley strolled out of hearing, sure of two things—that she felt rather sorry for Stanton, and that his course of love did not augur well for smooth running. What queer creatures were women! Carley had seen several million coquettes, she believed; and assuredly Flo Hutter belonged to the species.

Upon Carley's return to the cabin she found Stanton and Flo waiting for her to accompany them on a ride up the foothill. She was so stiff and sore that she could hardly mount into the saddle; and the first mile of riding was something like a nightmare. She lagged behind Flo and Stanton, who apparently forgot her in their quarrel.

The riders soon struck the base of a long incline of rocky ground that led up to the slope of the foothill. Here rocks and gravel gave place to black cinders out of which grew a scant bleached grass. This desert verdure was what lent the soft gray shade to the foothill when seen from a distance. The slope was gentle, so that the ascent did not entail any hardship. Carley was amazed at the length of the slope, and also to see how high over the desert she was getting. She felt lifted out of a monotonous level. A green-gray league-long cedar forest extended down toward Oak Creek. Behind her the magnificent bulk of the mountains reached up into the stormy clouds, showing white slopes of snow under the gray pall.

The hoofs of the horses sank in the cinders. A fine choking dust assailed Carley's nostrils. Presently, when there appeared at least a third of the ascent still to be accomplished, Flo dismounted to walk, leading their horses. Carley had no choice but to do likewise. At first walking was a relief. Soon, however, the soft yielding cinders began to drag at her feet. At every step she slipped back a few inches, a very annoying feature of climbing. When her legs seemed to grow dead, Carley paused for a little rest. The last of the ascent, over a few hundred yards of looser cinders, taxed her remaining strength to the limit. She grew hot and wet and out of breath. Her heart labored. An unreasonable antipathy seemed to attend her efforts. Only her ridiculous vanity held her to this task. She wanted to please Glenn, but not so earnestly that she would have kept on plodding up this ghastly bare mound of cinders. Carley did not mind being a tenderfoot, but she hated the thought of these Westerners considering her a weakling. So she bore the pain of raw blisters and the miserable sensation of staggering on under a leaden weight.

Several times she noted that Flo and Stanton halted to face each other in rather heated argument. At least Stanton's red face and forceful gestures attested to heat on his part. Flo evidently was weary of argument, and in answer to a sharp reproach she retorted, "Shore I was different after he came." To which Stanton responded by a quick passionate shrinking as if he had been stung.

Carley had her own reaction to this speech she could not help hearing; and inwardly, at least, her feeling must have been similar to Stanton's. She forgot the object of this climb and looked off to her right at the green level without really seeing it. A vague sadness weighed upon her soul. Was there to be a tangle of fates here, a conflict of wills, a crossing of loves? Flo's terse confession could not be taken lightly. Did she mean that she loved Glenn? Carley began to fear it. Only another reason why she must persuade Glenn to go back East! But the closer Carley came to what she divined must be an ordeal the more she dreaded it. This raw, crude West might have confronted her with a situation beyond her control. And as she dragged her weighted feet through the cinders, kicking up little puffs of black dust, she felt what she admitted to be an unreasonable resentment toward these Westerners and their barren, isolated, and boundless world.

"Carley," called Flo, "come—looksee, as the Indians say. Here is Glenn's Painted Desert, and I reckon it's shore worth seeing."

To Carley's surprise, she found herself upon the knob of the foothill. And when she looked out across a suddenly distinguishable void, she seemed struck by the immensity of something she was unable to grasp. She dropped her bridle; she gazed slowly, as if drawn, hearing Flo's voice.

"That thin green line of cottonwoods down there is the Little Colorado River," Flo was saying. "Reckon it's sixty miles, all down hill. The Painted Desert begins there and also the Navajo Reservation. You see the white strips, the red veins, the yellow bars, the black lines. They are all desert steps leading up and up for miles. That sharp black peak is called Wildcat. It's about a hundred miles. You see the desert stretching away to the right, growing dim—lost in distance? We don't know that country. But that north country we know as landmarks, anyway. Look at that saw-tooth range. The Indians call it Echo Cliffs. At the far end it drops off into the Colorado River. Lee's Ferry is there—about one hundred and sixty miles. That ragged black rent is the Grand Canyon. Looks like a thread, doesn't it? But Carley, it's some hole, believe me. Away to the left you see the tremendous wall rising and turning to come this way. That's the north wall of the Canyon. It ends at the great bluff—Greenland Point. See the black fringe above the bar of gold. That's a belt of pine trees. It's about eighty miles across this ragged old stone washboard of a desert. . . . Now turn and look straight and strain your sight over Wildcat. See the rim purple dome. You must look hard. I'm glad it's clear and the sun is shining. We don't often get this view. . . . That purple dome is Navajo Mountain, two hundred miles and more away!"

Carley yielded to some strange drawing power and slowly walked forward until she stood at the extreme edge of the summit.

What was it that confounded her sight? Desert slope—down and down—color—distance—space! The wind that blew in her face seemed to have the openness of the whole world back of it. Cold, sweet, dry, exhilarating, it breathed of untainted vastness. Carley's memory pictures of the Adirondacks faded into pastorals; her vaunted images of European scenery changed to operetta settings. She had nothing with which to compare this illimitable space.

"Oh!—America!" was her unconscious tribute.

Stanton and Flo had come on to places beside her. The young man laughed. "Wal, now Miss Carley, you couldn't say more. When I was in camp trainin' for service overseas I used to remember how this looked. An' it seemed one of the things I was goin' to fight for. Reckon I didn't like the idea of the Germans havin' my Painted Desert. I didn't get across to fight for it, but I shore was willin'."

"You see, Carley, this is our America," said Flo, softly.

Carley had never understood the meaning of the word. The immensity of the West seemed flung at her. What her vision beheld, so far-reaching and boundless, was only a dot on the map.

"Does any one live—out there?" she asked, with slow sweep of hand.

"A few white traders and some Indian tribes," replied Stanton. "But you can ride all day an' next day an' never see a livin' soul."

What was the meaning of the gratification in his voice? Did Westerners court loneliness? Carley wrenched her gaze from the desert void to look at her companions. Stanton's eyes were narrowed; his expression had changed; lean and hard and still, his face resembled bronze. The careless humor was gone, as was the heated flush of his quarrel with Flo. The girl, too, had subtly changed, had responded to an influence that had subdued and softened her. She was mute; her eyes held a light, comprehensive and all-embracing; she was beautiful then. For Carley, quick to read emotion, caught a glimpse of a strong, steadfast soul that spiritualized the brown freckled face.

Carley wheeled to gaze out and down into this incomprehensible abyss, and on to the far up-flung heights, white and red and yellow, and so on to the wonderful mystic haze of distance. The significance of Flo's designation of miles could not be grasped by Carley. She could not estimate distance. But she did not need that to realize her perceptions were swallowed up by magnitude. Hitherto the power of her eyes had been unknown. How splendid to see afar! She could see—yes—but what did she see? Space first, annihilating space, dwarfing her preconceived images, and then wondrous colors! What had she known of color? No wonder artists failed adequately and truly to paint mountains, let alone the desert space. The toiling millions of the crowded cities were ignorant of this terrible beauty and sublimity. Would it have helped them to see? But just to breathe that untainted air, just to see once the boundless open of colored sand and rock—to realize what the freedom of eagles meant—would not that have helped anyone?

And with the thought there came to Carley's quickened and struggling mind a conception of freedom. She had not yet watched eagles, but she now gazed out into their domain. What then must be the effect of such environment on people whom it encompassed? The idea stunned Carley. Would such people grow in proportion to the nature with which they were in conflict? Hereditary influence could not be comparable to such environment in the shaping of character.

"Shore I could stand here all day," said Flo. "But it's beginning to cloud over and this high wind is cold. So we'd better go, Carley."

"I don't know what I am, but it's not cold," replied Carley.

"Wal, Miss Carley, I reckon you'll have to come again an' again before you get a comfortable feelin' here," said Stanton.

It surprised Carley to see that this young Westerner had hit upon the truth. He understood her. Indeed she was uncomfortable. She was oppressed, vaguely unhappy. But why? The thing there—this infinitude of open sand and rock—was beautiful, wonderful, even glorious. She looked again.

Steep black-cindered slope, with its soft gray patches of grass, sheered down and down, and out in rolling slope to merge upon a cedar-dotted level. Nothing moved below, but a red-tailed hawk sailed across her vision. How still—how gray the desert floor as it reached away, losing its black dots, and gaining bronze spots of stone! By plain and prairie it fell away, each inch of gray in her sight magnifying into its league-long roll, on and on, and down across dark lines that were steppes, and at last blocked and changed by the meandering green thread which was the verdure of a desert river. Beyond stretched the white sand, where whirlwinds of dust sent aloft their funnel-shaped spouts; and it led up to the horizon wide ribs and ridges of red and walls of yellow and mountains of black, to the dim mound of purple so ethereal and mystic against the deep-blue cloud-curtained band of sky.

And on the moment the sun was obscured and that world of colorful flame went out, as if a blaze had died.

Deprived of its fire, the desert seemed to retreat, to fade coldly and gloomily, to lose its great landmarks in dim obscurity. Closer, around to the north, the canyon country yawned with innumerable gray jaws, ragged and hard, and the riven earth took on a different character. It had no shadows. It grew flat and, like the sea, seemed to mirror the vast gray cloud expanse. The sublime vanished, but the desolate remained. No warmth—no movement—no life! Dead stone it was, cut into a million ruts by ruthless ages. Carley felt that she was gazing down into chaos.

At this moment, as before, a hawk had crossed her vision, so now a raven sailed by, black as coal, uttering a hoarse croak.

"Quoth the raven—" murmured Carley, with a half-bitter laugh, as she turned away shuddering in spite of an effort of self-control. "Maybe he meant this wonderful and terrible West is never for such as I. . . . Come, let us go."

Carley rode all that afternoon in the rear of the caravan, gradually succumbing to the cold raw wind and the aches and pains to which she had subjected her flesh. Nevertheless, she finished the day's journey, and, sorely as she needed Glenn's kindly hand, she got off her horse without aid.

Camp was made at the edge of the devastated timber zone that Carley had found so dispiriting. A few melancholy pines were standing, and everywhere, as far as she could see southward, were blackened fallen trees and stumps. It was a dreary scene. The few cattle grazing on the bleached grass appeared as melancholy as the pines. The sun shone fitfully at sunset, and then sank, leaving the land to twilight and shadows.

Once in a comfortable seat beside the camp fire, Carley had no further desire to move. She was so far exhausted and weary that she could no longer appreciate the blessing of rest. Appetite, too, failed her this meal time. Darkness soon settled down. The wind moaned through the pines. She was indeed glad to crawl into bed, and not even the thought of skunks could keep her awake.

Morning disclosed the fact that the gray clouds had been blown away. The sun shone bright upon a white-frosted land. The air was still. Carley labored at her task of rising, and brushing her hair, and pulling on her boots; and it appeared her former sufferings were as naught compared with the pangs of this morning. How she hated the cold, the bleak, denuded forest land, the emptiness, the roughness, the crudeness! If this sort of feeling grew any worse she thought she would hate Glenn. Yet she was none the less set upon going on, and seeing the sheep-dip, and riding that fiendish mustang until the trip was ended.

Getting in the saddle and on the way this morning was an ordeal that made Carley actually sick. Glenn and Flo both saw how it was with her, and they left her to herself. Carley was grateful for this understanding. It seemed to proclaim their respect. She found further matter for satisfaction in the astonishing circumstance that after the first dreadful quarter of an hour in the saddle she began to feel easier. And at the end of several hours of riding she was not suffering any particular pain, though she was weaker.

At length the cut-over land ended in a forest of straggling pines, through which the road wound southward, and eventually down into a wide shallow canyon. Through the trees Carley saw a stream of water, open fields of green, log fences and cabins, and blue smoke. She heard the chug of a gasoline engine and the baa-baa of sheep. Glenn waited for her to catch up with him, and he said: "Carley, this is one of Hutter's sheep camps. It's not a—a very pleasant place. You won't care to see the sheep-dip. So I'm suggesting you wait here—"

"Nothing doing, Glenn," she interrupted. "I'm going to see what there is to see."

"But, dear—the men—the way they handle sheep—they'll—really it's no sight for you," he floundered.

"Why not?" she inquired, eying him.

"Because, Carley—you know how you hate the—the seamy side of things. . . . And the stench—why, it'll make you sick!"

"Glenn, be on the level," she said. "Suppose it does. Wouldn't you think more of me if I could stand it?"

"Why, yes," he replied, reluctantly, smiling at her, "I would. But I wanted to spare you. This trip has been hard. I'm sure proud of you. And, Carley—you can overdo it. Spunk is not everything. You simply couldn't stand this."

"Glenn, how little you know a woman!" she exclaimed. "Come along and show me your old sheep-dip."

They rode out of the woods into an open valley that might have been picturesque if it had not been despoiled by the work of man. A log fence ran along the edge of open ground and a mud dam held back a pool of stagnant water, slimy and green. As Carley rode on, the baa-baa of sheep became so loud that she could scarcely hear Glenn talking.

Several log cabins, rough hewn and gray with age, stood down inside the enclosure; and beyond there were large corrals. From the other side of these corrals came sounds of rough voices of men, a trampling of hoofs, heavy splashes, the beat of an engine, and the incessant baaing of the sheep.

At this point the members of Hutter's party dismounted and tied their horses to the top log of the fence. When Carley essayed to get off, Glenn tried to stop her, saying she could see well enough from there. But Carley got down and followed Flo. She heard Hutter call to Glenn: "Say, Ryan is short of men. We'll lend a hand for a couple of hours."

Presently Carley reached Flo's side and the first corral that contained sheep. They formed a compact woolly mass, rather white in color, with a tinge of pink. When Flo climbed up on the fence the flock plunged as one animal and with a trampling roar ran to the far side of the corral. Several old rams with wide curling horns faced around; and some of the ewes climbed up on the densely packed mass. Carley rather enjoyed watching them. She surely could not see anything amiss in this sight.

The next corral held a like number of sheep, and also several Mexicans who were evidently driving them into a narrow lane that led farther down. Carley saw the heads of men above other corral fences, and there was also a thick yellowish smoke rising from somewhere.

"Carley, are you game to see the dip?" asked Flo, with good nature that yet had a touch of taunt in it.

"That's my middle name," retorted Carley, flippantly.

Both Glenn and this girl seemed to be bent upon bringing out Carley's worst side, and they were succeeding. Flo laughed. The ready slang pleased her.

She led Carley along that log fence, through a huge open gate, and across a wide pen to another fence, which she scaled. Carley followed her, not particularly overanxious to look ahead. Some thick odor had begun to reach Carley's delicate nostrils. Flo led down a short lane and climbed another fence, and sat astride the top log. Carley hurried along to clamber up to her side, but stood erect with her feet on the second log of the fence.

Then a horrible stench struck Carley almost like a blow in the face, and before her confused sight there appeared to be drifting smoke and active men and running sheep, all against a background of mud. But at first it was the odor that caused Carley to close her eyes and press her knees hard against the upper log to keep from reeling. Never in her life had such a sickening nausea assailed her. It appeared to attack her whole body. The forerunning qualm of seasickness was as nothing to this. Carley gave a gasp, pinched her nose between her fingers so she could not smell, and opened her eyes.

Directly beneath her was a small pen, open at one end, into which sheep were being driven from the larger corral. The drivers were yelling. The sheep in the rear plunged into those ahead of them, forcing them on. Two men worked in this small pen. One was a brawny giant in undershirt and overalls that appeared filthy. He held a cloth in his hand and strode toward the nearest sheep. Folding the cloth round the neck of the sheep, he dragged it forward, with an ease which showed great strength, and threw it into a pit that yawned at the side. Souse went the sheep into a murky, muddy pool and disappeared. But suddenly its head came up and then its shoulders. And it began half to walk and half swim down what appeared to be a narrow boxlike ditch that contained other floundering sheep. Then Carley saw men on each side of this ditch bending over with poles that had crooks at the end, and their work was to press and pull the sheep along to the end of the ditch, and drive them up a boarded incline into another corral where many other sheep huddled, now a dirty muddy color like the liquid into which they had been immersed. Souse! Splash! In went sheep after sheep. Occasionally one did not go under. And then a man would press it under with the crook and quickly lift its head. The work went on with precision and speed, in spite of the yells and trampling and baa-baas, and the incessant action that gave an effect of confusion.

Carley saw a pipe leading from a huge boiler to the ditch. The dark fluid was running out of it.

From a rusty old engine with a big smokestack poured the strangling smoke. A man broke open a sack of yellow powder and dumped it into the ditch. Then he poured an acid-like liquid after it.

"Sulphur and nicotine," yelled Flo up at Carley. "The dip's poison. If a sheep opens his mouth he's usually a goner. But sometimes they save one."

Carley wanted to tear herself away from this disgusting spectacle. But it held her by some fascination. She saw Glenn and Hutter fall in line with the other men, and work like beavers. These two pacemakers in the small pen kept the sheep coming so fast that every worker below had a task cut out for him. Suddenly Flo squealed and pointed.

"There! that sheep didn't come up," she cried. "Shore he opened his mouth."

Then Carley saw Glenn energetically plunge his hooked pole in and out and around until he had located the submerged sheep. He lifted its head above the dip. The sheep showed no sign of life. Down on his knees dropped Glenn, to reach the sheep with strong brown hands, and to haul it up on the ground, where it flopped inert. Glenn pummeled it and pressed it, and worked on it much as Carley had seen a life-guard work over a half-drowned man. But the sheep did not respond to Glenn's active administrations.

"No use, Glenn," yelled Hutter, hoarsely. "That one's a goner."

Carley did not fail to note the state of Glenn's hands and arms and overalls when he returned to the ditch work. Then back and forth Carley's gaze went from one end to the other of that scene. And suddenly it was arrested and held by the huge fellow who handled the sheep so brutally. Every time he dragged one and threw it into the pit he yelled: "Ho! Ho!" Carley was impelled to look at his face, and she was amazed to meet the rawest and boldest stare from evil eyes that had ever been her misfortune to incite. She felt herself stiffen with a shock that was unfamiliar. This man was scarcely many years older than Glenn, yet he had grizzled hair, a seamed and scarred visage, coarse, thick lips, and beetling brows, from under which peered gleaming light eyes. At every turn he flashed them upon Carley's face, her neck, the swell of her bosom. It was instinct that caused her hastily to close her riding coat. She felt as if her flesh had been burned. Like a snake he fascinated her. The intelligence in his bold gaze made the beastliness of it all the harder to endure, all the stronger to arouse.

"Come, Carley, let's rustle out of this stinkin' mess," cried Flo.

Indeed, Carley needed Flo's assistance in clambering down out of the choking smoke and horrid odor.

"*Adios,* pretty eyes," called the big man from the pen.

"Well," ejaculated Flo, when they got out, "I'll bet I call Glenn good and hard for letting you go down there."

"It was—my—fault," panted Carley. "I said I'd stand it."

"Oh, you're game, all right. I didn't mean the dip. . . . That sheep-slinger is Haze Ruff, the toughest *hombre* on this range. Shore, now, wouldn't I like to take a shot at him? . . . I'm going to tell dad and Glenn."

"Please don't," returned Carley, appealingly.

"I shore am. Dad needs hands these days. That's why he's lenient. But Glenn will cowhide Ruff and I want to see him do it."

In Flo Hutter then Carley saw another and a different spirit of the West, a violence unrestrained and fierce that showed in the girl's even voice and in the piercing light of her eyes.

They went back to the horses, got their lunches from the saddlebags, and, finding comfortable seats in a sunny, protected place, they ate and talked. Carley had to force herself to swallow. It seemed that the horrid odor of dip and sheep had permeated everything. Glenn had known her better than she had known herself, and he had wished to spare her an unnecessary and disgusting experience. Yet so stubborn was Carley that she did not regret going through with it.

"Carley, I don't mind telling you that you've stuck it out better than any tenderfoot we ever had here," said Flo.

"Thank you. That from a Western girl is a compliment I'll not soon forget," replied Carley.

"I shore mean it. We've had rotten weather. And to end the little trip at this sheep-dip hole! Why, Glenn certainly wanted you to stack up against the real thing!"

"Flo, he did not want me to come on the trip, and especially here," protested Carley.

"Shore I know. But he *let* you."

"Neither Glenn nor any other man could prevent me from doing what I wanted to do."

"Well, if you'll excuse me," drawled Flo, "I'll differ with you. I reckon Glenn Kilbourne is not the man you knew before the war."

"No, he is not. But that does not alter the case."

"Carley, we're not well acquainted," went on Flo, more carefully feeling her way, "and I'm—not your kind. I don't know your Eastern ways. But I know what the West does to a man. The war ruined your friend—both his body and mind. . . . How sorry mother and I were for Glenn—those days when it looked he'd sure 'go west,' for good! . . . Did you know he'd been gassed and that he had five hemorrhages?"

"Oh! I knew his lungs had been weakened by gas. But he never told me about having hemorrhages."

"Well, he shore had them. The last one I'll never forget. Every time he'd cough it would fetch the blood. I could tell! . . . Oh, it was awful. I begged him *not* to cough. He smiled—like a ghost smiling—and he whispered, 'I'll quit.' . . . And he did. The doctor came from Flagstaff and packed him in ice. Glenn sat propped up all night and never moved a muscle. Never coughed again! And the bleeding stopped. After that we put him out on the porch where he could breathe fresh air all the time. There's something wonderfully healing in Arizona air. It's from the dry desert and here it's full of cedar and pine. Anyway Glenn got well. And I think the West has cured his mind, too."

"Of what?" queried Carley, in an intense curiosity she could scarcely hide.

"Oh, God only knows!" exclaimed Flo, throwing up her gloved hands. "I never could understand. But I *hated* what the war did to him."

Carley leaned back against the log, quite spent. Flo was unwittingly torturing her. Carley wanted passionately to give in to jealousy of this Western girl, but she could not do it. Flo Hutter deserved better than that. And Carley's baser nature seemed in conflict with all that was noble in her. The victory did not yet go to either side. This was a bad hour for Carley. Her strength had about played out, and her spirit was at low ebb.

"Carley, you're all in," declared Flo. "You needn't deny it. I'm shore you've made good with me as a tenderfoot who stayed the limit. But there's no sense in your killing yourself, nor in me letting you. So I'm going to tell dad we want to go home."

She left Carley there. The word home had struck strangely into Carley's mind and remained there. Suddenly she realized what it was to be homesick. The comfort, the ease, the luxury, the rest, the sweetness, the pleasure, the cleanliness, the gratification to eye and ear—to all the senses—how these thoughts came to haunt her! All of Carley's will power had been needed to sustain her on this trip to keep her from miserably failing. She had not failed. But contact with the West had affronted, disgusted, shocked, and alienated her. In that moment she could not be fair minded; she knew it; she did not care.

Carley gazed around her. Only one of the cabins was in sight from this position. Evidently it was a home for some of these men. On one side the peaked rough roof had been built out beyond the wall, evidently to serve as a kind of porch. On that wall hung the motliest assortment of things Carley had ever seen—utensils, sheep and cow hides, saddles, harness, leather clothes, ropes, old sombreros, shovels, stove pipe, and many other articles for which she could find no name. The most striking characteristic manifest in this collection was that of service. How they had been used! They had enabled people to live under primitive conditions. Somehow this fact inhibited Carley's sense of repulsion at their rude and uncouth appearance. Had any of her forefathers ever been pioneers? Carley did not know, but the thought was disturbing. It was thought-provoking. Many times at home, when she was dressing for dinner, she had gazed into the mirror at the graceful lines of her throat and arms, at the proud poise of her head, at the alabaster whiteness of her skin, and wonderingly she had asked of her image: "Can it be possible that I am a descendant of cavemen?" She had never been able to realize it, yet she knew it was true. Perhaps somewhere not far back along her line there had been a great-great-grandmother who had lived some kind of a primitive life, using such implements and necessaries as hung on this cabin wall, and thereby helped some man to conquer the wilderness, to live in it, and reproduce his kind. Like flashes Glenn's words came back to Carley—"Work and children!"

Some interpretation of his meaning and how it related to this hour held aloof from Carley. If she would ever be big enough to understand it and broad enough to accept it, the time was far distant. Just now she was sore and sick physically, and therefore certainly not in a receptive state of mind. Yet how could she have keener impressions than these she was receiving? It was all a problem. She grew tired of thinking. But even then her mind pondered on, a stream of consciousness over which she had no control. This dreary woods was deserted. No birds, no squirrels, no creatures such as fancy anticipated! In another direction, across the canyon, she saw cattle, gaunt, ragged, lumbering, and stolid. And on the moment the scent of sheep came on the breeze. Time seemed to stand still here, and what Carley wanted most was for the hours and days to fly, so that she would be home again.

At last Flo returned with the men. One quick glance at Glenn convinced Carley that Flo had not yet told him about the sheep dipper, Haze Ruff.

"Carley, you're a real sport," declared Glenn, with the rare smile she loved. "It's a dreadful mess. And to think you stood it! . . . Why, old Fifth Avenue, if you needed to make another hit with me you've done it!"

His warmth amazed and pleased Carley. She could not quite understand why it would have made any difference to him whether she had stood the ordeal or not. But then every day she seemed to drift a little farther from a real understanding of her lover. His praise gladdened her, and fortified her to face the rest of this ride back to Oak Creek.

Four hours later, in a twilight so shadowy that no one saw her distress, Carley half slipped and half fell from her horse and managed somehow to mount the steps and enter the bright living room. A cheerful red fire blazed on the hearth; Glenn's hound, Moze, trembled eagerly at sight of her and looked up with humble dark eyes; the white-clothed dinner table steamed with savory dishes. Flo stood before the blaze, warming her hands. Lee Stanton leaned against the mantel, with eyes on her, and every line of his lean, hard face expressed his devotion to her. Hutter was taking his seat at the head of the table. "Come an' get it—you-all," he called, heartily. Mrs. Hutter's face beamed with the spirit of that home. And lastly, Carley saw Glenn waiting for her, watching her come, true in this very moment to his stern hope for her and pride in her, as she dragged her weary, spent body toward him and the bright fire.

By these signs, or the effect of them, Carley vaguely realized that she was incalculably changing, that this Carley Burch had become a vastly bigger person in the sight of her friends, and strangely in her own a lesser creature.

CHAPTER
6

*I*F spring came at all to Oak Creek Canyon it
warmed into summer before Carley had time
to languish with the fever characteristic of early
June in the East.

As if by magic it seemed the green grass sprang
up, the green buds opened into leaves, the bluebells
and primroses bloomed, the apple and peach blossoms burst exquisitely white and pink against the blue
sky. Oak Creek fell to a transparent, beautiful brook,
leisurely eddying in the stonewalled nooks, hurrying
with murmur and babble over the little falls. The mornings broke clear and fragrantly cool, the noon hours
seemed to lag under a hot sun, the nights fell like
dark mantles from the melancholy star-sown sky.

Carley had stubbornly kept on riding and climbing until she killed her secret doubt that she was really a thoroughbred, until she satisfied her own insistent vanity that she could train to a point where this
outdoor life was not too much for her strength. She
lost flesh despite increase of appetite; she lost her
pallor for a complexion of gold-brown she knew her

Eastern friends would admire; she wore out the blisters and aches and pains; she found herself growing firmer of muscle, lither of line, deeper of chest. And in addition to these physical manifestations there were subtle intimations of a delight in a freedom of body she had never before known, of an exhilaration in action that made her hot and made her breathe, of a sloughing off of numberless petty and fussy and luxurious little superficialities which she had supposed were necessary to her happiness. What she had undertaken in vain conquest of Glenn's pride and Flo Hutter's Western tolerance, she had found to be a boomerang. She had won Glenn's admiration; she had won the Western girl's recognition. But her passionate, stubborn desire had been ignoble, and was proved so by the rebound of her achievement, coming home to her with a sweetness she had not the courage to accept. She forced it from her. This West with its rawness, its ruggedness, she hated.

Nevertheless, the June days passed, growing dreamily swift, growing more incomprehensibly full; and still she had not broached to Glenn the main object of her visit—to take him back East. Yet a little while longer! She hated his work and had not talked of that. Yet an honest consciousness told her that as time flew by she feared more and more to tell him that he was wasting his life there and that she could not bear it. Still—was he wasting it? Once in a while a timid and unfamiliar Carley Burch voiced a pregnant query. Perhaps what held Carley back most was the happiness she achieved in her walks and rides with Glenn. She lingered because of them. Every day she loved him more, and yet—there was something. Was it in her or in him? She had a woman's assurance

of his love and sometimes she caught her breath—
so sweet and strong was the tumultuous emotion it
stirred. She preferred to enjoy while she could, to
dream instead of think. But it was not possible to
hold a blank, dreamy, lulled consciousness all the
time. Thought would return. And not always could
she drive away a feeling that Glenn would never
be her slave. She divined something in his mind
that kept him gentle and kindly, restrained always,
sometimes melancholy and aloof, as if he were an
impassive destiny waiting for the iron consequences
he knew inevitably must fall. What was this that he
knew which she did not know? The idea haunted her.
Perhaps it was that which compelled her to use all her
woman's wiles and charms on Glenn. Still, though it
thrilled her to see she made him love her more as the
days passed, she could not blind herself to the truth
that no softness or allurement of hers changed this
strange restraint in him. How that baffled her! Was
it resistance or knowledge or nobility or doubt?

Flo Hutter's twentieth birthday came along the
middle of June, and all the neighbors and range hands
for miles around were invited to celebrate it.

For the second time during her visit, Carley put on
the white gown that had made Flo gasp with delight,
and had stunned Mrs. Hutter, and had brought a reluctant compliment from Glenn. Carley liked to create a
sensation. What were exquisite and expensive gowns
for, if not that?

It was twilight on this particular June night when
she was ready to go downstairs, and she tarried a
while on the long porch. The evening star, so lonely
and radiant, so cold and passionless in the dusky
blue, had become an object she waited for and

watched, the same as she had come to love the dreaming, murmuring melody of the waterfall. She lingered there. What had the sights and sounds and smells of this wild canyon come to mean to her? She could not say. But they had changed immeasurably.

Her soft slippers made no sound on the porch, and as she turned the corner of the house, where shadows hovered thick, she heard Lee Stanton's voice:

"But, Flo, you loved me before Kilbourne came."

The content, the pathos, of his voice chained Carley to the spot. Some situations, like fate, were beyond resisting.

"Shore I did," replied Flo, dreamily. This was the voice of a girl who was being confronted by happy and sad thoughts on her birthday.

"Don't you—love me—still?" he asked, huskily.

"Why, of course, Lee! *I* don't change," she said.

"But then, why—" There for the moment his utterance or courage failed.

"Lee, do you want the honest to God's truth?"

"I reckon—I do."

"Well, I love you just as I always did," replied Flo, earnestly. "But, Lee, I love—*him* more than you or anybody."

"My Heaven! Flo—you'll ruin us all!" he exclaimed, hoarsely.

"No, I won't either. You can't say I'm not level headed. I hated to tell you this, Lee, but you made me."

"Flo, you love me an' him—two men?" queried Stanton, incredulously.

"I shore do," she drawled, with a soft laugh. "And it's no fun."

"Reckon I don't cut much of a figure alongside Kilbourne," said Stanton, disconsolately.

"Lee, you could stand alongside any man," replied Flo, eloquently. "You're Western, and you're steady and loyal, and you'll—well, some day you'll be like dad. Could I say more? . . . But, Lee, this man is *different*. He is wonderful. I can't explain it, but I feel it. He has been through hell's fire. Oh! will I ever forget his ravings when he lay so ill? He means more to me than just *one* man. He's American. You're American, too, Lee, and you trained to be a soldier, and you would have made a grand one—if I know old Arizona. But you were not called to France. . . . Glenn Kilbourne went. God only knows what that means. But he *went*. And there's the difference. I saw the wreck of him. I did a little to save his life and his mind. I wouldn't be an American girl if I *didn't* love him. . . . Oh, Lee, can't you understand?"

"I reckon so. I'm not begrudging Glenn what— what you care. I'm only afraid I'll lose you."

"I never promised to marry you, did I?"

"Not in words. But kisses ought to—"

"Yes, kisses mean a lot," she replied. "And so far I stand committed. I suppose I'll marry you some day and be blamed lucky. I'll be happy, too—don't you overlook that hunch. . . . You needn't worry. Glenn is in love with Carley. She's beautiful, rich—and of his class. How could he ever see me?"

"Flo, you can never tell," replied Stanton, thoughtfully. "I didn't like her at first. But I'm comin' round. The thing is, Flo, does she love him as you love him?"

"Oh, I think so—I hope so," answered Flo, as if in distress.

"I'm not so shore. But then I can't savvy her. Lord knows I hope so, too. If she doesn't—if she goes back East an' leaves him here—I reckon my case—"

"Hush! I know she's out here to take him back. Let's go downstairs now."

"Aw, wait—Flo," he begged. "What's your hurry? Come—give me—"

"There! That's all you get, birthday or no birthday," replied Flo, gayly.

Carley heard the soft kiss and Stanton's deep breath, and then footsteps as they walked away in the gloom toward the stairway. Carley leaned against the log wall. She felt the rough wood—smelled the rusty pine rosin. Her other hand pressed her bosom where her heart beat with unwonted vigor. Footsteps and voices sounded beneath her. Twilight had deepened into night. The low murmur of the waterfall and the babble of the brook floated to her strained ears.

Listeners never heard good of themselves. But Stanton's subtle doubt of any depth to her, though it hurt, was not so conflicting as the ringing truth of Flo Hutter's love for Glenn. This unsought knowledge powerfully affected Carley. She was forewarned and forearmed now. It saddened her, yet did not lessen her confidence in her hold on Glenn. But it stirred to perplexing pitch her curiosity in regard to the mystery that seemed to cling round Glenn's transformation of character. This Western girl really knew more about Glenn than his fiancée knew. Carley suffered a humiliating shock when she realized that she had been thinking of herself, of her love, her life, her needs, her wants instead of Glenn's. It took no keen intelligence or insight into human nature to see that Glenn needed her more than she needed him.

Thus unwontedly stirred and upset and flung back upon pride of herself, Carley went downstairs to meet the assembled company. And never had she shown to greater contrast, never had circumstance and state of mind contrived to make her so radiant and gay and unbending. She heard many remarks not intended for her far-reaching ears. An old grizzled Westerner remarked to Hutter: "Wall, she's shore an unbroke filly." Another of the company—a woman—remarked: "Sweet an' pretty as a columbine. But I'd like her better if she was dressed decent." And a gaunt range rider, who stood with others at the porch door, looking on, asked a comrade: "Do you reckon that's style back East?" To which the other replied: "Mebbe, but I'd gamble they're short on silk back East an' likewise sheriffs."

Carley received some meed of gratification out of the sensation she created, but she did not carry her craving for it to the point of overshadowing Flo. On the contrary, she contrived to have Flo share the attention she received. She taught Flo to dance the fox-trot and got Glenn to dance with her. Then she taught it to Lee Stanton. And when Lee danced with Flo, to the infinite wonder and delight of the onlookers, Carley experienced her first sincere enjoyment of the evening.

Her moment came when she danced with Glenn. It reminded her of days long past and which she wanted to return again. Despite war tramping and Western labors Glenn retained something of his old grace and lightness. But just to dance with him was enough to swell her heart, and for once she grew oblivious to the spectators.

"Glenn, would you like to go to the Plaza with me again, and dance between dinner courses, as we used to?" she whispered up to him.

"Sure I would—unless Morrison knew you were to be there," he replied.

"Glenn! . . . I would not even see him."

"Any old time you wouldn't see Morrison!" he exclaimed, half mockingly.

His doubt, his tone grated upon her. Pressing closer to him, she said, "Come back and I'll prove it."

But he laughed and had no answer for her. At her own daring words Carley's heart had leaped to her lips. If he had responded, even teasingly, she could have burst out with her longing to take him back. But silence inhibited her, and the moment passed.

At the end of that dance Hutter claimed Glenn in the interest of neighboring sheep men. And Carley, crossing the big living room alone, passed close to one of the porch doors. Some one, indistinct in the shadow, spoke to her in low voice: "Hello, pretty eyes!"

Carley felt a little cold shock go tingling through her. But she gave no sign that she had heard. She recognized the voice and also the epithet. Passing to the other side of the room and joining the company there, Carley presently took a casual glance at the door. Several men were lounging there. One of them was the sheep dipper, Haze Ruff. His bold eyes were on her now, and his coarse face wore a slight, meaning smile, as if he understood something about her that was a secret to others. Carley dropped her eyes. But she could not shake off the feeling that wherever she moved this man's gaze followed her.

The unpleasantness of this incident would have been nothing to Carley had she at once forgotten it. Most unaccountably, however, she could not make herself unaware of this ruffian's attention. It did no good for her to argue that she was merely the cynosure of all eyes. This Ruff's tone and look possessed something heretofore unknown to Carley. Once she was tempted to tell Glenn. But that would only cause a fight, so she kept her counsel. She danced again, and helped Flo entertain her guests, and passed that door often; and once stood before it, deliberately, with all the strange and contrary impulse so inscrutable in a woman, and never for a moment wholly lost the sense of the man's boldness. It dawned upon her, at length, that the singular thing about this boldness was its difference from any which had ever before affronted her. The fool's smile meant that he thought she saw his attention, and, understanding it perfectly, had secret delight in it. Many and various had been the masculine egotisms which had come under her observation. But quite beyond Carley was this brawny sheep dipper, Haze Ruff. Once the party broke up and the guests had departed, she instantly forgot both man and incident.

Next day, late in the afternoon, when Carley came out on the porch, she was hailed by Flo, who had just ridden in from down the canyon.

"Hey Carley, come down. I shore have something to tell you," she called.

Carley did not lose any time pattering down that rude porch stairway. Flo was dusty and hot, and her chaps carried the unmistakable scent of sheep-dip.

"Been over to Ryan's camp an' shore rode hard to beat Glenn home," drawled Flo.

"Why?" queried Carley, eagerly.

"Reckon I wanted to tell you something Glenn swore he wouldn't let me tell. . . . He makes me tired. He thinks you can't stand things."

"Oh! Has he been—hurt?"

"He's skinned an' bruised up some, but I reckon he's not hurt."

"Flo—what happened?" demanded Carley, anxiously.

"Carley, do you know Glenn can fight like the devil?" asked Flo.

"No, I don't. But I remember he used to be athletic. Flo, you make me nervous. Did Glenn fight?"

"I reckon he did," drawled Flo.

"With whom?"

"Nobody else but that big *hombre,* Haze Ruff."

"Oh!" gasped Carley, with a violent start. "That—that ruffian! Flo, did you see—were you there?"

"I shore was, an' next to a horse race I like a fight," replied the Western girl. "Carley, why didn't you tell me Haze Ruff insulted you last night?"

"Why, Flo—he only said, 'Hello, pretty eyes,' and I let it pass!" said Carley, lamely.

"You never want to let anything pass, out West. Because next time you'll get worse. This turn your other cheek doesn't go in Arizona. But we shore thought Ruff said worse than that. Though from him that's aplenty."

"How did you know?"

"Well, Charley told it. He was standing out here by the door last night an' he heard Ruff speak to you. Charley thinks a heap of you an' I reckon he hates Ruff. Besides, Charley stretches things. He shore riled Glenn, an' I want to say, my dear, you missed the best thing that's happened since you got here."

"Hurry—tell me," begged Carley, feeling the blood come to her face.

"I rode over to Ryan's place for dad, an' when I got there I knew nothing about what Ruff said to you," began Flo, and she took hold of Carley's hand. "Neither did dad. You see, Glenn hadn't got there yet. Well, just as the men had finished dipping a bunch of sheep Glenn came riding down, lickety cut."

" 'Now what the hell's wrong with Glenn?' " said dad, getting up from where we sat.

"Shore I knew Glenn was mad, though I never before saw him that way. He looked sort of grim an' black. . . . Well, he rode right down on us an' piled off. Dad yelled at him an' so did I. But Glenn made for the sheep pen. You know where we watched Haze Ruff an' Lorenzo slinging the sheep into the dip. Ruff was just about to climb out over the fence when Glenn leaped up on it."

" 'Say, Ruff,' he said, sort of hard, 'Charley an' Ben tell me they heard you speak disrespectfully to Miss Burch last night.' "

"Dad an' I ran to the fence, but before we could catch hold of Glenn he'd jumped down into the pen."

" 'I'm not carin' much for what them herders say,' replied Ruff."

" 'Do you deny it?' demanded Glenn."

" 'I ain't denyin' nothin', Kilbourne,' growled Ruff. 'I might argue against me bein' disrespectful. That's a matter of opinion.' "

" 'You'll apologize for speaking to Miss Burch or I'll beat you up an' have Hutter fire you.' "

" 'Wal, Kilbourne, I never eat my words,' replied Ruff."

"Then Glenn knocked him flat. You ought to have heard that crack. Sounded like Charley hitting a steer with a club. Dad yelled: 'Look out, Glenn. He packs a gun!'—Ruff got up mad clear through I reckon. Then they mixed it. Ruff got in some swings, but he couldn't reach Glenn's face. An' Glenn batted him right an' left, every time in his ugly mug. Ruff got all bloody an' he cussed something awful. Glenn beat him against the fence an' then we all saw Ruff reach for a gun or knife. All the men yelled. An' shore I screamed. But Glenn saw as much as we saw. He got fiercer. He beat Ruff down to his knees an' swung on him hard. Deliberately knocked Ruff into the dip ditch. What a splash! It wet all of us. Ruff went out of sight. Then he rolled up like a huge hog. We were all scared now. That dip's rank poison, you know. Reckon Ruff knew that. He floundered along an' crawled up at the end. Anyone could see that he had mouth an' eyes tight shut. He began to grope an' feel around, trying to find the way to the pond. One of the men led him out. It was great to see him wade in the water an' wallow an' souse his head under. When he came out the men got in front of him an' stopped him. He shore looked bad. . . . An' Glenn called to him, 'Ruff, that sheep-dip won't go through your tough hide, but a bullet will!' "

Not long after this incident Carley started out on her usual afternoon ride, having arranged with Glenn to meet her on his return from work.

Toward the end of June Carley had advanced in her horsemanship to a point where Flo lent her one of her own mustangs. This change might not have had all to do with a wonderful difference in riding,

but it seemed so to Carley. There was as much difference in horses as in people. This mustang she had
ridden of late was of Navajo stock, but he had been
born and raised and broken at Oak Creek. Carley had
not yet discovered any objection on his part to do
as she wanted him to. He liked what she liked, and
most of all he liked to go. His color resembled a pat-
tern of calico, and in accordance with Western ways
his name was therefore Calico. Left to choose his
own gait, Calico always dropped into a gentle pace
which was so easy and comfortable and swinging
that Carley never tired of it. Moreover, he did not
shy at things lying in the road or rabbits darting
from bushes or at the upwhirring of birds. Carley
had grown attached to Calico before she realized
she was drifting into it; and for Carley to care for
anything or anybody was a serious matter, because
it did not happen often and it lasted. She was exceedingly tenacious of affection.

June had almost passed and summer lay upon the
lonely land. Such perfect and wonderful weather had
never before been Carley's experience. The dawns
broke cool, fresh, fragrant, sweet, and rosy, with
a breeze that seemed of heaven rather than earth,
and the air seemed tremulously full of the murmur of
falling water and the melody of mocking birds. At the
solemn noontides the great white sun glared down
hot—so hot that it burned the skin, yet strangely
was a pleasant burn. The waning afternoons were
Carley's especial torment, when it seemed the sounds
and winds of the day were tiring, and all things were
seeking repose, and life must soften to an unthinking
happiness. These hours troubled Carley because she
wanted them to last, and because she knew for her

this changing and transforming time could not last. So long as she did not think she was satisfied.

Maples and sycamores and oaks were in full foliage, and their bright greens contrasted softly with the dark shine of the pines. Through the spaces between brown tree trunks and the white-spotted boles of the sycamores gleamed the amber water of the creek. Always there was a murmur of little rills and the musical dash of little rapids. On the surface of still, shady pools trout broke to make ever-widening ripples. Indian paintbrush, so brightly carmine in color, lent a touch of fire to the green banks, and under the oaks, in cool dark nooks where mossy bowlders lined the stream, there were stately nodding yellow columbines. And high on the rock ledges shot up the wonderful mescal stalks, beginning to blossom, some with tints of gold and others with tones of red.

Riding along down the canyon, under its looming walls, Carley wondered that if unawares to her these physical aspects of Arizona could have become more significant than she realized. The thought had confronted her before. Here, as always, she fought it and denied it by the simple defense of elimination. Yet refusing to think of a thing when it seemed ever present was not going to do forever. Insensibly and subtly it might get a hold on her, never to be broken. Yet it was infinitely easier to dream than to think.

But the thought encroached upon her that it was not a dreamful habit of mind she had fallen into of late. When she dreamed or mused she lived vaguely and sweetly over past happy hours or dwelt in enchanted fancy upon a possible future. Carley had been told by a Columbia professor that she was a type of the present age—a modern young woman of materialistic mind. Be that as it might, she knew many things seemed loosening from the narrowness and tightness of her character, sloughing away like scales, exposing a new and strange and susceptible softness of fiber. And this blank habit of mind, when she did not think, and now realized that she was not dreaming, seemed to be the body of Carley Burch and her heart and soul stripped of a shell. Nerve and emotion and spirit received something from her surroundings. She absorbed her environment. She felt. It was a delightful state. But when her own consciousness caused it to elude her, then she both resented and regretted. Anything that approached permanent attachment to this crude and untenanted West, Carley would not tolerate for a moment. Reluctantly she admitted it had bettered her health, quickened her blood, and quite relegated Florida and the Adirondacks to little consideration.

"Well, as I told Glenn," soliloquized Carley, "every time I'm almost won over a little to Arizona she gives me a hard jolt. I'm getting near being mushy to-day. Now let's see what I'll get. I suppose that's my pessimism or materialism. Funny how Glenn keeps saying its the jolts, the hard knocks, the fights that are best to remember afterward. I don't get that at all."

Five miles below West Fork a road branched off and climbed the left side of the canyon. It was a rather steep road, long and zigzaging, and full of rocks and ruts. Carley did not enjoy ascending it, but she preferred the going up to coming down. It took half an hour to climb.

Once up on the flat cedar-dotted desert she was met, full in the face, by a hot dusty wind coming from the south. Carley searched her pockets for her goggles, only to ascertain that she had forgotten them. Nothing, except a freezing sleety wind, annoyed and punished Carley so much as a hard puffy wind, full of sand and dust. Somewhere along the first few miles of this road she was to meet Glenn. If she turned back for any cause he would be worried, and, what concerned her more vitally, he would think she had not the courage to face a little dust. So Carley rode on.

The wind appeared to be gusty. It would blow hard awhile, then lull for a few moments. On the whole, however, it increased in volume and persistence until she was riding against a gale. She had now come to a bare, flat, gravelly region, scant of cedars and brush, and far ahead she could see a dull yellow pall rising high into the sky. It was a duststorm and it was sweeping down on the wings of that gale. Carley remembered that somewhere along this flat there was a log cabin which had before provided shelter for her and Flo when they were caught in a rainstorm. It seemed unlikely that she had passed by this cabin.

Resolutely she faced the gale and knew she had a task to find that refuge. If there had been a big rock or bushy cedar to offer shelter she would have welcomed it. But there was nothing. When the hard dusty gusts hit her, she found it absolutely necessary to shut her eyes. At intervals less windy she opened them, and rode on, peering through the yellow gloom for the cabin. Thus she got her eyes full of dust— an alkali dust that made them sting and smart. The fiercer puffs of wind carried pebbles large enough to hurt severely. Then the dust clogged her nose and sand got between her teeth. Added to these annoyances was a heat like a blast from a furnace. Carley

perspired freely and that caked the dust on her face.
She rode on, gradually growing more uncomfortable
and miserable. Yet even then she did not utterly lose
a sort of thrilling zest in being thrown upon her own
responsibility. She could hate an obstacle, yet feel
something of pride in holding her own against it.

Another mile of buffeting this increasing gale so
exhausted Carley and wrought upon her nerves that
she became nearly panic-stricken. It grew harder and
harder not to turn back. At last she was about to give
up when right at hand through the flying dust she
espied the cabin. Riding behind it, she dismounted
and tied the mustang to a post. Then she ran around
to the door and entered.

What a welcome refuge! She was all right now,
and when Glenn came along she would have added to
her already considerable list another feat for which
he would commend her. With aid of her handkerchief, and the tears that flowed so copiously, Carley
presently freed her eyes of the blinding dust. But
when she essayed to remove it from her face she
discovered she would need a towel and soap and
hot water.

The cabin appeared to be enveloped in a soft,
swishing, hollow sound. It seeped and rustled. Then
the sound lulled, only to rise again. Carley went to
the door, relieved and glad to see that the duststorm
was blowing by. The great sky-high pall of yellow
had moved on to the north. Puffs of dust were whipping along the road, but no longer in one continuous
cloud. In the west, low down the sun was sinking, a
dull magenta in hue, quite weird and remarkable.

"I knew I'd get the jolt all right," soliloquized
Carley, wearily, as she walked to a rude couch of

poles and sat down upon it. She had begun to cool off. And there, feeling dirty and tired, and slowly wearing to the old depression, she composed herself to wait.

Suddenly she heard the clip-clop of hoofs. "There! that's Glenn," she cried, gladly, and rising, she ran to the door.

She saw a big bay horse bearing a burly rider. He discovered her at the same instant, and pulled his horse.

"Ho! Ho! if it ain't Pretty Eyes!" he called out, in a gay, coarse voice.

Carley recognized the voice, and then the epithet, before her sight established the man as Haze Ruff. A singular stultifying shock passed over her.

"Wal, by all thet's lucky!" he said, dismounting. "I knowed we'd meet some day. I can't say I just laid fer you, but I kept my eyes open."

Manifestly he knew she was alone, for he did not glance into the cabin.

"I'm waiting for—Glenn," she said, with lips she tried to make stiff.

"Shore I reckoned thet," he replied, genially. "But he won't be along yet awhile."

He spoke with a cheerful inflection of tone, as if the fact designated was one that would please her; and his swarthy, seamy face expanded into a good-humored, meaning smile. Then without any particular rudeness he pushed her back from the door, into the cabin, and stepped across the threshold.

"How dare—you!" cried Carley. A hot anger that stirred in her seemed to be beaten down and smothered by a cold shaking internal commotion, threatening collapse. This man loomed over her, huge, somehow monstrous in his brawny uncouth presence. And his knowing smile, and the hard, glinting twinkle of his light eyes, devilishly intelligent and keen, in no wise lessened the sheer brutal force of him physically. Sight of his bulk was enough to terrorize Carley.

"Me! Aw, I'm a darin' *hombre* an' a devil with the wimmin," he said, with a guffaw.

Carley could not collect her wits. The instant of his pushing her back into the cabin and following her had shocked her and almost paralyzed her will. If she saw him now any the less fearful she could not so quickly rally her reason to any advantage.

"Let me out of here," she demanded.

"Nope. I'm a-goin' to make a little love to you," he said, and he reached for her with great hairy hands.

Carley saw in them the strength that had so easily swung the sheep. She saw, too, that they were dirty, greasy hands. And they made her flesh creep.

"Glenn will kill—you," she panted.

"What fer?" he queried, in real or pretended surprise. "Aw, I know wimmin. You'll never tell him."

"Yes, I will."

"Wal, mebbe. I reckon you're lyin', Pretty Eyes," he replied, with a grin. "Anyhow, I'll take a chance."

"I tell you—he'll kill you," repeated Carley, backing away until her weak knees came against the couch.

"What fer, I ask you?" he demanded.

"For this—this insult."

"Huh! I'd like to know who's insulted you. Can't a man take an invitation to kiss an' hug a girl—without insultin' her?"

"Invitation! . . . Are you crazy?" queried Carley, bewildered.

"Nope, I'm not crazy, an' I shore said invitation. . . . I meant thet white shimmy dress you wore the night of Flo's party. Thet's my invitation to get a little fresh with you, Pretty Eyes!"

Carley could only stare at him. His words seemed to have some peculiar, unanswerable power.

"Wal, if it wasn't an invitation, what was it?" he asked, with another step that brought him within reach of her. He waited for her answer, which was not forthcoming.

"Wal, you're gettin' kinda pale around the gills," he went on, derisively. "I reckoned you was a real sport. . . . Come here."

He fastened one of his great hands in the front of her coat and gave her a pull. So powerful was it that Carley came hard against him, almost knocking her breathless. There he held her a moment and then put his other arm round her. It seemed to crush both breath and sense out of her. Suddenly limp, she sank strengthless. She seemed reeling in darkness. Then she felt herself thrust away from him with violence. She sank on the couch and her head and shoulders struck the wall.

"Say, if you're a-goin' to keel over like thet—I pass," declared Ruff, in disgust. "Can't you Eastern wimmin stand nothin'?"

Carley's eyes opened and beheld this man in an attitude of supremely derisive protest.

"You look like a sick kitten," he added. "When I get me a sweetheart or wife I want her to be a wild cat."

His scorn and repudiation of her gave Carley intense relief. She sat up and endeavored to collect her shattered nerves. Ruff gazed down at her with great disapproval and even disappointment.

"Say, did you have some fool idee I was a-goin' to kill you?" he queried, gruffly.

"I'm afraid—I did," faltered Carley. Her relief was a release; it was so strange that it was gratefulness.

"Wal, I reckon I wouldn't have hurt you. None of these flop-over Janes for me! . . . An' I'll give you a hunch, Pretty Eyes. You might have run acrost a fellar thet was no gentleman!"

Of all the amazing statements that had ever been made to Carley, this one seemed the most remarkable.

"What'd you wear thet onnatural white dress fer?" he demanded, as if he had a right to be her judge.

"Unnatural?" echoed Carley.

"Shore. Thet's what I said. Any woman's dress without top or bottom is onnatural. It's not right. Why, you looked like—like"—here he floundered for adequate expression—"like one of the devil's angels. An' I want to hear why you wore it."

"For the same reason I'd wear any dress," she felt forced to reply.

"Pretty Eyes, thet's a lie. An' you know it's a lie. You wore thet white dress to knock the daylights out of men. Only you ain't honest enough to say so. . . . Even me or my kind! Even us, who're dirt under your little feet. But all the same we're men, an' mebbe better men than you think. If you had to put that dress on, why didn't you stay in your room? Naw, you had to come down an' strut around an' show off your beauty. An' I ask you—if you're a nice girl like Flo Hutter—what'd you wear it fer?"

Carley not only was mute; she felt rise and burn in her a singular shame and surprise.

"I'm only a sheep dipper," went on Ruff, "but I ain't no fool. A fellar doesn't have to live East an' wear swell clothes to have sense. Mebbe you'll learn thet the West is bigger 'n you think. A man's a man East or West. But if your Eastern men stand for such dresses as thet white one they'd do well to come out West awhile, like your lover, Glenn Kilbourne. I've been rustlin' round here ten years, an' I never before seen a dress like yours—an' I never heerd of a girl bein' insulted, either. Mebbe you think I insulted you. Wal, I didn't. Fer I reckon *nothin'* could insult you in thet dress. . . . An' my last hunch is this, Pretty Eyes. You're not what a *hombre* like me calls either square or game. *Adios.*"

His bulky figure darkened the doorway, passed out, and the light of the sky streamed into the cabin again. Carley sat staring. She heard Ruff's spurs tinkle, then the ring of steel on stirrup, a sodden leathery sound as he mounted, and after that a rapid pound of hoofs, quickly dying away.

He was gone. She had escaped something raw and violent. Dazedly she realized it, with unutterable relief. And she sat there slowly gathering the nervous force that had been shattered. Every word that he had uttered was stamped in startling characters upon her consciousness. But she was still under the deadening influence of shock. This raw experience was the worst the West had yet dealt her. It brought back former states of revulsion and formed them in one whole irrefutable and damning judgment that seemed to blot out the vaguely dawning and growing happy susceptibilities. It was, perhaps, just as well to have her mind reverted to realistic fact. The presence of Haze Ruff, the astounding truth of the contact with his huge sheep-defiled hands, had been profanation and degradation under which she sickened with fear and shame. Yet hovering back of her shame and rising anger seemed to be a pale, monstrous, and indefinable thought, insistent and accusing, with which she must sooner or later reckon. It might have been the voice of the new side of her nature, but at that moment of outraged womanhood, and of revolt against the West, she would not listen. It might, too, have been the still small voice of conscience. But decision of mind and energy coming to her then, she threw off the burden of emotion and perplexity, and forced herself into composure before the arrival of Glenn.

The dust had ceased to blow, although the wind had by no means died away. Sunset marked the west in old rose and gold, a vast flare. Carley espied a horseman far down the road, and presently recognized both rider and steed. He was coming fast. She went out and, mounting her mustang, she rode out to meet Glenn. It did not appeal to her to wait for him at the cabin; besides hoof tracks other than those made by her mustang might have been noticed by Glenn. Presently he came up to her and pulled his loping horse.

"Hello! I sure was worried," was his greeting, as his gloved hand went out to her. "Did you run into that sandstorm?"

"It ran into me, Glenn, and buried me," she laughed.

His fine eyes lingered on her face with glad and warm glance, and the keen, apprehensive penetration of a lover.

"Well, under all that dust you look scared," he said.

"Scared!" I was worse than that. When I first ran into the flying dirt I was only afraid I'd lose my way—and my complexion. But when the worst of the storm hit me—then I feared I'd lose my breath.

"Did you face that sand and ride through it all?" he queried.

"No, not all. But enough. I went through the worst of it before I reached the cabin," she replied.

"Wasn't it great?"

"Yes—great bother and annoyance," she said, laconically.

Whereupon he reached with long arm and wrapped it round her as they rode side by side. Demonstrations of this nature were infrequent with Glenn. Despite losing one foot out of a stirrup and her seat in the saddle Carley rather encouraged it. He kissed her dusty face, and then set her back.

"By George! Carley, sometimes I think you've changed since you've been here," he said, with warmth. "To go through that sandstorm without one kick—one knock at my West!"

"Glenn, I always think of what Flo says—the worst is yet to come," replied Carley, trying to hide her unreasonable and tumultuous pleasure at words of praise from him.

"Carley Burch, you don't know yourself," he declared, enigmatically.

"What woman knows herself? But do you know me?"

"Not I. Yet sometimes I see depths in you—wonderful possibilities—submerged under your poise—under your fixed, complacent idle attitude toward life."

This seemed for Carley to be dangerously skating near thin ice, but she could not resist a retort: "Depths in me? Why I am a shallow, transparent stream like your West Fork! . . . And as for possibilities—may I ask what of them you imagine you see?"

"As a girl, before you were claimed by the world, you were earnest at heart. You had big hopes and dreams. And you had intellect, too. But you have wasted your talents, Carley. Having money, and spending it, living for pleasure, you have not realized your powers. . . . Now, don't look hurt. I'm not censuring you. It's just the way of modern life. And most of your friends have been more careless, thoughtless, useless than you. The aim of their existence is to be comfortable, free from work, worry, pain. They want pleasure, luxury. And what a pity it is! The best of you girls regard marriage as an escape, instead of responsibility. You don't marry to get your shoulders square against the old wheel of American progress—to help some man make good—to bring a troop of healthy American kids into the world. You bare your shoulders to the gaze of the multitude and like it best if you are strung with pearls."

"Glenn, you distress me when you talk like this," replied Carley, soberly. "You did not use to talk so. It seems to me you are bitter against women."

"Oh no, Carley! I am only sad," he said. "I only see where once I was blind. American women are the finest on earth, but as a race, if they don't change, they're doomed to extinction."

"How can you say such things?" demanded Carley, with spirit.

"I say them because they are true. Carley, on the level now, tell me how many of your immediate friends have children."

Put to a test, Carley rapidly went over in her mind her circle of friends, with the result that she was somewhat shocked and amazed to realize how few of them were even married, and how the babies of her acquaintance were limited to three. It was not easy to admit this to Glenn.

"My dear," replied he, "if that does not show you the handwriting on the wall, nothing ever will."

"A girl has to find a husband, doesn't she?" asked Carley, roused to defense of her sex. "And if she's anybody she has to find one in her set. Well, husbands are not plentiful. Marriage certainly is not the end of existence these days. We have to get along somehow. The high cost of living is no inconsiderable factor to-day. Do you know that most of the better-class apartment houses in New York will not take children? Women are not all to blame. Take the speed mania. Men must have automobiles. I know one girl who wanted a baby, but her husband wanted a car. They couldn't afford both."

"Carley, I'm not blaming women more than men," returned Glenn. "I don't know that I blame them as a class. But in my own mind I have worked it all out. Every man or woman who is genuinely American should read the signs of the times, realize the crisis, and meet it in an American way. Otherwise we are done as a race. Money is God in the older countries. But it should never become God in America.

If it does, we will make the fall of Rome pale into insignificance."

"Glenn, let's put off the argument," appealed Carley. "I'm not—just up to fighting you today. Oh—you needn't smile. I'm not showing a yellow streak, as Flo puts it. I'll fight you some other time."

"You're right, Carley," he assented. "Here we are loafing six or seven miles from home. Let's rustle along."

Riding fast with Glenn was something Carley had only of late added to her achievements. She had greatest pride in it. So she urged her mustang to keep pace with Glenn's horse and gave herself up to the thrill of the motion and feel of wind and sense of flying along. At a good swinging lope Calico covered ground swiftly and did not tire. Carley rode the two miles to the rim of the canyon, keeping alongside of Glenn all the way. Indeed, for one long level stretch she and Glenn held hands. When they arrived at the descent, which necessitated slow and careful riding, she was hot and tingling and breathless, worked by the action into an exuberance of pleasure. Glenn complimented her riding as well as her rosy cheeks. There was indeed a sweetness in working at a task as she had worked to learn to ride in Western fashion. Every turn of her mind seemed to confront her with sobering antitheses of thought. Why had she come to love to ride down a lonely desert road, through ragged cedars where the wind whipped her face with fragrant wild breath, if at the same time she hated the West? Could she hate a country, however barren and rough, if it had saved the health and happiness of her future husband? Verily there were problems for Carley to solve.

Early twilight purple lay low in the hollows and clefts of the canyon. Over the western rim a pale ghost of the evening star seemed to smile at Carley, to bid her look and look. Like a strain of distant music, the dreamy hum of falling water, the murmur and melody of the stream, came again to Carley's sensitive ear.

"Do you love this?" asked Glenn, when they reached the green-forested canyon floor, with the yellow road winding away into the purple shadows.

"Yes, both the ride—and you," flashed Carley, contrarily. She knew he had meant the deep-walled canyon with its brooding solitude.

"But I want you to love Arizona," he said.

"Glenn, I'm a faithful creature. You should be glad of that. I love New York."

"Very well, then. Arizona to New York," he said, lightly brushing her cheek with his lips. And swerving back into his saddle, he spurred his horse and called back over his shoulder: "That mustang and Flo have beaten me many a time. Come on."

It was not so much his words as his tone and look that roused Carley. Had he resented her loyalty to the city of her nativity? Always there was a little rift in the lute. Had his tone and look meant that Flo might catch him if Carley could not? Absurd as the idea was, it spurred her to recklessness. Her mustang did not need any more than to know she wanted him to run. The road was of soft yellow earth flanked with green foliage and overspread by pines. In a moment she was racing at a speed she had never before half attained on a horse. Down the winding road Glenn's big steed sped, his head low, his stride tremendous, his action beautiful. But Carley saw the distance between them diminishing. Calico was overtaking the bay. She cried out in the thrilling excitement of the moment. Glenn saw her gaining and pressed his mount to greater speed. Still he could not draw away from Calico. Slowly the little mustang gained. It seemed to Carley that riding him required no effort at all. And at such fast pace, with the wind roaring in her ears, the walls of green vague and continuous in her sight, the sting of pine tips on cheek and neck, the yellow road streaming toward her, under her, there rose out of the depths of her, out of the tumult of her breast, a sense of glorious exultation. She closed in on Glenn. From the flying hoofs of his horse shot up showers of damp sand and gravel that covered Carley's riding habit and spattered in her face. She had to hold up a hand before her eyes. Perhaps this caused her to lose something of her confidence, or her swing in the saddle, for suddenly she realized she was not riding well. The pace was too fast for her inexperience. But nothing could have stopped her then. No fear or awkwardness of hers should be allowed to hamper that thoroughbred mustang. Carley felt that Calico understood the situation; or at least he knew he could catch and pass this big bay horse, and he intended to do it. Carley was hard put to it to hang on and keep the flying sand from blinding her.

When Calico drew alongside the bay horse and brought Carley breast to breast with Glenn, and then inch by inch forged ahead of him, Carley pealed out an exultant cry. Either it frightened Calico or inspired him, for he shot right ahead of Glenn's horse. Then he lost the smooth, wonderful action. He seemed hurtling through space at the expense of tremendous muscular action. Carley could feel it. She lost her equilibrium. She seemed rushing through a blurred green and black aisle of the forest with a gale in her face. Then, with a sharp jolt, a break, Calico plunged to the sand. Carley felt herself propelled forward out of the saddle into the air, and down to strike with a sliding, stunning force that ended in sudden dark oblivion.

Upon recovering consciousness she first felt a sensation of oppression in her chest and a dull numbness of her whole body. When she opened her eyes she saw Glenn bending over her, holding her head on his knee. A wet, cold, reviving sensation evidently came from the handkerchief with which he was mopping her face.

"Carley, you can't be hurt—really!" he was ejaculating, in eager hope. "It was some spill. But you lit on the sand and slid. You can't be hurt."

The look of his eyes, the tone of his voice, the feel of his hands were such that Carley chose for a moment to pretend to be very badly hurt indeed. It was worth taking a header to get so much from Glenn Kilbourne. But she believed she had suffered no more than a severe bruising and scraping.

"Glenn—dear," she whispered, very low and very eloquently. "I think—my back—is broken. . . . You'll be free—soon."

Glenn gave a terrible start and his face turned a deathly white. He burst out with quavering, inarticulate speech.

Carley gazed up at him and then closed her eyes. She could not look at him while carrying on such deceit. Yet the sight of him and the feel of him then were inexpressibly blissful to her. What she needed most was assurance of his love. She had it. Beyond doubt, beyond morbid fancy, the truth had proclaimed itself, filling her heart with joy.

Suddenly she flung her arms up around his neck. "Oh—Glenn! It was too good a chance to miss! . . . I'm not hurt a bit."

CHAPTER

7

*T*HE day came when Carley asked Mrs. Hutter: "Will you please put up a nice lunch for Glenn and me? I'm going to walk down to his farm where he's working, and surprise him."

"That's a downright fine idea," declared Mrs. Hutter, and forthwith bustled away to comply with Carley's request.

So presently Carley found herself carrying a bountiful basket on her arm, faring forth on an adventure that both thrilled and depressed her. Long before this hour something about Glenn's work had quickened her pulse and given rise to an inexplicable admiration. That he was big and strong enough to do such labor made her proud; that he might want to go on doing it made her ponder and brood.

The morning resembled one of the rare Eastern days in June, when the air appeared flooded by rich thick amber light. Only the sun here was hotter and the shade cooler.

Carley took to the trail below where West Fork emptied its golden-green waters into Oak Creek. The red walls seemed to dream and wait under the blaze of the sun; the heat lay like a blanket over the still foliage; the birds were quiet; only the murmuring stream broke the silence of the canyon. Never had Carley felt more the isolation and solitude of Oak Creek Canyon. Far indeed from the madding crowd! Only Carley's stubbornness kept her from acknowledging the sense of peace that enveloped her—that and the consciousness of her own discontent. What would it be like to come to this canyon—to give up to its enchantments? That, like many another disturbing thought, had to go unanswered, to be driven into the closed chambers of Carley's mind, there to germinate subconsciously, and stalk forth some day to overwhelm her.

The trail led along the creek, threading a maze of bowlders, passing into the shade of cottonwoods, and crossing sun-flecked patches of sand. Carley's every step seemed to become slower. Regrets were assailing her. Long indeed had she overstayed her visit to the West. She must not linger there indefinitely. And mingled with misgiving was a surprise that she had not tired of Oak Creek. In spite of all, and of the dislike she vaunted to herself, the truth stared at her—she was not tired.

The long-delayed visit to see Glenn working on his own farm must result in her talking to him about his work; and in a way not quite clear she regretted the necessity for it. To disapprove of Glenn! She received faint intimations of wavering, of uncertainty, of vague doubt. But these were cried down by the dominant and habitable voice of her personality.

Presently through the shaded and shadowed breadth of the belt of forest she saw gleams of a sunlit clearing. And crossing this space to the border of trees she peered forth, hoping to espy Glenn at his labors. She saw an old shack, and irregular lines of rude fence built of poles of all sizes and shapes, and several plots of bare yellow ground, leading up toward the west side of the canyon wall. Could this clearing be Glenn's farm? Surely she had missed it or had not gone far enough. This was not a farm, but a slash in the forested level of the canyon floor, bare and somehow hideous. Dead trees were standing in the lots. They had been ringed deeply at the base by an ax, to kill them, and so prevent their foliage from shading the soil. Carley saw a long pile of rocks that evidently had been carried from the plowed ground. There was no neatness, no regularity, although there was abundant evidence of toil. To clear that rugged space, to fence it, and plow it, appeared at once to Carley an extremely strenuous and useless task. Carley persuaded herself that this must be the plot of ground belonging to the herder Charley, and she was about to turn on down the creek when far up under the bluff she espied a man. He was stalking along and bending down, stalking along and bending down. She recognized Glenn. He was planting something in the yellow soil.

Curiously Carley watched him, and did not allow her mind to become concerned with a somewhat painful swell of her heart. What a stride he had! How vigorous he looked, and earnest! He was as intent upon this job as if he had been a rustic. He might have been failing to do it well, but he most certainly was doing it conscientiously. Once he had said to her that a man should never be judged by the result of his labors, but by the nature of his effort. A man might strive with all his heart and strength, yet fail. Carley watched him striding along and bending down, absorbed in his task, unmindful of the glaring hot sun, and somehow to her singularly detached from the life wherein he had once moved and to which she yearned to take him back. Suddenly an unaccountable flashing query assailed her conscience: How dare she want to take him back? She seemed as shocked as if some stranger had accosted her. What was this dimming of her eye, this inward tremulousness; this dammed tide beating at an unknown and riveted gate of her intelligence? She felt more then than she dared to face. She struggled against something in herself. The old habit of mind instinctively resisted the new, the strange. But she did not come off wholly victorious. The Carley Burch whom she recognized as of old, passionately hated this life and work of Glenn Kilbourne's, but the rebel self, an unaccountable and defiant Carley, loved him all the better for them.

Carley drew a long deep breath before she called Glenn. This meeting would be momentous and she felt no absolute surety of herself.

Manifestly he was surprised to hear her call, and, dropping his sack and implement, he hurried across the tilled ground, sending up puffs of dust. He vaulted the rude fence of poles, and upon sight of her called out lustily. How big and virile he looked! Yet he was gaunt and strained. It struck Carley that he had not looked so upon her arrival at Oak Creek. Had she worried him? The query gave her a pang.

"Sir Tiller of the Fields," said Carley, gayly, "see, your dinner! *I* brought it and *I* am going to share it."

"You old darling!" he replied, and gave her an embrace that left her cheek moist with the sweat of his. He smelled of dust and earth and his body was hot. "I wish to God it could be true for always!"

His loving, bearish onslaught and his words quite silenced Carley. How at critical moments he always said the thing that hurt her or inhibited her! She essayed a smile as she drew back from him.

"It's sure good of you," he said, taking the basket. "I was thinking I'd be through work sooner to-day, and was sorry I had not made a date with you. . . . Come, we'll find a place to sit."

Whereupon he led her back under the trees to a half-sunny, half-shady bench of rock overhanging the stream. Great pines overshadowed a still, eddying pool. A number of brown butterflies hovered over the water, and small trout floated like spotted feathers just under the surface. Drowsy summer enfolded the sylvan scene.

Glenn knelt at the edge of the brook, and, plunging his hands in, he splashed like a huge dog and bathed his hot face and head, and then turned to Carley with gay words and laughter, while he wiped himself dry with a large red scarf. Carley was not proof against the virility of him then, and at the moment, no matter what it was that had made him the man he looked, she loved it.

"I'll sit in the sun," he said, designating a place. "When you're hot you mustn't rest in the shade, unless you've coat or sweater. But you sit here in the shade."

"Glenn, that 'll put us too far apart," complained Carley. "I'll sit in the sun with you."

The delightful simplicity and happiness of the ensuing hour was something Carley believed she would never forget.

"There! we've licked the platter clean," she said. "What starved bears we were! I wonder if I shall enjoy eating—when I get home. I used to be so finnicky and picky."

"Carley, don't talk about home," said Glenn, appealingly.

"You dear old farmer, I'd love to stay here—and just dream—forever," replied Carley, earnestly. "But I came on purpose to talk seriously."

"Oh, you did! About what?" he returned, with some quick, indefinable change of tone and expression.

"Well, first about your work. I know I hurt your feelings when I wouldn't listen. But I wasn't ready. I wanted to—to just be gay with you for a while. Don't think I wasn't interested. I was. And now, I'm ready to hear all about it—and everything."

She smiled at him bravely, and she knew that unless some unforeseen shock upset her composure, she would be able to conceal from him anything which might hurt his feelings.

"You do look serious," he said, with keen eyes on her.

"Just what are your business relations with Hutter?" she inquired.

"I'm simply working for him," replied Glenn. "My aim is to get an interest in his sheep, and I expect to, some day. We have some plans. And one of them is the development of that Deep Lake section. You remember—you were with us. The day Spillbeans spilled you?"

"Yes, I remember. It was a pretty place," she replied.

Carley did not tell him that for a month past she had owned the Deep Lake section of six hundred and forty acres. She had, in fact, instructed Hutter to purchase it, and to keep the transaction a secret for the present. Carley had never been able to understand the impulse that prompted her to do it. But as Hutter had assured her it was a remarkably good investment on very little capital, she had tried to persuade herself of its advantages. Back of it all had been an irresistible desire to be able some day to present to Glenn this ranch site he loved. She had concluded he would never wholly dissociate himself from this West; and as he would visit it now and then, she had already begun forming plans of her own. She could stand a month in Arizona at long intervals.

"Hutter and I will go into cattle raising some day," went on Glenn. "And that Deep Lake place is what I want for myself."

"What work are you doing for Hutter?" asked Carley.

"Anything from building fence to cutting timber," laughed Glenn. "I've not yet the experience to be a foreman like Lee Stanton. Besides, I have a little business all my own. I put all my money in that."

"You mean here—this—this farm?"

"Yes. And the stock I'm raising. You see I have to feed corn. And believe me, Carley, those cornfields represent some job."

"I can well believe that," replied Carley. "You—you looked it."

"Oh, the hard work is over. All I have to do now is to plant and keep the weeds out."

"Glenn, do sheep eat corn?"

"I plant corn to feed my hogs."

"Hogs?" she echoed, vaguely.

"Yes, hogs," he said, with quiet gravity. "The first day you visited my cabin I told you I raised hogs, and I fried my own ham for your dinner."

"Is that what you—put your money in?"

"Yes. And Hutter says I've done well."

"*Hogs!*" ejaculated Carley, aghast.

"My dear, are you growing dull of comprehension?" retorted Glenn. "H-o-g-s." He spelled the word out. "I'm in the hog-raising business, and pretty blamed well pleased over my success so far."

Carley caught herself in time to quell outwardly a shock of amaze and revulsion. She laughed, and exclaimed against her stupidity. The look of Glenn was no less astounding than the content of his words. He was actually proud of his work. Moreover, he showed not the least sign that he had any idea such information might be startlingly obnoxious to his fiancée.

"Glenn! It's so—so queer," she ejaculated. "That you—Glenn Kilbourne—should ever go in for—for hogs! It's unbelievable. How'd you ever—ever happen to do it?"

"By Heaven! you're hard on me!" he burst out, in sudden dark, fierce passion. "How'd I ever happen to do it? *What* was there left for me? I gave my soul and heart and body to the government—to fight for my country. I came home a wreck. *What* did my government do for me? *What* did my employers do for me? *What* did the people I fought for do for me? Nothing—so help me God—*nothing!* I got a ribbon and a bouquet—a little applause for an hour—and then the sight of me sickened my countrymen. I was broken and used. I was absolutely forgotten. . . . But my body, my life, my soul meant *all* to me. My future was ruined, but I wanted to live. I had killed men who never harmed me—I was not fit to die. . . . I *tried* to live. So I fought out my battle alone. Alone! . . . No one understood. No one cared. . . . I came West to keep from dying of consumption in sight of the indifferent mob for whom I had sacrificed myself. I chose to die on my feet away off alone somewhere. . . . But I got well. And what *made* me well—and *saved* my soul— was the first work that offered. *Raising and tending hogs!*"

The dead whiteness of Glenn's face, the lightning scorn of his eyes, the grim, stark strangeness of him then had for Carley a terrible harmony with this passionate denunciation of her, of her kind, of the America for whom he had lost all.

"Oh, Glenn!—forgive—me!" she faltered. "I was only—talking. What do I know? Oh, I am blind— blind and little!"

She could not bear to face him for a moment, and she hung her head. Her intelligence seemed concentrating swift, wild thoughts round the shock to her consciousness. By that terrible expression of his face, by those thundering words of scorn, would she come to realize the mighty truth of his descent into the abyss and his rise to the heights. Vaguely she began to see. An awful sense of her deadness, of her soul-blighting selfishness, began to dawn upon her as something monstrous out of dim, gray obscurity. She trembled under the reality of thoughts that were not new. How she had babbled about Glenn and the crippled soldiers! How she had imagined she sympathized! But she had only been a vain, worldly, complacent, effusive little fool. She had here the shock of her life, and she sensed a greater one, impossible to grasp.

"Carley, that was coming to you," said Glenn, presently, with a deep, heavy expulsion of breath.

"I only know I love you—more—more," she cried, wildly, looking up and wanting desperately to throw herself in his arms.

"I guess you do—a little," he replied. "Sometimes I feel you are a kid. Then again you represent the world—your world with its age-old custom—its unalterable. . . . But, Carley, let's get back to my work."

"Yes—yes," exclaimed Carley, gladly. "I'm ready to—to go pet your hogs—anything."

"By George! I'll take you up," he declared. "I'll bet you won't go near one of my hogpens."

"Lead me to it!" she replied, with a hilarity that was only a nervous reversion of her state.

"Well, maybe I'd better hedge on the bet," he said, laughing again. "You have more in you than I suspect. You sure fooled me when you stood for the sheep-dip. But, come on, I'll take you anyway."

So that was how Carley found herself walking arm in arm with Glenn down the canyon trail. A few moments of action gave her at least an appearance of outward composure. And the state of her emotion was so strained and intense that her slightest show of interest must deceive Glenn into thinking her eager, responsive, enthusiastic. It certainly appeared to loosen his tongue. But Carley knew she was farther from normal than ever before in her life, and that the subtle, inscrutable woman's intuition of her presaged another shock. Just as she had seemed to change, so had the aspects of the canyon undergone some illusive transformation. The beauty of green foliage and amber stream and brown tree trunks and gray rocks and red walls was there; and the summer drowsiness and languor lay as deep; and the loneliness and solitude brooded with its same eternal significance. But some nameless enchantment, perhaps of hope, seemed no longer to encompass her. A blow had fallen upon her, the nature of which only time could divulge.

Glenn led her around the clearing and up to the base of the west wall, where against a shelving portion of the cliff had been constructed a rude fence of poles. It formed three sides of a pen, and the fourth side was solid rock. A bushy cedar tree stood in the center. Water flowed from under the cliff, which accounted for the boggy condition of the red earth. This pen was occupied by a huge sow and a litter of pigs.

Carley climbed on the fence and sat there while Glenn leaned over the top pole and began to wax eloquent on a subject evidently dear to his heart. To-day of all days Carley made an inspiring listener. Even the shiny, muddy, suspicious old sow in no wise daunted her fictitious courage. That filthy pen of mud a foot deep, and of odor rancid, had no terrors for her. With an arm round Glenn's shoulder she watched the rooting and squealing little pigs, and was amused and interested, as if they were far removed from the vital issue of the hour. But all the time as she looked and laughed, and encouraged Glenn to talk, there seemed to be a strange, solemn, oppressive knocking at her heart. Was it only the beat—beat—beat of blood?

"There were twelve pigs in that litter," Glenn was saying, "and now you see there are only nine. I've lost three. Mountain lions, bears, coyotes, wild cats are all likely to steal a pig. And at first I was sure one of these varmints had been robbing me. But as I could not find any tracks, I knew I had to lay the blame on something else. So I kept watch pretty closely in daytime, and at night I shut the pigs up in the corner there, where you see I've built a pen. Yesterday I heard squealing—and, by George! I saw an eagle flying off with one of my pigs. Say, I was mad. A great old bald-headed eagle—the regal bird you see with America's stars and stripes—had degraded himself to the level of a coyote. I ran for my rifle, and I took some quick shots at him as he flew up. Tried to hit him, too, but I failed. And the old rascal hung on to my pig. I watched him carry it to that sharp crag way up there on the rim."

"Poor little piggy!" exclaimed Carley. "To think of our American emblem—our stately bird of noble warlike mien—our symbol of lonely grandeur and freedom of the heights—think of him being a robber of pigpens!—Glenn, I begin to appreciate the many-sidedness of things. Even my hide-bound narrowness is susceptible to change. It's never too late to learn. This should apply to the Society for the Preservation of the American Eagle."

Glenn led her along the base of the wall to three other pens, in each of which was a fat old sow with a litter. And at the last enclosure, that owing to dry soil was not so dirty, Glenn picked up a little pig and held it squealing out to Carley as she leaned over the fence. It was fairly white and clean, a little pink and fuzzy, and certainly cute with its curled tail.

"Carley Burch, take it in your hands," commanded Glenn.

The feat seemed monstrous and impossible of accomplishment for Carley. Yet such was her temper at the moment that she would have undertaken anything.

"Why, shore I will, as Flo says," replied Carley, extending her ungloved hands. "Come here, piggy. I christen you Pinky." And hiding an almost insupportable squeamishness from Glenn, she took the pig in her hands and fondled it.

"By George!" exclaimed Glenn, in huge delight. "I wouldn't have believed it. Carley, I hope you tell your fastidious and immaculate Morrison that you held one of my pigs in your beautiful hands."

"Wouldn't it please you more to tell him yourself?" asked Carley.

"Yes, it would," declared Glenn, grimly.

This incident inspired Glenn to a Homeric narration of his hog-raising experience. In spite of herself the content of his talk interested her. And as for the effect upon her of his singular enthusiasm, it was deep and compelling. The little-boned Berkshire razor-back hogs grew so large and fat and heavy that their bones broke under their weight. The Duroc Jerseys were the best breed in that latitude, owing to their larger and stronger bones, that enabled them to stand up under the greatest accumulation of fat.

Glenn told of his droves of pigs running wild in the canyon below. In summertime they fed upon vegetation, and at other seasons on acorns, roots, bugs, and grubs. Acorns, particularly, were good and fattening feed. They ate cedar and juniper berries, and piñon nuts. And therefore they lived off the land, at little or no expense to the owner. The only loss was from beasts and birds of prey. Glenn showed Carley how a profitable business could soon be established. He meant to fence off side canyons and to segregate droves of his hogs, and to raise an abundance of corn for winter feed. At that time there was a splendid market for hogs, a condition Hutter claimed would continue indefinitely in a growing country. In conclusion Glenn eloquently told how in his necessity he had accepted gratefully the humblest of labors, to find in the hard pursuit of it a rejuvenation of body and mind, and a promise of independence and prosperity.

When he had finished, and excused himself to go repair a weak place in the corral fence, Carley sat silent, wrapped in strange meditation.

Whither had faded the vulgarity and ignominy she had attached to Glenn's raising of hogs? Gone— like other miasmas of her narrow mind! Partly she understood him now. She shirked consideration of his sacrifice to his country. That must wait. But she thought of his work, and the more she thought the less she wondered.

First he had labored with his hands. What infinite meaning lay unfolding to her vision! Somewhere out of it all came the conception that man was intended to earn his bread by the sweat of his brow. But there was more to it than that. By that toil and sweat, by the friction of horny palms, by the expansion and contraction of muscle, by the acceleration of blood, something great and enduring, something physical and spiritual, came to a man. She understood then why she would have wanted to surrender herself to a man made manly by toil; she understood how a woman instinctively leaned toward the protection of a man who had used his hands—who had strength and red blood and virility—who could fight like the progenitors of the race. Any toil was splendid that served this end for any man. It all went back to the survival of the fittest. And suddenly Carley thought of Morrison. He could dance and dangle attendance upon her, and amuse her—but how would he have acquitted himself in a moment of peril? She had her doubts. Most assuredly he could not have beaten down for her a ruffian like Haze Ruff. What then should be the significance of a man for a woman?

Carley's querying and answering mind reverted to Glenn. He had found a secret in this seeking for something through the labor of hands. All development of body must come through exercise of muscles. The virility of cell in tissue and bone depended upon that. Thus he had found in toil the pleasure and reward athletes had in their desultory training. But when a man learned this secret the need of work must become permanent. Did this explain the law of the Persians—that every man was required to sweat every day?

Carley tried to picture to herself Glenn's attitude of mind when he had first gone to work here in the West. Resolutely she now denied her shrinking, cowardly sensitiveness. She would go to the root of this matter, if she had intelligence enough. Crippled, ruined in health, wrecked and broken by an inexplicable war, soul-blighted by the heartless, callous neglect of government and public, on the verge of madness at the insupportable facts, he had yet been wonderful enough, true enough to himself and God, to fight for life with the instinct of a man, to fight for his mind with a noble and unquenchable faith. Alone—indeed he had been alone! And by some miracle beyond the power of understanding he had found day by day in his painful efforts some hope and strength to go on. He could not have had any illusions. For Glenn Kilbourne, the health and happiness and success most men held so dear must have seemed impossible. His slow, daily, tragic, and terrible task must have been something he owed himself. Not for Carley Burch! She like all the others had failed him. How Carley shuddered in confession of that! Not for the country which had used him and cast him off! Carley divined now, as if by a flash of lightning, the meaning of Glenn's strange, cold, scornful, and aloof manner when he had encountered young men of his station, as capable and as strong as he, who had escaped the service of the army. For him these men did not exist. They were less than nothing. They had waxed fat on lucrative jobs; they had basked in the presence of girls whose brothers and lovers were in the trenches or on the turbulent sea, exposed to the ceaseless dread and almost ceaseless toil of war. If Glenn's spirit had lifted him to endurance of war for the sake of others, how then could it fail him in a precious duty of fidelity to himself? Carley could see him day by day toiling in his lonely canyon—plodding to his lonely cabin. He had been playing the game—fighting it out alone as surely he knew his brothers of like misfortune were fighting.

So Glenn Kilbourne loomed heroically in Carley's transfigured sight. He was one of Carlyle's battle-scarred warriors. Out of his travail he had climbed on stepping-stones of his dead self. *Resurgam!* That had been his unquenchable cry. Who had heard it? Only the solitude of his lonely canyon, only the waiting, dreaming, watching walls, only the silent midnight shadows, only the white, blinking, passionless stars, only the wild creatures of his haunts, only the moaning wind in the pines—only these had been with him in his agony. How near were these things to God?

Carley's heart seemed full to bursting. Not another single moment could her mounting love abide in a heart that held a double purpose. How bitter the assurance that she had not come West to help him! It was self, self, all self that had actuated her. Unworthy indeed was she of the love of this man. Only a lifetime of devotion to him could acquit her in the eyes of her better self. Sweetly and madly raced the thrill and tumult of her blood. There must be only one outcome to her romance. Yet the next instant there came a dull throbbing—an oppression which was pain—an impondering vague thought of catastrophe. Only the fearfulness of love perhaps!

She saw him complete his task and wipe his brown moist face and stride toward her, coming nearer, tall and erect with something added to his soldierly bearing, with a light in his eyes she could no longer bear.

The moment for which she had waited more than two months had come at last.

"Glenn—when will you get back East?" she asked, tensely and low.

The instant the words were spent upon her lips she realized that he had always been waiting and prepared for this question that had been so terrible for her to ask.

"Carley," he replied gently, though his voice rang, "I am never going back East."

An inward quivering hindered her articulation.

"*Never?*" she whispered.

"Never to live, or stay any while," he went on. "I might go some time for a little visit. . . . But never to live."

"Oh—Glenn!" she gasped, and her hands fluttered out to him. The shock was driving home. No amaze, no incredulity succeeded her reception of the fact. It was a slow stab. Carley felt the cold blanch of her skin. "Then—this is it—the something I felt strange between us?"

"Yes, I knew—and you never asked me," he replied.

"That was it? All the time you knew," she whispered, huskily. "You knew. . . . *I'd never—marry you—never live out here?*"

"Yes, Carley, I knew you'd never be woman enough—*American enough*—to help me reconstruct my broken life out here in the West," he replied, with a sad and bitter smile.

That flayed her. An insupportable shame and wounded vanity and clamoring love contended for dominance of her emotions. Love beat down all else.

"Dearest—I beg of you—don't break my heart," she implored.

"I love you, Carley," he answered, steadily, with piercing eyes on hers.

"Then come back—home—home with me."

"No. If you love me you will be my wife."

"Love you! Glenn, I worship you," she broke out, passionately. "But I could not live here—*I could not.*"

"Carley, did you ever read of the woman who said, 'Whither thou goest, there will I go' . . . ?"

"Oh, don't be ruthless! Don't judge me. . . . I never dreamed of this. I came West to take you back."

"My dear, it was a mistake," he said, gently, softening to her distress. "I'm sorry I did not write you more plainly. But, Carley, I could not ask you to share this—this wilderness home with me. I don't ask it now. I always knew you couldn't do it. Yet you've changed so—that I hoped against hope. Love makes us blind even to what we see."

"Don't try to spare me. I'm slight and miserable. I stand abased in my own eyes. I thought I loved you. But I must love best the crowd—people—luxury—fashion—the damned round of things I was born to."

"Carley, you will realize their insufficiency too late," he replied, earnestly. "The things you were born to are love, work, children, happiness."

"Don't! don't! . . . they are hollow mockery for me," she cried, passionately. "Glenn, it is the end. It must come—quickly. . . . You are free."

"I do not ask to be free. Wait. Go home and look at it again with different eyes. Think things over. Remember what came to me out of the West. I will always love you—and I will be here—hoping—"

"I—I cannot listen," she returned, brokenly, and she clenched her hands tightly to keep from wringing them. "I—I cannot face you. . . . Here is—your ring. . . . You—are—free. . . . Don't stop me—don't come. . . . Oh, Glenn, good-by!"

With breaking heart she whirled away from him and hurried down the slope toward the trail. The shade of the forest enveloped her. Peering back through the trees, she saw Glenn standing where she had left him, as if already stricken by the loneliness that must be his lot. A sob broke from Carley's throat. She hated herself. She was in a terrible state of conflict. Decision had been wrenched from her, but she sensed unending strife. She dared not look back again. Stumbling and breathless, she hurried on. How changed the atmosphere and sunlight and shadow of the canyon! The looming walls had pitiless eyes for her flight. When she crossed the mouth of West Fork an almost irresistible force breathed to her from under the stately pines.

An hour later she had bidden farewell to the weeping Mrs. Hutter, and to the white-faced Flo, and Lolomi Lodge, and the murmuring waterfall, and the haunting loneliness of Oak Creek Canyon.

CHAPTER

8

A T Flagstaff, where Carley arrived a few minutes before train time, she was too busily engaged with tickets and baggage to think of herself or of the significance of leaving Arizona. But as she walked into the Pullman she overheard a passenger remark, "Regular old Arizona sunset," and that shook her heart. Suddenly she realized she had come to love the colorful sunsets, to watch and wait for them. And bitterly she thought how that was her way—to learn the value of something when it was gone.

The jerk and start of the train affected her with singular depressing shock. She had burned her last bridge behind her. Had she unconsciously hoped for some incredible reversion of Glenn's mind or of her own? A sense of irreparable loss flooded over her— the first check to shame and humiliation.

From her window she looked out to the southwest. Somewhere across the cedar and pine-greened uplands lay Oak Creek Canyon, going to sleep in its purple and gold shadows of sunset. Banks of broken clouds hung to the horizon, like continents and islands and reefs set in a turquoise sea. Shafts of sunlight streaked down through creamy-edged and purple-centered clouds. A vast flare of gold dominated the sunset background.

When the train rounded a curve, Carley's strained vision became filled with the upheaved bulk of the San Francisco Mountains. Ragged gray grass slopes and green forests on end, and black fringed sky lines, all pointed to the sharp clear peaks spearing the sky. And as she watched, the peaks slowly flushed with sunset hues, and the sky flared golden, and the strength of the eternal mountains stood out in sculptured sublimity. Every day for two months and more Carley had watched these peaks, at all hours, in every mood; and they had unconsciously become a part of her thought. The train was relentlessly whirling her eastward. Soon they must become a memory. Tears blurred her sight. Poignant regret seemed added to the anguish she was suffering. Why had she not learned sooner to see the glory of the mountains, to appreciate the beauty and solitude? Why had she not understood herself?

The next day through New Mexico she followed magnificent ranges and valleys—so different from the country she had seen coming West—so supremely beautiful that she wondered if she had only acquired the harvest of a seeing eye.

But it was at sunset of the following day, when the train was speeding down the continental slope of prairie land beyond the Rockies, that the West took its ruthless revenge.

Masses of strange cloud and singular light upon the green prairie, and a luminosity in the sky, drew

Carley to the platform of her car, which was the last of the train. There she stood, gripping the iron gate, feeling the wind whip her hair and the iron-tracked ground speed from under her, spellbound and stricken at the sheer wonder and glory of the firmament, and the mountain range that it canopied so exquisitely.

A rich and mellow light, singularly clear, seemed to flood out of some unknown source. For the sun was hidden. The clouds just above Carley hung low, and they were like thick, heavy smoke, mushrooming, coalescing, forming and massing, of strange yellow cast of mauve. It shaded westward into heliotrope and this into a purple so royal, so matchless and rare that Carley understood why the purple of the heavens could never be reproduced in paint. Here the cloud mass thinned and paled, and a tint of rose began to flush the billowy, flowery, creamy white. Then came the surpassing splendor of this cloud pageant—a vast canopy of shell pink, a sun-fired surface like an opal sea, rippled and webbed, with the exquisite texture of an Oriental fabric, pure, delicate, lovely as no work of human hands could be. It mirrored all the warm, pearly tints of the inside whorl of the tropic nautilus. And it ended abruptly, a rounded depth of bank, on a broad stream of clear sky, intensely blue, transparently blue, as if through the lambent depths shone the infinite firmament. The lower edge of this stream took the golden lightning of the sunset and was notched for all its horizon-long length by the wondrous white glistening-peaked range of the Rockies. Far to the north, standing aloof from the range, loomed up the grand black bulk and noble white dome of Pikes Peak.

Carley watched the sunset transfiguration of cloud and sky and mountain until all were cold and gray. And then she returned to her seat, thoughtful and sad, feeling that the West had mockingly flung at her one of its transient moments of loveliness.

Nor had the West wholly finished with her. Next day the mellow gold of the Kansas wheat fields, endless and boundless as a sunny sea, rich, waving in the wind, stretched away before her aching eyes for hours and hours. Here was the promise fulfilled, the bountiful harvest of the land, the strength of the West. The great middle state had a heart of gold.

East of Chicago Carley began to feel that the long days and nights of riding, the ceaseless turning of the wheels, the constant and wearing stress of emotion, had removed her an immeasurable distance of miles and time and feeling from the scene of her catastrophe. Many days seemed to have passed. Many had been the hours of her bitter regret and anguish.

Indiana and Ohio, with their green pastoral farms, and numberless villages, and thriving cities, denoted a country far removed and different from the West, and an approach to the populous East. Carley felt like a wanderer coming home. She was restlessly and impatiently glad. But her weariness of body and mind, and the close atmosphere of the car, rendered her extreme discomfort. Summer had laid its hot hand on the low country east of the Mississippi.

Carley had wired her aunt and two of her intimate friends to meet her at the Grand Central Station. This reunion soon to come affected Carley in recurrent emotions of relief, gladness, and shame. She did not sleep well, and arose early, and when the train reached Albany she felt that she could hardly endure the tedious hours. The majestic Hudson and the palatial mansions on the wooded bluffs proclaimed to Carley that she was back in the East. How long a time seemed to have passed! Either she was not the same or the aspect of everything had changed. But she believed that as soon as she got over the ordeal of meeting her friends, and was home again, she would soon see things rationally.

At last the train sheered away from the broad Hudson and entered the environs of New York. Carley sat perfectly still, to all outward appearances a calm, superbly-poised New York woman returning home, but inwardly raging with contending tides. In her own sight she was a disgraceful failure, a prodigal sneaking back to the ease and protection of loyal friends who did not know her truly. Every familiar landmark in the approach to the city gave her a thrill, yet a vague unsatisfied something lingered after each sensation.

Then the train with rush and roar crossed the Harlem River to enter New York City. As one waking from a dream Carley saw the blocks and squares of gray apartment houses and red buildings, the miles of roofs and chimneys, the long hot glaring streets full of playing children and cars. Then above the roar of the train sounded the high notes of a hurdy-gurdy. Indeed she was home. Next to startle her was the dark tunnel, and then the slowing of the train to a stop. As she walked behind a porter up the long incline toward the station gate her legs seemed to be dead.

In the circle of expectant faces beyond the gate she saw her aunt's, eager and agitated, then the handsome pale face of Eleanor Harmon, and beside her the sweet thin one of Beatrice Lovell. As they saw her how quick the change from expectancy to joy! It seemed they all rushed upon her, and embraced her, and exclaimed over her together. Carley never recalled what she said. But her heart was full.

"Oh, how perfectly stunning you look!" cried Eleanor, backing away from Carley and gazing with glad, surprised eyes.

"Carley!" gasped Beatrice. "You wonderful golden-skinned goddess! . . . You're *young* again, like you were in our school days."

It was before Aunt Mary's shrewd, penetrating, loving gaze that Carley quailed.

"Yes, Carley, you look well—better than I ever saw you, but—but—"

"But I don't look happy," interrupted Carley. "I am happy to get home—to see you all . . . but—my—my heart is broken!"

A little shocked silence ensued, then Carley found herself being led across the lower level and up the wide stairway. As she mounted to the vast-domed cathedral-like chamber of the station a strange sensation pierced her with a pang. Not the old thrill of leaving New York or returning! Nor was it welcome sight of the hurrying, well-dressed throng of travelers and commuters, nor the stately beauty of the station. Carley shut her eyes, and then she knew. The dim light of vast space above, the looming gray walls, shadowy with tracery of figures, the lofty dome like the blue sky, brought back to her the walls of Oak Creek Canyon and the great caverns under the ramparts. As suddenly as she had shut her eyes Carley opened them to face her friends.

"Let me get it over—quickly," she burst out, with hot blood surging to her face. "I—I hated the West. It was so raw—so violent—so big. I think I hate it more—now.... But it changed me—made me over physically—and did something to my soul—God knows what.... And it has saved Glenn. Oh! he is wonderful! You would never know him.... For long I had not the courage to tell him I came to bring him back East. I kept putting it off. And I rode, I climbed, I camped, I lived outdoors. At first it nearly killed me. Then it grew bearable, and easier, until I forgot. I wouldn't be honest if I didn't admit now that somehow I had a wonderful time, in spite of all.... Glenn's business is raising hogs. He has a hog ranch. Doesn't it sound sordid? But things are not always what they sound—or seem. Glenn is absorbed in his work. I hated it—I expected to ridicule it. But I ended by infinitely respecting him. I learned through his hog-raising the real nobility of work.... Well, at last I found courage to ask him when he was coming back to New York. He said—'*never*!' ... I realized then my blindness, my selfishness. I could not be his wife and live there. I could not. I was too small, too miserable, too comfort-loving—too spoiled. And all the time he knew this—*knew* I'd never be big enough to marry him.... That broke my heart.... I left him free—and here I am.... I beg you—don't ask me any more—and never to mention it to me—so I can forget."

The tender unspoken sympathy of women who loved her proved comforting in that trying hour. With the confession ruthlessly made, the hard compression in Carley's breast subsided, and her eyes cleared of a hateful dimness. When they reached the taxi stand outside the station Carley felt a rush of hot devitalized air from the street. She seemed not to be able to get air into her lungs.

"Isn't it dreadfully hot?" she asked.

"This is a cool spell to what we had last week," replied Eleanor.

"Cool!" exclaimed Carley, as she wiped her moist face. "I wonder if you Easterners know the real significance of words."

Then they entered a taxi, to be whisked away apparently through a labyrinthine maze of cars and streets, where pedestrians had to run and jump for their lives. A congestion of traffic at Fifth Avenue and Forty-second Street halted their taxi for a few moments, and here in the thick of it Carley had full assurance that she was back in the metropolis. Her sore heart eased somewhat at sight of the streams of people passing to and fro. How they rushed! Where were they going? What was their story? And all the while her aunt held her hand, and Beatrice and Eleanor talked as fast as their tongues could wag. Then the taxi clad on up the avenue, to turn down a side street and presently stop at Carley's home. It was a modest three-story brown-stone house. Carley had been so benumbed by sensations that she did not imagine she could experience a new one. But peering out of the taxi, she gazed dubiously at the brownish-red stone steps and front of her home.

"I'm going to have it painted," she muttered, as if to herself.

Her aunt and her friends laughed, glad and relieved to hear such a practical remark from Carley. How were they to divine that this brownish-red stone was the color of desert rocks and canyon walls?

In a few more moments Carley was inside the house, feeling a sense of protection in the familiar rooms that had been her home for seventeen years. Once in the sanctity of her room, which was exactly as she had left it, her first action was to look in the mirror at her weary, dusty, heated face. Neither the brownness of it nor the shadow appeared to harmonize with the image of her that haunted the mirror.

"Now!" she whispered low. "It's done.... I'm home. The old life—or a new life? How to meet either. Now!"

Thus she challenged her spirit. And her intelligence rang at her the imperative necessity for action, for excitement, for effort that left no time for rest or memory or wakefulness. She accepted the issue. She was glad of the stern fight ahead of her. She set her will and steeled her heart with all the pride and vanity and fury of a woman who had been defeated but who scorned defeat. She was what birth and breeding and circumstance had made her. She would seek what the old life held.

What with unpacking and chatting and telephoning and lunching, the day soon passed. Carley went to dinner with friends and later to a roof garden. The color and light, the gayety and music, the news of acquaintances, the humor of the actors—all, in fact, except the unaccustomed heat and noise, were most welcome and diverting. That night she slept the sleep of weariness.

Awakening early, she inaugurated a habit of getting up at once, instead of lolling in bed, and breakfasting there, and reading her mail, as had been her wont before going West. Then she went over business matters with her aunt, called on her lawyer and banker, took lunch with Rose Maynard, and spent the afternoon shopping. Strong as she was, the unaccustomed heat and the hard pavements and the jostle of shoppers and the continual rush of sensations wore her out so completely that she did not want any dinner. She talked to her aunt a while, then went to bed.

Next day Carley motored through Central Park, and out of town into Westchester County, finding some relief from the stifling heat. But she seemed to look at the dusty trees and the worn greens without really seeing them. In the afternoon she called on friends, and had dinner at home with her aunt, and then went to a theatre. The musical comedy was good, but the almost unbearable heat and the vitiated air spoiled her enjoyment. That night upon arriving home at midnight she stepped out of the taxi, and involuntarily, without thought, looked up to see the stars. But there were no stars. A murky yellow-tinged blackness hung low over the city. Carley recollected that stars, and sunrises and sunsets, and untainted air, and silence were not for city dwellers. She checked any continuation of the thought.

A few days sufficed to swing her into the old life. Many of Carley's friends had neither the leisure nor the means to go away from the city during the summer. Some there were who might have afforded that if they had seen fit to live in less showy apartments, or to dispense with cars. Other of her best friends were on their summer outings in the Adirondacks. Carley decided to go with her aunt to Lake Placid about the first of August. Meanwhile she would keep going and doing.

She had been a week in town before Morrison telephoned her and added his welcome. Despite the gay gladness of his voice, it irritated her. Really, she scarcely wanted to see him. But a meeting was inevitable, and besides, going out with him was in accordance with the plan she had adopted. So she made an engagement to meet him at the Plaza for dinner. When with slow and pondering action she hung up the receiver it occurred to her that she resented the idea of going to the Plaza. She did not dwell on the reason why.

When Carley went into the reception room of the Plaza that night Morrison was waiting for her—the same slim, fastidious, elegant, sallow-faced Morrison whose image she had in mind, yet somehow different. He had what Carley called the New York masculine face, blasé and lined, with eyes that gleamed, yet had no fire. But at sight of her his face lighted up.

"By Jove! but you've come back a peach!" he exclaimed, clasping her extended hand. "Eleanor told me you looked great. It's worth missing you to see you like this."

"Thanks, Larry," she replied. "I must look pretty well to win that compliment from you. And how are you feeling? You don't seem robust for a golfer and horseman. But then I'm used to husky Westerners."

"Oh, I'm fagged with the daily grind," he said. "I'll be glad to get up in the mountains next month. Let's go down to dinner."

They descended the spiral stairway to the grill-room, where an orchestra was playing jazz, and dancers gyrated on a polished floor, and diners in evening dress looked on over their cigarettes.

"Well, Carley, are you still finicky about the eats?" he queried, consulting the menu.

"No. But I prefer plain food," she replied.

"Have a cigarette," he said, holding out his silver monogrammed case.

"Thanks, Larry. I—I guess I'll not take up smoking again. You see, while I was West I got out of the habit."

"Yes, they told me you had changed," he returned. "How about drinking?"

"Why, I thought New York had gone dry!" she said, forcing a laugh.

"Only on the surface. Underneath it's wetter than ever."

"Well, I'll obey the law."

He ordered a rather elaborate dinner, and then turning his attention to Carley, gave her closer scrutiny. Carley knew then that he had become acquainted with the fact of her broken engagement. It was a relief not to need to tell him.

"How's that big stiff, Kilbourne?" asked Morrison, suddenly. "Is it true he got well?"

"Oh—yes! He's fine," replied Carley with eyes cast down. A hot knot seemed to form deep within her and threatened to break and steal along her veins. "But if you please—I do not care to talk of him."

"Naturally. But I must tell you that one man's loss is another's gain."

Carley had rather expected renewed courtship from Morrison. She had not, however, been prepared for the beat of her pulse, the quiver of her nerves, the uprising of hot resentment at the mere mention of Kilbourne. It was only natural that Glenn's former rivals should speak of him, and perhaps disparagingly. But from this man Carley could not bear even a casual reference. Morrison had escaped the army service. He had been given a high-salaried post at the ship-yards—the duties of which, if there had been any, he performed wherever he happened to be. Morrison's father had made a fortune in leather during the war. And Carley remembered Glenn telling her he had seen two whole blocks in Paris piled twenty feet deep with leather army goods that were never used and probably had never been intended to be used. Morrison represented the not inconsiderable number of young men in New York who had gained at the expense of the valiant legion who had lost. But what had Morrison gained? Carley raised her eyes to gaze steadily at him. He looked well-fed, indolent, rich, effete, and supremely self-satisfied. She could not see that he had gained anything. She would rather have been a crippled ruined soldier.

"Larry, I fear gain and loss are mere words," she said. "The thing that counts with me is what you *are*."

He stared in well-bred surprise, and presently talked of a new dance which had lately come into vogue. And from that he passed on to gossip of the theatres. Once between courses of the dinner he asked Carley to dance, and she complied. The music would have stimulated an Egyptian mummy, Carley thought, and the subdued rose lights, the murmur of gay voices, the glide and grace and distortion of the dancers, were exciting and pleasurable. Morrison had the suppleness and skill of a dancing-master. But he held Carley too tightly, and so she told him, and added, "I imbibed some fresh pure air while I was out West—something you haven't here—and I don't want it all squeezed out of me."

* * *

The latter days of July Carley made busy—so busy that she lost her tan and appetite, and something of her splendid resistance to the dragging heat and late hours. Seldom was she without some of her friends. She accepted almost any kind of an invitation, and went even to Coney Island, to baseball games, to the motion pictures, which were three forms of amusement not customary with her. At Coney Island, which she visited with two of her younger girl friends, she had the best time since her arrival home. What had put her in accord with ordinary people? The baseball games, likewise pleased her. The running of the players and the screaming of the spectators amused and excited her. But she hated the motion pictures with their salacious and absurd misrepresentations of life, in some cases capably acted by skillful actors, and in others a silly series of scenes featuring some doll-faced girl.

But she refused to go horseback riding in Central Park. She refused to go to the Plaza. And these refusals she made deliberately, without asking herself why.

On August 1st she accompanied her aunt and several friends to Lake Placid, where they established themselves at a hotel. How welcome to Carley's strained eyes were the green of mountains, the soft gleam of amber water! How sweet and refreshing a breath of cool pure air! The change from New York's glare and heat and dirt, and iron-red insulating walls, and thronging millions of people, and ceaseless roar and rush, was tremendously relieving to Carley. She had burned the candle at both ends. But the beauty of the hills and vales, the quiet of the forest, the sight of the stars, made it harder to forget. She had to rest. And when she rested she could not always converse, or read, or write.

For the most part her days held variety and pleasure. The place was beautiful, the weather pleasant, the people congenial. She motored over the forest roads, she canoed along the margin of the lake, she played golf and tennis. She wore exquisite gowns to dinner and danced during the evenings. But she seldom walked anywhere on the trails and, never alone, and she never climbed the mountains and never rode a horse.

Morrison arrived and added his attentions to those of other men. Carley neither accepted nor repelled them. She favored the association with married couples and older people, and rather shunned the pairing off peculiar to vacationists at summer hotels. She had always loved to play and romp with children, but here she found herself growing to avoid them, somehow hurt by the sounds of pattering feet and joyous laughter. She filled the days as best she could, and usually earned quick slumber at night. She staked all on present occupation and the truth of flying time.

CHAPTER
9

*T*HE latter part of September Carley returned to New York.

Soon after her arrival she received by letter a formal proposal of marriage from Elbert Harrington, who had been quietly attentive to her during her sojourn at Lake Placid. He was a lawyer of distinction, somewhat older than most of her friends, and a man of means and fine family. Carley was quite surprised. Harrington was really one of the few of her acquaintances whom she regarded as somewhat behind the times, and liked him the better for that. But she could not marry him, and replied to his letter in as kindly a manner as possible. Then he called personally.

"Carley, I've come to ask you to reconsider," he said, with a smile in his gray eyes. He was not a tall or handsome man, but he had what women called a nice strong face.

"Elbert, you embarrass me," she replied, trying to laugh it out. "Indeed I feel honored, and I thank you. But I can't marry you."

"Why not?" he asked, quietly.

"Because I don't love you," she replied.

"I did not expect you to," he said. "I hoped in time you might come to care. I've known you a good many years, Carley. Forgive me if I tell you I see you are breaking—wearing yourself down. Maybe it is not a husband you need so much now, but you do need a home and children. You are wasting your life."

"All you say may be true, my friend," replied Carley, with a helpless little upflinging of hands. "Yet it does not alter my feelings."

"But you will marry sooner or later?" he queried, persistently.

This straightforward question struck Carley as singularly as if it was one she might never have encountered. It forced her to think of things she had buried.

"I don't believe I ever will," she answered, thoughtfully.

"That is nonsense, Carley," he went on. "You'll have to marry. What else can you do? With all due respect to your feelings—that affair with Kilbourne is ended—and you're not the wishy-washy heartbreak kind of a girl."

"You can never tell what a woman will do," she said, somewhat coldly.

"Certainly not. That's why I refuse to take no. Carley, be reasonable. You like me—respect me, do you not?"

"Why, of course I do!"

"I'm only thirty-five, and I could give you all any sensible woman wants," he said. "Let's make a real American home. Have you thought at all about that, Carley? Something is wrong to-day. Men are not marrying. Wives are not having children. Of all the friends I have, not one has a real American home. Why, it is a terrible fact! But, Carley, you are not a sentimentalist, or a melancholiac. Nor are you a waster. You have fine qualities. You need something to do—some one to care for."

"Pray do not think me ungrateful, Elbert," she replied, "nor insensible to the truth of what you say. But my answer is no!"

When Harrington had gone Carley went to her room, and precisely as upon her return from Arizona she faced her mirror skeptically and relentlessly. "I am such a liar that I'll do well to look at myself," she meditated. "Here I am again. Now! The world expects me to marry. But *what* do I expect?"

There was a raw unhealed wound in Carley's heart. Seldom had she permitted herself to think about it, let alone to probe it with hard materialistic queries. But custom to her was as inexorable as life. If she chose to live in the world she must conform to its customs. For a woman, marriage was the aim and the end and the all of existence. Nevertheless, for Carley it could not be without love. Before she had gone West she might have had many of the conventional modern ideas about women and marriage. But because out there in the wilds her love and perception had broadened, now her arraignment of herself and her sex was bigger, sterner, more exacting. The months she had been home seemed fuller than all the months of her life. She had tried to forget and enjoy, she had not succeeded; but she had looked with far-seeing eyes at her world. Glenn Kilbourne's tragic fate had opened her eyes. Either the world was all wrong or the people in it were. But if that were an extravagant and erroneous supposition, there certainly was proof positive that her own small individual world was wrong. The women did not do any real work; they did not bear children; they lived on excitement and luxury. They had no ideals. How greatly were men to blame? Carley doubted her judgment here. But as men could not live without the smiles and comradeship and love of women, it was only natural that they should give the women what they wanted. Indeed, they had no choice. It was give or go without. How much of real love entered into the marriages among her acquaintances? Before marriage Carley wanted a girl to be sweet, proud, aloof, with a heart of golden fire. Not attainable except through love! It would be better that no children be born at all unless born of such beautiful love. Perhaps that was why so few children were born. Nature's balance and revenge! In Arizona Carley had learned something of the ruthlessness and inevitableness of nature. She was finding out she had learned this with many other staggering facts.

"I love Glenn still," she whispered, passionately, with trembling lips, as she faced the tragic-eyed image of herself in the mirror. "I love him more— more. Oh, my God! If I were honest I'd cry out the truth! It is terrible. . . . I will always love him. How then could I marry any other man? I would be a lie, a cheat. If I could only forget him—only kill that love. Then I might love another man—and if I did love him—no matter what I had felt or done before, I would be worthy. I could feel worthy. I could give him just as much. But without such love I'd give only a husk—a body without soul."

Love, then, was the sacred and holy flame of life that sanctioned the begetting of children. Marriage might be a necessity of modern time, but it was not the vital issue. Carley's anguish revealed strange and hidden truths. In some inexplicable way Nature struck a terrible balance—revenged herself upon a people who had no children, or who brought into the world children not created by the divinity of love, unyearned for, and therefore somehow doomed to carry on the blunders and burdens of life.

Carley realized how right and true it might be for her to throw herself away upon an inferior man, even a fool or a knave, if she loved him with that great and natural love of woman; likewise it dawned upon her how false and wrong and sinful it would be to marry the greatest or the richest or the noblest man unless she had that supreme love to give him, and knew it was reciprocated.

"What am I going to do with my life?" she asked, bitterly and aghast. "I have been—I am a waster. I've lived for nothing but pleasurable sensation. I'm utterly useless. I do absolutely no good on earth."

Thus she saw how Harrington's words rang true—how they had precipitated a crisis for which her unconscious brooding had long made preparation.

"Why not give up ideals and be like the rest of my kind?" she soliloquized.

That was one of the things which seemed wrong with modern life. She thrust the thought from her with passionate scorn. If poor, broken, ruined Glenn Kilbourne could cling to an ideal and fight for it, could not she, who had all the world esteemed worth while, be woman enough to do the same? The direction of her thought seemed to have changed. She had been ready for rebellion. Three months of the old life had shown her that for her it was empty, vain, farcical, without one redeeming feature. The naked truth was brutal, but it cut clean to wholesome consciousness. Such so-called social life as she had plunged into deliberately to forget her unhappiness had failed her utterly. If she had been shallow and frivolous it might have done otherwise. Stripped of all guise, her actions must have been construed by a penetrating and impartial judge as a mere parading of her decorated person before a number of males with the purpose of ultimate selection.

"I've got to find some work," she muttered, soberly.

At the moment she heard the postman's whistle outside; and a little later the servant brought up her mail. The first letter, large, soiled, thick, bore the postmark Flagstaff, and her address in Glenn Kilbourne's writing.

Carley stared at it. Her heart gave a great leap. Her hand shook. She sat down suddenly as if the strength of her legs was inadequate to uphold her.

"Glenn has—written me!" she whispered, in slow, halting realization. "For what? Oh, why?"

The other letters fell off her lap, to lie unnoticed. This big thick envelope fascinated her. It was one of the stamped envelopes she had seen in his cabin. It contained a letter that had been written on his rude table, before the open fire, in the light of the doorway, in that little log cabin under the spreading pines of West Fork Canyon. Dared she read it? The shock to her heart passed; and with mounting swell, seemingly too full for her breast, it began to beat and throb a wild gladness through all her being. She tore the envelope apart and read:

Dear Carley:

I'm surely glad for a good excuse to write you.

Once in a blue moon I get a letter, and to-day Hutter brought me one from a soldier pard of mine who was with me in the Argonne. His name is Virgil Rust—queer name, don't you think?—and he's from Wisconsin. Just a rough-diamond sort of chap, but fairly well educated. He and I were in some pretty hot places, and it was he who pulled me out of a shell crater. I'd "gone west" sure then if it hadn't been for Rust.

Well, he did all sorts of big things during the war. Was down several times with wounds. He liked to fight and he was a holy terror. We all thought he'd get medals and a promotion. But he didn't get either. These much-desired things did not always go where they were best deserved.

Rust is now lying in a hospital in Bedford Park. His letter is pretty blue. All he says about why he's there is that he's knocked out. But he wrote a heap about his girl. It seems he was in love with a girl in his hometown—a pretty, big-eyed lass whose picture I've seen—and while he was overseas she married one of the chaps who got out of fighting. Evidently Rust is deeply hurt. He wrote: "I'd not care so . . . if she'd thrown me down to marry an old man or a boy who couldn't have gone to war." You see, Carley, servicemen feel queer about that sort of thing. It's something we got over there, and none of us will ever outlive it. Now, the point of this is that

I am asking you to go see Rust, and cheer him up, and do what you can for the poor devil. It's a good deal to ask of you, I know, especially as Rust saw *your* picture many a time and knows you were my girl. But you needn't tell him that you—we couldn't make a go of it.

And, as I am writing this to you, I see no reason why I shouldn't go on in behalf of myself.

The fact is, Carley, I miss writing to you more than I miss anything of my old life. I'll bet you have a trunkful of letters from me— unless you've destroyed them. I'm not going to say how I miss *your* letters. But I will say you wrote the most charming and fascinating letters of anyone I ever knew, quite aside from any sentiment. You knew, of course, that I had no other girl correspondent. Well, I got along fairly well before you came West, but I'd be an awful liar if I denied I didn't get lonely for you and your letters. It's different now that you've been to Oak Creek. I'm alone most of the time and I dream a lot, and I'm afraid I see you here in my cabin, and along the brook, and under the pines, and riding Calico—which you came to do well—and on my hogpen fence—and, oh, everywhere! I don't want you to think I'm down in the mouth, for I'm not. I'll take my medicine. But, Carley, you spoiled me, and I miss hearing from you, and I don't see why it wouldn't be all right for you to send me a friendly letter occasionally.

It is autumn now. I wish you could see Arizona canyons in their gorgeous colors. We have had frost right along and the mornings are great. There's a broad zigzag belt of gold halfway up the San Francisco peaks, and that is the aspen thickets taking on their fall coat. Here in the canyon you'd think there was blazing fire everywhere. The vines and the maples are red, scarlet, carmine, cerise, magenta, all the hues of flame. The oak leaves are turning russet gold, and the sycamores are yellow green. Up on the desert the other day I rode across a patch of asters, lilac and lavender, almost purple. I had to get off and pluck a handful. And then what do you think? I dug up the whole bunch, roots and all, and planted them on the sunny side of my cabin. I rather guess your love of flowers engendered this remarkable susceptibility in me.

I'm home early most every afternoon now, and I like the couple of hours loafing around. Guess it's bad for me, though. You know I seldom hunt, and the trout in the pool here are so tame now they'll almost eat out of my hand. I haven't the heart to fish for them. The squirrels, too, have grown tame and friendly. There's a red squirrel that climbs up on my table. And there's a chipmunk who lives in my cabin and runs over my bed. I've a new pet—the little pig you christened Pinky. After he had the wonderful good fortune to be caressed and named by you I couldn't think of letting him grow up in an ordinary piglike manner. So I fetched him home. My dog, Moze, was jealous at first and did not like this intrusion, but now they are good friends and sleep together. Flo has a kitten she's going to give me, and then, as Hutter says, I'll be "Jake."

My occupation during these leisure hours perhaps would strike my old friends East as idle, silly, mawkish. But I believe you will understand me.

I have the pleasure of doing nothing, and of catching now and then a glimpse of supreme joy in the strange state of *thinking* nothing. Tennyson came close to this in his "Lotus Eaters." Only to see—only to feel is enough!

Sprawled on the warm sweet pine needles, I breathe through them the breath of the earth and am somehow no longer lonely. I cannot, of course, see the sunset, but I watch for its coming on the eastern wall of the canyon. I see the shadow slowly creep up, driving the gold before it, until at last the canyon rim and pines are turned to golden fire. I watch the sailing eagles as they streak across the gold, and swoop up into the blue, and pass out of sight. I watch the golden flush fade to gray, and then the canyon slowly fills with purple shadows. This hour of twilight is the silent and melancholy one. Seldom is there any sound save the soft rush of the water over the stones, and that seems to die away. For a moment, perhaps, I am Hiawatha alone in his forest home, or a more primitive savage, feeling the great, silent pulse of nature, happy in unconsciousness, like a beast of the wild. But only for an instant do I ever catch this fleeting state. Next I am Glenn Kilbourne of West Fork, doomed and haunted by memories of the past. The great looming walls then become no longer blank. They are vast pages of the history of my life, with its past and present, and, alas!

its future. Everything time does is written on the stones. And my stream seems to murmur the sad and ceaseless flow of human life, with its music and its misery.

Then, descending from the sublime to the humdrum and necessary, I heave a sigh, and pull myself together, and go in to make biscuits and fry ham. But I should not forget to tell you that before I do go in, very often my looming, wonderful walls and crags weave in strange shadowy characters the beautiful and unforgettable face of Carley Burch!

I append what little news Oak Creek affords.

That blamed old bald eagle stole another of my pigs.

I am doing so well with my hog-raising that Hutter wants to come in with me, giving me an interest in his sheep.

It is rumored some one has bought the Deep Lake section I wanted for a ranch. I don't know who. Hutter was rather noncommittal.

Charley, the herder, had one of his queer spells the other day, and swore to me he had a letter from you. He told the blamed lie with a sincere and placid eye, and even a smile of pride. Queer guy, that Charley!

Flo and Lee Stanton had another quarrel—the worst yet, Lee tells me. Flo asked a girl friend out from Flag and threw her in Lee's way, so to speak, and when Lee retaliated by making love to the girl Flo got mad. Funny creatures, you girls! Flo rode with me from High Falls to West Fork, and never showed the slightest sign of trouble. In fact she was delightfully gay. She rode Calico, and beat me bad in a race.

Adios, Carley. Won't you write me?

Glenn.

No sooner had Carley read the letter through to the end than she began it all over again, and on this second perusal she lingered over passages—only to reread them. That suggestion of her face sculptured by shadows on the canyon walls seemed to thrill her very soul.

She leaped up from the reading to cry out something that was unutterable. All the intervening weeks of shame and anguish and fury and strife and pathos, and the endless striving to forget, were as if by the magic of a letter made nothing but vain oblations.

"He loves me still!" she whispered, and pressed her breast with clenching hands, and laughed in wild exultance, and paced her room like a caged lioness. It was as if she had just awakened to the assurance she was beloved. That was the shibboleth—the cry by which she sounded the closed depths of her love and called to the stricken life of a woman's insatiate vanity.

Then she snatched up the letter, to scan it again, and, suddenly grasping the import of Glenn's request, she hurried to the telephone to find the number of the hospital in Bedford Park. A nurse informed her that visitors were received at certain hours and that any attention to disabled soldiers was most welcome.

Carley motored out there to find the hospital merely a long one-story frame structure, a barracks hastily thrown up for the care of invalided men of the service. The chauffeur informed her that it had been used for that purpose during the training period of the army, and later when injured soldiers began to arrive from France.

A nurse admitted Carley into a small bare anteroom. Carley made known her errand.

"I'm glad it's Rust you want to see," replied the nurse. "Some of these boys are going to die. And some will be worse off if they live. But Rust may get well if he'll only behave. You are a relative—or friend?"

"I don't know him," answered Carley. "But I have a friend who was with him in France."

The nurse led Carley into a long narrow room with a line of single beds down each side, a stove at each end, and a few chairs. Each bed appeared to have an occupant and those nearest Carley lay singularly quiet. At the far end of the room were soldiers on crutches, wearing bandages on their heads, carrying their arms in slings. Their merry voices contrasted discordantly with their sad appearance.

Presently Carley stood beside a bed and looked down upon a gaunt, haggard young man who lay propped up on pillows.

"Rust—a lady to see you," announced the nurse.

Carley had difficulty in introducing herself. Had Glenn ever looked like this? What a face! It's healed scar only emphasized the pallor and furrows of pain that assuredly came from present wounds. He had unnaturally bright dark eyes, and a flush of fever in his hollow cheeks.

"How do!" he said, with a wan smile. "Who're you?"

"I'm Glenn Kilbourne's fiancée," she replied, holding out her hand.

"Say, I ought to 've known you," he said, eagerly, and a warmth of light changed the gray shade of his face. "You're the girl Carley! You're almost like my— my own girl. By golly! you're some looker! It was good of you to come. Tell me about Glenn."

Carley took the chair brought by the nurse, and pulling it close to the bed, she smiled down upon him and said: "I'll be glad to tell you all I know—presently. But first you tell me about yourself. Are you in pain? What is your trouble? You must let me do everything I can for you, and these other men."

Carley spent a poignant and depth-stirring hour at the bedside of Glenn's comrade. At last she learned from loyal lips the nature of Glenn Kilbourne's service to his country. How Carley clasped to her sore heart the praise of the man she loved—the simple proofs of his noble disregard of self! Rust said little about his own service to country or to comrade. But Carley saw enough in his face. He had been like Glenn. By these two Carley grasped the compelling truth of the spirit and sacrifice of the legion of boys who had upheld American traditions. Their children and their children's children, as the years rolled by into the future, would hold their heads higher and prouder. Some things could never die in the hearts and the blood of a race. These boys, and the girls who had the supreme glory of being loved by them, must be the ones to revive the Americanism of their forefathers. Nature and God would take care of the slackers, the cowards who cloaked their shame with bland excuses of home service, of disability, and of dependence.

Carley saw two forces in life—the destructive and constructive. On the one side greed, selfishness, materialism: on the other generosity, sacrifice, and idealism. Which of them builded for the future? She saw men as wolves, sharks, snakes, vermin, and opposed to them men as lions and eagles. She saw women who did not inspire men to fare forth to seek, to imagine, to dream, to hope, to work, to fight. She began to have a glimmering of what a woman might be.

That night she wrote swiftly and feverishly, page after page, to Glenn, only to destroy what she had written. She could not keep her heart out of her words, nor a hint of what was becoming a sleepless and eternal regret. She wrote until a late hour, and at last composed a letter she knew did not ring true, so stilted and restrained was it in all passages save those concerning news of Glenn's comrade and of her own friends. "I'll never—never write him again," she averred with stiff lips, and next moment could have laughed in mockery at the bitter truth. If she had ever had any courage, Glenn's letter had destroyed it. But had it not been a kind of selfish, false courage, roused to hide her hurt, to save her own future? Courage should have a thought of others. Yet shamed one moment at the consciousness she would write Glenn again and again, and exultant the next with the clamouring love, she seemed to have climbed beyond the self that had striven to forget. She would remember and think though she died of longing.

Carley, like a drowning woman, caught at straws. What a relief and joy to give up that endless nagging at her mind! For months she had kept ceaselessly active, by associations which were of no help to her and which did not make her happy, in her determination to forget. Suddenly then she gave up to remembrance. She would cease trying to get over her love for Glenn, and think of him and dream about him as much as memory dictated. This must constitute the only happiness she could have.

The change from strife to surrender was so novel and sweet that for days she felt renewed. It was augmented by her visits to the hospital in Bedford Park. Through her bountiful presence Virgil Rust and his comrades had many dull hours of pain and weariness alleviated and brightened. Interesting herself in the condition of the seriously disabled soldiers and possibility of their future took time and work Carley gave willingly and gladly. At first she endeavored to get acquaintances with means and leisure to help the boys, but these overtures met with such little success that she quit wasting valuable time she could herself devote to their interests.

Thus several weeks swiftly passed by. Several soldiers who had been more seriously injured than Rust improved to the extent that they were discharged. But Rust gained little or nothing. The nurse and doctor both informed Carley that Rust brightened for her, but when she was gone he lapsed into somber indifference. He did not care whether he ate or not, or whether he got well or died.

"If I do pull out, where 'll I go and what 'll I do?" he once asked the nurse.

Carley knew that Rust's hurt was more than loss of a leg, and she decided to talk earnestly to him and try to win him to hope and effort. He had come to have a sort of reverence for her. So, biding her time, she at length found opportunity to approach his bed while his comrades were asleep or out of hearing. He endeavored to laugh her off, and then tried subterfuge, and lastly he cast off his mask and let her see his naked soul.

"Carley, I don't want your money or that of your kind friends—whoever they are—you say will help me to get into business," he said. "God knows I thank you and it warms me inside to find *some one* who appreciates what I've given. But I don't want charity. . . . And I guess I'm pretty sick of the game. I'm sorry the Boches didn't do the job right."

"Rust, that is morbid talk," replied Carley. "You're ill and you just can't see any hope. You must cheer up—fight *yourself;* and look at the brighter side. It's a horrible pity you must be a cripple, but Rust, indeed life can be worth living if you make it so."

"How could there be a brighter side when a man's only half a man?" he queried, bitterly.

"You can be just as much a man as ever," persisted Carley, trying to smile when she wanted to cry.

"Could you care for a man with only one leg?" he asked, deliberately.

"What a question! Why, of course I could!"

"Well, maybe you are different. Glenn always swore even if he was killed no slacker or no rich guy left at home could ever get you. Maybe you haven't any idea how much it means to us fellows to know there *are* true and faithful girls. But I'll tell you, Carley, we fellows who went across got to see things strange when we came home. The good old U. S. needs a lot of faithful girls just now, believe me."

"Indeed that's true," replied Carley. "It's a hard time for everybody, and particularly you boys who have lost so—so much."

"I lost *all,* except my life—and I wish to God I'd lost that," he replied, gloomily.

"Oh, don't talk so!" implored Carley in distress. "Forgive me, Rust, if I hurt you. But I must tell you—that—that Glenn wrote me—you'd lost your girl. Oh, I'm sorry! It is dreadful for you now. But if you got well—and went to work—and took up life where you left it—why soon your pain would grow easier. And you'd find some happiness yet."

"Never for me in this world."

"But why, Rust, *why?* You're no—no—Oh! I mean you have intelligence and courage. Why isn't there anything left for you?"

"Because something here's been killed," he replied, and put his hand to his heart.

"Your faith? Your love of—of everything? Did the war kill it?"

"I'd gotten over that, maybe," he said, drearily, with his somber eyes on space that seemed lettered for him. "But *she* half murdered it—and *they* did the rest."

"They? Whom do you mean, Rust?"

"Why, Carley, I mean the people I lost my leg for!" he replied, with terrible softness.

"The British? The French?" she queried, in bewilderment.

"*No!*" he cried, and turned his face to the wall.

Carley dared not ask him more. She was shocked. How helplessly impotent all her earnest sympathy! No longer could she feel an impersonal, however kindly, interest in this man. His last ringing word had linked her also to his misfortune and his suffering. Suddenly he turned away from the wall. She saw him swallow laboriously. How tragic that thin, shadowed face of agony! Carley saw it differently. But for the beautiful softness of light in his eyes, she would have been unable to endure gazing longer.

"Carley, I'm bitter," he said, "but I'm not rancorous and callous, like some of the boys. I know if you'd been my girl you'd have stuck to me."

"Yes," Carley whispered.

"That makes a difference," he went on, with a sad smile. "You see, we soldiers all had feelings. And in one thing we all felt alike. That was we were going to fight for our homes and our women. I should say women first. No matter what we read or heard about standing by our allies, fighting for liberty or civilization, the truth was we all felt the same, even if we never breathed it. . . . Glenn fought for you. I fought for Nell. . . . We were not going to let the Huns treat you as they treated French and Belgian girls. . . . And think! Nell was engaged to me—she *loved* me—and, by God! She married a slacker when I lay half dead on the battlefield!"

"She was not worth loving or fighting for," said Carley, with agitation.

"Ah! now you've said something," he declared. "If I can only hold to that truth! What does one girl amount to? *I* do not count. It is the sum that counts. We love America—our homes—our women! . . . Carley, I've had comfort and strength come to me through you. Glenn will have his reward in your love. Somehow I seem to share it, a little. Poor Glenn! He got his, too. Why, Carley, that guy wouldn't *let* you do what he could do *for you*. He was cut to pieces—"

"Please—Rust—don't say any more. I am unstrung," she pleaded.

"Why not? It's due you to know how splendid Glenn was. . . . I tell you, Carley, all the boys here love you for the way you've stuck to Glenn. Some of them knew him, and I've told the rest. We thought he'd never pull through. But he has, and we know how you helped. Going West to see him! He didn't write it to me, but I know. . . . I'm wise. I'm happy for him—the lucky dog. Next time you go West——"

"Hush!" cried Carley. She could endure no more. She could no longer be a lie.

"You're white—you're shaking," exclaimed Rust, in concern. "Oh, I—what did I say? Forgive me—"

"Rust, I am no more worth loving and fighting for than your Nell."

"What!" he ejaculated.

"I have not told you the truth," she said, swiftly. "I have let you believe a lie. . . . I shall never marry Glenn. I broke my engagement to him."

Slowly Rust sank back upon the pillow, his large luminous eyes piercingly fixed upon her, as if he would read her soul.

"I went West—yes—" continued Carley. "But it was selfishly. I wanted Glenn to come back here. . . . He had suffered as you have. He nearly died. But he fought—he fought—Oh! he went through hell! And after a long, slow, horrible struggle he began to mend. He worked. He went to raising hogs. He lived alone. He worked harder and harder. . . . The West and his work saved him, body and soul. . . . He had learned to love both the West and his work. I did not blame him. But I could not live out there. He needed me. But I was too little—too selfish. I could not marry him. I gave him up. . . . I left—him—alone!"

Carley shrank under the scorn in Rust's eyes.

"And there's another man," he said, "a clean, straight, unscarred fellow who wouldn't fight!"

"Oh, no—I—I swear there's not," whispered Carley.

"You, too," he replied, thickly. Then slowly he turned that worn dark face to the wall. His frail breast heaved. And his lean hand made her a slight gesture of dismissal, significant and imperious.

Carley fled. She could scarcely see to find the car. All her internal being seemed convulsed, and a deadly faintness made her sick and cold.

*C*ARLEY'S edifice of hopes, dreams, aspirations, and struggles fell in ruins about her. It had been built upon false sands. It had no ideal for foundation. It had to fall.

Something inevitable had forced her confession to Rust. Dissimulation had been a habit of her mind; it was more a habit of her class than sincerity. But she had reached a point in her mental strife where she could not stand before Rust and let him believe she was noble and faithful when she knew she was neither. Would not the next step in this painful metamorphosis of her character be a fierce and passionate repudiation of herself and all she represented?

She went home and locked herself in her room, deaf to telephone and servants. There she gave up to her shame. Scorned—despised—dismissed by that poor crippled flame-spirited Virgil Rust! He had reverenced her, and the truth had earned his hate. Would she ever forget his look—incredulous— shocked—bitter—and blazing with unutterable contempt? Carley Burch was only another Nell—a jilt— a mocker of the manhood of soldiers! Would she ever

cease to shudder at the memory of Rust's slight movement of hand? Go! Get out of my sight! Leave me to my
agony as you left Glenn Kilbourne alone to fight his!
Men such as I am do not want the smile of your face,
the touch of your hand! We gave for womanhood! Pass
on to lesser men who loved the fleshpots and who
would buy your charms! So Carley interpreted that
slight gesture, and writhed in her abasement.

Rust threw a white, illuminating light upon her
desertion of Glenn. She had betrayed him. She had left
him alone. Dwarfed and stunted was her narrow soul!
To a man who had given all for her she had returned
nothing. Stone for bread! Betrayal for love! Cowardice
for courage!

The hours of contending passions gave birth to
vague, slow-forming revolt.

She became haunted by memory pictures and
sounds and smells of Oak Creek Canyon. As from afar
she saw the great sculptured rent in the earth, green
and red and brown, with its shining, flashing ribbons
of waterfalls and streams. The mighty pines stood up
magnificent and stately. The walls loomed high, shadowed under the shelves, gleaming in the sunlight, and
they seemed dreaming, waiting, watching. For what?
For her return to their serene fastnesses—to the little
gray log cabin. The thought stormed Carley's soul.

Vivid and intense shone the images before her
shut eyes. She saw the winding forest floor, green
with grass and fern, colorful with flower and rock.
A thousand aisles, glades, nooks, and caverns called
her to come. Nature was every woman's mother.
The populated city was a delusion. Disease and
death and corruption stalked in the shadows of the
streets. But her canyon promised hard work, playful

hours, dreaming idleness, beauty, health, fragrance, loneliness, peace, wisdom, love, children, and long life. In the hateful shut-in isolation of her room, Carley stretched forth her arms as if to embrace the vision. Pale close walls, gleaming placid stretches of brook, churning amber and white rapids, mossy banks and pine-matted ledges, the towers and turrets and ramparts where the eagles wheeled—she saw them all as beloved images lost to her save in anguished memory.

She heard the murmur of flowing water, soft, low, now loud, and again lulling, hollow and eager, tinkling over rocks, bellowing into the deep pools, washing with silky seep of wind-swept waves the hanging willows. Shrill and piercing and far-aloft pealed the scream of the eagle. And she seemed to listen to a mocking bird while he mocked her with his melody of many birds. The bees hummed, the wind moaned, the leaves rustled, the waterfall murmured. Then came the sharp rare note of a canyon swift, most mysterious of birds, significant of the heights.

A breath of fragrance seemed to blow with her shifting senses. The dry, sweet, tangy canyon smells returned to her—of fresh-cut timber, of wood smoke, of the cabin fire with its steaming pots, of flowers and earth, and of the wet stones, of the redolent pines and the pungent cedars.

And suddenly, clearly, amazingly, Carley beheld in her mind's sight the hard features, the bold eyes, the slight smile, the coarse face of Haze Ruff. She had forgotten him. But he now returned. And with memory of him flashed a revelation as to his meaning in her life. He had appeared merely a clout, a ruffian, an animal with man's shape and intelligence.

But he was the embodiment of the raw, crude violence of the West. He was the eyes of the natural primitive man, believing what he saw. He had seen in Carley Burch the paraded charm, the unashamed and serene front, the woman seeking man. Haze Ruff had been neither vile nor base nor unnatural. It had been her subjection to the decadence of feminine dress that had been unnatural. But Ruff had found her a lie. She invited what she did not want. And his scorn had been commensurate with the falsehood of her. So might any man have been justified in his insult to her, in his rejection of her. Haze Ruff had found her unfit for his idea of dalliance. Virgil Rust had found her false to the ideals of womanhood for which he had sacrificed all but life itself. What then had Glenn Kilbourne found her? He possessed the greatness of noble love. He had loved her before the dark and changeful tide of war had come between them. How had he judged her? That last sight of him standing alone, leaning with head bowed, a solitary figure trenchant with suggestion of tragic resignation and strength, returned to flay Carley. He had loved, trusted, and hoped. She saw now what his hope had been—that she would have instilled into her blood the subtle, red, and revivifying essence of calling life in the open, the strength of the wives of earlier years, an emanation from canyon, desert, mountain, forest, of health, of spirit, of forward-gazing natural love, of the mysterious saving instinct he had gotten out of the West. And she had been too little—too steeped in the indulgence of luxurious life—too slight-natured and pale-blooded! And suddenly there pierced into the black storm of Carley's mind a blazing, white-streaked thought—she had left Glenn to the Western girl, Flo Hutter. Humiliated, and abased in her own sight, Carley fell prey to a fury of jealousy.

She went back to the old life. But it was in a bitter, restless, critical spirit, conscious of the fact that she could derive neither forgetfulness nor pleasure from it, nor see any release from the habit of years.

One afternoon, late in the fall, she motored out to a Long Island club where the last of the season's golf was being enjoyed by some of her most intimate friends. Carley did not play. Aimlessly she walked around the grounds, finding the autumn colors subdued and drab, like her mind. The air held a promise of early winter. She thought that she would go South before the cold came. Always trying to escape anything rigorous, hard, painful, or disagreeable! Later she returned to the clubhouse to find her party assembled on an enclosed porch, chatting and partaking of refreshment. Morrison was there. He had not taken kindly to her late habit of denying herself to him.

During a lull in the idle conversation Morrison addressed Carley pointedly. "Well, Carley, how's your Arizona hog-raiser?" he queried, with a little gleam in his usually lusterless eyes.

"I have not heard lately," she replied, coldly.

The assembled company suddenly quieted with a portent inimical to their leisurely content of the moment. Carley felt them all looking at her, and underneath the exterior she preserved with extreme difficulty, there burned so fierce an anger that she seemed to have swelling veins of fire.

"Queer how Kilbourne went into raising hogs," observed Morrison. "Such a low-down sort of work, you know."

"He had no choice," replied Carley. "Glenn didn't have a father who made tainted millions out of the war. He had to work. And I must differ with you about its being low-down. No honest work is that. It is idleness that is low down."

"But so foolish of Glenn when he might have married money," rejoined Morrison, sarcastically.

"The honor of soldiers is beyond your ken, Mr. Morrison."

He flushed darkly and bit his lip.

"You women make a man sick with this rot about soldiers," he said, the gleam in his eye growing ugly. "A uniform goes to a woman's head no matter what's inside it. I don't see where your vaunted honor of soldiers comes in—considering how they accepted the let-down of women during and after the war."

"How could you see when you stayed comfortably at home?" retorted Carley.

"All I could see was women falling into soldiers' arms," he said, sullenly.

"Certainly. Could an American girl desire any greater happiness—or opportunity to prove her gratitude?" flashed Carley, with proud uplift of head.

"It didn't look like gratitude to me," returned Morrison.

"Well, it *was* gratitude," declared Carley, ringingly. "If women of America did throw themselves at soldiers it was not owing to the moral lapse of the day. It was woman's instinct to save the race! Always, in every war, women have sacrificed themselves to the future. Not vile, but noble! . . . You insult both soldiers and women, Mr. Morrison. I wonder—did any American girls throw themselves at *you?*"

Morrison turned a dead white, and his mouth twisted to a distorted checking of speech, disagreeable to see.

"No, you were a slacker," went on Carley, with scathing scorn. "You let the other men go fight for American girls. Do you imagine one of them will ever *marry* you?. . . All your life, Mr. Morrison, you will be a marked man—outside the pale of friendship with real American men and the respect of real American girls."

Morrison leaped up, almost knocking the table over, and he glared at Carley as he gathered up his hat and cane. She turned her back upon him. From that moment he ceased to exist for Carley. She never spoke to him again.

Next day Carley called upon her dearest friend, whom she had not seen for some time.

"Carley dear, you don't look so very well," said Eleanor, after greetings had been exchanged.

"Oh, what does it matter how I look?" queried Carley, impatiently.

"You were so wonderful when you got home from Arizona."

"If I was wonderful and am now commonplace you can thank your old New York for it."

"Carley, don't you care for New York any more?" asked Eleanor.

"Oh, New York is all right, I suppose. It's I who am wrong."

"My dear, you puzzle me these days. You've changed. I'm sorry. I'm afraid you're unhappy."

"Me? Oh, impossible! I'm in a seventh heaven," replied Carley, with a hard little laugh. "What're you doing this afternoon? Let's go out—riding—or somewhere."

"I'm expecting the dressmaker."

"Where are you going to-night?"

"Dinner and theater. It's a party, or I'd ask you."

"What did you do yesterday and the day before, and the days before that?"

Eleanor laughed indulgently, and acquainted Carley with a record of her social wanderings during the last few days.

"The same old things—over and over again! Eleanor don't you get sick of it?" queried Carley.

"Oh yes, to tell the truth," returned Eleanor, thoughtfully. "But there's nothing else to do."

"Eleanor, I'm no better than you," said Carley, with disdain. "I'm as useless and idle. But I'm beginning to see myself—and you—and all this rotten crowd of ours. We're no good. But you're married, Eleanor. You're settled in life. You ought to *do something*. I'm single and at loose ends. Oh, I'm in revolt!... Think, Eleanor, just think. Your husband works hard to keep you in this expensive apartment. You have a car. He dresses you in silks and satins. You wear diamonds. You eat your breakfast in bed. You loll around in a pink dressing gown all morning. You dress for lunch or tea. You ride or golf or worse than waste your time on some lounge lizard, dancing till time to come home to dress for dinner. You let other men make love to you. Oh, don't get sore. You do.... And so goes the round of your life. What good on earth are you, anyhow? You're just a—a gratification to the senses of your husband. And at that you don't see much of *him*."

"Carley, how you rave!" exclaimed her friend. "What has gotten into you lately? Why, everybody tells me you're—you're queer! The way you insulted Morrison—how unlike you, Carley!"

"I'm glad I found the nerve to do it. What do you think, Eleanor?"

"Oh, I despise him. But you can't say the things you feel."

"You'd be bigger and truer if you did. Some day I'll break out and flay you and your friends alive."

"But, Carley, you're my friend and you're just exactly like we are. Or you were, quite recently."

"Of course, I'm your friend. I've always loved you, Eleanor," went on Carley, earnestly. "I'm as deep in this—this damned stagnant muck as you, or any-one. But I'm no longer *blind*. There's something terribly wrong with us women, and it's not what Morrison hinted."

"Carley, the only thing wrong with you is that you jilted poor Glenn—and are breaking your heart over him still."

"Don't—don't!" cried Carley, shrinking. "God knows that is true. But there's more wrong with me than a blighted love affair."

"Yes, you mean the modern feminine unrest?"

"Eleanor, I positively hate that phrase 'mod-ern feminine unrest!' It smacks of ultra—ultra— Oh! I don't know what. That phrase ought to be translated by a Western acquaintance of mine— one Haze Ruff. I'd not like to hurt your sensitive feelings with what he'd say. But this unrest means speed-mad, excitement-mad, fad-mad, dress-mad, or I should say *un*dress-mad, culture-mad, and Heaven only knows what else. The women of our set are idle, luxurious, selfish, pleasure-craving, lazy, useless, work-and-children shirking, absolutely no good."

"Well, if we are, who's to blame?" rejoined Eleanor, spiritedly. "Now, Carley Burch, you listen to me. I think the twentieth-century girl in America is the most wonderful female creation of all the ages of the universe. I admit it. That is why we are a prey to the evils attending greatness. Listen. Here is a crying sin—an infernal paradox. Take this twentieth-century girl, this American girl who is the finest creation of the ages. A young and healthy girl, the most perfect type of culture possible to the freest and greatest city on earth—New York! She holds absolutely an unreal, untrue position in the scheme of existence. Surrounded by parents, relatives, friends, suitors, and instructive schools of every kind, colleges, institutions, is she really happy, is she really living?"

"Eleanor," interrupted Carley, earnestly, "she is *not*. . . . And I've been trying to tell you why."

"My dear, let me get a word in, will you," complained Eleanor. "You don't know it all. There are as many different points of view as there are people. . . . Well, if this girl happened to have a new frock, and a new beau to show it to, she'd say, 'I'm the happiest girl in the world.' But she is nothing of the kind. Only she doesn't know that. She approaches marriage, or, for that matter, a more matured life, having had too much, having been too well taken care of, *knowing too much*. Her masculine satellites—father, brothers, uncles, friends, lovers—all utterly spoil her. Mind you, I mean, girls like us, of the middle class— which is to say the largest and best class of

Americans. We are spoiled.... This girl marries. And life goes on smoothly, as if its aim was to exclude friction and effort. Her husband makes it too easy for her. She is an ornament, or a toy, to be kept in a luxurious cage. To soil her pretty hands would be disgraceful! Even if she can't afford a maid, the modern devices of science make the care of her four-room apartment a farce. Electric dish-washer, clothes-washer, vacuum-cleaner, and the near-by delicatessen and the caterer simply rob a young wife of her housewifely heritage. If she has a baby—which happens occasionally, Carley, in spite of your assertion—it very soon goes to the kindergarten. Then what does she find to do with hours and hours? If she is not married, what on earth *can* she find to do?"

"She can work," replied Carley, bluntly.

"Oh yes, she can, but she doesn't," went on Eleanor. "*You* don't work. I never did. We both hated the idea. You're calling spades spades, Carley, but you seem to be riding a morbid, impractical thesis. Well, our young American girl or bride goes in for being rushed or she goes in for fads, the ultra stuff you mentioned. New York City gets all the great artists, lecturers, and surely the great fakirs. The New York women support them. The men laugh, but they furnish the money. They take the women to the theaters, but they cut out the reception to a Polish princess, a lecture by an Indian magician and mystic, or a benefit luncheon for a Home for Friendless Cats. The truth is most of our young girls or brides have a wonderful enthusiasm worthy of a better cause. What is to become of their surplus energy, the bottled-lightning spirit so characteristic of modern girls? Where is the outlet for intense feelings? What use can they make of education or of gifts? They just can't, that's all. I'm not taking into consideration the new-woman species, the faddist or the reformer. I mean normal girls like you and me. Just think, Carley. A girl's every wish, every need, is almost instantly satisfied without the slightest effort on her part to obtain it. No struggle, let alone work! If women crave to achieve something outside of the arts, you know, something universal and helpful which will make men acknowledge her worth, if not the equality, where is the opportunity?"

"Opportunities should be *made*," replied Carley.

"There are a million sides to this question of the modern young woman—the *fin-de-siècle* girl. I'm for her!"

"How about the extreme of style in dress for this remarkably-to-be-pitied American girl you champion so eloquently?" queried Carley, sarcastically.

"Immoral!" exclaimed Eleanor with frank disgust.

"You admit it?"

"To my shame, I do."

"Why do women wear extreme clothes? Why do you and I wear open-work silk stockings, skirts to our knees, gowns without sleeves or bodices?"

"We're slaves to fashion," replied Eleanor. "That's the popular excuse."

"Bah!" exclaimed Carley.

Eleanor laughed in spite of being half nettled. "Are you going to stop wearing what all the other women wear—and be looked at askance? Are you going to be dowdy and frumpy and old-fashioned?"

"No. But I'll never wear anything again that can be called immoral. I want to be able to say *why* I wear a dress. . . . You haven't answered my question yet. Why do you wear what you frankly admit is disgusting?"

"I don't know, Carley," replied Eleanor, helplessly. "How you harp on things! We must dress to make other women jealous and to attract men. To be a sensation! Perhaps the word 'immoral' is not what I mean. A woman will be shocking in her obsession to attract, but hardly more than that, if she knows it."

"Ah! So few women realize how they actually do look. Haze Ruff could tell them."

"Haze Ruff. Who in the world is he or she?" asked Eleanor.

"Haze Ruff is a he, all right," replied Carley, grimly.

"Well, who is he?"

"A sheep-dipper in Arizona," answered Carley, dreamily.

"Humph! And what can Mr. Ruff tell us?"

"He told *me* I looked like one of the devil's angels—and that I dressed to knock the daylights out of men."

"Well, Carley Burch, if that isn't rich!" exclaimed Eleanor, with a peal of laughter. "I dare say you appreciate that as an original compliment."

"No. . . . I wonder what Ruff would say about jazz—I just wonder," murmured Carley.

"Well, I wouldn't care what he said, and I don't care what *you* say," returned Eleanor. "The preachers and reformers and bishops and rabbis make me sick. They rave about jazz. Jazz—the discordant note of our decadence! Jazz—the harmonious expression of our musicless, mindless, soulless materialism!— The idiots! If they could be women for a while they would realize the error of their ways. But they will never, never abolish jazz—*never,* for it is the grandest, the most wonderful, the most absolutely necessary thing for women in this terrible age of smotheration."

"All right, Eleanor, we understand each other, even if we do not agree," said Carley. "You leave the future of women to chance, to life, to materialism, not to their own conscious efforts. I want to leave it to free will and idealism."

"Carley, you are getting a little beyond me," declared Eleanor, dubiously.

"What are you going to *do?* It all comes home to each individual woman. Her attitude toward life."

"I'll drift along with the current, Carley, and be a good sport," replied Eleanor, smiling.

"You don't care about the women and children of the future? You'll not deny yourself now, and think and work, and suffer a little, in the interest of future humanity?"

"How you put things, Carley!" exclaimed Eleanor, wearily. "Of course I care—when you make me think of such things. But what have *I* to do with the lives of people in the years to come?"

"Everything. America for Americans! While you dawdle, the life blood is being sucked out of our great nation. It is a man's job to fight, it is a woman's to save. . . . I think you've made your choice, though you don't realize it. I'm praying to God that I'll rise to mine."

* * *

Carley had a visitor one morning earlier than the usual or conventional time for calls.

"He wouldn't give no name," said the maid. "He wears soldier clothes, ma'am, and he's pale, and walks with a cane."

"Tell him I'll be right down," replied Carley.

Her hands trembled while she hurriedly dressed. Could this caller be Virgil Rust? She hoped so, but she doubted.

As she entered the parlor a tall young man in worn khaki rose to meet her. At first glance she could not name him, though she recognized the pale face and light-blue eyes, direct and steady.

"Good morning, Miss Burch," he said. "I hope you'll excuse so early a call. You remember me, don't you? I'm George Burton, who had the bunk next to Rust's."

"Surely I remember you, Mr. Burton, and I'm glad to see you," replied Carley, shaking hands with him. "Please sit down. Your being here must mean you're discharged from the hospital."

"Yes, I was discharged, all right," he said.

"Which means you're well again. That is fine. I'm very glad."

"I was put out to make room for a fellow in bad shape. I'm still shaky and weak," he replied. "But I'm glad to go. I've pulled through pretty good, and it'll not be long until I'm strong again. It was the 'flu' that kept me down."

"You must be careful. May I ask where you're going and what you expect to do?"

"Yes, that's what I came to tell you," he replied, frankly. "I want you to help me a little. I'm from

Illinois and my people aren't so badly off. But I don't want to go back to my home town down and out, you know. Besides, the winters are cold there. The doctor advises me to go to a little milder climate. You see, I was gassed, and got the 'flu' afterward. But I know I'll be all right if I'm careful. . . . Well, I've always had a leaning toward agriculture, and I want to go to Kansas. Southern Kansas. I want to travel around till I find a place I like, and there I'll get a job. Not too hard a job at first—that's why I'll need a little money. I know what to do. I want to lose myself in the wheat country and forget the—the war. I'll not be afraid of work, presently. . . . Now, Miss Burch, you've been so kind—I'm going to ask you to lend me a little money. I'll pay it back. I can't promise just when. But some day. Will you?"

"Assuredly I will," she replied, heartily. "I'm happy to have the opportunity to help you. How much will you need for immediate use? Five hundred dollars?"

"Oh no, not so much as that," he replied. "Just railroad fare home, and then to Kansas, and to pay board while I get well, you know, and look around."

"We'll make it five hundred, anyway," she replied, and, rising, she went toward the library. "Excuse me a moment." She wrote the check and, returning, gave it to him.

"You're very good," he said, rather low.

"Not at all," replied Carley. "You have no idea how much it means to me to be permitted to help you. Before I forget, I must ask you, can you cash that check here in New York?"

"Not unless you identify me," he said, ruefully. "I don't know anyone I could ask."

"Well, when you leave here go at once to my bank—it's on Thirty-fourth Street—and I'll telephone the cashier. So you'll not have any difficulty. Will you leave New York at once?"

"I surely will. It's an awful place. Two years ago when I came here with my company I thought it was grand. But I guess I lost something over there. . . . I want to be where it's quiet. Where I won't see many people."

"I think I understand," returned Carley. "Then I suppose you're in a hurry to get home? Of course you have a girl you're just dying to see?"

"No, I'm sorry to say I haven't," he replied, simply. "I was glad I didn't have to leave a sweetheart behind, when I went to France. But it wouldn't be so bad to have one to go back to—now."

"Don't you worry!" exclaimed Carley. "You can take your choice presently. You have the open sesame to every real American girl's heart."

"And what is that?" he asked, with a blush.

"Your service to your country," she said, gravely.

"Well," he said, with a singular bluntness, "considering I didn't get any medals or bonuses, I'd like to draw a nice girl."

"You will," replied Carley, and made haste to change the subject. "By the way, did you meet Glenn Kilbourne in France?"

"Not that I remember," rejoined Burton, as he got up, rising rather stiffly by aid of his cane. "I must go, Miss Burch. Really I can't thank you enough. And I'll never forget it."

"Will you write me how you are getting along?" asked Carley, offering her hand.

"Yes."

Carley moved with him out into the hall and to the door. There was a question she wanted to ask, but found it strangely difficult of utterance. At the door Burton fixed a rather penetrating gaze upon her.

"You didn't ask me about Rust," he said.

"No, I—I didn't think of him—until now, in fact," Carley lied.

"Of course then you couldn't have heard about him. I was wondering."

"I have heard nothing."

"It was Rust who told me to come to you," said Burton. "We were talking one day, and he—well, he thought you were true blue. He said he knew you'd trust me and lend me money. I couldn't have asked you but for him."

"True blue! He believed that. I'm glad. . . . Has he spoken of me to you since I was last at the hospital?"

"Hardly," replied Burton, with the straight, strange glance on her again.

Carley met this glance and suddenly a coldness seemed to envelop her. It did not seem to come from within though her heart stopped beating. Burton had not changed—the warmth, the gratitude still lingered about him. But the light of his eyes! Carley had seen it in Glenn's, in Rust's—a strange, questioning, far-off light, infinitely aloof and unutterably sad. Then there came a lift of her heart that released a pang. She whispered with dread, with a tremor, with an instinct of calamity.

"How about—Rust?"

"He's dead."

* * *

The winter came, with its bleak sea winds and cold rains and blizzards of snow. Carley did not go South. She read and brooded, and gradually avoided all save those true friends who tolerated her.

She went to the theater a good deal, showing preference for the drama of strife, and she did not go anywhere for amusement. Distraction and amusement seemed to be dead issues for her. But she could become absorbed in any argument on the good or evil of the present day. Socialism reached into her mind, to be rejected. She had never understood it clearly, but it seemed to her a state of mind where dissatisfied men and women wanted to share what harder working or more gifted people possessed. There were a few who had too much of the world's goods and many who had too little. A readjustment of such inequality and injustice must come, but Carley did not see the remedy in Socialism.

She devoured books on the war with a morbid curiosity and hope that she would find some illuminating truth as to the uselessness of sacrificing young men in the glory and prime of their lives. To her, war appeared a matter of human nature rather than politics. Hate really was an effect of war. In her judgment future wars could be avoided only in two ways—by men becoming honest and just or by women refusing to have children to be sacrificed. As there seemed no indication whatever of the former, she wondered how soon all women of all races would meet on a common height, with the mounting spirit that consumed her own heart. Such time must come. She granted every argument for war and flung against it one ringing passionate truth—agony of mangled soldiers and agony of women and children. There was no justification for offensive war. It was monstrous and hideous. If nature and evolution proved the absolute need of strife, war, blood, and death in the progress of animal and man toward perfection, then it would be better to abandon this Christless code and let the race of man die out.

All through these weeks she longed for a letter from Glenn. But it did not come. Had he finally roused to the sweetness and worth and love of the western girl, Flo Hutter? Carley knew absolutely, through both intelligence and intuition, that Glenn Kilbourne would never love Flo. Yet such was her intensity and stress at times, especially in the darkness of waking hours, that jealousy overcame her and insidiously worked its havoc. Peace and a strange kind of joy came to her in dreams of her walks and rides and climbs in Arizona, of the lonely canyon where it always seemed afternoon, of the tremendous colored vastness of that Painted Desert. But she resisted these dreams now because when she awoke from them she suffered such a yearning that it became unbearable. Then she knew the feeling of the loneliness and solitude of the hills. Then she knew the sweetness of the murmur of falling water, the wind in the pines, the song of birds, the white radiance of the stars, the break of day and its gold-flushed close. But she had not yet divined their meaning. It was not all love for Glenn Kilbourne. Had city life palled upon her solely because of the absence of her lover? So Carley plodded on, like one groping in the night, fighting shadows.

One day she received a card from an old schoolmate, a girl who had married out of Carley's set, and had been ostracized. She was living down on Long Island, at a little country place named Wading River. Her husband was an electrician—something of an inventor. He worked hard. A baby boy had just come to them. Would not Carley run down on the train to see the youngster?

That was a strong and trenchant call. Carley went. She found indeed a country village, and on the outskirts of it a little cottage that must have been pretty in summer, when the green was on the vines and trees. Her old schoolmate was rosy, plump, bright-eyed, and happy. She saw in Carley no change—a fact that somehow rebounded sweetly on Carley's consciousness. Elsie prattled of herself and her husband and how they had worked to earn this little home, and then the baby.

When Carley saw the adorable dark-eyed, pink-toed, curly-fisted baby she understood Elsie's happiness and reveled in it. When she felt the soft, warm, living little body in her arms, against her breast, then she absorbed some incalculable and mysterious strength. What were the trivial, sordid, and selfish feelings that kept her in tumult compared to this welling emotion? Had she the secret in her arms? Babies and Carley had never become closely acquainted in those infrequent meetings that were usually the result of chance. But Elsie's baby nestled to her breast and cooed to her and clung to her finger. When at length the youngster was laid in his crib it seemed to Carley that the fragrance and the soul of him remained with her.

"A real American boy!" she murmured.

"You can just bet he is," replied Elsie. "Carley you ought to see his dad."

"I'd like to meet him," said Carley, thoughtfully. "Elsie, was he in the service?"

"Yes. He was on one of the navy transports that took munitions to France. Think of me, carrying this baby, with my husband on a boat full of explosives and with German submarines roaming the ocean! Oh, it was horrible!"

"But he came back, and now all's well with you," said Carley, with a smile of earnestness. "I'm very glad, Elsie."

"Yes—but I shudder when I think of a possible war in the future. I'm going to raise boys, and girls, too, I hope—and the thought of war is torturing."

Carley found her return train somewhat late, and she took advantage of the delay to walk out to the wooded headlands above the Sound.

It was a raw March day, with a steely sun going down in a pale-gray sky. Patches of snow lingered in sheltered brushy places. This bit of woodland had a floor of soft sand that dragged at Carley's feet. There were sere and brown leaves still fluttering on the scrub-oaks. At length Carley came out on the edge of the bluff with the gray expanse of seat beneath her, and a long wandering shore line, ragged with wreckage or driftwood. The surge of water rolled in—a long, low, white, creeping line that softly roared on the beach and dragged the pebbles gratingly back. There was neither boat nor living creature in sight.

Carley felt the scene ease a clutching hand within her breast. Here was loneliness and solitude vastly different from that of Oak Creek Canyon, yet it held the same intangible power to soothe. The swish of the surf, the moan of the wind in the evergreens, were voices that called to her. How many more miles of lonely land than peopled cities! Then the sea—how vast! And over that the illimitable and infinite sky, and beyond, the endless realms of space. It helped her somehow to see and hear and feel the eternal presence of nature. In communion with nature the significance of life might be realized. She remembered Glenn quoting: "The world is too much with us. . . . Getting and spending, we lay waste our powers." What were our powers? What did God intend men to do with hands and bodies and gifts and souls? She gazed back over the bleak land and then out across the broad sea. Only a millionth part of the surface of the unsubmerged earth knew the populous abodes of man. And the lonely sea, inhospitable to stable homes of men, was thrice the area of the land. Were men intended, then, to congregate in few places, to squabble and to bicker and breed the discontents that led to injustice, hatred, and war? What a mystery it all was! But Nature was neither false nor little, however cruel she might be.

Once again Carley fell under the fury of her ordeal. Wavering now, restless and sleepless, given to violent starts and slow spells of apathy, she was wearing to defeat.

That spring day, one year from the day she had left New York for Arizona, she wished to spend alone. But her thoughts grew unbearable. She summed up the endless year. Could she live another like it? Something must break within her.

She went out. The air was warm and balmy, carrying that subtle current which caused the mild madness of spring fever. In the Park the greening of the grass, the opening of buds, the singing of birds, the gladness of children, the light on the water, the warm sun—all seemed to reproach her. Carley fled from the Park to the home of Beatrice Lovell; and there, unhappily, she encountered those of her acquaintance with whom she had least patience. They forced her to think too keenly of herself. They appeared carefree while she was miserable.

Over teacups there were waging gossip and argument and criticism. When Carley entered with Beatrice there was a sudden hush and then a murmur.

"Hello, Carley! Now say it to our faces," called out Geralda Conners, a fair, handsome young woman of thirty, exquisitely gowned in the latest mode, and whose brilliantly tinted complexion was not the natural one of health.

"Say what, Geralda?" asked Carley. "I certainly would not say anything behind your backs that I wouldn't repeat here."

"Eleanor has been telling us how you simply burned us up."

"We did have an argument. And I'm not sure I said all I wanted to."

"Say the rest here," drawled a lazy, mellow voice. "For Heaven's sake, stir us up. If I could get a kick out of *anything* I'd bless it."

"Carley, go on the stage," advised another. "You've got Elsie Ferguson tied to the mast for looks. And lately you're surely tragic enough."

"I wish you'd go somewhere far off," observed a third. "My husband is dippy about you."

"Girls, do you know that you actually have not one sensible idea in your heads?" retorted Carley.

"Sensible? I should hope not. Who wants to be sensible?"

Geralda battered her teacup on a saucer. "Listen," she called. "I wasn't kidding Carley. I am good and sore. She goes around knocking everybody and saying New York backs Sodom off the boards. I want her to come out with it right here."

"I dare say I've talked too much," returned Carley. "It's been a rather hard winter on me. Perhaps, indeed, I've tried the patience of my friends."

"See here, Carley," said Geralda, deliberately, "just because you've had life turn to bitter ashes in your mouth you've no right to poison it for us. We all find it pretty sweet. You're an *un*satisfied woman and if you don't marry somebody you'll end by being a reformer or fanatic."

"I'd rather end that way than rot in a shell," retorted Carley.

"I declare, you make me see red, Carley," flashed Geralda, angrily. "No wonder Morrison roasts you to everybody. He says Glenn Kilbourne threw you down for some Western girl. If that's true it's pretty small of you to vent your spleen on us."

Carley felt the gathering of a mighty resistless force. But Geralda Conners was nothing to her except the target for a thunderbolt.

"I have no spleen," she replied, with a dignity of passion. "I have only pity. I was as blind as you. If heartbreak tore the scales from my eyes, perhaps that is well for me. For I see something terribly wrong in myself, in you, in all of us, in the life of to-day."

"You keep your pity to yourself. You need it," answered Geralda, with heat. "There's nothing wrong with me or my friends or life in good old New York."

"Nothing wrong!" cried Carley. "Listen. Nothing wrong in you or life to-day—nothing for you women to make right? You are blind as bats—as dead to living truth as if you were buried. Nothing wrong when thousands of crippled soldiers have no homes— no money—no friends—no work—in many cases no food or bed? . . . Splendid young men who went away in their prime to fight for *you* and came back ruined, suffering! Nothing wrong when sane women with the vote might rid politics of partisanship, greed, crookedness? Nothing wrong when prohibition is mocked by women—when the greatest boon ever granted this country is derided and beaten down and cheated? Nothing wrong when there are half a million defective children in this city? Nothing wrong when there are not enough schools and teachers to educate our boys and girls, when those teachers are shamefully underpaid? Nothing wrong when the mothers of this great country let their youngsters go to the dark motion-picture halls and night after night in thousands of towns over all this broad land see pictures that the juvenile court and the educators and keepers of reform schools say make burglars, crooks, and murderers of our boys and vampires of our girls? Nothing wrong when these young adolescent girls ape *you* and wear stockings rolled under their knees below their skirts and use a lip stick and paint their faces and darken their eyes and pluck their eyebrows and absolutely do not know what shame is? Nothing wrong when you may find in any city women standing at street corners distributing booklets on birth control? Nothing wrong when great magazines print no page or picture without its sex appeal? Nothing wrong when the automobile, so convenient for the innocent little run out of town, presents the greatest evil that ever menaced American girls! Nothing wrong when money is God—when luxury, pleasure, excitement, speed are the striven for? Nothing wrong when some of your husbands spend more of their time with other women than with you? Nothing wrong with jazz—where the lights go out in the dance hall and the dancers jiggle and toddle and wiggle in a frenzy? Nothing wrong in a country where the greatest college cannot report birth of one child to each graduate in ten years? Nothing wrong with race suicide and the incoming horde of foreigners? . . . Nothing wrong with you women who cannot or will not stand childbirth? Nothing wrong with most of you, when if you *did* have a child, you could not nurse it? . . . Oh, my God, there's nothing wrong with America except that she staggers under a Titanic burden that only mothers of sons can remove! . . . You doll women, you parasites, you toys of men, you silken-wrapped geisha girls, you painted, idle, purring cats, you parody of the females of your species—find brains enough if you can to see the doom hanging over you and revolt before it is too late!"

*C*ARLEY burst in upon her aunt.

"Look at me, Aunt Mary!" she cried, radiant and exultant. "I'm going back out West to marry Glenn and live his life!"

The keen old eyes of her aunt softened and dimmed. "Dear Carley, I've known that for a long time. You've found yourself at last."

Then Carley breathlessly babbled her hastily formed plans, every word of which seemed to rush her onward.

"You're going to surprise Glenn again?" queried Aunt Mary.

"Oh, I must! I want to see his face when I tell him."

"Well, I hope he won't surprise *you,*" declared the old lady. "When did you hear from him last?"

"In January. It seems ages—but—Aunt Mary, you don't imagine Glenn—"

"I imagine nothing," interposed her aunt. "It will turn out happily and I'll have some peace in my old age. But, Carley, what's to become of me?"

"Oh, I never thought!" replied Carley, blankly. "It will be lonely for you. Auntie, I'll come back in the fall for a few weeks. Glenn will let me."

"*Let* you? Ye gods! So you've come to that? Imperious Carley Burch! . . . Thank Heaven, you'll now be satisfied to be let do things."

"I'd—I'd crawl for him," breathed Carley.

"Well, child, as you can't be practical, I'll have to be," replied Aunt Mary, seriously. "Fortunately for you I am a woman of quick decision. Listen. I'll go West with you. I want to see the Grand Canyon. Then I'll go on to California, where I have old friends I've not seen for years. When you get your new home all fixed up I'll spend awhile with you. And if I want to come back to New York now and then I'll go to a hotel. It is settled. I think the change will benefit me."

"Auntie, you make me very happy. I could ask no more," said Carley.

Swiftly as endless tasks could make them the days passed. But those on the train dragged interminably.

Carley sent her aunt through to the Canyon while she stopped off at Flagstaff to store innumerable trunks and bags. The first news she heard of Glenn and the Hutters was that they had gone to the Tonto Basin to buy hogs and would be absent at least a month. This gave birth to a new plan in Carley's mind. She would doubly surprise Glenn. Wherefore she took council with some Flagstaff businessmen and engaged them to set a force of men at work on the Deep Lake property, making the improvements she desired, and hauling lumber, cement, bricks, machinery, supplies—all the necessaries for building construction. Also she instructed them to throw up a tent house for her to live in during the work, and to engage a reliable Mexican man with his wife for servants. When she left for the Canyon she was happier than ever before in her life.

It was near the coming of sunset when Carley first looked down into the Grand Canyon. She had forgotten Glenn's tribute to this place. In her rapturous excitement of preparation and travel the Canyon had been merely a name. But now she saw it and she was stunned.

What a stupendous chasm, gorgeous in sunset color on the heights, purpling into mystic shadows in the depths! There was a wonderful brightness of all the millions of red and yellow and gray surfaces still exposed to the sun. Carley did not feel a thrill, because feeling seemed inhibited. She looked and looked, yet was reluctant to keep on looking. She possessed no image in mind with which to compare this grand and mystic spectacle. A transformation of color and shade appeared to be going on swiftly, as if gods were changing the scenes of a Titanic stage. As she gazed the dark fringed line of the north rim turned to burnished gold, and she watched that with fascinated eyes. It turned rose, it lost its fire, it faded to quiet cold gray. The sun had set.

Then the wind blew cool through the piñons on the rim. There was a sweet tang of cedar and sage on the air and that indefinable fragrance peculiar to the canyon country of Arizona. How it brought back to Carley remembrance of Oak Creek! In the west, across the purple notches of the abyss, a dull gold flare showed where the sun had gone down.

In the morning at eight o'clock there were great irregular black shadows under the domes and peaks and escarpments. Bright Angel Canyon was all dark, showing dimly its ragged lines. At noon there were no shadows and all the colossal gorge lay glaring under the sun. In the evening Carley watched the Canyon as again the sun was setting.

Deep dark-blue shadows, like purple sails of immense ships, in wonderful contrast with the bright sunlit slopes, grew and rose toward the east, down the canyons and up the walls that faced the west. For a long while there was no red color, and the first indication of it was a dull bronze. Carley looked down into the void, at the sailing birds, at the precipitous slopes, and the dwarf spruces and the weathered old yellow cliffs. When she looked up again the shadows out there were no longer dark. They were clear. The slopes and depths and ribs of rock could be seen through them. Then the tips of the highest peaks and domes turned bright red. Far to the east she discerned a strange shadow, slowly turning purple. One instant it grew vivid, then began to fade. Soon after that all the colors darkened and slowly the pale gray stole over all.

At night Carley gazed over and into the black void. But for the awful sense of depth she would not have known the Canyon to be there. A soundless movement of wind passed under her. The chasm seemed a grave of silence. It was as mysterious as the stars and as aloof and as inevitable. It had held her senses of beauty and proportion in abeyance.

At another sunrise the crown of the rim, a broad belt of bare rock, turned pale gold under its fringed dark line of pines. The tips of the peak gleamed opal. There was no sunrise red, no fire. The light in the east was a pale gold under a steely green-blue sky. All the abyss of the Canyon was soft, gray, transparent, and the belt of gold broadened downward, making shadows on the west slopes of the mesas and escarpments. Far down in the shadows she discerned the river, yellow, turgid, palely gleaming. By straining her ears Carley heard a low dull roar as of distant storm. She stood fearfully at the extreme edge of a stupendous cliff, where it sheered dark and forbidding, down and down, into what seemed the red and boundless depths of Hades. She saw gold spots of sunlight on the dark shadows, proving that somewhere, impossible to discover, the sun was shining through wind-worn holes in the sharp ridges. Every instant Carley grasped a different effect. Her studied gaze absorbed an endless changing. And at last she realized that sun and light and stars and moon and night and shade, all working incessantly and mutably over shapes and lines and angles and surfaces too numerous and too great for the sight of man to hold, made an ever-changing spectacle of supreme beauty and colorful grandeur.

She talked very little while at the Canyon. It silenced her. She had come to see it at the critical time of her life and in the right mood. The superficialities of the world shrunk to their proper insignificance. Once she asked her aunt: "Why did not Glenn bring me here?" As if this Canyon proved the nature of all things!

But in the end Carley found that the rending strife of the transformation of her attitude toward life had insensibly ceased. It had ceased during the long watching of this cataclysm of nature, this canyon of gold-banded black-fringed ramparts, and red-walled mountains which sloped down to be lost in purple depths. That was final proof of the strength of nature to soothe, to clarify, to stabilize the tried and weary and upward-gazing soul. Stronger than the recorded deeds of saints, stronger than the eloquence of the gifted uplifters of men, stronger than any words ever written, was the grand, brooding, sculptured aspect of nature. And it must have been so because thousands of years before the age of saints or preachers—before the fret and symbol and figure were cut in stone—man must have watched with thought-developing sight the wonders of the earth, the monuments of time, the glooming of the dark-blue sea, the handiwork of God.

In May, Carley returned to Flagstaff to take up with earnest inspiration the labors of homebuilding in a primitive land.

It required two trucks to transport her baggage and purchases out to Deep Lake. The road was good for eighteen miles of the distance, until it branched off to reach her land, and from there it was desert rock and sand. But eventually they made it; and Carley found herself and belongings dumped out into the windy and sunny open. The moment was singularly thrilling and full of transport. She was free. She had shaken off the shackles. She faced lonely, wild, barren desert that must be made habitable by the genius of her direction and the labor of her hands. Always a thought of Glenn hovered tenderly, dreamily in the back of her consciousness, but she welcomed the opportunity to have a few weeks of work and activity and solitude before taking up her life with him. She wanted to adapt herself to the metamorphosis that had been wrought in her.

To her amazement and delight, a very considerable progress had been made with her plans. Under a sheltered red cliff among the cedars had been erected the tents where she expected to live until the house was completed. These tents were large, with broad floors high off the ground, and there were four of them. Her living tent had a porch under a wide canvas awning. The bed was a boxlike affair, raised off the floor two feet, and it contained a great, fragrant mass of cedar boughs upon which the blankets were to be spread. At one end was a dresser with large mirror, and a chiffonier. There were table and lamp, a low rocking chair, a shelf for books, a row of hooks upon which to hang things, a washstand with its necessary accessories, a little stove and a neat stack of cedar chips and sticks. Navajo rugs on the floor lent brightness and comfort.

Carley heard the rustling of cedar branches over her head, and saw where they brushed against the tent roof. It appeared warm and fragrant inside, and protected from the wind, and a subdued white light filtered through the canvas. Almost she felt like reproving herself for the comfort surrounding her. For she had come West to welcome the hard knocks of primitive life.

It took less than an hour to have her trunks stored in one of the spare tents, and to unpack clothes and necessaries for immediate use. Carley donned the comfortable and somewhat shabby outdoor garb she had worn at Oak Creek the year before; and it seemed to be the last thing needed to make her fully realize the glorious truth of the present.

"I'm here," she said to her pale, yet happy face in the mirror. "The impossible has happened. I have accepted Glenn's life. I have answered that strange call out of the West."

She wanted to throw herself on the sunlit woolly blankets of her bed and hug them, to think and think of the bewildering present happiness, to dream of the future, but she could not lie or sit still, nor keep her mind from grasping at actualities and possibilities of this place, nor her hands from itching to do things.

It developed, presently, that she could not have idled away the time even if she had wanted to, for the Mexican woman came for her, with smiling gesticulation and jabber that manifestly meant dinner. Carley could not understand many Mexican words, and herein she saw another task. This swarthy woman and her sloe-eyed husband favorably impressed Carley.

Next to claim her was Hoyle, the superintendent. "Miss Burch," he said, "in the early days we could run up a log cabin in a jiffy. Axes, horses, strong arms, and a few pegs—that was all we needed. But this house you've planned is different. It's good you've come to take the responsibility."

Carley had chosen the site for her home on top of the knoll where Glenn had taken her to show her the magnificent view of mountains and desert. Carley climbed it now with beating heart and mingled emotions. A thousand times already that day, it seemed, she had turned to gaze up at the noble white-clad peaks. They were closer now, apparently looming over her, and she felt a great sense of peace and protection in the thought that they would always be there. But she had not yet seen the desert that had haunted her for a year. When she reached the summit of the knoll and gazed out across the open space it seemed that she must stand spellbound. How green the cedared foreground—how gray and barren the downward slope—how wonderful the painted steppes! The vision that had lived in her memory shrank to nothingness. The reality was immense, more than beautiful, appalling in its isolation, beyond comprehension with its lure and strength to uplift.

But the superintendent drew her attention to the business at hand.

Carley had planned an L-shaped house of one story. Some of her ideas appeared to be impractical, and these she abandoned. The framework was up and half a dozen carpenters were lustily at work with saw and hammer.

"We'd made better progress if this house was in an ordinary place," explained Hoyle. "But you see the wind blows here, so the framework had to be made as solid and strong as possible. In fact, it's bolted to the sills."

Both living room and sleeping room were arranged so that the Painted Desert could be seen from one window, and on the other side the whole of the San Francisco Mountains. Both rooms were to have open fireplaces. Carley's idea was for service and durability. She thought of comfort in the severe winters of that high latitude, but elegance and luxury had no more significance in her life.

Hoyle made his suggestions as to changes and adaptations, and, receiving her approval, he went on to show her what had been already accomplished.

Back on higher ground a reservoir of concrete was being constructed near an everflowing spring of snow water from the peaks. This water was being piped by gravity to the house, and was a matter of greatest satisfaction to Hoyle, for he claimed that it would never freeze in winter, and would be cold and abundant during the hottest and driest of summers. This assurance solved the most difficult and serious problem of ranch life in the desert.

Next Hoyle led Carley down off the knoll to the wide cedar valley adjacent to the lake. He was enthusiastic over its possibilities. Two small corrals and a large one had been erected, the latter having a low flat barn connected with it. Ground was already being cleared along the lake where alfalfa and hay were to be raised. Carley saw the blue and yellow smoke from burning brush, and the fragrant odor thrilled her. Mexicans were chopping the cleared cedars into firewood for winter use.

The day was spent before she realized it. At sunset the carpenters and mechanics left in two old Ford cars for town. The Mexicans had a camp in the cedars, and the Hoyles had theirs at the spring under the knoll where Carley had camped with Glenn and the Hutters. Carley watched the golden rosy sunset, and as the day ended she breathed deeply as if in unutterable relief. Supper found her with appetite she had long since lost. Twilight brought cold wind, the staccato bark of coyotes, the flicker of camp fires through the cedars. She tried to embrace all her sensations, but they were so rapid and many that she failed.

The cold, clear, silent night brought back the charm of the desert. How flaming white the stars!

The great spire-pointed peaks lifted cold pale-gray outlines up into the deep star-studded sky. Carley walked a little to and fro, loath to go to her tent, though tired. She wanted calm. But instead of achieving calmness she grew more and more towards a strange state of exultation.

Westward, only a matter of twenty or thirty miles, lay the deep rent in the level desert—Oak Creek Canyon. If Glenn had been there, this night would have been perfect, yet almost unendurable. She was again grateful for his absence. What a surprise she had in store for him! And she imagined his face in its change of expression when she met him. If only he never learned of her presence in Arizona until she made it known in person! That she most longed for. Chances were against it, but then her luck had changed. She looked to the eastward where a pale luminosity of afterglow shone in the heavens. Far distant seemed the home of her childhood, the friends she had scorned and forsaken, the city of complaining and striving millions. If only some miracle might illumine the minds of her friends, as she felt that hers was to be illumined here in the solitude. But she well realized that not all problems could be solved by a call out of the West. Any open and lonely land that might have saved Glenn Kilbourne would have sufficed for her. It was the spirit of the thing and not the letter. It was work of any kind and not only that of ranch life. Not only the raising of hogs!

Carley directed stumbling steps toward the light of her tent. Her eyes had not been used to such black shadow along the ground. She had, too, squeamish feminine fears of hydrophobia skunks, and nameless animals or reptiles that were imagined denizens of the darkness. She gained her tent and entered. The Mexican, Gino, as he called himself, had lighted her lamp and fire. Carley was chilled through, and the tent felt so warm and cozy that she could scarcely believe it. She fastened the screen door, laced the flaps across it, except at the top, and then gave herself up to the lulling and comforting heat.

There were plans to perfect; innumerable things to remember; a car and accessories, horses, saddles, outfits to buy. Carley knew she should sit down at her table and write and figure, but she could not do it then.

For a long time she sat over the little stove, toasting her knees and hands, adding some chips now and then to the red coals. And her mind seemed a kaleidoscope of changing visions, thoughts, feelings. At last she undressed and blew out the lamp and went to bed.

Instantly a thick blackness seemed to enfold her and silence as of a dead world settled down upon her. Drowsy as she was, she could not close her eyes nor refrain from listening. Darkness and silence were tangible things. She felt them. And they seemed suddenly potent with magic charm to still the tumult of her, to soothe and rest, to create thoughts she had never thought before. Rest was more than selfish indulgence. Loneliness was necessary to gain consciousness of the soul. Already far back in the past seemed Carley's other life.

By and by the dead stillness awoke to faint sounds not before perceptible to her—a low, mournful sough of the wind in the cedars, then the faint far-distant note of a coyote, sad as the night and infinitely wild.

*   *   *

Days passed. Carley worked in the mornings with her hands and her brains. In the afternoons she rode and walked and climbed with a double object, to work herself into fit physical condition and to explore every nook and corner of her six hundred and forty acres.

Then what she had expected and deliberately induced by her efforts quickly came to pass. Just as the year before she had suffered excruciating pain from aching muscles, and saddle blisters, and walking blisters, and a very rending of her bones, so now she fell victim to them again. In sunshine and rain she faced the desert. Sunburn and sting of sleet were equally to be endured. And that abomination, the hateful blinding sandstorm, did not daunt her. But the weary hours of abnegation to this physical torture at least held one consoling recompense as compared with her experience of last year, and it was that there was no one interested to watch for her weaknesses and failures and blunders. She could fight it out alone.

Three weeks of this self-imposed strenuous training wore by before Carley was free enough from weariness and pain to experience other sensations. Her general health, evidently, had not been so good as when she had first visited Arizona. She caught cold and suffered other ills attendant upon an abrupt change of climate and condition. But doggedly she kept at her task. She rode when she should have been in bed; she walked when she should have ridden; she climbed when she should have kept to level ground. And finally by degrees so gradual as not to be noticed except in the sum of them she began to mend.

Meanwhile the construction of her house went on with uninterrupted rapidity. When the low, slanting, wide-eaved roof was completed, Carley lost further concern about rainstorms. Let them come. When the plumbing was all in and Carley saw verification of Hoyle's assurance that it would mean a gravity supply of water ample and continual, she lost her last concern as to the practicability of the work. That, and the earning of her endurance, seemed to bring closer a wonderful reward, still nameless and spiritual, that had been unattainable, but now breathed to her on the fragrant desert wind and in the brooding silence.

The time came when each afternoon's ride or climb called to Carley with increasing delight. But the fact that she must soon reveal to Glenn her presence and transformation did not seem to be all the cause. She could ride without pain, walk without losing her breath, work without blistering her hands; and in this there was compensation. The building of the house that was to become a home, the development of water resources and land that meant the making of a ranch—these did not altogether constitute the anticipation of content. To be active, to accomplish things, to recall to mind her knowledge of manual training, of domestic science, of designing and painting, to learn to cook—these were indeed measures full of reward, but they were not all. In her wondering, pondering meditation she arrived at the point where she tried to assign to her love the growing fullness of her life. This, too, splendid and all-pervading as it was, she had to reject. Some exceedingly illusive and vital significance of life had insidiously come to Carley.

One afternoon, with the sky full of white and black rolling clouds and a cold wind sweeping through the cedars, she halted to rest and escape the chilling gale for a while. In a sunny place, under the lee of a gravel bank, she sought refuge. It was warm here because of the reflected sunlight and the absence of wind. The sand at the bottom of the bank held a heat that felt good to her cold hands. All about her and over her swept the keen wind, rustling the sage, seeping the sand, swishing the cedars, but she was out of it, protected and insulated. The sky above showed blue between the threatening clouds. There were no birds or living creatures in sight. Certainly the place had little of color or beauty or grace, nor could she see beyond a few rods. Lying there, without any particular reason that she was conscious of, she suddenly felt shot through and through with exhilaration.

Another day, the warmest of the spring so far, she rode a Navajo mustang she had recently bought from a passing trader; and at the farthest end of her section, in rough wooded and ridged ground she had not explored, she found a canyon with red walls and pine trees and gleaming streamlet and glades of grass and jumbles of rock. It was a miniature canyon, to be sure, only a quarter of a mile long, and as deep as the height of a lofty pine, and so narrow that it seemed only the width of a lane, but it had all the features of Oak Creek Canyon, and so sufficed for the exultant joy of possession. She explored it. The willow brakes and oak thickets harbored rabbits and birds. She saw the white flags of deer running away down the open. Up at the head where the canyon boxed she flushed a flock of wild turkeys. They ran like ostriches and flew like great brown chickens. In a cavern Carley found the den of a bear, and in another place the bleached bones of a steer.

She lingered here in the shaded depths with a feeling as if she were indeed lost to the world. These big brown and seamy-barked pines with their spreading gnarled arms and webs of green needles belonged to her, as also the tiny brook, the blue bells smiling out of the ferns, the single stalk of mescal on a rocky ledge.

Never had sun and earth, tree and rock, seemed a part of her being until then. She would become a sun-worshiper and a lover of the earth. That canyon had opened there to sky and light for millions of years; and doubtless it had harbored sheep herders, Indians, cliff dwellers, barbarians. She was a woman with white skin and a cultivated mind, but the affinity for them existed in her. She felt it, and that an understanding of it would be good for body and soul.

Another day she found a little grove of jack pines growing on a flat mesalike bluff, the highest point on her land. The trees were small and close together, mingling their green needles overhead and their discarded brown ones on the ground. From here Carley could see afar to all points of the compass—the slow green descent to the south and the climb to the black-timbered distance; the ridged and canyoned country to the west, red vents choked with green and rimmed with gray; to the north the grand upflung mountain kingdom crowned with snow; and to the east the vastness of illimitable space, the openness and wildness, the chased and beaten mosaic of colored sands and rocks.

Again and again she visited this lookout and came to love its isolation, its command of wondrous prospects, its power of suggestion to her thoughts. She became a creative being, in harmony with the live things around her. The great life-dispensing sun poured its rays down upon her, as if to ripen her; and the earth seemed warm, motherly, immense with its all-embracing arms. She no longer plucked the bluebells to press to her face, but leaned to them. Every blade of gramma grass, with its shining bronze-tufted seed head, had significance for her. The scents of the desert began to have meaning for her. She sensed within her the working of a great leveling process through which supreme happiness would come.

June! The rich, thick, amber light, like a transparent reflection from some intense golden medium, seemed to float in the warm air. The sky became an azure blue. In the still noontides, when the bees hummed drowsily and the flies buzzed, vast creamy-white columnar clouds rolled up from the horizon, like colossal ships with bulging sails. And summer with its rush of growing things was at hand.

Carley rode afar, seeking in strange places the secret that eluded her. Only a few days now until she would ride down to Oak Creek Canyon! There was a low, singing melody of wind in the cedars. The earth became too beautiful in her magnified sight. A great truth was dawning upon her—that the sacrifice of what she had held as necessary to the enjoyment of life—that the strain of conflict, the labor of hands, the forcing of weary body, the enduring of pain, the contact with the earth—had served somehow to rejuvenate her blood, quicken her pulse, intensify her sensorial faculties, thrill her very soul, lead her into the realm of enchantment.

One afternoon a dull, lead-black-colored cinder knoll tempted her to explore its bare heights. She rode up until her mustang sank to his knees and could climb no farther. From there she essayed the ascent on foot. It took labor. But at last she gained the summit, burning, sweating, panting.

The cinder hill was an extinct crater of a volcano. In the center of it lay a deep bowl, wondrously symmetrical, and of a dark lusterless hue. Not a blade of grass was there, nor a plant. Carley conceived a desire to go to the bottom of this pit. She tried the cinders of the edge of the slope. They had the same consistency as those of the ascent she had overcome. But here there was a steeper incline. A tingling rush of daring seemed to drive her over the rounded rim, and, once started down, it was as if she wore seven-league boots. Fear left her. Only an exhilarating emotion consumed her. If there were danger, it mattered not. She strode down with giant steps, she plunged, she started avalanches to ride them until they stopped, she leaped, and lastly she fell, to roll over the soft cinders to the pit.

There she lay. It seemed a comfortable resting place. The pit was scarcely six feet across. She gazed upward and was astounded. How steep was the rounded slope on all sides! There were no sides; it was a circle. She looked up at a round lake of deep translucent sky. Such depth of blue, such exquisite rare color! Carley imagined she could gaze through it to the infinite beyond.

She closed her eyes and rested. Soon the laboring of heart and breath calmed to normal, so that she could not hear them. Then she lay perfectly motionless. With eyes shut she seemed still to look, and what she saw was the sunlight through the blood and flesh of her eyelids. It was red, as rare a hue as the blue of sky. So piercing did it grow that she had to shade her eyes with her arm.

Again the strange, rapt glow suffused her body. Never in all her life had she been so absolutely alone. She might as well have been in her grave. She might have been dead to all earthy things and reveling in spirit in the glory of the physical that had escaped her in life. And she abandoned herself to this influence.

She loved these dry, dusty cinders; she loved the crater here hidden from all save birds; she loved the desert, the earth—above all, the sun. She was a product of the earth—a creation of the sun. She had been an infinitesimal atom of inert something that had quickened to life under the blazing magic of the sun. Soon her spirit would abandon her body and go on, while her flesh and bone returned to dust. This frame of hers, that carried the divine spark, belonged to the earth. She had only been ignorant, mindless, feelingless, absorbed in the seeking of gain, blind to the truth. She had to give. She had been created a woman; she belonged to nature; she was nothing save a mother of the future. She had loved neither Glenn Kilbourne nor life itself. False education, false standards, false environment had developed her into a woman who imagined she must feed her body on the milk and honey of indulgence.

She was abased now—woman as animal, though saved and uplifted by her power of immortality. Transcendental was her female power to link life with the future. The power of the plant seed, the power of the earth, the heat of the sun, the inscrutable creation—

spirit of nature, almost the divinity of God—these were all hers because she was a woman. That was the great secret, aloof so long. That was what had been wrong with life—the woman blind to her meaning, her power, her mastery.

So she abandoned herself to the woman within her. She held out her arms to the blue abyss of heaven as if to embrace the universe. She was Nature. She kissed the dusty cinders and pressed her breast against the warm slope. Her heart swelled to bursting with a glorious and unutterable happiness.

That afternoon as the sun was setting under a gold-white scroll of cloud Carley got back to Deep Lake.

A familiar lounging figure crossed her sight. It approached to where she had dismounted. Charley, the sheep herder of Oak Creek!

"Howdy!" he drawled, with his queer smile. "So it was you-all who had this Deep Lake section?"

"Yes. And how are you, Charley?" she replied, shaking hands with him.

"Me? Aw, I'm tip-top. I'm shore glad you got this ranch. Reckon I'll hit you for a job."

"I'd give it to you. But aren't you working for the Hutters?"

"Nope. Not any more. Me an' Stanton had a row with them."

How droll and dry he was! His lean, olive-brown face, with its guileless clear eyes and his lanky figure in blue jeans vividly recalled Oak Creek to Carley.

"Oh, I'm—sorry," returned she haltingly, somehow checked in her warm rush of thought. "Stanton? . . . Did he quit too?"

"Yep. He sure did."

"What was the trouble?"

"Reckon because Flo made up to Kilbourne," replied Charley, with a grin.

"Ah! I—I see," murmured Carley. A blankness seemed to wave over her. It extended to the air without, to the sense of the golden sunset. It passed. What should she ask—what out of a thousand sudden flashing queries? "Are—are the Hutters back?"

"Sure. Been back several days. I reckoned Hoyle told you. Mebbe he didn't know, though. For nobody's been to town."

"How is—how are they all?" faltered Carley. There was a strange wall here between her thought and her utterance.

"Everybody satisfied, I reckon," replied Charley.

"Flo—how is she?" burst out Carley.

"Aw, Flo's loony over her husband," drawled Charley, his clear eyes on Carley's.

"Husband!" she gasped.

"Sure. Flo's gone an' went an' done what I swore on."

"Who?" whispered Carley, and the query was a terrible blade piercing her heart.

"Now who'd you reckon on?" asked Charley, with his slow grin.

Carley's lips were mute.

"Wal, it was your old beau thet you wouldn't have," returned Charley, as he gathered up his long frame, evidently to leave. "Kilbourne! He an' Flo came back from the Tonto all hitched up."

CHAPTER
12

V AGUE sense of movement, of darkness, and of cold attended Carley's consciousness for what seemed endless time.

A fall over rocks and a severe thrust from a sharp branch brought an acute appreciation of her position, if not of her mental state. Night had fallen. The stars were out. She had stumbled over a low ledge. Evidently she had wandered around, dazedly and aimlessly, until brought to her senses by pain. But for a gleam of camp fires through the cedars she would have been lost. It did not matter. She was lost, anyhow. What was it that had happened?

Charley, the sheep herder! Then the thunderbolt of his words burst upon her, and she collapsed to the cold stones. She lay quivering from head to toe. She dug her fingers into the moss and lichen. "Oh, God, to think—after all—it happened!" she moaned. There had been a rending within her breast, as of physical violence, from which she now suffered anguish. There were a thousand stinging nerves. There was a mortal sickness of horror, of insupportable heart-breaking loss. She could not endure it. She could not live under it.

She lay there until energy supplanted shock. Then she rose to rush into the darkest shadows of the cedars, to grope here and there, hanging her head, wringing her hands, beating her breast. "It can't be true," she cried. "Not after my struggle—my victory— not *now!*" But there had been no victory. And now it was too late. She was betrayed, ruined, lost. That wonderful love had wrought transformation in her— and now havoc. Once she fell against the branches of a thick cedar that upheld her. The fragrance which had been sweet was now bitter. Life that had been bliss was now hateful! She could not keep still for a single moment.

Black night, cedars, brush, rocks, washes, seemed not to obstruct her. In a frenzy she rushed on, tearing her dress, her hands, her hair. Violence of some kind was imperative. All at once a pale gleaming open space, shimmering under the stars, lay before her. It was water. Deep Lake! And instantly a hideous terrible longing to destroy herself obsessed her. She had no fear. She could have welcomed the cold, slimy depths that meant oblivion. But could they really bring oblivion? A year ago she would have believed so, and would no longer have endured such agony. She had changed. A cursed strength had come to her, and it was this strength that now augmented her torture. She flung wide her arms to the pitiless white stars and looked up at them. "My hope, my faith, my love have failed me," she whispered. "They have been a lie. I went through hell for them. And now I've nothing to live for. . . . Oh, let me end it all!"

If she prayed to the stars for mercy, it was denied her. Passionlessly they blazed on. But she could not kill herself. In that hour death would have been the only relief and peace left to her. Stricken by the cruelty of her fate, she fell back against the stones and gave up to grief. Nothing was left but fierce pain. The youth and vitality and intensity of her then locked arms with anguish and torment and a cheated, unsatisfied love. Strength of mind and body involuntarily resisted the ravages of this catastrophe. Will power seemed nothing, but the flesh of her, that medium of exquisite sensation, so full of life, so prone to joy, refused to surrender. The part of her that felt, fought terribly for its heritage.

All night long Carley lay there. The crescent moon went down, the stars moved on their course, the coyotes ceased to wail, the wind died away, the lapping of the waves along the lake shore wore to a gentle splash, the whispering of the insects stopped as the cold of dawn approached. The darkest hour fell—hour of silence, solitude, and melancholy, when the desert lay tranced, cold, waiting, mournful without light of moon or stars or sun.

In the gray dawn Carley dragged her bruised and aching body back to her tent, and, fastening the door, she threw off her wet clothes and boots and fell upon her bed. Slumber of exhaustion came to her.

When she awoke the tent was light and the moving shadows of cedar boughs on the white canvas told that the sun was straight above. Carley ached as never before. A deep pang seemed invested in every bone. Her heart felt swollen out of proportion to its space in her breast. Her breathing came slow and it hurt. Her blood was sluggish. Suddenly she shut her eyes. She loathed the light of day. What was it that had happened?

Then the brutal truth flashed over her again, in aspect new, with all the old bitterness. For an instant she experienced a suffocating sensation as if the canvas had sagged under the burden of heavy air and was crushing her breast and heart. Then wave after wave of emotion swept over her. The storm winds of grief and passion were loosened again. And she writhed in her misery.

Some one knocked on her door. The Mexican woman called anxiously. Carley awoke to the fact that her presence was not solitary on the physical earth, even if her soul seemed stricken to eternal loneliness. Even in the desert there was a world to consider. Vanity that had bled to death, pride that had been crushed, availed her not here. But something else came to her support. The lesson of the West had been to endure, not to shirk—to face an issue, not to hide. Carley got up, bathed, dressed, brushed and arranged her dishevelled hair. The face she saw in the mirror excited her amaze and pity. Then she went out in answer to the call for dinner. But she could not eat. The ordinary functions of life appeared to be deadened.

The day happened to be Sunday, and therefore the workmen were absent. Carley had the place to herself. How the half-completed house mocked her! She could not bear to look at it. What use could she make of it now? Flo Hutter had become the working comrade of Glenn Kilbourne, the mistress of his cabin. She was his wife and she would be the mother of his children.

That thought gave birth to the darkest hour of

Carley Burch's life. She became possessed as by a thousand devils. She became merely a female robbed of her mate. Reason was not in her, nor charity, nor justice. All that was abnormal in human nature seemed coalesced in her, dominant, passionate, savage, terrible. She hated with an incredible and insane ferocity. In the seclusion of her tent, crouched on her bed, silent, locked, motionless, she yet was the embodiment of all terrible strife and storm in nature. Her heart was a maelstrom and would have whirled and sucked down to hell all the beings that were men. Her soul was a bottomless gulf, filled with the gales and the fires of jealousy, superhuman to destroy.

That fury consumed all her remaining strength, and from the relapse she sank to sleep.

Morning brought the inevitable reaction. However long her other struggles, this monumental and final one would be brief. She realized that, yet was unable to understand how it could be possible, unless shock or death or mental aberration ended the fight. An eternity of emotion lay back between this awakening of intelligence and the hour of her fall into the clutches of primitive passion.

That morning she faced herself in the mirror and asked, "Now—what do I owe *you?*" It was not her voice that answered. It was beyond her. But it said: "Go on! You are cut adrift. You are alone. You owe none but yourself! . . . Go on! Not backward—nor to the depths—but up—upward!"

She shuddered at such a decree. How impossible for her! All animal, all woman, all emotion, how could she live on the cold, pure heights? Yet she owed something intangible and inscrutable to herself. Was it the thing that woman lacked physically, yet contained hidden in her soul? An element of eternal spirit to rise! Because of heartbreak and ruin and irreparable loss must she fail? Was loss of love and husband and children only a test? The present hour would be swallowed in the sum of life's trials. She could not go back. She would not go down. There was wrenched from her tried and sore heart an unalterable and unquenchable decision—to make her own soul prove the evolution of woman. Vessel of blood and flesh she might be, doomed by nature to the reproduction of her kind, but she had in her the supreme spirit and power to carry on the progress of the ages—the climb of woman out of the darkness.

Carley went out to the workmen. The house should be completed and she would live in it. Always there was the stretching and illimitable desert to look at, and the grand heave upward of the mountains. Hoyle was full of zest for the practical details of the building. He saw nothing of the havoc wrought in her. Nor did the other workmen glance more than casually at her. In this Carley lost something of a shirking fear that her loss and grief were patent to all eyes.

That afternoon she mounted the most spirited of the mustangs she had purchased from the Indians. To govern him and stick on him required all her energy. And she rode him hard and far, out across the desert, across mile after mile of cedar forest, clear to the foothills. She rested there, absorbed in gazing desertward, and upon turning back again, she ran him over the level stretches. Wind and branch threshed her seemingly to ribbons. Violence seemed good for her. A fall had no fear for her now. She reached camp at dusk, hot as fire, breathless and strengthless. But she had earned something. Such action required constant use of muscle and mind. If need be she could drive both to the very furthermost limit. She could ride and ride—until the future, like the immensity of the desert there, might swallow her. She changed her clothes and rested a while. The call to supper found her hungry. In this fact she discovered mockery of her grief. Love was not the food of life. Exhausted nature's need of rest and sleep was no respecter of a woman's emotion.

Next day Carley rode northward, wildly and fearlessly, as if this conscious activity was the initiative of an endless number of rides that were to save her. As before the foothills called her, and she went on until she came to a very high one.

Carley dismounted from her panting horse, answering the familiar impulse to attain heights by her own effort.

"Am I only a weakling?" she asked herself. "Only a creature mined by the fever of the soul! . . . Thrown from one emotion to another? Never the same. Yearning, suffering, sacrificing, hoping, and changing—forever the same! What is it that drives *me?* A great city with all its attractions has failed to help me realize my life. So have friends failed. So has the world. What can solitude and grandeur do? . . . All this obsession of mine—all this strange feeling for simple elemental earthly things likewise will fail me. Yet I am driven. . . . They would call me a mad woman."

It took Carley a full hour of slow body-bending labor to climb to the summit of that hill. High, steep, and rugged, it resisted ascension. But at last she surmounted it and sat alone on the heights, with naked eyes, and an unconscious prayer on her lips.

What was it that had happened? Could there

be here a different answer from that which always mocked her?

She had been a girl, not accountable for loss of mother, for choice of home and education. She had belonged to a class. She had grown to womanhood in it. She had loved, and in loving had escaped the evil of her day, if not its taint. She had lived only for herself. Conscience had awakened—but, alas! too late. She had overthrown the sordid, self-seeking habit of life; she had awakened to real womanhood; she had fought the insidious spell of modernity and she had defeated it; she had learned the thrill of taking root in new soil, the pain and joy of labor, the bliss of solitude, the promise of home and love and motherhood. But she had gathered all these marvelous things to her soul too late for happiness.

"*Now* it is answered," she declared aloud. "That is what has happened? . . . And all that is *past*. . . . Is there anything left? If so—*what?*"

She flung her query out to the winds of the desert. But the desert seemed too gray, too vast, too remote, too aloof, too measureless. It was not concerned with her little life. Then she turned to the mountain kingdom.

It seemed overpoweringly near at hand. It loomed above her to pierce the fleecy clouds. It was only a stupendous upheaval of earth-crust, grown over at the base by leagues and leagues of pine forest, belted along the middle by vast slanting zigzag slopes of aspen, rent and riven toward the heights into canyon and gorge, bared above to cliffs and corners of craggy rock, whitened at the sky-piercing peaks by snow. Its beauty and sublimity were lost upon Carley now; she was concerned with its travail, its age, its endurance, its strength. And she studied it with magnified sight.

What incomprehensible subterranean force had swelled those immense slopes and lifted the huge bulk aloft to the clouds? Cataclysm of nature—the expanding or shrinking of the earth—vast volcanic action under the surface! Whatever it had been, it had left its expression of the travail of the universe. This mountain mass had been hot gas when flung from the parent sun, and now it was solid granite. What had it endured in the making? What indeed had been its dimensions before the millions of years of its struggle?

Eruption, earthquake, avalanche, the attrition of glacier, the erosion of water, the cracking of frost, the weathering of rain and wind and snow—these it had eternally fought and resisted in vain, yet still it stood magnificent, frowning, battle-scarred and undefeated. Its sky-piercing peaks were as cries for mercy to the Infinite. This old mountain realized its doom. It had to go, perhaps to make room for a newer and better kingdom. But it endured because of the spirit of nature. The great notched circular line of rock below and between the peaks, in the body of the mountains, showed where in ages past the heart of living granite had blown out, to let loose on all the near surrounding desert the streams of black lava and the hills of black cinders. Despite its fringe of green it was hoary with age. Every looming gray-faced wall, massive and sublime, seemed a monument of its mastery over time. Every deep-cut canyon, showing the skeleton ribs, the caverns and caves, its avalanche-carved slides, its long, fan-shaped, spreading taluses, carried conviction to the spectator that it was but a frail bit of rock, that its life was little and brief, that upon it had been laid the merciless curse of nature. Change! Change must unknit the very knots of the center of the earth. So its strength lay in the sublimity of its defiance. It meant to endure to the last rolling grain of sand. It was a dead mountain of rock, without spirit, yet it taught a grand lesson to the seeing eye.

Life was only a part, perhaps an infinitely small part of nature's plan. Death and decay were just as important to her inscrutable design. The universe had not been created for life, ease, pleasure, and happiness of a man creature developed from lower organisms. If nature's secret was the developing of a spirit through all time, Carley divined that she had it within her. So the present meant little.

"I have no right to be unhappy," concluded Carley. "I had no right to Glenn Kilbourne. I failed him. In that I failed myself. Neither life nor nature failed me—nor love. It is no longer a mystery. Unhappiness is only a change. Happiness itself is only change. So what does it matter? The great thing is to see life—to understand—to feel—to work—to fight—to endure. It is not my fault I am here. But it is my fault if I leave this strange old earth the poorer for my failure. . . . I will no longer be little. I will find strength. I will endure. . . . I still have eyes, ears, nose, taste. I can feel the sun, the wind, the nip of frost. Must I slink like a craven because I've lost the love of *one* man? Must I hate Flo Hutter because she will make Glenn happy? Never! . . . All of this seems better so, because through it I am changed. I might have lived on, a selfish clod!"

Carley turned from the mountain kingdom and faced her future with the profound and sad and far-seeing look that had come with her lesson. She knew what to give. Sometime and somewhere there would be recompense. She would hide her wound in the faith that time would heal it. And the ordeal she set herself, to prove her sincerity and strength, was to ride down to Oak Creek Canyon.

Carley did not wait many days. Strange how the old vanity held her back until something of the havoc in her face should be gone!

One morning she set out early, riding her best horse, and she took a sheep trail across country. The distance by road was much farther. The June morning was cool, sparkling, fragrant. Mocking birds sang from the topmost twig of cedars; doves cooed in the pines; sparrow hawks sailed low over the open grassy patches. Desert primroses showed their rounded pink clusters in sunny places, and here and there burned the carmine of Indian paint-brush. Jack rabbits and cotton-tails bounded and scampered away through the sage. The desert had life and color and movement this June day. And as always there was the dry fragrance on the air.

Her mustang had been inured to long and consistent travel over the desert. Her weight was nothing to him and he kept to the swinging lope for miles. As she approached Oak Creek Canyon, however, she drew him to a trot, and then a walk. Sight of the deep red-walled and green-floored canyon was a shock to her.

The trail came out on the road that led to Ryan's sheep camp, at a point several miles west of the cabin where Carley had encountered Haze Ruff. She remembered the curves and stretches, and especially the steep jump-off where the road led down off the rim into the canyon. Here she dismounted and walked. From the foot of this descent she knew every rod of the way would be familiar to her, and, womanlike, she wanted to turn away and fly from them. But she kept on and mounted again at level ground.

The murmur of the creek suddenly assailed her ears—sweet, sad, memorable, strangely powerful to hurt. Yet the sound seemed of long ago. Down here summer had advanced. Rich thick foliage overspread the winding road of sand. Then out of the shade she passed into the sunnier regions of isolated pines. Along here she had raced Calico with Glenn's bay; and here she had caught him, and there was the place she had fallen. She halted a moment under the pine tree where Glenn had held her in his arms. Tears dimmed her eyes. If only she had known then the truth, the reality! But regrets were useless.

By and by a craggy red wall loomed above the trees, and its pipe-organ conformation was familiar to Carley. She left the road and turned to go down to the creek. Sycamores and maples and great bowlders, and mossy ledges overhanging the water, and a huge sentinel pine marked the spot where she and Glenn had eaten their lunch that last day. Her mustang splashed into the clear water and halted to drink. Beyond, through the trees, Carley saw the sunny red-earthed clearing that was Glenn's farm. She looked, and fought herself, and bit her quivering lip until she tasted blood. Then she rode out into the open.

The whole west side of the canyon had been cleared and cultivated and plowed. But she gazed no farther. She did not want to see the spot where she had given Glenn his ring and had parted from him. She rode on. If she could pass West Fork she believed her courage would rise to the completion of this ordeal. Places were what she feared. Places that she had loved while blindly believing she hated! There the narrow gap of green and blue split the looming red wall. She was looking into West Fork. Up there stood the cabin. How fierce a pang rent her breast! She faltered at the crossing of the branch stream, and almost surrendered. The water murmured, the leaves rustled, the bees hummed, the birds sang—all with some sad sweetness that seemed of the past.

Then the trail leading up West Fork was like a barrier. She saw horse tracks in it. Next she descried boot tracks the shape of which was so well-remembered that it shook her heart. There were fresh tracks in the sand, pointing in the direction of the Lodge. Ah! that was where Glenn lived now. Carley strained at her will to keep it fighting her memory. The glory and the dream were gone!

A touch of spur urged her mustang into a gallop. The splashing ford of the creek—the still, eddying pool beyond—the green orchards—the white lacy waterfall—and Lolomi Lodge!

Nothing had altered. But Carley seemed returning after many years. Slowly she dismounted—slowly she climbed the porch steps. Was there no one at home? Yet the vacant doorway, the silence— something attested to the knowledge of Carley's presence. Then suddenly Mrs. Hutter fluttered out with Flo behind her.

"You dear girl—I'm so glad!" cried Mrs. Hutter, her voice trembling.

"I'm glad to see you, too," said Carley, bending to receive Mrs. Hutter's embrace. Carley saw dim eyes— the stress of agitation, but no surprise.

"Oh, Carley!" burst out the Western girl, with voice rich and full, yet tremulous.

"Flo, I've come to wish you happiness," replied Carley, very low.

Was it the same Flo? This seemed more of a woman—strange now—white and strained—beautiful, eager, questioning. A cry of gladness burst from her. Carley felt herself enveloped in strong close clasp—and then a warm, quick kiss of joy. It shocked her, yet somehow thrilled. Sure was the welcome here. Sure was the strained situation, also, but the voice rang too glad a note for Carley. It touched her deeply, yet she could not understand. She had not measured the depth of Western friendship.

"Have you—seen Glenn?" queried Flo, breathlessly.

"Oh no, indeed not," replied Carley, slowly gaining composure. The nervous agitation of these women had stilled her own. "I just rode up the trail. Where is he?"

"He was here—a moment ago," panted Flo. "Oh, Carley, we sure are locoed. . . . Why, we only heard an hour ago—that *you* were at Deep Lake. . . . Charley rode in. He told us. . . . I thought my heart would break. Poor Glenn! When he heard it. . . . But never mind *me*. Jump your horse and run to West Fork!"

The spirit of her was like the strength of her arms as she hurried Carley across the porch and shoved her down the steps.

"Climb on and run, Carley," cried Flo. "If you only knew how glad he'll be that you came!"

Carley leaped into the saddle and wheeled the mustang. But she had no answer for the girl's singular, almost wild exultance. Then like a shot the spirited mustang was off down the lane. Carley wondered with swelling heart. Was her coming such a wondrous surprise—so unexpected and big in generosity—something that would make Kilbourne as glad as it had seemed to make Flo? Carley thrilled to this assurance.

Down the lane she flew. The red walls blurred and the sweet wind whipped her face. At the trail she swerved the mustang, but did not check his gait. Under the great pines he sped and round the bulging wall. At the rocky incline leading to the creek she pulled the fiery animal to a trot. How low and clear the water! As Carley forded it fresh cool drops splashed into her face. Again she spurred her mount and again trees and walls rushed by. Up and down the yellow bits of trail—on over the brown mats of pine needles—until there in the sunlight shone the little gray log cabin with a tall form standing in the door. One instant the canyon tilted on end for Carley and she was riding into the blue sky. Then some magic of soul sustained her, so that she saw clearly. Reaching the cabin she reined in her mustang.

"Hello, Glenn! Look who's here!" she cried, not wholly failing of gayety.

He threw up his sombrero.

"Whoopee!" he yelled, in stentorian voice that rolled across the canyon and bellowed in hollow echo and then clapped from wall to wall. The unexpected Western yell, so strange from Glenn, disconcerted Carley. Had he only answered her spirit of greeting? Had hers rung false?

But he was coming to her. She had seen the bronze of his face turn to white. How gaunt and worn he looked. Older he appeared, with deeper lines and whiter hair. His jaw quivered.

"Carley Burch, so it was *you?*" he queried, hoarsely.

"Glenn, I reckon it was," she replied. "I bought your Deep Lake ranch site. I came back too late. . . . But it is never too late for some things. . . . I've come to wish you and Flo all the happiness in the world—and to say we must be friends."

The way he looked at her made her tremble. He strode up beside the mustang, and he was so tall that his shoulder came abreast of her. He placed a big warm hand on hers, as it rested, ungloved, on the pommel of the saddle.

"Have you seen Flo?" he asked.

"I just left her. It was funny—the way she rushed me off after you. As if there weren't two—"

Was it Glenn's eyes or the movement of his hand that checked her utterance? His gaze pierced her soul. His hand slid along her arm—to her waist—around it. Her heart seemed to burst.

"Kick your feet out of the stirrups," he ordered.

Instinctively she obeyed. Then with a strong pull he hauled her half out of the saddle, pellmell into his arms. Carley had no resistance. She sank limp, in an agony of amaze. Was this a dream? Swift and hard his lips met hers—and again—and again. . . .

"Oh, my God!—Glenn, are—you—mad?" she whispered, almost swooning.

"Sure—I reckon I am," he replied, huskily, and pulled her all the way out of the saddle.

Carley would have fallen but for his support. She could not think. She was all instinct. Only the amaze—the sudden horror—drifted—faded as before fires of her heart!

"Kiss me!" he commanded.

She would have kissed him if death were the penalty. How his face blurred in her dimmed sight! Was that a strange smile? Then he held her back from him.

"Carley—you came to wish Flo and me happiness?" he asked.

"Oh, yes—yes. . . . Pity me, Glenn—let me go. I meant well. . . . I should—never have come."

"Do you love me?" he went on, with passionate, shaking clasp.

"God help me—I do—I do! . . . And now it will kill me!"

"What did that damned fool Charley tell you?"

The strange content of his query, the trenchant force of it, brought her upright, with sight suddenly cleared. Was this giant the tragic Glenn who had strode to her from the cabin door?

"Charley told me—you and Flo—were married," she whispered.

"You didn't *believe* him!" returned Glenn.

She could no longer speak. She could only see her lover, as if transfigured, limned dark against the looming red wall.

"That was one of Charley's queer jokes. I told you to beware of him. Flo is married, yes—and very happy. . . . I'm unutterably happy, too—but I'm *not* married. Lee Stanton was the lucky bridegroom. . . . Carley, the moment I saw you I knew you had come back to me."

Zane Grey, author of over 80 books, was born in Ohio in 1872. His writing career spanned over 35 years until his death in 1939. Estimates of Zane Grey's audience exceed 250 million readers.

Zane Grey, author of over 80 books, was born in Ohio in 1872. His writing career spanned over 35 years until his death in 1939. Estimates of Zane Grey's audience exceed 250 million readers.

ZANE GREY

THE MYSTERIOUS RIDER

HarperPaperbacks
A Division of HarperCollinsPublishers

HarperPaperbacks   *A Division of* HarperCollins*Publishers*
10 East 53rd Street, New York, N.Y. 10022

THE CALL OF THE CANYON. Copyright © 1921, 1922, 1924 by Zane Grey. Copyright renewed 1949, 1950, 1952 by Lina Elise Grey.

THE MYSTERIOUS RIDER. Copyright © 1921 by Harper & Brothers. Copyright renewed 1949 by Lina Elise Grey.

THE CALL OF THE CANYON/THE MYSTERIOUS RIDER. Copyright © 1995 by Lina Elise Grey.

All rights reserved. No part of this book may be used or reproduced in any manner whatsoever without written permission of the publisher, except in the case of brief quotations embodied in critical articles and reviews. For information address HarperCollins*Publishers*, 10 East 53rd Street, New York, N.Y. 10022.

Cover art courtesy of H. Armstrong Roberts, Inc. and the Bettman Archive

First HarperPaperbacks Zane Grey double western printing: May 1995

The Call of the Canyon was published by HarperPaperbacks in March 1992. *The Mysterious Rider* was published by HarperPaperbacks in January 1991.

Printed in the United States of America

HarperPaperbacks and colophon are trademarks of HarperCollins*Publishers*

10 9 8 7 6 5 4 3 2 1

THE MYSTERIOUS RIDER

A SEPTEMBER sun, losing some of its heat if not its brilliance, was dropping low in the west over the black Colorado range. Purple haze began to thicken in the timbered notches. Gray foothills, round and billowy, rolled down from the higher country. They were smooth, sweeping, with long velvety slopes and isolated patches of aspens that blazed in autumn gold. Splotches of red vine colored the soft gray of sage. Old White Slides, a mountain scarred by avalanche, towered with bleak rocky peak above the valley, sheltering it from the north.

A girl rode along the slope, with gaze on the sweep and range and color of the mountain fastness that was her home. She followed an old trail which led to a bluff overlooking an arm of the valley. Once it had been a familiar lookout for her, but she had not visited the place of late. It was associated with serious hours of her life. Here seven years before, when she was twelve, she had made a hard choice to please her guardian—the old rancher whom she loved and called father, who had indeed been a father to her. That choice had been to go to school in Denver. Four years she had lived away from her beloved gray hills and black mountains. Only once since her return had she climbed to this height, and that occasion, too, was memorable as an unhappy hour. It had been three years ago. To-day girlish ordeals and griefs seemed back in the past: she was a woman at nineteen and face to face with the first great problem in her life.

The trail came up back of the bluff, through a clump of aspens with white trunks and yellow fluttering leaves, and led across a level bench of luxuriant grass and wild flowers to the rocky edge.

She dismounted and threw the bridle. Her mustang, used to being petted, rubbed his sleek, dark head against her and evidently expected like demonstration in return, but as none was forthcoming he bent his nose to the grass and began grazing. The girl's eyes were intent upon some waving, slender, white-and-blue flowers. They smiled up wanly, like pale stars, out of the long grass that had a tinge of gold.

"Columbines," she mused, wistfully, as she plucked several of the flowers and held them up to gaze wonderingly at them, as if to see in them some revelation of the mystery that shrouded her birth and her name. Then she stood with dreamy gaze upon the distant ranges.

"Columbine! . . . So they named me—those miners

who found me—a baby—lost in the woods—asleep among the columbines." She spoke aloud, as if the sound of her voice might convince her.

So much of the mystery of her had been revealed that day by the man she had always called father. Vaguely she had always been conscious of some mystery, something strange about her childhood, some relation never explained.

"No name but Columbine," she whispered, sadly, and now she understood a strange longing of her heart.

Scarcely an hour back, as she ran down the wide porch of White Slides ranch-house, she had encountered the man who had taken care of her all her life. He had looked upon her as kindly and fatherly as of old, yet with a difference. She seemed to see him as old Bill Belllounds, pioneer and rancher, of huge frame and broad face, hard and scarred and grizzled, with big eyes of blue fire.

"Collie," the old man had said, "I reckon hyar's news. A letter from Jack....He's comin' home."

Belllounds had waved the letter. His huge hand trembled as he reached to put it on her shoulder. The hardness of him seemed strangely softened. Jack was his son. Buster Jack, the range had always called him, with other terms, less kind, that never got to the ears of his father. Jack had been sent away three years ago, just before Columbine's return from school. Therefore she had not seen him for over seven years. But she remembered him well—a big, rangy boy, handsome and wild, who had made her childhood almost unendurable.

"Yes—my son—Jack—he's comin' home," said

Belllounds, with a break in his voice. "An', Collie—now I must tell you somethin'."

"Yes, dad," she had replied, with strong clasp of the heavy hand on her shoulder.

"Thet's just it, lass. I ain't your dad. I've tried to be a dad to you an' I've loved you as my own. But you're not flesh an' blood of mine. An' now I must tell you."

The brief story followed. Seventeen years ago miners working a claim of Belllounds's in the mountains above Middle Park had found a child asleep in the columbines along the trail. Near that point Indians, probably Arapahoes coming across the mountains to attack the Utes, had captured or killed the occupants of a prairie-schooner. There was no other clue. The miners took the child to their camp, fed and cared for it, and, after the manner of their kind, named it Columbine. Then they brought it to Belllounds.

"Collie," said the old rancher, "it needn't never have been told, an' wouldn't but fer one reason. I'm gettin' old. I reckon I'd never split my property between you an' Jack. So I mean you an' him to marry. You always steadied Jack. With a wife like you'll be—wal, mebbe Jack'll—"

"Dad!" burst out Columbine. "Marry Jack! . . . Why I—I don't even remember him!"

"Haw! Haw!" laughed Belllounds. "Wal, you doggone soon will. Jack's in Kremmlin', an' he'll be hyar tonight or to-morrow."

"But—I—I don't l-love him," faltered Columbine.

The old man lost his mirth; the strong-lined face resumed its hard cast; the big eyes smoldered. Her appealing objection had wounded him. She was reminded of how sensitive the old man had always been to any reflection cast upon his son.

"Wal, thet's onlucky," he replied, gruffly. "Mebbe you'll change. I reckon no girl could help a boy much, onless she cared for him. Anyway, you an' Jack will marry."

He had stalked away and Columbine had ridden her mustang far up the valley slope where she could be alone. Standing on the verge of the bluff, she suddenly became aware that the quiet and solitude of her lonely resting-place had been disrupted. Cattle were bawling below her and along the slope of old White Slides and on the grassy uplands above. She had forgotten that the cattle were being driven down into the lowlands for the fall round-up. A great red-and-white-spotted herd was milling in the park just beneath her. Calves and yearlings were making the dust fly along the mountain slope; wild old steers were crashing in the sage, holding level, unwilling to be driven down; cows were running and lowing for their lost ones. Melodious and clear rose the clarion calls of the cowboys. The cattle knew those calls and only the wild steers kept up-grade.

Columbine also knew each call and to which cowboy it belonged. They sang and yelled and swore, but it was all music to her. Here and there along the slope, where the aspen groves clustered, a horse would flash across an open space; the dust would fly, and a cowboy would peal out a lusty yell that rang along the slope and echoed under the bluff and lingered long after the daring rider had vanished in the steep thickets.

"I wonder which is Wils," murmured Columbine,

as she watched and listened, vaguely conscious of a little difference, a strange check in her remembrance of this particular cowboy. She felt the change, yet did not understand. One after one she recognized the riders on the slopes below, but Wilson Moore was not among them. He must be above her, then, and she turned to gaze across the grassy bluff, up the long, yellow slope, to where the gleaming aspens half hid a red bluff of mountain, towering aloft. Then from far to her left, high up a scrubby ridge of the slope, rang down a voice that thrilled her: "Go—aloong—you—ooooo." Red cattle dashed pell-mell down the slope, raising the dust, tearing the brush, rolling rocks, and letting out hoarse bawls.

"Whoop-ee!" High-pitched and pealing came a clearer yell.

Columbine saw a white mustang flash out on top of the ridge, silhouetted against the blue, with mane and tail flying. His gait on that edge of steep slope proved his rider to be a reckless cowboy for whom no heights or depths had terrors. She would have recognized him from the way he rode, if she had not known the slim, erect figure. The cowboy saw her instantly. He pulled the mustang, about to plunge down the slope, and lifted him, rearing and wheeling. Then Columbine waved her hand. The cowboy spurred his horse along the crest of the ridge, disappeared behind the grove of aspens, and came in sight again around to the right, where on the grassy bench he slowed to a walk in descent to the bluff.

The girl watched him come, conscious of an unfamiliar sense of uncertainty in this meeting, and of the fact that she was seeing him differently from any other time in the years he had been a playmate, a friend, almost like a brother. He had ridden for Belllounds for years, and was a cowboy because he loved cattle well and horses better, and above all a life in the open. Unlike most cowboys, he had been to school; he had a family in Denver that objected to his wild range life, and often importuned him to come home; he seemed aloof sometimes and not readily understood.

While many thoughts whirled through Columbine's mind she watched the cowboy ride slowly down to her, and she became more concerned with a sudden restraint. How was Wilson going to take the news of this forced change about to come in her life? That thought leaped up. It gave her a strange pang. But she and he were only good friends. As to that, she reflected, of late they had not been the friends and comrades they formerly were. In the thrilling uncertainty of this meeting she had forgotten his distant manner and the absence of little attentions she had missed.

By this time the cowboy had reached the level, and with the lazy grace of his kind slipped out of the saddle. He was tall, slim, round-limbed, with the small hips of a rider, and square, though not broad shoulders. He stood straight like an Indian. His eyes were hazel, his features regular, his face bronzed. All men of the open had still, lean, strong faces, but added to this in him was a steadiness of expression, a restraint that seemed to hide sadness.

"Howdy, Columbine!" he said. "What are you doing up here? You might get run over."

"Hello, Wils!" she replied, slowly. "Oh, I guess I can keep out of the way."

"Some bad steers in that bunch. If any of them run over here Pronto will leave you to walk home. That mustang hates cattle. And he's only half broke, you know."

"I forgot you were driving to-day," she replied, and looked away from him. There was a moment's pause—long, it seemed to her.

"What'd you come for?" he asked, curiously.

"I wanted to gather columbines. See." She held out the nodding flowers toward him. "Take one....Do you like them?"

"Yes. I like columbine," he replied, taking one of them. His keen hazel eyes, softened, darkened. "Colorado's flower."

"Columbine!...It is my name."

"Well, could you have a better? It sure suits you."

"Why?" she asked, and she looked at him again.

"You're slender—graceful. You sort of hold your head high and proud. Your skin is white. Your eyes are blue. Not bluebell blue, but columbine blue—and they turn purple when you're angry."

"Compliments! Wilson, this is new kind of talk for you," she said.

"You're different to-day."

"Yes, I am." She looked across the valley toward the westering sun, and the slight flush faded from her cheeks. "I have no right to hold my head proud. No one knows who I am—where I came from."

"As if that made any difference!" he exclaimed.

"Belllounds is not my dad. I have no dad. I was a

waif. They found me in the woods—a baby—lost among the flowers. Columbine Belllounds I've always been. But that is not my name. No one can tell what my name really is."

"I knew your story years ago, Columbine," he replied, earnestly. "Everybody knows. Old Bill ought to have told you long before this. But he loves you. So does—everybody. You must not let this knowledge sadden you.... I'm sorry you've never known a mother or a sister. Why, I could tell you of many orphans who—whose stories were different."

"You don't understand. I've been happy. I've not longed for any—any one except a mother. It's only—"

"What don't I understand?"

"I've not told you all."

"No? Well, go on," he said, slowly.

Meaning of the hesitation and the restraint that had obstructed her thought now flashed over Columbine. It lay in what Wilson Moore might think of her prospective marriage to Jack Belllounds. Still she could not guess why that should make her feel strangely uncertain of the ground she stood on or how it could cause a constraint she had to fight herself to hide. Moreover, to her annoyance, she found that she was evading his direct request for the news she had withheld.

"Jack Belllounds is coming home to-night or tomorrow," she said. Then, waiting for her companion to reply, she kept an unseeing gaze upon the scanty pines fringing Old White Slides. But no reply appeared to be forthcoming from Moore. His silence compelled her to turn to him. The cowboy's face had subtly altered; it was darker with a tinge of red under the bronze; and his lower lip was released from his teeth, even as she looked. He had his eyes intent upon the lasso he was coiling. Suddenly he faced her and the dark fire of his eyes gave her a shock.

"I've been expecting that shorthorn back for months." he said, bluntly.

"You—never—liked Jack?" queried Columbine, slowly. That was not what she wanted to say, but the thought spoke itself.

"I should smile I never did."

"Ever since you and he fought—long ago—all over—"

His sharp gesture made the coiled lasso loosen.

"Ever since I licked him good—don't forget that," interrupted Wilson. The red had faded from the bronze.

"Yes, you licked him," mused Columbine. "I remember that. And Jack's hated you ever since."

"There's been no love lost."

"But, Wils, you never before talked this way—spoke out so—against Jack," she protested.

"Well, I'm not the kind to talk behind a fellow's back. But I'm not mealy-mouthed, either, and—and—"

He did not complete the sentence and his meaning was enigmatic. Altogether Moore seemed not like himself. The fact disturbed Columbine. Always she had confided in him. Here was a most complex situation—she burned to tell him, yet somehow feared to—she felt an incomprehensible satisfaction in his bitter reference to Jack—she seemed to realize that she valued Wilson's friendship more than she had known, and now for some strange reason it was slipping from her.

"We—we were such good friends—pards," said Columbine, hurriedly and irrelevantly.

"Who?" He stared at her.

"Why, you—and me."

"Oh!" His tone softened, but there was still disapproval in his glance. "What of that?"

"Something has happened to make me think I've missed you—lately—that's all."

"Ahuh!" His tone held finality and bitterness, but he would not commit himself. Columbine sensed a pride in him that seemed the cause of his aloofness.

"Wilson, why have you been different lately?" she asked, plaintively.

"What's the good to tell you now?" he queried, in reply.

That gave her a blank sense of actual loss. She had lived in dreams and he in realities. Right now she could not dispel her dream—see and understand all that he seemed to. She felt like a child, then, growing old swiftly. The strange past longing for a mother surged up in her like a strong tide. Some one to lean on, some one who loved her, some one to help her in this hour when fatality knocked at the door of her youth—how she needed that!

"It might be bad for me—to tell me, but tell me, anyhow," she said, finally, answering as some one older than she had been an hour ago—to something feminine that leaped up. She did not understand this impulse, but it was in her.

"No!" declared Moore, with dark red staining his face. He slapped the lasso against his saddle, and tied it with clumsy hands. He did not look at her. His tone expressed anger and amaze.

"Dad says I must marry Jack," she said, with a sudden return to her natural simplicity.

"I heard him tell that months ago," snapped Moore.

"You did! Was that—why?" she whispered.

"It was," he answered, ringingly.

"But that was no reason for you to be—be—to stay away from me," she declared, with rising spirit.

He laughed shortly.

"Wils, didn't you like me any more after dad said that?" she queried.

"Columbine, a girl nineteen years and about to—to get married—ought not be a fool," he replied, with sarcasm

"I'm not a fool," she rejoined, hotly.

"You ask fool questions."

"Well, you *didn't* like me afterward or you'd never have mistreated me."

"If you say I mistreated you—you say what's untrue," he replied, just as hotly.

They had never been so near a quarrel before. Columbine experienced a sensation new to her—a commingling of fear, heat, and pang, it seemed, all in one throb. Wilson was hurting her. A quiver ran all over her, along her veins, swelling and tingling.

"You mean I lie?" she flashed.

"Yes, I do—if—"

But before he could conclude she slapped his face. It grew pale then, while she began to tremble.

"Oh—I didn't intend that. Forgive me," she faltered.

He rubbed his cheek. The hurt had not been great,

so far as the blow was concerned. But his eyes were dark with pain and anger.

"Oh, don't distress yourself," he burst out. "You slapped me before—once, years ago—for kissing you. I—I apologize for saying you lied. You're only out of your head. So am I."

That poured oil upon the troubled waters. The cowboy appeared to be hesitating between sudden flight and the risk of staying longer.

"Maybe that's it," replied Columbine, with a half-laugh. She was not far from tears and fury with herself. "Let us make up—be friends again."

Moore squared around aggressively. He seemed to fortify himself against something in her. She felt that. But his face grew harder and older than she had ever seen it.

"Columbine, do *you* know where Jack Belllounds has been for these three years?" he asked, deliberately, entirely ignoring her overtures of friendship.

"No. Somebody said Denver. Some one else said Kansas City. I never asked dad, because I knew Jack had been sent away. I've supposed he was working—making a man of himself."

"Well, I hope to Heaven—for your sake—what you suppose comes true," returned Moore, with exceeding bitterness.

"Do *you* know where he has been?" asked Columbine. Some strange feeling prompted that. There was a mystery here. Wilson's agitation seemed strange and deep.

"Yes, I do." The cowboy bit that out through closing

teeth, as if locking them against an almost overmastering temptation.

Columbine lost her curiosity. She was woman enough to realize that there might well be facts which would only make her situation harder.

"Wilson," she began, hurriedly, "I owe all I am to dad. He has cared for me—sent me to school. He has been so good to me. I've loved him always. It would be a shabby return for all his protection and love if—if I refused—"

"Old Bill is the best man ever," interrupted Moore, as if to repudiate any hint of disloyalty to his employer. "Everybody in Middle Park and all over owes Bill something. He's sure good. There never was anything wrong with him except his crazy blindness about his son. Buster Jack—the—the—"

Columbine put a hand over Moore's lips.

"The man I must marry," she said, solemnly.

"You must—you will?" he demanded.

"Of course. What else could I do? I never thought of refusing."

"Columbine!" Wilson's cry was so poignant, his gesture so violent, his dark eyes so piercing that Columbine sustained a shock that held her trembling and mute. "How can you love Jack Belllounds? You were twelve years old when you saw him last. How can you love him?"

"I don't," replied Columbine.

"Then how could you marry him?"

"I owe dad obedience. It's his hope that I can steady Jack."

"*Steady Jack!*" exclaimed Moore, passionately.

"Why, you girl—you white-faced flower! *You* with your innocence and sweetness steady that damned pup! My Heavens! He was a gambler and a drunkard. He—"

"Hush!" implored Columbine.

"He cheated at cards," declared the cowboy, with a scorn that placed that vice as utterly base.

"But Jack was only a wild boy," replied Columbine, trying with brave words to champion the son of the man she loved as her father. "He has been sent away to work. He'll have outgrown that wildness. He'll come home a man."

"Bah!" cried Moore, harshly.

Columbine felt a sinking within her. Where was her strength? She, who could walk and ride so many miles, to become sick with an inward quaking! It was childish. She struggled to hide her weakness from him.

"It's not like you to be this way," she said. "You used to be generous. Am I to blame? Did I choose my life?"

Moore looked quickly away from her, and, standing with a hand on his horse, he was silent for a moment. The squaring of his shoulders bore testimony to his thought. Presently he swung up into the saddle. The mustang snorted and champed the bit and tossed his head, ready to bolt.

"Forget my temper," begged the cowboy, looking down upon Columbine. "I take it all back. I'm sorry. Don't let a word of mine worry you. I was only jealous."

"Jealous!" exclaimed Columbine, wonderingly.

"Yes. That makes a fellow see red and green. Bad medicine! You never felt it."

"What were you jealous of?" asked Columbine.

The cowboy had himself in hand now and he regarded her with a grim amusement.

"Well, Columbine, it's like a story," he replied. "I'm the fellow disowned by his family—a wanderer of the wilds—no good—and no prospects....Now our friend Jack, he's handsome and rich. He has a doting old dad. Cattle, horses—ranches! He wins the girl. See!"

Spurring his mustang, the cowboy rode away. At the edge of the slope he turned in the saddle. "I've got to drive in this bunch of cattle. It's late. You hurry home." Then he was gone. The stones cracked and rolled down under the side of the bluff.

Columbine stood where he had left her; dubious, yet with the blood still hot in her cheeks.

"Jealous?...He wins the girl?" she murmured in repetition to herself. "What ever could he have meant? He didn't mean—he didn't—"

The simple, logical interpretation of Wilson's words opened Columbine's mind to a disturbing possibility of which she had never dreamed. That he might love her! If he did, why had he not said so? Jealous, maybe, but he did not love her! The next throb of thought was like a knock at a door of her heart—a door never yet opened, inside which seemed a mystery of feeling, of hope, despair, unknown longing, and clamorous voices. The woman just born in her, instinctive and self-preservative, shut that door before she had more than a glimpse inside. But then she felt her heart swell with its nameless burdens.

Pronto was grazing near at hand. She caught him and mounted. It struck her then that her hands were numb with cold. The wind had ceased fluttering the aspens, but the yellow leaves were falling, rustling. Out on the brow of the slope she faced home and the west.

A glorious Colorado sunset had just reached the wonderful height of its color and transformation. The sage slopes below her seemed rosy velvet; the golden aspens on the farther reaches were on fire at the tips; the foothills rolled clear and mellow and rich in the light; the gulf of distance on to the great black range was veiled in mountain purple; and the dim peaks beyond the range stood up, sunset-flushed and grand. The narrow belt of blue sky between crags and clouds was like a river full of fleecy sails and wisps of silver. Above towered a pall of dark cloud, full of the shades of approaching night.

"Oh, beautiful!" breathed the girl, with all her worship of nature. That wild world of sunset grandeur and loneliness and beauty was hers. Over there, under a peak of the black range, was the place where she had been found, a baby, lost in the forest. She belonged to that, and so it belonged to her. Strength came to her from the glory of light on the hills.

Pronto shot up his ears and checked his trot.

"What is it, boy?" called Columbine. The trail was getting dark. Shadows were creeping up the slope as she rode down to meet them. The mustang had keen sight and scent. She reined him to a halt.

All was silent. The valley had begun to shade on the far side and the rose and gold seemed fading from the nearer. Below, on the level floor of the valley, lay the rambling old ranch-house, with the cabins nestling around, and the corrals leading out to the soft hay-fields, misty and gray in the twilight. A single light gleamed. It was like a beacon.

The air was cold with a nip of frost. From far on the other side of the ridge she had descended came the bawls of the last straggling cattle of the round-up. But surely Pronto had not shot up his ears for them. As if in answer a wild sound pealed down the slope, making the mustang jump. Columbine had heard it before.

"Pronto, it's only a wolf," she soothed him.

The peal was loud, rather harsh at first, then softened to a mourn, wild, lonely, haunting. A pack of coyotes barked in angry answer, a sharp, staccato, yelping chorus, the more piercing notes biting on the cold night air. These mountain mourns and yelps were music to Columbine. She rode on down the trail in the gathering darkness, less afraid of the night and its wild denizens than of what awaited her at White Slides Ranch.

DARKNESS settled down like a black mantle over the valley. Columbine rather hoped to find Wilson waiting to take care of her horse, as used to be his habit, but she was disappointed. No light showed from the cabin in which the cowboys lived; he had not yet come in from the round-up. She unsaddled, and turned Pronto loose in the pasture.

The windows of the long, low ranch-house were bright squares in the blackness, sending cheerful rays afar. Columbine wondered in trepidation if Jack Bell-lounds had come home. It required effort of will to approach the house. Yet since she must meet him, the sooner the ordeal was over the better. Nevertheless she tiptoed past the bright windows, and went all the length of the long porch, and turned around and went back, and then hesitated, fighting a slow drag of her spirit, an oppression upon her heart. The door was crude and heavy. It opened hard.

Columbine entered a big room lighted by a lamp on the upper table and by blazing logs in a huge stone fireplace. This was the living-room, rather gloomy in the corners, and bare, but comfortable, for all simple needs. The logs were new and the chinks between them filled with clay, still white, showing that the house was of recent build.

The rancher, Belllounds, sat in his easy-chair before the fire, his big, horny hands extended to the warmth. He was in his shirt-sleeves, a gray, bold-faced man, of over sixty years, still muscular and rugged.

At Columbine's entrance he raised his drooping head, and so removed the suggestion of sadness in his posture.

"Wal, lass, hyar you are," was his greeting. "Jake has been hollerin' thet chuck was ready. Now we can eat."

"Dad—did—did your son come?" asked Columbine.

"No. I got word jest at sundown. One of Baker's cowpunchers from up the valley. He rode up from Kremmlin' an' stopped to say Jack was celebratin' his arrival by too much red liquor. Reckon he won't be home to-night. Mebbe to-morrow."

Belllounds spoke in an even, heavy tone, without any apparent feeling. Always he was mercilessly frank and never spared the truth. But Columbine, who knew him well, felt how this news flayed him. Resentment stirred in her toward the wayward son, but she knew better than to voice it.

"Natural like, I reckon, fer Jack to feel gay on gettin' home. I ain't holdin' thet ag'in' him. These last three years must have been gallin' to thet boy."

Columbine stretched her hands to the blaze.

"It's cold, dad," she averred. "I didn't dress warmly, so I nearly froze. Autumn is here and there's frost in the air. Oh, the hills were all gold and red—the aspen leaves were falling. I love autumn, but it means winter is so near."

"Wal, wal, time flies," sighed the old man. "Where'd you ride?"

"Up the west slope to the bluff. It's far. I don't go there often."

"Meet any of the boys? I sent the outfit to drive stock down from the mountain. I've lost a good many head lately. They're eatin' some weed thet poisons them. They swell up an' die. Wuss this year than ever before."

"Why, that is serious, dad! Poor things! That's worse than eating loco.... Yes, I met Wilson Moore driving down the slope."

"Ahuh! Wal, let's eat."

They took seats at the table which the cook, Jake, was loading with steaming victuals. Supper appeared to be a rather sumptuous one this evening, in honor of the expected guest, who had not come. Columbine helped the old man to his favorite dishes, stealing furtive glances at his lined and shadowed face. She sensed a subtle change in him since the afternoon, but could not see any sign of it in his look or demeanor. His appetite was as hearty as ever.

"So you met Wils. Is he still makin' up to you?"

asked Belllounds, presently.

"No, he isn't. I don't see that he ever did—that— dad," she replied.

"You're a kid in mind an' a woman in body. Thet cowpuncher has been lovesick over you since you were a little girl. It's what kept him hyar ridin' fer me."

"Dad, I don't believe it," said Columbine, feeling the blood at her temples. "You always imagined such things about Wilson, and the other boys as well."

"Ahuh! I'm an old fool about wimmen, hey? Mebbe I was years ago. But I can see now. . . . Didn't Wils always get ory-eyed when any of the other boys shined up to you?"

"I can't remember that he did," replied Columbine. She felt a desire to laugh, yet the subject was anything but amusing to her.

"Wal, you've always been innocent-like. Thank the Lord you never leaned to tricks of most pretty lasses, makin' eyes at all the men. Anyway, a matter of three months ago I told Wils to keep away from you—thet you were not fer any poor cowpuncher."

"You never liked him. Why? Was it fair, taking him as boys come?"

"Wal, I reckon it wasn't," replied Belllounds, and as he looked up his broad face changed to ruddy color. "Thet boy's the best rider an' roper I've had in years. He ain't the bronco-bustin' kind. He never drank. He was honest an' willin'. He saves his money. He's good at handlin' stock. Thet boy will be a rich rancher some day."

"Strange, then, you never liked him," murmured

Columbine. She felt ashamed of the good it did her to hear Wilson praised.

"No, it ain't strange. I have my own reasons," replied Belllounds, gruffly, as he resumed eating.

Columbine believed she could guess the cause of the old rancher's unreasonable antipathy for this cowboy. Not improbably it was because Wilson had always been superior in every way to Jack Belllounds. The boys had been natural rivals in everything pertaining to life on the range. What Bill Belllounds admired most in men was paramount in Wilson and lacking in his own son.

"Will you put Jack in charge of your ranches, now?" asked Columbine.

"Not much. I reckon I'll try him hyar at White Slides as foreman. An' if he runs the outfit, then I'll see."

"Dad, he'll never run the White Slides outfit," asserted Columbine.

"Wal, it is a hard bunch, I'll agree. But I reckon the boys will stay, exceptin', mebbe, Wils. An' it'll be jest as well fer him to leave."

"It's not good business to send away your best cowboy. I've heard you complain lately of lack of men."

"I sure do need men," replied Belllounds, seriously. "Stock gettin' more 'n we can handle. I sent word over the range to Meeker, hopin' to get some men there. What I need most jest now is a fellar who knows dogs an' who'll hunt down the wolves an' lions an' bears thet're livin' off my cattle."

"Dad, you need a whole outfit to handle the packs of hounds you've got. Such an assortment of them! There must be a hundred. Only yesterday some man brought a lot of mangy, long-eared canines. It's funny.

Why, dad, you're the laughing-stock of the range!"

"Yes, an' the range'll be thankin' me when I rid it of all these varmints," declared Belllounds. "Lass, I swore I'd buy every dog fetched to me, until I had enough to kill off the coyotes an' lofers an' lions. I'll do it, too. But I need a hunter."

"Why not put Wilson Moore in charge of the hounds? He's a hunter."

"Wal, lass, thet might be a good idee," replied the rancher, nodding his grizzled head. "Say, you're sort of wantin' me to keep Wils on."

"Yes, dad."

"Why? Do you like him so much?"

"I like him—of course. He has been almost a brother to me."

"Ahuh! Wal, are you sure you don't like him more'n you ought—considerin' what's in the wind?"

"Yes, I'm sure I don't," replied Columbine, with tingling cheeks.

"Wal, I'm glad of thet. Reckon it'll be no great matter whether Wils stays or leaves. If he wants to I'll give him a job with the hounds."

That evening Columbine went to her room early. It was a cozy little blanketed nest which she had arranged and furnished herself. There was a little square window cut through the logs and through which many a night the snow had blown in upon her bed. She loved her little isolated refuge. This night it was cold, the first time this autumn, and the lighted lamp, though brightening the room, did not make it appreciably warmer. There was a stone fireplace, but as she had neglected to bring in wood she could not start a fire. So she undressed, blew out the lamp, and went to bed.

Columbine was soon warm, and the darkness of her little room seemed good to her. Sleep she felt never would come that night. She wanted to think; she could not help but think; and she tried to halt the whirl of her mind. Wilson Moore occupied the foremost place in her varying thoughts—a fact quite remarkable and unaccountable. She tried to change it. In vain! Wilson persisted—on his white mustang flying across the ridgetop—coming to her as never before—with his anger and disapproval—his strange, poignant cry, "Columbine!" that haunted her—with his bitter smile and his resignation and his mocking talk of jealousy. He persisted and grew with the old rancher's frank praise.

"I must not think of him," she whispered. "Why, I'll be—be married soon. . . . Married!"

That word transformed her thought, and where she had thrilled she now felt cold. She revolved the fact in mind.

"It's true, I'll be married, because I ought—I must," she said, half aloud. "Because I can't help myself. I ought to want to—for dad's sake. . . . But I don't—I don't."

She longed above all things to be good, loyal, loving, helpful, to show her gratitude for the home and the affection that had been bestowed upon a nameless waif. Bill Belllounds had not been under any obligation to succor a strange, lost child. He had done it because he was big, noble. Many splendid deeds had been laid at the old rancher's door. She was not of an ungrateful nature. She meant to pay. But the significance of the price began to dawn upon her.

"It will change my whole life," she whispered, aghast.

But how? Columbine pondered. She must go over the details of that change. No mother had ever taught her. The few women that had been in the Belllounds home from time to time had not been sympathetic or had not stayed long enough to help her much. Even her school life in Denver had left her still a child as regarded the serious problems of women.

"If I'm his wife," she went on, "I'll have to be with him—I'll have to give up this little room—I'll never be free—alone—happy, any more."

That was the first detail she enumerated. It was also the last. Realization came with a sickening little shudder. And that moment gave birth to the nucleus of an unconscious revolt.

The coyotes were howling. Wild, sharp, sweet notes! They soothed her troubled, aching head, lulled her toward sleep, reminded her of the gold-and-purple sunset, and the slopes of sage, the lonely heights, and the beauty that would never change. On the morrow, she drowsily thought, she would persuade Wilson not to kill all the coyotes; to leave a few, because she loved them.

Bill Belllounds had settled in Middle Park in 1860. It was wild country, a home of the Ute Indians, and a natural paradise for elk, deer, antelope, buffalo. The mountain ranges harbored bear. These ranges sheltered the rolling valley land which some explorer had named Middle Park in earlier days.

Much of this inclosed table-land was prairie, where

long grass and wild flowers grew luxuriantly. Belllounds was a a a cattleman, and he saw the possibilities there. To which end he sought the friendship of Piah, chief of the Utes. This noble red man was well disposed toward the white settlers, and his tribe, during those troublous times, kept peace with these invaders of their mountain home.

In 1868 Belllounds was instrumental in persuading the Utes to relinquish Middle Park. The slopes of the hills were heavily timbered; gold and silver had been found in the mountains. It was a country that attracted prospectors, cattlemen, lumbermen. The summer season was not long enough to grow grain, and the nights too frosty for corn; otherwise Middle Park would have increased rapidly in population.

In the years that succeeded the departure of the Utes Bill Belllounds developed several cattle-ranches and acquired others. White Slides Ranch lay some twenty-odd miles from Middle Park, being a winding arm of the main valley land. Its development was a matter of later years, and Belllounds lived there because the country was wilder. The rancher, as he advanced in years, seemed to want to keep the loneliness that had been his in earlier days. At the time of the return of his son to White Slides Belllounds was rich in cattle and land, but he avowed frankly that he had not saved any money, and probably never would. His hand was always open to every man and he never remembered an obligation. He trusted every one. A proud boast of his was that neither white man nor red man had ever betrayed his trust. His cowboys took advantage of him, his neighbors imposed upon him, but none were there who did not make good their debts of service or stock. Belllounds was one of the great pioneers of the frontier days to whom the West owed its settlement; and he was finer than most, because he proved that the Indians, if not robbed or driven, would respond to friendliness.

Belllounds was not seen at his customary tasks on the day he expected his son. He walked in the fields and around the corrals; he often paced up and down the porch, scanning the horizon below, where the road from Kremmling showed white down the valley; and part of the time he stayed indoors.

It so happened that early in the afternoon he came out in time to see a buckboard, drawn by dust-and-lather-stained horses, pull into the yard. And then he saw his son. Some of the cowboys came running. There were greetings to the driver, who appeared well known to them.

Jack Belllounds did not look at them. He threw a bag out of the buckboard and then clambered down slowly, to go toward the porch.

"Wal, Jack—-my son—I'm sure glad you're back home," said the old rancher, striding forward. His voice was deep and full, singularly rich. But that was the only sign of feeling he showed.

"Howdy—dad!" replied the son, not heartily, as he put out his hand to his father's.

Jack Belllounds's form was tall, with a promise of his father's bulk. But he did not walk erect; he slouched a little. His face was pale, showing he had not of late been used to sun and wind. Any stranger would have seen the resemblance of boy to man would have granted the handsome boldness, but denied the strength. The lower part of Jack Belllounds's face was weak.

The constraint of this meeting was manifest mostly in the manner of the son. He looked ashamed, almost sullen. But if he had been under the influence of liquor at Kremmling, as reported the day before, he had entirely recovered.

"Come on in," said the rancher.

When they got into the big living-room, and Belllounds had closed the doors, the son threw down his baggage and faced his father aggressively.

"Do they all know where I've been?" he asked, bitterly. Broken pride and shame flamed in his face.

"Nobody knows. The secret's been kept." replied Belllounds.

Amaze and relief transformed the young man. "Aw, now, I'm—glad—" he exclaimed, and he sat down, half covering his face with shaking hands.

"Jack, we'll start over," said Belllounds, earnestly, and his big eyes shone with a warm and beautiful light. "Right hyar. We'll never speak of where you've been these three years. Never again!"

Jack gazed up, then, with all the sullenness and shadow gone.

"Father, you were wrong about—doing me good. It's done me harm. But now, if nobody knows—why, I'll try to forget it."

"Mebbe I blundered," replied Belllounds, pathetically. "Yet, God knows I meant well. You sure were— But thet's enough palaver.... You'll go to work as foreman of White Slides. An' if you make a success of it I'll be only too glad to have you boss the ranch. I'm gettin' along in years, son. An' the last year has made me poorer. Hyar's a fine range, but I've less stock this year than last. There's been some rustlin' of cattle, an' a big loss from wolves an' lions an' poison-weed.... What d'you say, son?"

"I'll run White Slides," replied Jack, with a wave of his hand. "I hadn't hoped for such a chance. But it's due me. Who's in the outfit I know?"

"Reckon no one, except Wils Moore."

"Is that cowboy here yet? I don't want him."

"Wal, I'll put him to chasin' varmints with the hounds. An' say, son, this outfit is bad. You savvy—it's bad. You can't run that bunch. The only way you can handle them is to get up early an' come back late. Sayin' little, but sawin' wood. Hard work."

Jack Belllounds did not evince any sign of assimilating the seriousness of his father's words.

"I'll show them," he said. "They'll find out who's boss. Oh, I'm aching to get into boots and ride and tear around."

Belllounds stroked his grizzled beard and regarded his son with mingled pride and doubt. Not at this moment, most assuredly, could he get away from the wonderful fact that his only son was home.

"Thet's all right, son. But you've been off the range fer three years. You'll need advice. Now listen. Be gentle with hosses. You used to be mean with a hoss. Some cowboys jam their hosses around an' make 'em pitch an' bite. But it ain't the best way. A hoss has got sense. I've some fine stock, an' don't want it spoiled. An' be easy an' quiet with the boys. It's hard to get help these days. I'm short on hands now.... You'd do best, son, to stick to your dad's ways with hosses an' men."

"Dad, I've seen you kick horses an' shoot at men" replied Jack.

"Right, you have. But them was particular bad cases. I'm not advisin' thet way. . . . Son, it's close to my heart—this hope I have thet you'll—"

The full voice quavered and broke. It would indeed have been a hardened youth who could not have felt something of the deep and unutterable affection in the old man. Jack Belllounds put an arm around his father's shoulder.

"Dad, I'll make you proud of me yet. Give me a chance. And don't be sore if I can't do wonders right at first."

"Son, you shall have every chance. An' thet reminds me. Do you remember Columbine?"

"I should say so," replied Jack, eagerly. "They spoke of her in Kremmling. Where is she?"

"I reckon somewheres about. Jack, you an' Columbine are to marry."

"Marry! Columbine and me?" he ejaculated.

"Yes. You're my son an' she's my adopted daughter. I won't split my property. An' it's right she had a share. A fine, strong, quiet, pretty lass, Jack, an' she'll make a good wife. I've set my heart on the idee."

"But Columbine always hated me."

"Wal, she was a kid then an' you teased her. Now she's a woman, an' willin' to please me. Jack, you'll not buck ag'in' this deal?"

"That depends," replied Jack. "I'd marry 'most any girl you wanted me to. But if Columbine were to flout me as she used to—why, I'd buck sure enough. . . . Dad, are you sure she knows nothing, suspects nothing of where you—you sent me?"

"Son, I swear she doesn't."

"Do you mean you'd want us to marry soon?"

"Wal, yes, as soon as Collie would think reasonable. Jack, she's shy an' strange, an' deep, too. If you ever win her heart you'll be richer than if you owned all the gold in the Rockies. I'd say go slow. But contrariwise, it'd mebbe be surer to steady you, keep you home, if you married right off."

"Married right off!" echoed Jack, with a laugh. "It's like a story. But wait till I see her."

At that very moment Columbine was sitting on the topmost log of a high corral, deeply interested in the scene before her.

Two cowboys were in the corral with a saddled mustang. One of them carried a canvas sack containing tools and horseshoes. As he dropped it with a metallic clink the mustang snorted and jumped and rolled the whites of his eyes. He knew what that clink meant.

"Miss Collie, air you-all goin' to sit up thar?" inquired the taller cowboy, a lean, supple, and powerful fellow, with a rough, red-blue face, hard as a rock, and steady, bright eyes.

"I sure am, Jim," she replied, imperturbably.

"But we've gotta hawg-tie him," protested the cowboy.

"Yes, I know. And you're going to be gentle about it."

Jim scratched his sandy head and looked at his comrade, a little gnarled fellow, like the bleached root of a tree. He seemed all legs.

"You hear, you Wyomin' galoot," he said to Jim. "Them shoes goes on Whang right gentle."

Jim grinned, and turned to speak to his mustang. "Whang, the law's laid down an' we wanta see how much hoss sense you hev."

The shaggy mustang did not appear to be favorably impressed by this speech. It was a mighty distrustful look he bent upon the speaker.

"Jim, seein' as how this here job's aboot the last Miss Collie will ever boss us on, we gotta do it without Whang turnin' a hair," drawled the other cowboy.

"Lem, why is this the last job I'll ever boss you boys?" demanded Columbine, quickly.

Jim gazed quizzically at her, and Lem assumed that blank, innocent face Columbine always associated with cowboy deviltry.

"Wal, Miss Collie, we reckon the new boss of White Slides rode in to-day."

"You mean Jack Belllounds came home," said Columbine. "Well, I'll boss you boys the same as always."

"Thet'd be mighty fine for us, but I'm feared it ain't writ in the fatal history of White Slides," replied Jim.

"Buster Jack will run over the ole man an' marry you," added Lem.

"Oh, so that's your idea," rejoined Columbine, lightly. "Well, if such a thing did come to pass I'd be your boss more than ever."

"I reckon no, Miss Collie, for we'll not be ridin' fer White Slides," said Jim, simply.

Columbine had sensed this very significance long before when the possibility of Buster Jack's return had been rumored. She knew cowboys. As well try to change the rocks of the hills!

"Boys, the day you leave White Slides will be a sad one for me," sighed Columbine.

"Miss Collie, we 'ain't gone yet," put in Lem, with awkward softness. "Jim has long hankered fer Wyomin' an' he jest talks thet way."

Then the cowboys turned to the business in hand. Jim removed the saddle, but left the bridle on. This move, of course, deceived Whang. He had been broken to stand while his bridle hung, and, like a horse that would have been good if given a chance, he obeyed as best he could, shaking in every limb. Jim, apparently to hobble Whang, roped his forelegs together, low down, but suddenly slipped the rope over the knees. Then Whang knew he had been deceived. He snorted fire, let out a scream, and, rearing on his hind legs, he pawed the air savagely. Jim hauled on the rope while Whang screamed and fought with his fore-feet high in the air. Then Jim, with a powerful jerk, pulled Whang down and threw him, while Lem, seizing the bridle, hauled him over on his side and sat upon his head. Whereupon Jim slipped the loop off one front hoof and pulled the other leg back across one of the hind ones, where both were secured by a quick hitch. Then the lasso was wound and looped around front and back hoofs together. When this had been done the mustang was rolled over on his other side, his free front hoof lassoed and pulled back to the hind one, where both were secured, as had been the others. This rendered the mustang powerless, and the shoeing proceeded.

Columbine hated to sit by and watch it, but she

always stuck to her post, when opportunity afforded, because she knew the cowboys would not be brutal while she was there.

"Wal, he'll step high to-morrer," said Lem, as he got up from his seat on the head of Whang.

"Ahuh! An', like a mule, he'll be my friend fer twenty years jest to get a chance to kick me," replied Jim.

For Columbine, the most interesting moment of this incident was when the mustang raised his head to look at his legs, in order to see what had been done to them. There was something almost human in that look. It expressed intelligence and fear and fury.

The cowboys released his legs and let him get up. Whang stamped his iron-shod hoofs.

"It was a mean trick, Whang," said Columbine. "If I owned you that'd never be done to you."

"I reckon you can have him fer the askin'," said Jim, as he threw on the saddle. "Nobody but me can ride him. Do you want to try?"

"Not in these clothes," replied Columbine, laughing.

"Wal, Miss Collie, you're shore dressed up fine to-day, fer some reason or other," said Lem, shaking his head, while he gathered up the tools from the ground.

"Ahuh! An' here comes the reason," exclaimed Jim, in low, hoarse whisper.

Columbine heard the whisper and at the same instant a sharp footfall on the gravel road. She quickly turned, almost losing her balance. And she recognized Jack Belllounds. The boy Buster Jack she remembered so well was approaching, now a young man, taller, heavier, older, with paler face and bolder look. Col-

umbine had feared this meeting, had prepared herself
for it. But all she felt when it came was annoyance at
the fact that he had caught her sitting on top of the
corral fence, with little regard for dignity. It did not
occur to her to jump down. She merely sat straight,
smoothed down her skirt, and waited.

Jim led the mustang out of the corral and Lem
followed. It looked as if they wanted to avoid the young
man, but he prevented that.

"Howdy, boys! I'm Jack Belllounds," he said, rather
loftily. But his manner was nonchalant. He did not offer
to shake hands.

Jim mumbled something, and Lem said, "Hod do."

"That's an ornery-looking bronc," went on Belllounds, and he reached with careless hand for the mustang. Whang jerked so hard that he pulled Jim half over.

"Wal, he ain't a bronc, but I reckon he's all the
rest," drawled Jim.

Both cowboys seemed slow, careless. They were
neither indifferent nor responsive. Columbine saw their
keen, steady glances go over Belllounds. Then she took
a second and less hasty look at him. He wore high-
heeled, fancy-topped boots, tight-fitting trousers of dark
material, a heavy belt with silver buckle, and a white,
soft shirt, with wide collar, open at the neck. He was
bareheaded.

"I'm going to run White Slides," he said to the cowboys. "What're your names?"

Columbine wanted to giggle, which impulse she
smothered. The idea of any one asking Jim his name!
She had never been able to find out.

"My handle is Lemuel Archibawld Billings," replied

Lem, blandly. The middle name was an addition no one had ever heard.

Belllounds then directed his glance and steps toward the girl. The cowboys dropped their heads and shuffled on their way.

"There's only one girl on the ranch," said Belllounds, "so you must be Columbine."

"Yes. And you're Jack," she replied, and slipped off the fence. "I'm glad to welcome you home."

She offered her hand, and he held it until she extricated it. There was genuine surprise and pleasure in his expression.

"Well, I'd never have known you," he said, surveying her from head to foot. "It's funny. I had the clearest picture of you in mind. But you're not at all like I imagined. The Columbine I remember was thin, white-faced, and all eyes."

"It's been a long time. Seven years," she replied. "But I knew you. You're older, taller, bigger, but the same Buster Jack."

"I hope not," he said, frankly condemning that former self. "Dad needs me. He wants me to take charge here—to be a man. I'm back now. It's good to be home. I never was worth much. Lord! I hope I don't disappoint him again."

"I hope so, too," she murmured. To hear him talk frankly, seriously, like this counteracted the unfavorable impression she had received. He seemed earnest. He looked down at the ground, where he was pushing little pebbles with the toe of his boot. She had a good opportunity to study his face, and availed herself of it. He did look like his father, with his big, handsome head,

and his blue eyes, bolder perhaps from their promi-
nence than from any direct gaze or fire. His face was
pale, and shadowed by worry or discontent. It seemed
as though a repressed character showed there. His
mouth and chin were undisciplined. Columbine could
not imagine that she despised anything she saw in the
features of this young man. Yet there was something
about him that held her aloof. She had made up her
mind to do her part unselfishly. She would find the best
in him, like him for it, be strong to endure and to help.
Yet she had no power to control her vague and strange
perceptions. Why was it that she could not feel in him
what she liked in Jim Montana or Lem or Wilson Moore?

"This was my second long stay away from home,"
said Belllounds. "The first was when I went to school
in Kansas City. I liked that. I was sorry when they turned
me out—sent me home. . . . But the last three years were
hell."

His face worked, and a shade of dark blood rippled
over it.

"Did you work?" queried Columbine.

"Work! It was worse than work. . . . Sure I worked,"
he replied.

Columbine's sharp glance sought his hands. They
looked as soft and unscarred as her own. What kind of
work had he done, if he told the truth?

"Well, if you work hard for dad, learn to handle the
cowboys, and never take up those old bad habits—"

"You mean drink and cards? I swear I'd forgotten
them for three years—until yesterday. I reckon I've the
better of them."

"Then you'll make dad and me happy. You'll be happy, too."

Columbine thrilled at the touch of fineness coming out in him. There was good in him, whatever the mad, wild pranks of his boyhood.

"Dad wants us to marry," he said, suddenly, with shyness and a strange, amused smile. "Isn't that funny? You and me—who used to fight like cat and dog! Do you remember the time I pushed you into the old mud-hole? And you lay in wait for me, behind the house, to hit me with a rotten cabbage?"

"Yes, I remember," replied Columbine, dreamily. "It seems so long ago."

"And the time you ate my pie, and how I got even by tearing off your little dress, so you had to run home almost without a stitch on?"

"Guess I've forgotten that," replied Columbine, with a blush. "I must have been very little then."

"You were a little devil.... Do you remember the fight I had with Moore—about you?"

She did not answer, for she disliked the fleeting expression that crossed his face. He remembered too well.

"I'll settle that score with Moore," he went on. "Besides, I won't have him on the ranch."

"Dad needs good hands," she said, with her eyes on the gray sage slopes. Mention of Wilson Moore augmented the aloofness in her. An annoyance pricked along her veins.

"Before we get any farther I'd like to know something. Has Moore ever made love to you?"

Columbine felt that prickling augment to a hot,

sharp wave of blood. Why was she at the mercy of strange, quick, unfamiliar sensations? Why did she hesitate over that natural query from Jack Belllounds?

"No. He never has," she replied, presently.

"That's damn queer. You used to like him better than anybody else. You sure hated me....Columbine, have you outgrown that?"

"Yes, of course," she answered. "But I hardly hated you."

"Dad said you were willing to marry me. Is that so?"

Columbine dropped her head. His question, kindly put, did not affront her, for it had been expected. But his actual presence, the meaning of his words, stirred in her an unutterable spirit of protest. She had already in her will consented to the demand of the old man; she was learning now, however, that she could not force her flesh to consent to a surrender it did not desire.

"Yes, I'm willing," she replied, bravely.

"Soon?" he flashed, with an eager difference in his voice.

"If I had my way it'd not be—too soon," she faltered. Her downcast eyes had seen the stride he had made closer to her, and she wanted to run.

"Why? Dad thinks it'd be good for me," went on Belllounds, now, with strong, self-centered thought. "It'd give me responsibility. I reckon I need it. Why not soon?"

"Wouldn't it be better to wait awhile?" she asked. "We do not know each other—let alone care—"

"Columbine, I've fallen in love with you." he declared, hotly.

"Oh, how could you!" cried Columbine, incredulously.

"Why, I always was moony over you—when we were kids," he said. "And now to meet you grown up like this—so pretty and sweet—such a—a healthy, blooming girl....And dad's word that you'd be my wife soon—*mine*—why, I just went off my head at sight of you."

Columbine looked up at him and was reminded of how, as a boy, he had always taken a quick, passionate longing for things he must and would have. And his father had not denied him. It might really be that Jack had suddenly fallen in love with her.

"Would you want to take me without my—my love?" she asked, very low. "I don't love you now. I might some time, if you were good—if you made dad happy—if you conquered—"

"Take you! I'd take you if you—if you hated me," he replied, now in the grip of passion.

"I'll tell dad how I feel," she said, faintly, "and—and marry you when he says."

He kissed her, would have embraced her had she not put him back.

"Don't! Some—some one will see."

"Columbine, we're engaged," he asserted, with a laugh of possession. "Say, you needn't look so white and scared. I won't eat you. But I'd like to....Oh, you're a sweet girl! Here I was hating to come home. And look at my luck!"

Then with a sudden change, that seemed significant of his character, he lost his ardor, dropped the half-bold, half-masterful air, and showed the softer side.

"Collie, I never was any good," he said. "But I want to be better. I'll prove it. I'll make a clean breast of everything. I won't marry you with any secret between us. You might find out afterward and hate me....Do you have any idea where I've been these last three years?"

"No," answered Columbine.

"I'll tell you right now. But you must promise never to mention it to any one—or throw it up to me—ever."

He spoke hoarsely, and had grown quite white. Suddenly Columbine thought of Wilson Moore! He had known where Jack had spent those years. He had resisted a strong temptation to tell her. That was as noble in him as the implication of Jack's whereabouts had been base.

"Jack, that is big of you," she replied, hurriedly. "I respect you—like you for it. But you needn't tell me. I'd rather you didn't. I'll take the will for the deed."

Belllounds evidently experienced a poignant shock of amaze, of relief, of wonder, of gratitude. In an instant he seemed transformed.

"Collie, if I hadn't loved you before I'd love you now. That was going to be the hardest job I ever had— to tell you my—my story. I meant it. And now I'll not have to feel your shame for me and I'll not feel I'm a cheat or a liar....But I will tell you this—if you love me you'll make a man of me!"

CHAPTER 3

*T*HE rancher thought it best to wait till after the roundup before he turned over the foremanship to his son. This was wise, but Jack did not see it that way. He showed that his old, intolerant spirit had, if anything, grown during his absence. Belllounds patiently argued with him, explaining what certainly should have been clear to a young man brought up in Colorado. The fall round-up was the most important time of the year, and during the strenuous drive the appointed foreman should have absolute control. Jack gave in finally with a bad grace.

It was unfortunate that he went directly from his father's presence out to the corrals. Some of the cowboys who had ridden all the day before and stood guard all night had just come in. They were begrimed with dust, weary, and sleepy-eyed.

"This hyar outfit won't see my tracks no more," said one, disgustedly. "I never kicked on doin' two men's work. But when it comes to rustlin' day and night, all the time, I'm a-goin' to pass."

"Turn in, boys, and sleep till we get back with the chuck-wagon," said Wilson Moore. "We'll clean up that bunch to-day."

"Ain't you tired, Wils?" queried Bludsoe, a squat, bowlegged cowpuncher who appeared to be crippled or very lame.

"Me? Naw!" grunted Moore, derisively. "Blud, you sure ask fool questions.... Why, you——mahogany-colored, stump-legged, biped of a cowpuncher, I've had three hours' sleep in four nights!"

"What's a biped?" asked Bludsoe, dubiously.

Nobody enlightened him.

"Wils, you-all air the only eddicated cowman I ever loved, but I'm a son-of-a-gun if we ain't agoin' to come to blows some day," declared Bludsoe.

"He shore can sling English," drawled Lem Billings. "I reckon he swallowed a dictionary onct."

"Wal, he can sling a rope, too, an' thet evens up," added Jim Montana.

Just at this moment Jack Belllounds appeared upon the scene. The cowboys took no notice of him. Jim was bandaging a leg of his horse; Bludsoe was wearily gathering up his saddle and trappings; Lem was giving his tired mustang a parting slap that meant much. Moore evidently awaited a fresh mount. A Mexican lad had come in out of the pasture leading several horses, one of which was the mottled white mustang that Moore rode most of the time.

Belllounds lounged forward with interest as Moore whistled, and the mustang showed his pleasure. Manifestly he did not like the Mexican boy and he did like Moore.

"Spottie, it's drag yearlings around for you to-day," said the cowboy, as he caught the mustang. Spottie tossed his head and stepped high until the bridle was on. When the saddle was thrown and strapped in place the mustang showed to advantage. He was beautiful, but not too graceful or sleek or fine-pointed or prancing to prejudice any cowboy against his qualities for work.

Jack Belllounds admiringly walked all around the mustang, a little too close to please Spottie.

"Moore, he's a fair-to-middling horse," said Belllounds, with the air of judge of horseflesh. "What's his name?"

"Spottie," replied Moore, shortly, as he made ready to mount.

"Hold on, will you!" ordered Jack, peremptorily. "I like this horse. I want to look him over."

When he grasped the bridle-reins out of the cowboy's hand Spottie jumped as if he had been shot at. Belllounds jerked at him and went closer. The mustang reared, snorting, plunging to get loose. Then Jack Belllounds showed the sudden temper for which he was noted. Red stained his pale cheeks.

"Damn you—come down!" he shouted, infuriated at the mustang, and with both hands he gave a powerful lunge. Spottie came down, and stood there, trembling all over, his ears laid back, his eyes showing fright and pain. Blood dripped from his mouth where the bit had cut him.

"I'll teach you to stand," said Belllounds, darkly. "Moore, lend me your spurs. I want to try him out."

"I don't lend my spurs—or my horse, either," replied the cowboy, quietly, with a stride that put him within reach of Spottie.

The other cowboys had dropped their trappings and stood at attention, with intent gaze and mute lips.

"Is he your horse?" demanded Jack, with a quick flush.

"I reckon so," replied Moore, slowly. "No one but me ever rode him."

"Does my father own him or do you own him?"

"Well, if that's the way you figure—he belongs to White Slides," returned the cowboy. "I never bought him. I only raised him from a colt, broke him, and rode him."

"I thought so. Moore, he's mine, and I'm going to ride him now. Lend me spurs, one of you cowpunchers."

Nobody made any motion to comply. There seemed to be a suspense at hand that escaped Belllounds.

"I'll ride him without spurs," he declared, presently, and again he turned to mount the mustang.

"Belllounds, it'd be better for you not to ride him now," said Moore, coolly.

"Why, I'd like to know?" demanded Belllounds, with the temper of one who did not tolerate opposition.

"He's the only horse left for me to ride," answered the cowboy. "We're branding to-day. Hudson was hurt yesterday. He was foreman, and he appointed me to fill his place. I've got to rope yearlings. Now, if you get up on Spottie you'll excite him. He's high-strung, nervous.

That'll be bad for him, as he hates cutting-out and roping."

The reasonableness of this argument was lost upon Belllounds.

"Moore, maybe it'd interest you to know that I'm foreman of White Slides," he asserted, not without loftiness.

His speech manifestly decided something vital for the cowboy.

"Ahuh!....I'm sure interested this minute," replied Moore, and then, stepping to the side of the mustang, with swift hands he unbuckled the cinch, and with one sweep he drew saddle and blanket to the ground.

The action surprised Belllounds. He stared. There seemed something boyish in his lack of comprehension. Then his temper flamed.

"What do you mean by that?" he demanded, with a strident note in his voice. "Put that saddle back."

"Not much. It's my saddle. Cost sixty dollars at Kremmling last year. Good old hard-earned saddle!... And you can't ride it. Savvy?"

"Yes, I savvy," replied Belllounds, violently. "Now you'll savvy what I say. I'll have you discharged."

"Nope. Too late," said Moore, with cool, easy scorn. "I figured that. And I quit a minute ago—when you showed what little regard you had for a horse."

"You quit!...Well, it's damned good riddance. I wouldn't have you in the outfit."

"You couldn't have kept me, Buster Jack."

The epithet must have been an insult to Belllounds. "Don't you dare call me that," he burst out, furiously.

Moore pretended surprise. "Why not? It's your

range name. We all get a handle, whether we like it or not. There's Montana and Blud and Lemme Two Bits. They call me Professor. Why should you kick on yours?"

"I won't stand it now. Not from any one—especially not you."

"Ahuh! Well, I'm afraid it'll stick," replied Moore, with sarcasm. "It sure suits you. Don't you bust everything you monkey with? Your old dad will sure be glad to see you bust the round-up to-day—and I reckon the outfit to-morrow."

"You insolent cowpuncher!" shouted Belllounds, growing beside himself with rage. "If you don't shut up I'll bust your face."

"Shut up! . . . Me? Nope. It can't be did. This is a free country, Buster Jack." There was no denying Moore's cool, stinging repetition of the epithet that had so affronted Belllounds.

"I always hated you!" he rasped out, hoarsely. Striking hard at Moore, he missed, but a second effort landed a glancing blow on the cowboy's face.

Moore staggered back, recovered his balance, and, hitting out shortly, he returned the blow. Belllounds fell against the corral fence, which upheld him.

"Buster Jack—you're crazy!" cried the cowboy, his eyes flashing. "Do you think you can lick me—after where you've been these three years?"

Like a maddened boy Belllounds leaped forward, this time his increased violence and wildness of face expressive of malignant rage. He swung his arms at random. Moore avoided his blows and planted a fist squarely on his adversary's snarling mouth. Belllounds fell with a thump. He got up with clumsy haste, but did not rush forward again. His big, prominent eyes held a dark and ugly look. His lower jaw wabbled as he panted for breath and speech at once.

"Moore—I'll kill—you!" he hissed, with glance flying everywhere for a weapon. From ground to cowboys he looked. Bludsoe was the only one packing a gun. Belllounds saw it, and he was so swift in bounding forward that he got a hand on it before Bludsoe could prevent.

"Let go! Give me—that gun! By God! I'll fix him!" yelled Belllounds, as Bludsoe grappled with him.

There was a sharp struggle. Bludsoe wrenched the other's hands free, and, pulling the gun, he essayed to throw it. But Belllounds blocked his action and the gun fell at their feet.

"Grab it!" sang out Bludsoe, ringingly. "Quick, somebody! The damned fool'll kill Wils."

Lem, running in, kicked the gun just as Belllounds reached for it. When it rolled against the fence Jim was there to secure it. Lem likewise grappled with the struggling Belllounds.

"Hyar, you Jack Belllounds," said Lem, "couldn't you see Wils wasn't packin' no gun? A-r'arin' like thet! ...Stop your rantin' or we'll sure handle you rough."

"The old man's comin'," called Jim, warningly.

The rancher appeared. He strode swiftly, ponderously. His gray hair waved. His look was as stern as that of an eagle.

"What the hell's goin' on?" he roared.

The cowboys released Jack. That worthy, sullen and downcast, muttering to himself, stalked for the house.

"Jack, stand your ground," called old Belllounds.

But the son gave no heed. Once he looked back over his shoulder, and his dark glance saw no one save Moore.

"Boss, thar's been a little argyment," explained Jim, as with swift hand he hid Bludsoe's gun. "Nuthin' much."

"Jim, you're a liar," replied the old rancher.

"Aw!" exclaimed Jim, crestfallen.

"What're you hidin'? . . . You've got somethin' there. Gimme thet gun."

Without more ado Jim handed the gun over.

"It's mine, boss," put in Bludsoe.

"Ahuh? Wal, what was Jim hidin' it fer?" demanded Belllounds.

"Why, I jest tossed it to him—when I—sort of j'ined in with the argyment. We was tusslin' some an' I didn't want no gun."

How characteristic of cowboys that they lied to shield Jack Belllounds! But it was futile to attempt to deceive the old rancher. Here was a man who had been forty years dealing with all kinds of men and events.

"Bludsoe, you can't fool me," said old Bill, calmly. He had roared at them, and his eyes still flashed like blue fire, but he was calm and cool. Returning the gun to its owner, he continued: "I reckon you'd spare my feelin's an' lie about some trick of Jack's. Did he bust out?"

"Wal, tolerable like," replied Bludsoe, dryly.

"Ahuh! Tell me, then—an' no lies."

Belllounds's shrewd eyes had rested upon Wilson Moore. The cowboy's face showed the red marks of battle and the white of passion.

"I'm not going to lie, you can bet on that," he declared, forcefully.

"Ahuh! I might hev knowed you an' Jack'd clash," said Belllounds, gruffly. "What happened?"

"He hurt my horse. If it hadn't been for that there'd been no trouble."

A light leaped up in the old man's bold eyes. He was a lover of horses. Many hard words, and blows, too, he had dealt cowboys for being brutal.

"What'd he do?"

"Look at Spottie's mouth."

The rancher's way of approaching a horse was singularly different from his son's, notwithstanding the fact that Spottie knew him and showed no uneasiness. The examination took only a moment.

"Tongue cut bad. Thet's a damn shame. Take thet bridle off.... There. If it'd been an ornery hoss, now.... Moore, how'd this happen?"

"We just rode in," replied Wilson, hurriedly. "I was saddling Spottie when Jack came up. He took a shine to the mustang and wanted to ride him. When Spottie reared—he's shy with strangers—why, Jack gave a hell of a jerk on the bridle. The bit cut Spottie.... Well, that made me mad, but I held in. I objected to Jack riding Spottie. You see, Hudson was hurt yesterday and he appointed me foreman for to-day. I needed Spottie. But your son couldn't see it, and that made me sore. Jack said the mustang was his—"

"His?" interrupted Belllounds.

"Yes. He claimed Spottie. Well, he wasn't really mine, so I gave in. When I threw off the saddle, which *was* mine, Jack began to roar. He said he was foreman and he'd have me discharged. But I said I'd quit already. We both kept getting sorer and I called him Buster Jack. . . . He hit me first. Then we fought. I reckon I was getting the best of him when he made a dive for Bludsoe's gun. And that's all."

"Boss, as sure as I'm a born cowman," put in Bludsoe, "he'd hev plugged Wils if he'd got my gun. At thet he damn near got it!"

The old man stroked his scant gray beard with his huge, steady hand, apparently not greatly concerned by the disclosure.

"Montana, what do you say?" he queried, as if he held strong store by that quiet cowboy's opinion.

"Wal, boss," replied Jim, reluctantly, "Buster Jack's temper was bad onct, but now it's plumb wuss."

Whereupon Belllounds turned to Moore with a gesture and a look of a man who, in justice to something in himself, had to speak.

"Wils, it's onlucky you clashed with Jack right off," he said. "But thet was to be expected. I reckon Jack was in the wrong. Thet hoss was yours by all a cowboy holds right an' square. Mebbe by law Spottie belonged to White Slides Ranch—to me. But he's yours now, fer I give him to you."

"Much obliged, Belllounds. I sure do appreciate that," replied Moore, warmly. "It's what anybody 'd gamble Bill Belllounds would do."

"Ahuh! An' I'd take it as a favor if you'd stay on to-day an' get thet brandin' done."

"All right, I'll do that for you," replied Moore. "Lem, I guess you won't get your sleep till to-night. Come on."

"Aw!" sighed Lem, as he picked up his bridle.

*   *   *

Late that afternoon Columbine sat upon the porch, watching the sunset. It had been a quiet day for her, mostly indoors. Once only had she seen Jack, and then he was riding by toward the pasture, whirling a lasso round his head. Jack could ride like one born to the range, but he was not an adept in the use of a rope. Nor had Columbine seen the old rancher since breakfast. She had heard his footsteps, however, pacing slowly up and down his room.

She was watching the last rays of the setting sun rimming with gold the ramparts of the mountain eastward, and burning a crown for Old White Slides peak. A distant bawl and bellow of cattle had died away. The branding was over for that fall. How glad she felt! The wind, beginning to grow cold as the sun declined, cooled her hot face. In the solitude of her room Columbine had cried enough that day to scald her cheeks.

Presently, down the lane between the pastures, she saw a cowboy ride into view. Very slowly he came, leading another horse. Columbine recognized Lem a second before she saw that he was leading Pronto. That struck her as strange. Another glance showed Pronto to be limping. Apparently he could just get along, and that was all. Columbine ran out in dismay, reaching the corral gate before Lem did. At first she had eyes only for her beloved mustang.

"Oh, Lem—Pronto's hurt!" she cried.

"Wal, I should smile he is," replied Lem.

But Lem was not smiling. And when he wore a serious face for Columbine something had indeed happened. The cowboy was the color of dust and so tired that he reeled.

"Lem, he's all bloody!" exclaimed Columbine, as she ran toward Pronto.

"Hyar, you jest wait," ordered Lem, testily. "Pronto's all cut up, an' you gotta hustle some linen an' salve."

Columbine flew away to do his bidding, and so quick and violent was she that when she got back to the corral she was out of breath. Pronto whinnied as she fell, panting, on her knees beside Lem, who was examining bloody gashes on the legs of the mustang.

"Wal, I reckon no great harm did," said Lem, with relief. "But he shore hed a close shave. Now you help me doctor him up."

"Yes—I'll help," panted Columbine. "I've done this kind—of thing often—but never—to Pronto.... Oh, I was afraid—he'd been gored by a steer."

"Wal, he come damn near bein'," replied Lem, grimly. "An' if it hedn't been fer ridin' you don't see every day, why thet ornery Texas steer'd hev got him."

"Who was riding? Lem, was it you? Oh, I'll never be able to do enough for you!"

"Wuss luck, it weren't me," said Lem.

"No? Who, then?"

"Wal, it was Wils, an' he made me swear to tell you nuthin'—leastways about him."

"Wils! Did *he* save Pronto? ... And didn't want you to tell me? Lem, something has happened. You're not like yourself."

"Miss Collie, I reckon I'm nigh all in," replied Lem, wearily. "When I git this bandagin' done I'll fall right off my hoss."

"But you're on the ground now, Lem," said Columbine, with a nervous laugh. "What happened?"

"Did you hear about the argyment this mawnin'?"

"No. What—who—"

"You can ask Ole Bill aboot thet. The way Pronto was hurt come off like this. Buster Jack rode out to where we was brandin' an' jumped his hoss over a fence into the pasture. He hed a rope an' he got to chasin' some hosses over thar. One was Pronto, an' the son-of-a-gun somehow did git the noose over Pronto's head. But he couldn't hold it, or didn't want to, fer Pronto broke loose an' jumped the fence. This wasn't so bad as far as it went. But one of them bad steers got after Pronto. He run an' sure stepped on the rope, an' fell. The big steer nearly piled on him. Pronto broke some records then. He shore was scared. Howsoever he picked out rough ground an' run plumb into some dead brush. Reckon thar he got cut up. We was all a good ways off. The steer went bawlin' an' plungin' after Pronto. Wils yelled fer a rifle, but nobody hed one. Nor a six-shooter, either.... I'm goin' back to packin' a gun. Wal, Wils did some ridin' to git over thar in time to save Pronto."

"Lem, that is not all," said Columbine, earnestly, as the cowboy concluded. Her knowledge of the range told her that Lem had narrated nothing so far which could have been cause for his cold, grim, evasive manner; and her woman's intuition divined a catastrophe.

"Nope.... Wil's hoss fell on him."

Lem broke that final news with all a cowboy's bluntness.

"Was he hurt—*Lem!*" cried Columbine.

"Say, Miss Collie," remonstrated Lem, "we're doctorin' up your hoss. You needn't drop everythin' an' grab me like thet. An' you're white as a sheet, too. It ain't nuthin' much fer a cowboy to hev a hoss fall on him."

"Lem Billings, I'll hate you if you don't tell me quick," flashed Columbine, fiercely.

"Ahuh! So thet's how the land lays," replied Lem, shrewdly. "Wal, I'm sorry to tell you thet Wils was bad hurt. Now, not *real* bad! . . . The hoss fell on his leg an' broke it. I cut off his boot. His foot was all smashed. But thar wasn't any other hurt—honest! They're takin' him to Kremmlin'."

"Ah!" Columbine's low cry sounded strangely in her ears, as if some one else had uttered it.

"Buster Jack made two bursts this hyar day," concluded Lem, reflectively. "Miss Collie, I ain't shore how you're regardin' thet individool, but I'm tellin' you this, fer your own good. He's bad medicine. He has his old man's temper thet riles up at nuthin' an' never felt a halter. Wusser'n thet, he's spoiled an' he acts like a colt thet 'd tasted loco. The idee of his ropin' Pronto right thar near the round-up! Any one would think he jest come West. Old Bill is no fool. But he wears blinders when he looks at his son. I'm predictin' bad days fer White Slides Ranch."

ONLY one man at Meeker appeared to be attracted by the news that Rancher Bill Belllounds was offering employment. This was a little cadaverous-looking fellow, apparently neither young nor old, who said his name was Bent Wade. He had drifted into Meeker with two poor horses and a pack.

"Whar you from?" asked the innkeeper, observing how Wade cared for his horses before he thought of himself. The query had to be repeated.

"Cripple Creek. I was cook for some miners an' I panned gold between times," was the reply.

"Humph! Thet oughter been a better-payin' job than any to be hed hereabouts."

"Yes, got big pay there," said Wade, with a sigh.

"What'd you leave fer?"

"We hed a fight over the diggin's an' I was the only one left. I'll tell you...." Whereupon Wade sat down on a box, removed his old sombrero, and began to talk. An idler sauntered over, attracted by something. Then a miner happened by to halt and join the group.

Next, old Kemp, the patriarch of the village, came and listened attentively. Wade seemed to have a strange magnetism, a magic tongue.

He was small of stature, but wiry and muscular. His garments were old, soiled, worn. When he removed the wide-brimmed sombrero he exposed a remarkable face. It was smooth except for a drooping mustache, and pallid, with drops of sweat standing out on the high, broad forehead; gaunt and hollow-cheeked, with an enormous nose, and cavernous eyes set deep under shaggy brows. These features, however, were not so striking in themselves. Long, sloping, almost invisible lines of pain, the shadow of mystery and gloom in the deep-set, dark eyes, a sad harmony between features and expression, these marked the man's face with a record no keen eye could miss.

Wade told a terrible tale of gold and blood and death. It seemed to relieve him. His face changed, and lost what might have been called its tragic light, its driven intensity.

His listeners shook their heads in awe. Hard tales were common in Colorado, but this one was exceptional. Two of the group left without comment. Old Kemp stared with narrow, half-recognizing eyes at the newcomer.

"Wal! Wal!" ejaculated the innkeeper. "It do beat

hell what can happen!...Stranger, will you put up your hosses an' stay?"

"I'm lookin' for work," replied Wade.

It was then that mention was made of Belllounds sending to Meeker for hands.

"Old Bill Belllounds that settled Middle Park an' made friends with the Utes," said Wade, as if certain of his facts.

"Yep, you have Bill to rights. Do you know him?"

"I seen him once twenty years ago."

"Ever been to Middle Park? Belllounds owns ranches there," said the innkeeper.

"He ain't livin' in the Park now," interposed Kemp. "He's at White Slides, I reckon, these last eight or ten years. Thet's over the Gore Range."

"Prospected all through that country," said Wade.

"Wal, it's a fine part of Colorado. Hay an' stock country—too high fer grain. Did you mean you'd been through the Park?"

"Once—long ago," replied Wade, staring with his great, cavernous eyes into space. Some memory of Middle Park haunted him.

"Wal, then, I won't be steerin' you wrong," said the innkeeper. "I like thet country. Some people don't. An' I say if you can cook or pack or punch cows or 'most anythin' you'll find a bunk with Old Bill. I understand he was needin' a hunter most of all. Lions an' wolves bad! Can you hunt?"

"Hey?" queried Wade, absently, as he inclined his ear. "I'm deaf on one side."

"Are you a good man with dogs an' guns?" shouted his questioner.

"Tolerable," replied Wade.

"Then you're sure of a job."

"I'll go. Much obliged to you."

"Not a-tall. I'm doin' Belllounds a favor. Reckon you'll put up here to-night?"

"I always sleep out. But I'll buy feed an' supplies," replied Wade, as he turned to his horses.

Old Kemp trudged down the road, wagging his gray head as if he was contending with a memory sadly failing him. An hour later when Bent Wade rode out of town he passed Kemp, and hailed him. The old-timer suddenly slapped his leg: "By Golly! I knowed I'd met him before!"

Later, he said with a show of gossipy excitement to his friend the innkeeper, "Thet fellar was Bent Wade!"

"So he told me," returned the other.

"But didn't you never hear of him? *Bent Wade?*"

"Now you tax me, thet name do 'pear familiar. But dash take it, I can't remember. I knowed he was somebody, though. Hope I didn't wish a gun-fighter or outlaw on Old Bill. Who was he, anyhow?"

"They call him Hell-Bent Wade. I seen him in Wyomin', whar he were a stage-driver. But I never heerd who he was an' what he was till years after. Thet was onct I dropped down into Boulder. Wade was thar, all shot up, bein' nussed by Sam Coles. Sam's dead now. He was a friend of Wade's an' knowed him fer long. Wal, I heerd all thet anybody ever heerd about him, I reckon. Accordin' to Coles this hyar Hell-Bent Wade was a strange, wonderful sort of fellar. He had the most amazin' ways. He could do anythin' under the sun better 'n any one else. Bad with guns! He never stayed in one place fer long. He never hunted trouble, but trouble follered him. As I remember Coles, thet was Wade's queer idee—he couldn't shake trouble. No matter whar he went, always thar was hell. Thet's what gave him the name Hell-Bent....An' Coles swore thet Wade was the whitest man he ever knew. Heart of gold, he said. Always savin' somebody, helpin' somebody, givin' his money or time—never thinkin' of himself a-tall....When he began to tell thet story about Cripple Creek then my ole head begun to ache with rememberin'. Fer I'd heerd Bent Wade talk before. Jest the same kind of story he told hyar, only wuss. Lordy! but thet fellar has seen times. An' queerest of all is thet idee he has how hell's on his trail an' everywhere he roams it ketches up with him, an' thar he meets the man who's got to hear his tale!"

Sunset found Bent Wade far up the valley of White River under the shadow of the Flat Top Mountains.

It was beautiful country. Grassy hills, with colored aspen groves, swelled up on his left, and across the brawling stream rose a league-long slope of black spruce, above which the bare red-and-gray walls of the range towered, glorious with the blaze of sinking sun. White patches of snow showed in the sheltered nooks. Wade's gaze rested longest on the colored heights.

By and by the narrow valley opened into a park, at the upper end of which stood a log cabin. A few cattle and horses grazed in an inclosed pasture. The trail led by the cabin. As Wade rode up a bushy-haired man came out of the door, rifle in hand. He might have been going out to hunt, but his scrutiny of Wade was that of a lone settler in a wild land.

"Howdy, stranger!" he said.

"Good evenin'," replied Wade. "Reckon you're Blair an' I'm nigh the headwaters of this river?"

"Yep, a matter of three miles to Trapper's Lake."

"My name's Wade. I'm packin' over to take a job with Bill Belllounds."

"Git down an' come in," returned Blair. "Bill's man stopped with me some time ago."

"Obliged, I'm sure, but I'll be goin' on," responded Wade. "Do you happen to have a hunk of deer meat? Game powerful scarce comin' up this valley."

"Lots of deer an' elk higher up. I chased a bunch of more 'n thirty, I reckon, right out of my pasture this mornin'."

Blair crossed to an open shed near by and returned with half a deer haunch, which he tied upon Wade's packhorse.

"My ole woman's ailin'. Do you happen to hev some terbaccer?"

"I sure do—both smokin' an' chewin', an' I can spare more chewin'. A little goes a long ways with me."

"Wal, gimme some of both, most chewin,'" replied Blair, with evident satisfaction.

"You acquainted with Belllounds?" asked Wade, as he handed over the tobacco.

"Wal, yes, everybody knows Bill. You'd never find a whiter boss in these hills."

"Has he any family?"

"Now, I can't say as to thet," replied Blair. "I heerd

he lost a wife years ago. Mebbe he married ag'in. But Bill's gittin' along."

"Good day to you, Blair," said Wade, and took up his bridle.

"Good day an' good luck. Take the right-hand trail. Better trot up a bit, if you want to make camp before dark."

Wade soon entered the spruce forest. Then he came to a shallow, roaring river. The horses drank the water, foaming white and amber around their knees, and then with splash and thump they forded it over the slippery rocks. As they cracked out upon the trail a covey of grouse whirred up into the low branches of spruce-trees. They were tame.

"That's somethin' like," said Wade. "First birds I've seen this fall. Reckon I can have stew any day."

He halted his horse and made a move to dismount, but with his eyes on the grouse he hesitated. "Tame as chickens, an' they sure are pretty."

Then he rode on, leading his pack-horse. The trail was not steep, although in places it had washed out, thus hindering a steady trot. As he progressed the forest grew thick and darker, and the fragrance of pine and spruce filled the air. A dreamy roar of water rushing over rocks rang in the traveler's ears. It receded at times, then grew louder. Presently the forest shade ahead lightened and he rode out into a wide space where green moss and flags and flowers surrounded a wonderful spring-hole. Sunset gleams shone through the trees to color the wide, round pool. It was shallow all along the margin, with a deep, large green hole in the middle, where the water boiled up. Trout were feeding on gnats and playing on the surface, and some big ones left wakes behind them as they sped to deeper water. Wade had an appreciative eye for all this beauty, his gaze lingering longest upon the flowers.

"Wild woods is the place for me," he soliloquized, as the cool wind fanned his cheeks and the sweet tang of evergreen tingled his nostrils. "But sure I'm most haunted in these lonely, silent places."

Bent Wade had the look of a haunted man. Perhaps the consciousness he confessed was part of his secret.

Twilight had come when again he rode out into the open. Trapper's Lake lay before him, a beautiful sheet of water, mirroring the black slopes and the fringed spruces and the flat peaks. Over all its gray, twilight-softened surface showed little swirls and boils and splashes where the myriads of trout were rising. The trail led out over open grassy shores, with a few pines straggling down to the lake, and clumps of spruces raising dark blurs against the background of gleaming lake. Wade heard a sharp crack of hoofs on rock, and he knew he had disturbed deer at their drinking; also he heard a ring of horns on the branch of a tree, and was sure an elk was slipping off through the woods. Across the lake he saw a camp-fire and a pale, sharp-pointed object that was a trapper's tent or an Indian's tepee.

Selecting a camp-site for himself, he unsaddled his horse, threw the pack off the other, and, hobbling both animals, he turned them loose. His roll of bedding, roped in canvas tarpaulin, he threw under a spruce-tree. Then he opened his oxhide-covered packs and laid out utensils and bags, little and big. All his movements were methodical, yet swift, accurate, habitual. He was not thinking about what he was doing. It took him some little time to find a suitable log to split for fire-wood, and when he had started a blaze night had fallen, and the light as it grew and brightened played fantastically upon the isolating shadows.

Lid and pot of the little Dutch oven he threw separately upon the sputtering fire, and while they heated he washed his hands, mixed the biscuits, cut slices of meat off the deer haunch, and put water on to boil. He broiled his meat on the hot, red coals, and laid it near on clean pine chips, while he waited for bread to bake and coffee to boil. The smell of wood-smoke and odorous steam from pots and the fragrance of spruce mingled together, keen, sweet, appetizing. Then he ate his simple meal hungrily, with the content of the man who had fared worse.

After he had satisfied himself he washed his utensils and stowed them away, with the bags. Whereupon his movements acquired less dexterity and speed. The rest hour had come. Still, like the long-experienced man in the open, he looked around for more to do, and his gaze fell upon his weapons, lying on his saddle. His rifle was a Henry—shiny and smooth from long service and care. His small gun was a Colt's .45. It had been carried in a saddle holster. Wade rubbed the rifle with his hands, and then with a greasy rag which he took from the sheath. After that he held the rifle to the heat of the fire. A squall of rain had overtaken him that day, wetting his weapons. A subtle and singular difference seemed to show in the way he took up the Colt's. His action was slow, his look reluctant. The small gun was not merely a thing of steel and powder and ball. He dried it and rubbed it with care, but not with love, and then he stowed it away.

Next Wade unrolled his bed under the spruce, with one end of the tarpaulin resting on the soft mat of needles. On top of that came the two woolly sheepskins, which he used to lie upon, then his blankets, and over all the other end of the tarpaulin.

This ended his tasks for the day. He lighted his pipe and composed himself beside the camp-fire to smoke and rest awhile before going to bed. The silence of the wilderness enfolded lake and shore; yet presently it came to be a silence accentuated by near and distant sounds, faint, wild, lonely—the low hum of falling water, the splash of tiny waves on the shore, the song of insects, and the dismal hoot of owls.

"Bill Belllounds—an' he needs a hunter," soliloquized Bent Wade, with gloomy, penetrating eyes, seeing far through the red embers. "That will suit me an' change my luck, likely. Livin' in the woods, away from people—I could stick to a job like that....But if this White Slides is close to the old trail I'll never stay."

He sighed, and a darker shadow, not from flickering fire, overspread his cadaverous face. Eighteen years ago he had driven the woman he loved away from him, out into the world with her baby girl. Never had he rested beside a camp-fire that that old agony did not recur! Jealous fool! Too late he had discovered his fatal blunder; and then had begun a search over Colorado, ending not a hundred miles across the wild mountains from where he brooded that lonely hour—a search ended by news of the massacre of a wagon-train by Indians.

That was Bent Wade's secret.

And no earthly sufferings could have been crueler than his agony and remorse, as through the long years he wandered on and on. The very good that he tried to do seemed to foment evil. The wisdom that grew out of his suffering opened pitfalls for his wandering feet. The wildness of men and the passion of women somehow waited with incredible fatality for that hour when chance led him into their lives. He had toiled, he had given, he had fought, he had sacrificed, he had killed, he had endured for the human nature which in his savage youth he had betrayed. Yet out of his supreme and endless striving to undo, to make reparation, to give his life, to find God, had come, it seemed to Wade in his abasement, only a driving torment.

But though his thought and emotion fluctuated, varying, wandering, his memory held a fixed and changeless picture of a woman, fair and sweet, with eyes of nameless blue, and face as white as a flower.

"Baby would have been—let's see—'most nineteen years old now—if she'd lived," he said. "A big girl, I reckon, like her mother. . . . Strange how, as I grow older, I remember better!"

The night wind moaned through the spruces; dark clouds scudded across the sky, blotting out the bright stars; a steady, low roar of water came from the outlet of the lake. The camp-fire flickered and burned out, so that no sparks blew into the blackness, and the red embers glowed and paled and crackled. Wade at length got up and made ready for bed. He threw back tarpaulin and blankets, and laid his rifle alongside where he could cover it. His coat served for a pillow and he put the Colt's gun under that; then pulling off his boots, he slipped into bed, dressed as he was, and, like all men in the open, at once fell asleep.

For Wade, and for countless men like him, who for many years had roamed the West, this sleeping alone in wild places held both charm and peril. But the fascination of it was only a vague realization, and the danger was laughed at.

Over Bent Wade's quiet form the shadows played, the spruce boughs waved, the piny needles rustled down, the wind moaned louder as the night advanced. By and by the horses rested from their grazing; the insects ceased to hum; and the continuous roar of water dominated the solitude. If wild animals passed Wade's camp they gave it a wide berth.

Sunrise found Wade on the trail, climbing high up above the lake, making for the pass over the range. He walked, leading his horses up a zigzag trail that bore the tracks of recent travelers. Although this country was sparsely settled, yet there were men always riding from camp to camp or from one valley town to another. Wade never tarried on a well-trodden trail.

As he climbed higher the spruce-trees grew smaller, no longer forming a green aisle before him, and at length they became dwarfed and stunted, and at last failed altogether. Soon he was above timber-line and out upon a flat-topped mountain range, where in both directions the land rolled and dipped, free of tree or shrub, colorful with grass and flowers. The elevation exceeded eleven thousand feet. A whipping wind swept across the plain-land. The sun was pale-bright in the east, slowly being obscured by gray clouds. Snow began to fall, first in scudding, scanty flakes, but increasing until the air was full of a great, fleecy swirl. Wade rode along the rim of a mountain wall, watching a beautiful snow-storm falling into the brown gulf beneath him. Once as he headed round a break he caught sight of mountain-sheep cuddled under a protecting shelf. The snow-squall blew away, like a receding wall, leaving grass and flowers wet. As the dark clouds parted, the sun shone warmer out of the blue. Gray peaks, with patches of white, stood up above their black-timbered slopes.

Wade soon crossed the flat-topped pass over the range and faced a descent, rocky and bare at first, but yielding gradually to the encroachment of green. He left the cold winds and bleak trails above him. In an hour, when he was half down the slope, the forest had become warm and dry, fragrant and still. At length he rode out upon the brow of a last wooded bench above a grassy valley, where a bright, winding stream gleamed in the sun. While the horses rested Wade looked about him. Nature never tired him. If he had any peace it emanated from the silent places, the solemn hills, the flowers and animals of the wild and lonely land.

A few straggling pines shaded this last low hill above the valley. Grass grew luxuriantly there in the open, but not under the trees, where the brown needle-mats jealously obstructed the green. Clusters of columbines waved their graceful, sweet, pale-blue flowers that Wade felt a joy in seeing. He loved flowers—columbines, the glory of Colorado, came first, and next the many-hued purple asters, and then the flaunting spikes of paint-brush, and after them the nameless and numberless wild flowers that decked the mountain meadows and colored the grass of the aspen groves and peeped out of the edge of snow-fields.

"Strange how it seems good to live—when I look at a columbine—or watch a beaver at his work—or listen to the bugle of an elk!" mused Bent Wade. He wondered why, with all his life behind him, he could still find comfort in these things.

Then he rode on his way. The grassy valley, with its winding stream, slowly descended and widened, and left foothill and mountain far behind. Far across a wide plain rose another range, black and bold against the blue. In the afternoon Wade reached Elgeria, a small hamlet, but important by reason of its being on the main stage line, and because here miners and cattlemen bought supplies. It had one street, so wide it appeared to be a square, on which faced a line of bold board houses with high, flat fronts. Wade rode to the inn where the stagecoaches made headquarters. It suited him to feed and rest his horses there, and partake of a meal himself, before resuming his journey.

The proprietor was a stout, pleasant-faced little woman, loquacious and amiable, glad to see a stranger for his own sake rather than from considerations of possible profit. Though Wade had never before visited Elgeria, he soon knew all about the town, and the miners up in the hills, and the only happenings of moment— the arrival and departure of stages.

"Prosperous place," remarked Wade. "I saw that. An' it ought to be growin'."

"Not so prosperous fer me as it uster be," replied the lady. "We did well when my husband was alive, before our competitor come to town. He runs a hotel where miners can drink an' gamble. I don't....But I reckon I've no cause to complain. I live."

"Who runs the other hotel?"

"Man named Smith. Reckon thet's not his real name. I've had people here who—but it ain't no matter."

"Men change their names," replied Wade.

"Stranger, air you packin' through or goin' to stay?"

"On my way to White Slides Ranch, where I'm goin' to work for Belllounds. Do you know him?"

"Know Bill Belllounds? Me? Wal, he's the best friend I ever had when I was at Kremmlin'. I lived there several years. My husband had stock there. In fact, Bill started us in the cattle business. But we got out of there an' come here, where Bob died, an' I've been stuck ever since."

"Everybody has a good word for Belllounds," observed Wade.

"You'll never hear a bad one," replied the woman, with cheerful warmth. "Bill never had but one fault, an' people loved him fer thet."

"What was it?"

"He's got a wild boy thet he thinks the sun rises an' sets in. Buster Jack, they call him. He used to come here often. But Bill sent him away somewhere. The boy was spoiled. I saw his mother years ago—she's dead this long time—an' she was no wife fer Bill Belllounds. Jack took after her. An' Bill was thet woman's slave. When she died all his big heart went to the son, an' thet accounts. Jack will never be any good."

Wade thoughtfully nodded his head, as if he understood, and was pondering other possibilities.

"Is he the only child?"

"There's a girl, but she's not Bill's kin. He adopted her when she was a baby. An' Jack's mother hated this child—jealous, we used to think, because it might grow up an' get some of Bill's money."

"What's the girl's name?" asked Wade.

"Columbine. She was over here last summer with Old Bill. They stayed with me. It was then Bill had hard words with Smith across the street. Bill was resentin' somethin' Smith put in my way. Wal, the lass's the prettiest I ever seen in Colorado, an' as good as she's pretty. Old Bill hinted to me he'd likely make a match between her an' his son Jack. An' I ups an' told him, if Jack hadn't turned over a new leaf when he comes home, thet such a marriage would be tough on Columbine. Whew! but Old Bill was mad. He jest can't stand a word ag'in' thet Buster Jack."

"Columbine Belllounds," mused Wade. "Queer name."

"Oh, I've knowed three girls named Columbine. Don't you know the flower? It's common in these parts. Very delicate, like a sago lily, only paler."

"Were you livin' in Kremmlin' when Belllounds adopted the girl?" asked Wade.

"Laws no!" was the reply. "Thet was long before I come to Middle Park. But I heerd all about it. The baby was found by gold-diggers up in the mountains. Must have got lost from a wagon-train thet Indians set on soon after—so the miners said. Anyway, Old Bill took the baby an' raised her as his own."

"How old is she now?" queried Wade, with a singular change in his tone.

"Columbine's around nineteen."

Bent Wade lowered his head a little, hiding his features under the old, battered, wide-brimmed hat. The amiable innkeeper did not see the tremor that passed over him, nor the slight stiffening that followed, nor the gray pallor of his face. She went on talking until someone called her.

Wade went outdoors, and with bent head walked down the street, across a little river, out into green pasture-land. He struggled with an amazing possibility. Columbine Belllounds might be his own daughter. His heart leaped with joy. But the joy was short-lived. No such hope in this world for Bent Wade! This coincidence, however, left him with a strange, prophetic sense in his soul of a tragedy coming to White Slides Ranch. Wade possessed some power of divination, some strange gift to pierce the veil of the future. But he could not exercise this power at will; it came involuntarily, like a messenger of trouble in the dark night. Moreover, he had never yet been able to draw away from the fascination of this knowledge. It lured him on. Always his decision had been to go on, to meet this boding circumstance, or to remain and meet it, in the hope that he might take some one's burden upon his shoulders. He sensed it now, in the keen, poignant clairvoyance of the moment—the tangle of life that he was about to enter. Old Bill Belllounds, big and fine, victim of love for a wayward son; Buster Jack, the waster, the tearer-down, the destroyer, the wild youth at a wild time; Columbine, the girl of unknown birth, good and loyal, subject to a condition sure to ruin her. Wade's strange mind revolved a hundred outcomes to this conflict of characters, but not one of them was the one that was written. That remained dark. Never had he received so strong a call out of the unknown, nor had he ever felt such intense curiosity. Hope had long been dead in him, except the one that he might atone in some way for the wrong he had done his wife. So the pangs of emotion that recurred, in spite of reason and bitterness, were not recognized by him as lingering hopes. Wade denied the human in him, but he thrilled at the thought of meeting Columbine Belllounds. There was something here beyond all his comprehension.

"It *might*—be true!" he whispered. "I'll know when I see her."

Then he walked back toward the inn. On the way he looked into the barroom of the hotel run by Smith. It was a hard-looking place, half full of idle men, whose faces were as open pages to Bent Wade. Curiosity did not wholly control the impulse that made him wait at the door till he could have a look at the man Smith. Somewhere, at some time, Wade had met most of the veterans of western Colorado. So much he had traveled! But the impulse that held him was answered and explained when Smith came in—a burly man, with an ugly scar marring one eye. Bent Wade recognized Smith. He recognized the scar. For that scar was his own mark, dealt to this man, whose name was not Smith, and who had been as evil as he looked, and whose nomadic life was not due to remorse or love of travel.

Wade passed on without being seen. This recognition meant less to him than it would have ten years ago, as he was not now the kind of man who hunted old enemies for revenge or who went to great lengths to keep out of their way. Men there were in Colorado who would shoot at him on sight. There had been more than one that had shot to his cost.

That night Wade camped in the foothills east of Elgeria, and upon the following day, at sunrise, his horses were breaking the frosty grass and ferns of the timbered range. This he crossed, rode down into a valley where a lonely cabin nestled, and followed an old, blazed trail that wound up the course of a brook. The water was of a color that made rock and sand and moss seem like gold. He saw no signs or tracks of game. A gray jay now and then screeched his approach to un-seen denizens of the woods. The stream babbled past him over mossy ledges, under the dark shade of clumps of spruces, and it grew smaller as he progressed toward its source. At length it was lost in a swale of high, rank grass, and the blazed trail led on through heavy pine woods. At noon he reached the crest of the divide, and, halting upon an open, rocky eminence, he gazed down over a green and black forest, slow-descending to a great irregular park that was his destination for the night.

Wade needed meat, and to that end, as he went on, he kept a sharp lookout for deer, especially after he espied fresh tracks crossing the trail. Slipping along ahead of his horses, that followed him almost too closely to permit of his noiseless approach to game, he hunted all the way down to the great open park without getting a shot.

This park was miles across and miles long, covered with tall, waving grass, and it had straggling arms that led off into the surrounding belt of timber. It sloped gently toward the center, where a round, green acreage of grass gave promise of water. Wade rode toward this, keeping somewhat to the right, as he wanted to camp at the edge of the woods. Soon he rode out beyond one of the projecting peninsulas of forest to find the park spreading wider in that direction. He saw horses grazing with elk, and far down at the notch, where evidently the park had outlet in a narrow valley, he espied the black, hump-shaped, shaggy forms of buffalo. They bobbed off out of sight. Then the elk saw or scented him, and they trotted away, the antlered bulls ahead of the cows. Wade wondered if the horses were wild. They showed great interest, but no fear. Beyond them was a rising piece of ground, covered with pine, and it appeared to stand aloft from the forest on the far side as well as upon that by which he was approaching. Riding a mile or so farther he ascertained that this bit of wooded ground resembled an island in a lake. Presently he saw smoke arising above the treetops.

A tiny brook welled out of the green center of the park and meandered around to pass near the island of pines. Wade saw unmistakable signs of prospecting along this brook, and farther down, where he crossed it, he found tracks made that day.

The elevated plot of ground appeared to be several acres in extent, covered with small-sized pines, and at the far edge there was a little log cabin. Wade expected to surprise a lone prospector at his evening meal. As he rode up a dog ran out of the cabin, barking furiously. A man, dressed in fringed buckskin, followed. He was tall, and had long, iron-gray hair over his shoulders. His bronzed and weather-beaten face was a mass of fine wrinkles where the grizzled hair did not hide them, and his shining, red countenance proclaimed an honest, fearless spirit.

"Howdy, stranger!" he called, as Wade halted several rods distant. His greeting was not welcome, but it was civil. His keen scrutiny, however, attested to more than his speech.

"Evenin', friend," replied Wade. "Might I throw my pack here?"

"Sure. Get down," answered the other. "I calkilate I never seen you in these diggin's."

"No. I'm Bent Wade, an' on my way to White Slides to work for Belllounds."

"Glad to meet you. I'm new hereabouts, myself, but I know Belllounds. My name's Lewis. I was jest cookin' grub. An' it'll burn, too, if I don't rustle. Turn your hosses loose an' come in."

Wade presented himself with something more than his usual methodical action. He smelled buffalo steak, and he was hungry. The cabin had been built years ago, and was a ramshackle shelter at best. The stone fireplace, however, appeared well preserved. A bed of red coals glowed and cracked upon the hearth.

"Reckon I sure smelled buffalo meat," observed Wade, with much satisfaction. "It's long since I chewed a hunk of that."

"All ready. Now pitch in. . . . Yes, thar's some buffalo left in here. Not hunted much. Thar's lots of elk an' herds of deer. After a little snow you'd think a drove of sheep had been trackin' around. An' some bear."

Wade did not waste many words until he had enjoyed that meal. Later, while he helped his host, he recurred to the subject of game.

"If there's so many deer then there's lions an' wolves."

"You bet. I see tracks every day. Had a shot at a lofer not long ago. Missed him. But I reckon thar's more varmints over in the Troublesome country back of White Slides."

"Troublesome! Do they call it that?" asked Wade, with a queer smile.

"Sure. An' it *is* troublesome. Belllounds has been tryin' to hire a hunter. Offered me big wages to kill off the wolves an' lions."

"That's the job I'm goin' to take."

"Good!" exclaimed Lewis. "I'm sure glad. Belllounds is a nice fellar. I felt sort of cheap till I told him I wasn't really a hunter. You see, I'm prospectin' up here, an' pretendin' to be a hunter."

"What do you make that bluff for?" queried Wade. "You couldn't fool any one who'd ever prospected for gold. I saw your signs out here."

"Wal, you've sharp eyes, thet's all. Wade, I've some ondesirable neighbors over here. I'd just as lief they didn't see me diggin' gold. Lately I've had a hunch they're rustlin' cattle. Anyways, they've sold cattle in Kremmlin' thet came from over around Elgeria."

"Wherever there's cattle there's sure to be some stealin'," observed Wade.

"Wal, you needn't say anythin' to Belllounds, because mebbe I'm wrong. An' if I found out I was right I'd go down to White Slides an' tell it myself. Belllounds done me some favors."

"How far to White Slides?" asked Wade, with a puff on his pipe.

"Roundabout trail, an' rough, but you'll make it in one day, easy. Beautiful country. Open, big peaks an' ranges, with valleys an' lakes. Never seen such grass!"

"Did you ever see Belllounds's son?"

"No. Didn't know he hed one. But I seen his gal the fust day I was thar. She was nice to me. I went thar to be fixed up a bit. Nearly chopped my hand off. The gal— Columbine, she's called—doctored me up. Fact is, I owe considerable to thet White Slides Ranch. There's a cowboy, Wils somethin', who rode up here with some medicine fer me—some they didn't have when I was thar. You'll like thet boy. I seen he was sweet on the gal an' I sure couldn't blame him."

Bent Wade removed his pipe and let out a strange laugh, significant with its little note of grim confirmation.

"What's funny about thet?" demanded Lewis, rather surprised.

"I was only laughin'," replied Wade. "What you said about the cowboy bein' sweet on the girl popped into my head before you told it. Well, boys will be boys. I was young once an' had my day."

Lewis grunted as he bent over to lift a red coal to light his pipe, and as he raised his head he gave Wade a glance of sympathetic curiosity.

"Wal, I hope I'll see more of you," he said, as his guest rose, evidently to go.

"Reckon you will, as I'll be chasin' hounds all over. An' I want a look at them neighbors you spoke of that might be rustlers. . . . I'll turn in now. Good night."

CHAPTER
5

*B*ENT WADE rode out of the forest to look down upon the White Slides country at the hour when it was most beautiful.

"Never seen the beat of that!" he exclaimed, as he halted.

The hour was sunset, with the golden rays and shadows streaking ahead of him down the rolling sage hills, all rosy and gray with rich, strange softness. Groves of aspens stood isolated from one another—here crowning a hill with blazing yellow, and there fringing the brow of another with gleaming gold, and lower down reflecting the sunlight with brilliant red and purple. The valley seemed filled with a delicate haze, almost like smoke. White Slides Ranch was hidden from sight, as it lay in the bottomland. The gray old peak towered proud and aloof, clear-cut and sunset-flushed against the blue. The eastern slope of the valley was a vast sweep of sage and hill and grassy bench and aspen bench, on fire with the colors of autumn made molten by the last flashing of the sun. Great black slopes of forest gave sharp contrast, and led up to the red-walled ramparts of the mountain range.

Wade watched the scene until the fire faded, the golden shafts paled and died, the rosy glow on sage changed to cold steel gray. Then he rode out upon the foothills. The trail led up and down slopes of sage. Grass grew thicker as he descended. Once he startled a great flock of prairie-chickens, or sage-hens, large gray birds, lumbering-swift fliers, that whirred up, and soon plumped down again into the sage. Twilight found him on a last long slope of the foothills, facing the pasture-land of the valley, with the ranch still five miles distant, now showing misty and dim in the gathering shadows.

Wade made camp where a brook ran near an aspen thicket. He had no desire to hurry to meet events at White Slides Ranch, although he longed to see this girl that belonged to Belllounds. Night settled down over the quiet foothills. A pack of roving coyotes visited Wade, and sat in a half-circle in the shadows back of the campfire. They howled and barked. Nevertheless sleep visited Wade's tired eyelids the moment he lay down and closed them.

Next morning, rather late, Wade rode down to White Slides Ranch. It looked to him like the property of a rich rancher who held to the old and proven customs of his generation. The corrals were new, but their style was old. Wade reflected that it would be hard for rustlers or horse-thieves to steal out of those corrals. A long lane led from the pasture-land, following the brook that ran through the corrals and by the back door of the rambling, comfortable-looking cabin. A cowboy was leading horses across a wide square between the main ranch-house and a cluster of cabins and sheds. He saw the visitor and waited.

"Mornin'," said Wade, as he rode up.

"Hod do," replied the cowboy.

Then these two eyed each other, not curiously nor suspiciously, but with that steady, measuring gaze common to Western men.

"My name's Wade," said the traveler. "Come from Meeker way. I'm lookin' for a job with Belllounds."

"I'm Lem Billings," replied the other. "Ridin' fer White Slides fer years. Reckon the boss 'll be glad to take you on."

"Is he around?"

"Sure. I jest seen him," replied Billings, as he haltered his horses to a post. "I reckon I ought to give you a hunch."

"I'd take that as a favor."

"Wal, we're short of hands," said the cowboy. "Jest got the round-up over. Hudson was hurt an' Wils Moore got crippled. Then the boss's son has been put on as foreman. Three of the boys quit. Couldn't stand him. This hyar son of Belllounds is a son-of-a-gun! Me an' pards of mine, Montana an' Bludsoe, are stickin' on— wal, fer reasons thet ain't egzactly love fer the boss. But Old Bill's the best of bosses.... Now the hunch is—thet if you git on hyar you'll hev to do two or three men's work."

"Much obliged," replied Wade. "I don't shy at that."

"Wal, git down an' come in," added Billings, heartily.

He led the way across the square, around the corner of the ranch-house, and up on a long porch, where the arrangement of chairs and blankets attested to the hand of a woman. The first door was open, and from it issued voices; first a shrill, petulant boy's complaint, and then a man's deep, slow, patient reply.

Lem Billings knocked on the door-jamb.

"Wal, what's wanted?" called Belllounds.

"Boss, thar's a man wantin' to see you," replied Lem.

Heavy steps approached the doorway and it was filled with the large figure of the rancher. Wade remembered Belllounds and saw only a gray difference in years.

"Good mornin', Lem, an' good mornin' to you, stranger," was the rancher's greeting, his bold, blue glance, honest and frank and keen, with all his long experience of men, taking Wade in with one flash.

Lem discreetly walked to the end of the porch as another figure, that of the son who resembled the father, filled the doorway, with eyes less kind, bent upon the visitor.

"My name's Wade. I'm over from Meeker way, hopin' to find a job with you," said Wade.

"Glad to meet you," replied Belllounds, extending his huge hand to shake Wade's. "I need you, sure bad. What's your special brand of work?"

"I reckon any kind."

"Set down, stranger," replied Belllounds, pulling up a chair. He seated himself on a bench and leaned against the log wall. "Now, when a boy comes an' says he can do anythin', why I jest haw! haw! at him. But you're a man, Wade, an' one as has been there. Now I'm hard put fer hands. Jest speak out now fer yourself. No one else can speak fer you, thet's sure. An' this is bizness."

"Any work with stock, from punchin' steers to doctorin' horses," replied Wade, quietly. "Am fair carpenter an' mason. Good packer. Know farmin'. Can milk cows an' make butter. I've been cook in many outfits. Read an' write an' not bad at figures. Can do work on saddles an' harness, an—"

"Hold on!" yelled Belllounds, with a hearty laugh. "I ain't imposin' on no man, no matter how I need help. You're sure a jack of all range trades. An' I wish you was a hunter."

"I was comin' to that. You didn't give me time."

"Say, do you know hounds?" queried Belllounds, eagerly.

"Yes. Was raised where everybody had packs. I'm from Kentucky. An' I've run hounds off an' on for years. I'll tell you—"

Belllounds interrupted Wade.

"By all that's lucky! An' last, can you handle guns? We'ain't had a good shot on this range fer Lord knows how long. I used to hit plumb center with a rifle. My eyes are pore now. An' my son can't hit a flock of haystacks. An' the cowpunchers are 'most as bad. Sometimes right hyar where you could hit elk with a club we're out of fresh meat."

"Yes, I can handle guns," replied Wade, with a quiet

smile and a lowering of his head. "Reckon you didn't catch my name."

"Wal—no, I didn't," slowly replied Belllounds, and his pause, with the keener look he bestowed upon Wade, told how the latter's query had struck home.

"Wade—Bent Wade," said Wade, with quiet distinctness.

"*Not Hell-Bent Wade!*" ejaculated Belllounds.

"The same....I ain't proud of the handle, but I never sail under false colors."

"Wal, I'll be damned!" went on the rancher. "Wade, I've heerd of you fer years. Some bad, but most good, an' I reckon I'm jest as glad to meet you as if you'd been somebody else."

"You'll give me the job?"

"I should smile."

"I'm thankin' you. Reckon I was some worried. Jobs are hard for me to get an' harder to keep."

"Thet's not onnatural, considerin' the hell which's said to camp on your trail," replied Belllounds, dryly. "Wade, I can't say I take a hell of a lot of stock in such talk. Fifty years I've been west of the Missouri. I know the West an' I know men. Talk flies from camp to ranch, from diggin's to town, an' always some one adds a little more. Now I trust my judgment an' I trust men. No one ever betrayed me yet."

"I'm that way, too," replied Wade. "But it doesn't pay, an' yet I still kept on bein' that way....Belllounds, my name's as bad as good all over western Colorado. But as man to man I tell you—I never did a low-down trick in my life....Never but once."

"An' what was thet?" queried the rancher, gruffly.

"I killed a man who was innocent," replied Wade, with quivering lips, "an'—an' drove the woman I loved to her death."

"Aw! we all make mistakes some time in our lives," said Belllounds, hurriedly. "I made 'most as big a one as yours—so help me God! ..."

"I'll tell you—" interrupted Wade.

"You needn't tell me anythin'," said Belllounds, interrupting in his turn. "But at thet some time I'd like to hear about the Lascelles outfit over on the Gunnison. I knowed Lascelles. An' a pardner of mine down in Middle Park came back from the Gunnison with the dog-gondest story I ever heerd. Thet was five years ago this summer. Of course I knowed your name long before, but this time I heerd it powerful strong. You got in thet mix-up to your neck.... Wal, what consarns me now is this. Is there any sense in the talk thet wherever you land there's hell to pay?"

"Belllounds, there's no sense in it, but a lot of truth," confessed Wade, gloomily.

"Ahuh! ... Wal, Hell-Bent Wade, I'll take a chance on you," boomed the rancher's deep voice, rich with the intent of his big heart. "I've gambled all my life. An' the best friends I ever made were men I'd helped.... What wages do you ask?"

"I'll take what you offer."

"I'm payin' the boys forty a month, but thet's not enough fer you."

"Yes, that'll do."

"Good, it's settled," concluded Belllounds, rising. Then he saw his son standing inside the door. "Say, Jack, shake hands with Bent Wade, hunter an' all-around

man. Wade, this 's my boy. I've jest put him on as foreman of the outfit, an' while I'm at it I'll say thet you'll
take orders from me an' not from him."

Wade looked up into the face of Jack Belllounds,
returned his brief greeting, and shook his limp hand.
The contact sent a strange chill over Wade. Young Belllounds's face was marred by a bruise and shaded by a
sullen light.

"Get Billin's to take you out to thet new cabin an'
sheds I jest had put up," said the rancher. "You'll bunk
in the cabin....Aw, I know. Men like you sleep in the
open. But you can't do thet under Old White Slides in
winter. Not much! Make yourself to home, an' I'll walk
out after a bit an' we'll look over the dog outfit. When
you see thet outfit you'll holler fer help."

Wade bowed his thanks, and, putting on his sombrero, he turned away. As he did so he caught a sound
of light, quick footsteps on the far end of the porch.

"Hello, you-all!" cried a girl's voice, with melody
in it that vibrated piercingly upon Wade's sensitive ears.

"Mornin', Columbine," replied the rancher.

Bent Wade's heart leaped up. This girlish voice rang
upon the chord of memory. Wade had not the strength
to look at her then. It was not that he could not bear
to look, but that he could not bear the disillusion
sure to follow his first glimpse of this adopted daughter
of Belllounds. Sweet to delude himself! Ah! the years
were bearing sterner upon his head! The old dreams
persisted, sadder now for the fact that from long use
they had become half-realities! Wade shuffled slowly
across the green square to where the cowboy waited

for him. His eyes were dim, and a sickness attended the sinking of his heart.

"Wade, I ain't a bettin' fellar, but I'll bet Old Bill took you up," vouchsafed Billings, with interest.

"Glad to say he did," replied Wade. "You're to show me the new cabin where I'm to bunk."

"Come along," said Lem, leading off. "Air you agoin' to handle stock or chase coyotes?"

"My job's huntin'."

"Wal, it may be thet from sunup to sundown, but between times you'll be sure busy otherwise, I opine," went on Lem. "Did you meet the boss's son?"

"Yes, he was there. An' Belllounds made it plain I was to take orders from him an' not from his son."

"Thet'll make your job a million times easier," declared Lem, as if to make up for former hasty pessimism. He led the way past some log cabins, and sheds with dirt roofs, and low, flat-topped barns, out across another brook where willow-trees were turning yellow. Then the new cabin came into view. It was small, with one door and one window, and a porch across the front. It stood on a small elevation, near the swift brook, and overlooking the ranch-house perhaps a quarter of a mile below. Above it, and across the brook, had been built a high fence constructed of aspen poles laced closely together. The sounds therefrom proclaimed this stockade to be the dog-pen.

Lem helped Wade unpack and carry his outfit into the cabin. It contained one room, the corner of which was filled with blocks and slaps of pine, evidently left there after the construction of the cabin, and meant for firewood. The ample size of the stone fireplace attested to the severity of the winters.

"Real sawed boards on the floor!" exclaimed Lem, meaning to impress the new-comer. "I call this a plumb good bunk."

"Much too good for me," replied Wade.

"Wal, I'll look after your hosses," said Lem. "I reckon you'll fix up your bunk. Take my hunch an' ask Miss Collie to find you some furniture an' sich like. She's Ole Bill's daughter, an' she makes up fer—fer—wal, fer a lot we hev to stand. I'll fetch the boys over later."

"Do you smoke?" asked Wade. "I've somethin' fine I fetched up from Leadville."

"Smoke! Me? I'll give you a hoss right now for a cigar. I git one onct a year, mebbe."

"Here's a box I've been packin' for long," replied Wade, as he handed it up to Billings. "They're Spanish, all right. Too rich for my blood!"

A box of gold could not have made that cowboy's eyes shine any brighter.

"*Whoop-ee!*" he yelled. "Why, man, you're like the fairy in the kid's story! Won't I make the outfit wild? Aw, I forgot. Thar's only Jim an' Blud left. Wal, I'll divvy with them. Sure, Wade, you hit me right. I was dyin' fer a real smoke. An' I reckon what's mine is yours."

Then he strode out of the cabin, whistling a merry cowboy tune.

Wade was left sitting in the middle of the room on his roll of bedding, and for a long time he remained there motionless, with his head bent, his worn hands idly clasped. A heavy footfall outside aroused him from his meditation.

"Hey, Wade!" called the cheery voice of Belllounds.

Then the rancher appeared at the door. "How's this bunk suit you?"

"Much too fine for an old-timer like me," replied Wade.

"Old-timer! Say, you're young yet. Look at me. Sixty-eight last birthday! Wal, every dog has his day.... What're you needin' to fix this bunk comfortable like?"

"Reckon I don't need much."

"Wal, you've beddin' an' cook outfit. Go get a table, an' a chair an' a bench from thet first cabin. The boys thet had it are gone. Somethin' with a back to it, a rockin'-chair, if there's one. You'll find tools, an' boxes, an' stuff in the workshop, if you want to make a cupboard or anythin'."

"How about a lookin'-glass?" asked Wade. "I had a piece, but I broke it."

"Haw! Haw! Mebbe we can rustle thet, too. My girl's good on helpin' the boys fix up. Woman-like, you know. An' she'll fetch you some decorations on her own hook. Now let's take a look at the hounds."

Belllounds led the way out toward the crude dog-corral, and the way he leaped the brook bore witness to the fact that he was still vigorous and spry. The door of the pen was made of boards hung on wire. As Belllounds opened it there came a pattering rush of many padded feet, and a chorus of barks and whines. Wade's surprised gaze took in forty or fifty dogs, mostly hounds, browns and blacks and yellows, all sizes—a motley, mangy, hungry pack, if he had ever seen one.

"I swore I'd buy every hound fetched to me, till I'd cleaned up the varmints around White Slides. An' sure I was imposed on," explained the rancher.

"Some good-lookin' hounds in the bunch," replied Wade. "An' there's hardly too many. I'll train two packs, so I can rest one when the other's huntin'."

"Wal, I'll be dog-goned!" ejaculated Belllounds, with relief. "I sure thought you'd roar. All this rabble to take care of!"

"No trouble after I've got acquainted," said Wade. "Have they been hunted any?"

"Some of the boys took out a bunch. But they split on deer tracks an' elk tracks an' Lord knows what all. Never put up a lion! Then again Billings took some out after a pack of coyotes, an' gol darn me if the coyotes didn't lick the hounds. An' wuss! Jack, my son, got it into his head thet he was a hunter. The other mornin' he found a fresh lion track back of the corral. An' he ups an' puts the whole pack of hounds on the trail. I had a good many more hounds in the pack than you see now. Wal, anyway, it was great to hear the noise thet pack made. Jack lost every blamed hound of them. Thet night an' next day an' the followin' they straggled in. But twenty some never did come back."

Wade laughed. "They may come yet. I reckon, though, they've gone home where they came from. Are any of these hounds recommended?"

"Every consarned one of them," declared Belllounds.

"That's funny. But I guess it's natural. Do you know for sure whether you bought any good dogs?"

"Yes, I gave fifty dollars for two hounds. Got them of a friend in Middle Park whose pack killed off the lions there. They're good dogs, trained on lion, wolf, an' bear."

"Pick 'em out," said Wade.

With a throng of canines crowding and fawning round him, and snapping at one another, it was difficult for the rancher to draw the two particular ones apart so they could be looked over. At length he succeeded, and Wade drove back the rest of the pack.

"The big fellar's Sampson an' the other's Jim," said Belllounds.

Sampson was a huge hound, gray and yellow, with mottled black marks, very long ears, and big, solemn eyes. Jim, a good-sized dog, but small in comparison with the other, was black all over, except around the nose and eyes. Jim had many scars. He was old, yet not past a vigorous age, and he seemed a quiet, dignified, wise hound, quite out of his element in that mongrel pack.

"If they're as good as they look we're lucky," said Wade, as he tied the ends of his rope round their necks. "Now are there any more you know are good?"

"Denver, come hyar!" yelled Belllounds. A white, yellow-spotted hound came wagging his tail. "I'll swear by Denver. An' there's one more—Kane. He's half blood-hound, a queer, wicked kind of dog. He keeps to himself. ... Kane! Come hyar!"

Belllounds tramped around the corral, and finally found the hound in question, asleep in a dusty hole. Kane was the only beautiful dog in the lot. If half of him was bloodhound the other half was shepherd, for his black and brown hair was inclined to curl, and his head had the fine thoroughbred contour of the shepherd. His ears, long and drooping and thin, betrayed the hound in him. Kane showed no disposition to be friendly. His dark eyes, sad and mournful, burned with the fires of doubt.

Wade haltered Kane, Jim, and Sampson, which act almost precipitated a fight, and led them out of the corral. Denver, friendly and glad, followed at the rancher's heels.

"I'll keep them with me an' make lead dogs out of them," said Wade. "Belllounds, that bunch hasn't had enough to eat. They're half starved."

"Wal, thet's worried me more'n you'll guess," declared Belllounds, with irritation. "What do a lot of cowpunchin' fellars know about dogs? Why, they nearly ate Bludsoe up. He wouldn't feed 'em. An' Wils, who seemed good with dogs, was taken off bad hurt the other day. Lem's been tryin' to rustle feed fer them. Now we'll give back the dogs you don't want to keep, an' thet way thin out the pack."

"Yes, we won't need 'em all. An' I reckon I'll take the worry of this dog-pack off your mind."

"Thet's your job, Wade. My orders are fer you to kill off the varmints. Lions, wolves, coyotes. An' every fall some ole silvertip gits bad, an' now an' then other bears. Whatever you need in the way of supplies jest ask fer. We send regular to Kremmlin'. You can hunt fer two months yet, barrin' an onusual early winter.... I'm askin' you—if my son tramps on your toes—I'd take it as a favor fer you to be patient. He's only a boy yet, an' coltish."

Wade divined that was a favor difficult for Belllounds to ask. The old rancher, dominant and forceful and self-sufficient all his days, had begun to feel an encroachment of opposition beyond his control. If he but realized it, the favor he asked of Wade was an appeal.

"Belllounds, I get along with everybody," Wade assured him. "An' maybe I can help your son. Before I'd reached here I'd heard he was wild, an' so I'm prepared."

"If you'd do thet—wal, I'd never forgit it," replied the rancher, slowly. "Jack's been away fer three years. Only got back a week or so ago. I calkilated he'd be sobered, steadied, by—thet—thet work I put him to. But I'm not sure. He's changed. When he gits his own way he's all I could ask. But thet way he wants ain't always what it ought to be. An' so thar's been clashes. But Jack's a fine young man. An' he'll outgrow his temper an' crazy notions. Work'll do it."

"Boys will be boys," replied Wade, philosophically. "I've not forgotten when I was a boy."

"Neither hev I. Wal, I'll be goin', Wade. I reckon Columbine will be up to call on you. Bein' the only woman-folk in my house, she sort of runs it. An' she's sure interested in thet pack of hounds."

Belllounds trudged away, his fine old head erect, his gray hair shining in the sun.

Wade sat down upon the step of his cabin, pondering over the rancher's remarks about his son. Recalling the young man's physiognomy, Wade began to feel that it was familiar to him. He had seen Jack Belllounds before. Wade never made mistakes in faces, though he often had a task to recall names. And he began to go over the recent past, recalling all that he could remember of Meeker, and Cripple Creek, where he had worked for several months, and so on, until he had gone back as far as his last trip to Denver.

"Must have been there," mused Wade, thoughtfully, and he tried to recall all the faces he had seen. This was impossible, of course, yet he remembered many. Then he visualized the places in Denver that for one reason or another had struck him particularly. Suddenly into one of these flashed the pale, sullen, bold face of Jack Belllounds.

"It was *there!*" he exclaimed, incredulously. "Well! ...If thet's not the strangest yet! Could I be mistaken? No. I saw him.... Belllounds must have known it—must have let him stay there.... Maybe put him there! He's just the kind of a man to go to extremes to reform his son."

Singular as was this circumstance, Wade dwelt only momentarily on it. He dismissed it with the conviction that it was another strange happening in the string of events that had turned his steps toward White Slides Ranch. Wade's mind stirred to the probability of an early sight of Columbine Belllounds. He would welcome it, both as interesting and pleasurable, and surely as a relief. The sooner a meeting with her was over the better. His life had been one long succession of shocks, so that it seemed nothing the future held could thrill him, amaze him, torment him. And yet how well he knew that his heart was only the more responsive for all it had withstood! Perhaps here at White Slides he might meet with an experience dwarfing all others. It was possible; it was in the nature of events. And though he repudiated such a possibility, he fortified himself against a subtle divination that he might at last have reached the end of his long trail, where anything might happen.

Three of the hounds lay down at Wade's feet. Kane, the bloodhound, stood watching this new master, after the manner of a dog who was a judge of men. He sniffed at Wade. He grew a little less surly.

Wade's gaze, however, was on the path that led down along the border of the brook to disappear in the willows. Above this clump of yellowing trees could be seen the ranch-house. A girl with fair hair stepped off the porch. She appeared to be carrying something in her arms, and shortly disappeared behind the willows. Wade saw her and surmised that she was coming to his cabin. He did not expect any more or think any more. His faculties condensed to the objective one of sight.

The girl, when she reappeared, was perhaps a hundred yards distant. Wade bent on her one keen, clear glance. Then his brain and his blood beat wildly. He saw a slender girl in riding-costume, lithe and strong, with the free step of one used to the open. It was this form, this step that struck Wade. "My—God! how like Lucy!" he whispered, and he tried to pierce the distance to see her face. It gleamed in the sunshine. Her fair hair waved in the wind. She was coming, but so slowly! All of Wade that was physical and emotional seemed to wait—clamped. The moment was age-long, with nothing beyond it. While she was still at a distance her face became distinct. And Wade sustained a terrible shock. ...Then, as one in a dream, as in a blur of strained peering into a maze, he saw the face of his sweetheart, his wife, the Lucy of his early manhood. It moved him out of the past. Closer! Pang on pang quivered in his heart. Was this only a nightmare? Or had he at last gone mad! This girl raised her head. She was looking—she saw him. Terror mounted upon Wade's consciousness.

"That's Lucy's face!" he gasped. "So help—me, God!...It's for this—I wandered here! She's my flesh an' blood—my Lucy's child—my own!"

Fear and presentiment and blank amaze and stricken consciousness left him in the lightning-flash of divination that was recognition as well. A shuddering cataclysm enveloped him, a passion so stupendous that it almost brought oblivion.

The three hounds leaped up with barks and wagging tails. They welcomed this visitor. Kane lost still more of his canine aloofness.

Wade's breast heaved. The blue sky, the gray hills, the green willows, all blurred in his sight, that seemed to hold clear only the face floating closer.

"I'm Columbine Belllounds," said a voice.

It stilled the storm in Wade. It was real. It was a voice of twenty years ago. The burden on his breast lifted. Then flashed the spirit, the old self-control of a man whose life had held many terrible moments.

"Mornin', miss. I'm glad to meet you," he replied, and there was no break, no tone unnatural in his greeting.

So they gazed at each other, she with that instinctive look peculiar to women in its intuitive powers, but common to all persons who had lived far from crowds and to whom a new-comer was an event. Wade's gaze, intense and all-embracing, found that face now closer in resemblance to the imagined Lucy's—a pretty face, rather than beautiful, but strong and sweet—its striking qualities being a colorless fairness of skin that yet held a rose and golden tint, and the eyes of a rare and exquisite shade of blue.

"Oh! Are you feeling ill?" she asked. "You look so—so pale."

"No. I'm only tuckered out," replied Wade, easily, as he wiped the clammy drops from his brow. "It was a long ride to get here."

"I'm the lady of the house," she said, with a smile. "I'm glad to welcome you to White Slides, and hope you'll like it."

"Well, Miss Columbine, I reckon I will," he replied, returning the smile. "Now if I was younger I'd like it powerful much."

She laughed at that. "Men are all alike, young or old."

"Don't ever think so," said Wade, earnestly.

"No? I guess you're right about that. I've fetched you up some things for your cabin. May I peep in?"

"Come in," replied Wade, rising. "You must excuse my manners. It's long indeed since I had a lady caller."

She went in, and Wade, standing on the threshold, saw her survey the room with a woman's sweeping glance.

"I told dad to put some—"

"Miss, your dad told me to go get them, an' I've not done it yet. But I will presently."

"Very well. I'll leave these things and come back later," she replied, depositing a bundle upon the floor. "You won't mind if I try to—to make you a little comfortable. It's dreadful the way outdoor men live when they do get indoors."

"I reckon I'll be slow in lettin' you see what a good

housekeeper I am," he replied. "Because then, maybe, I'll see more of you."

"Weren't you a sad flatterer in your day?" she queried, archly.

Her intonation, the tilt of her head, gave Wade such a pang that he could not answer. And to hide his momentary restraint he turned back to the hounds. Then she came out upon the porch.

"I love hounds," she said, patting Denver, which caress immediately made Jim and Sampson jealous. "I've gotten on pretty well with these, but that Kane won't make up. Isn't he splendid? But he's afraid—no, not afraid of me, but he doesn't like me."

"It's mistrust. He's been hurt. I reckon he'll get over that after a while."

"You don't beat dogs?" she asked, eagerly.

"No, miss. That's not the way to get on with hounds or horses."

Her glance was a blue flash of pleasure.

"How glad that makes me! Why, I quit coming here to see and feed the dogs because somebody was always kicking them around."

Wade handed the rope to her. "You hold them, so when I come out with some meat they won't pile over me." He went inside, took all that was left of the deer haunch out of his pack, and, picking up his knife, returned to the porch. The hounds saw the meat and yelped. The pulled on the rope.

"You hounds behave," ordered Wade, as he sat down on the step and began to cut the meat. "Jim, you're the oldest an' hungriest. Here....Now you, Sampson. Here!"...The big hound snapped at the meat. Whereupon Wade slapped him. "Are you a pup or a wolf that you grab for it? Here." Sampson was slower to act, but he snapped again. Whereupon Wade hit him again, with open hand, not with violence or rancor, but a blow that meant Sampson must obey.

Next time the hound did not snap. Denver had to be cuffed several times before he showed deference to this new master. But the bloodhound Kane refused to take any meat out of Wade's hand. He growled and showed his teeth, and sniffed hungrily.

"Kane will have to be handled carefully," observed Wade. "He'd bite pretty quick."

"But he's so splendid," said the girl. "I don't like to think he's mean. You'll be good to him—try to win him?"

"I'll do my best with him."

"Dad's full of glee that he has a real hunter at White Slides at last. Now I'm glad, and sorry, too. I hate to think of little calves being torn and killed by lions and wolves. And it's dreadful to know bears eat grown-up cattle. But I love the mourn of a wolf and the yelp of a coyote. I can't help hoping you don't kill them all—quite."

"It's not likely, miss," he replied. "I'll be pretty sure to clean out the lions an' drive off the bears. But the wolf family can't be exterminated. No animal so cunnin' as a wolf!...I'll tell you....Some years ago I went to cook on a ranch north of Denver, on the edge of the plains. An' right off I began to hear stories about a big lobo—a wolf that was an old residenter. He'd been known for long, an' he got meaner an' wiser as he was hunted. His specialty got to be yearlings, an' the ranch-

ers all over rose up in arms against him. They hired all
the old hunters an' trappers in the country to kill him.
No good! Old Lobo went right on pullin' down yearlings.
Every night he'd get one or more. An' he was so cute
an' so swift that he'd work on different ranches on different nights. Finally he killed eleven yearlings for my
boss on one night. Eleven! Think of that. An' then I said
to my boss, 'I reckon you'd better let me go kill that
gray butcher.' An' my boss laughed at me. But he let
me go. He'd have tried anythin'. I took a hunk of meat,
a blanket, my gun, an' a pair of snow-shoes, an' I set
out on old Lobo's tracks....An', Miss Columbine, I
walked old Lobo to death in the snow!"

"Why, how wonderful!" exclaimed the girl, breathless and glowing with interest. "Oh, it seems a pity such
a splendid brute should be killed. Wild animals are
cruel. I wish it were different."

"Life is cruel, miss, an' I echo your wish," replied
Wade, sadly.

"You have had great experiences. Dad said to me,
'Collie, here at last is a man who can tell you enough
stories!'...But I don't believe you ever could."

"You like stories?" asked Wade, curiously.

"Love them. All kinds, but I like adventure best. *I*
should have been a boy. Isn't it strange, I can't hurt
anything myself or bear to see even a steer slaughtered?
But you can't tell too bloody and terrible stories for me.
Except I hate Indian stories. The very thought of Indians
makes me shudder....Some day I'll tell you a story."

Wade could not find his tongue readily.

"I must go now," she continued, and moved off the
porch. Then she hesitated, and turned with a smile that

was wistful and impulsive. "I—I believe we'll be good friends."

"Miss Columbine, we sure will, if I can live up to my part," replied Wade.

Her smile deepened, even while her gaze grew unconsciously penetrating. Wade felt how subtly they were drawn to each other. But she had no inkling of that.

"It takes two to make a bargain," she replied, seriously. "I've my part. Good-by."

Wade watched her lithe stride, and as she drew away the restraint he had put upon himself loosened. When she disappeared his feeling burst all bounds. Dragging the dogs inside, he closed the door. Then, like one broken and spent, he fell face against the wall, with the hoarsely whispered words, "I'm thankin' God!"

CHAPTER

6

SEPTEMBER'S glory of gold and red and purple began to fade with the autumnal equinox. It rained enough to soak the frost-bitten leaves, and then the mountain winds sent them flying and fluttering and scurrying to carpet the dells and spot the pools in the brooks and color the trails. When the weather cleared and the sun rose bright again many of the aspen thickets were leafless and bare, and the willows showed stark against the gray sage hills, and the vines had lost their fire. Hills and valleys had sobered with subtle change that left them none the less beautiful.

A mile or more down the road from White Slides, in a protected nook, nestled two cabins belonging to a cattleman named Andrews, who had formerly worked for Belllounds and had recently gone into the stock business for himself. He had a rather young wife, and several children, and a brother who rode for him. These people were the only neighbors of Belllounds for some ten miles on the road toward Kremmling.

Columbine liked Mrs. Andrews and often rode or walked down there for a little visit and a chat with her friend and a romp with the children.

Toward the end of September Columbine found herself combating a strong desire to go down to the Andrews ranch and try to learn some news about Wilson Moore. If anything had been heard at White Slides it certainly had not been told her. Jack Belllounds had ridden to Kremmling and back in one day, but Columbine would have endured much before asking him for information.

She did, however, inquire of the freighter who hauled Belllounds's supplies, and the answer she got was awkwardly evasive. That nettled Columbine. Also it raised a suspicion which she strove to subdue. Finally it seemed apparent that Wilson Moore's name was not to be mentioned to her.

First, in her growing resentment, she had an impulse to go to her new friend, the hunter Wade, and confide in him not only her longing to learn about Wilson, but also other matters that were growing daily more burdensome. How strange for her to feel that in some way Jack Belllounds had come between her and the old man she loved and called father! Columbine had not divined that until lately. She felt it now in the fact that she no longer sought the rancher as she used to, and he had apparently avoided her. But then, Columbine reflected, she might be entirely wrong, for when Belllounds did meet her at meal-times, or anywhere, he seemed just as affectionate as of old. Still he was not the same man. A chill, an atmosphere of shadow, had pervaded the once wholesome ranch. And so, feeling not yet well enough acquainted with Wade to confide so intimately in him, she stifled her impulses and resolved to make some effort herself to find out what she wanted to know.

As luck would have it, when she started out to walk down to the Andrews ranch she encountered Jack Belllounds.

"Where are you going?" he inquired, inquisitively.

"I'm going to see Mrs. Andrews," she replied.

"No, you're not!" he declared, quickly, with a flash.

Columbine felt a queer sensation deep within her, a hot little gathering that seemed foreign to her physical being, and ready to burst out. Of late it had stirred in her at words or acts of Jack Belllounds. She gazed steadily at him, and he returned her look with interest. What he was thinking she had no idea of, but for herself it was a recurrence and an emphasis of the fact that she seemed growing further away from this young man she had to marry. The weeks since his arrival had been the most worrisome she could remember.

"I *am* going," she replied, slowly.

"No!" he replied, violently. "I won't have you running off down there to—to gossip with that Andrews woman."

"Oh, *you* won't?" inquired Columbine, very quietly. How little he understood her!

"That's what I said."

"You're not my boss yet, Mister Jack Belllounds,"

she flashed, her spirit rising. He could irritate her as no one else.

"I soon will be. And what's a matter of a week or a month?" he went on, calming down a little.

"I've promised, yes," she said, feeling her face blanch, "and I keep my promises....But I didn't say when. If you talk like that to me it might be a good many weeks—or—or months before I name the day."

"*Columbine!*" he cried, as she turned away. There was genuine distress in his voice. Columbine felt again an assurance that had troubled her. No matter how she was reacting to this new relation, it seemed a fearful truth that Jack was really falling in love with her. This time she did not soften.

"I'll call dad to *make* you stay home," he burst out again, his temper rising.

Columbine wheeled as on a pivot.

"If you do you've got less sense than I thought."

Passion claimed him then.

"I know why you're going. It's to see that club-footed cowboy Moore!...Don't let me catch you with him!"

Columbine turned her back upon Bellounds and swung away, every pulse in her throbbing and smarting. She hurried on into the road. She wanted to run, not to get out of sight or hearing, but to fly from something, she knew not what.

"Oh! it's more than his temper!" she cried, hot tears in her eyes. "He's mean—*mean*—MEAN! What's the use of me denying that—any more—just because I love dad?...My life will be wretched....It *is* wretched!"

Her anger did not last long, nor did her resentment.

She reproached herself for the tart replies that had inflamed Jack. Never again would she forget herself!

"But he—he makes me furious," she cried, in sudden excuse for herself. "What did he say? 'That club-footed cowboy Moore'!...Oh, that was vile. He's heard, then, that poor Wilson has a bad foot, perhaps permanently crippled....If it's true...But why should he yell that he knew I wanted to see Wilson?...I did *not!* I *do* not....Oh, but I do, I do!"

And then Columbine was to learn straightway that she would forget herself again, that she had forgotten, and that a sadder, stranger truth was dawning upon her—she was discovering another Columbine within herself, a wilful, passionate, different creature who would no longer be denied.

Almost before Columbine realized that she had started upon the visit she was within sight of the Andrews ranch. So swiftly had she walked! It behooved her to hide such excitement as had dominated her. And to that end she slowed her pace, trying to put her mind on other matters.

The children saw her first and rushed upon her, so that when she reached the cabin door she could not well have been otherwise than rosy and smiling. Mrs. Andrews, ruddy and strong, looked the pioneer rancher's hard-working wife. Her face brightened at the advent of Columbine, and showed a little surprise and curiosity as well.

"Laws, but it's good to see you, Columbine," was her greeting. "You 'ain't been here for a long spell."

"I've been coming, but just put it off," replied Columbine.

And so, after the manner of women neighbors, they began to talk of the fall round-up, and the near approach of winter with its loneliness, and the children, all of which naturally led to more personal and interesting topics.

"An' is it so, Columbine, that you're to marry Jack Belllounds?" asked Mrs. Andrews, presently.

"Yes, I guess it is," replied Columbine, smiling.

"Humph! I'm nó relative of yours or even a particular, close friend, but I'd like to say—"

"Please don't," interposed Columbine.

"All right, my girl. I guess it's better I don't say anythin'. It's a pity, though, onless you love this Buster Jack. An' you never used to do that, I'll swan."

"No, I don't love Jack—yet—as I ought to love a husband. But I'll try, and if—if I—I never do—still, it's my duty to marry him."

"Some woman ought to talk to Bill Belllounds," declared Mrs. Andrews with a grimness that boded ill for the old rancher.

"Did you know we had a new man up at the ranch?" asked Columbine, changing the subject.

"You mean the hunter, Hell-Bent Wade?"

"Yes. But I hate that ridiculous name," said Columbine.

"It's queer, like lots of names men get in these parts. An' it'll stick. Wade's been here twice; once as he was passin' with the hounds, an' the other night. I like him, Columbine. He's true-blue, for all his strange name. My men-folks took to him like ducks to water."

"I'm glad. I took to him almost like that," rejoined Columbine. "He has the saddest face I ever saw."

"Sad? Wal, yes. That man has seen a good deal of what they tacked on to his name. I laughed when I seen him first. Little lame fellar, crooked-legged an' ragged, with thet awful homely face! But I forgot how he looked next time he came."

"That's just it. He's not much to look at, but you forget his homeliness right off," replied Columbine, warmly. "You feel something behind all his—his looks."

"Wal, you an' me are women, an' we feel different," replied Mrs. Andrews. "Now my men-folks take much store on what Wade can *do*. He fixed up Tom's gun, that's been out of whack for a year. He made our clock run ag'in, an' run better than ever. Then he saved our cow from that poison-weed. An' Tom gave her up to die."

"The boys up home were telling me Mr. Wade had saved some of our cattle. Dad was delighted. You know he's lost a good many head of stock from this poison-weed. I saw so many dead steers on my last ride up the mountain. It's too bad our new man didn't get here sooner to save them. I asked him how he did it, and he said he was a doctor."

"A cow-doctor," laughed Mrs. Andrews. "Wal, that's a new one on me. Accordin' to Tom, this here Wade, when he seen our sick cow, said she'd eat poison-weed—larkspur, I think he called it—an' then when she drank water it formed a gas in her stomach an' she swelled up turrible. Wade jest stuck his knife in her side a little an' let the gas out, and she got well."

"Ughh! . . . What cruel doctoring! But if it saves the cattle, then it's good."

"It'll save them if they can be got to right off," replied Mrs. Andrews.

"Speaking of doctors," went on Columbine, striving to make her query casual, "do you know whether or not Wilson Moore had his foot treated by a doctor at Kremmling?"

"He did not," answered Mrs. Andrews. "Wasn't no doctor there. They'd had to send to Denver, an', as Wils couldn't take that trip or wait so long, why, Mrs. Plummer fixed up his foot. She made a good job of it, too, as I can testify."

"Oh, I'm—very thankful!" murmured Columbine. "He'll not be crippled or—or club-footed, then?"

"I reckon not. You can see for yourself. For Wils's here. He was drove up night before last an' is stayin' with my brother-in-law—in the other cabin there."

Mrs. Andrews launched all this swiftly, with evident pleasure, but with more of woman's subtle motive. Her eyes were bent with shrewd kindness upon the younger woman.

"Here!" exclaimed Columbine, with a start, and for an instant she was at the mercy of conflicting surprise and joy and alarm. Alternately she flushed and paled.

"Sure he's here," replied Mrs. Andrews, now looking out of the door. "He ought to be in sight somewheres. He's walkin' with a crutch."

"Crutch!" cried Columbine, in dismay.

"Yes, crutch, an' he made it himself. . . . I don't see him nowheres. Mebbe he went in when he see you comin'. For he's powerful sensitive about that crutch."

"Then—if he's so—so sensitive, perhaps I'd better go," said Columbine, struggling with embarrassment and discomfiture. What if she happened to meet him! Would he imagine her purpose in coming there? Her heart began to beat unwontedly.

"Suit yourself, lass," replied Mrs. Andrews, kindly. "I know you and Wils quarreled, for he told me. An' it's a pity.... Wal, if you must go, I hope you'll come again before the snow flies. Good-by."

Columbine bade her a hurried good-by and ventured forth with misgivings. And almost around the corner of the second cabin, which she had to pass, and before she had time to recover her composure, she saw Wilson Moore, hobbling along on a crutch, holding a bandaged foot off the ground. He had seen her; he was hurrying to avoid a meeting, or to get behind the corrals there before she observed him.

"Wilson!" she called, involuntarily. The instant the name left her lips she regretted it. But too late! The cowboy halted, slowly turned.

Then Columbine walked swiftly up to him, suddenly as brave as she had been fearful. Sight of him had changed her.

"Wilson Moore, you meant to avoid me," she said, with reproach.

"Howdy, Columbine!" he drawled, ignoring her words.

"Oh, I was so sorry you were hurt!" she burst out. "And now I'm so glad—you're—you're ... Wilson, you're thin and pale—you've suffered!"

"It pulled me down a bit," he replied.

Columbine had never before seen his face anything except bronzed and lean and healthy, but now it bore testimony to pain and strain and patient endurance. He looked older. Something in the fine, dark, hazel eyes hurt her deeply.

"You never sent me word," she went on, reproachfully. "No one would tell me anything. The boys said they didn't know. Dad was angry when I asked him. I'd never have asked Jack. And the freighter who drove up—he lied to me. So I came down here to-day purposely to ask news of you, but I never dreamed you were here,...Now I'm glad I came."

What a singular, darkly kind, yet strange glance he gave her!

"That was like you, Columbine," he said. "I knew you'd feel badly about my accident. But how could I send word to you?"

"You saved—Pronto," she returned, with a strong tremor in her voice. "I can't thank you enough."

"That was a funny thing. Pronto went out of his head. I hope he's all right."

"He's almost well. It took some time to pick all the splinters out of him. He'll be all right soon—none the worse for that—that cowboy trick of Mister Jack Belllounds."

Columbine finished bitterly. Moore turned his thoughtful gaze away from her.

"I hope Old Bill is well," he remarked, lamely.

"Have you told your folks of your accident?" asked Columbine, ignoring his remark.

"No."

"Oh, Wilson, you ought to have sent for them, or have written at least."

"Me? To go crying for them when I got in trouble? I couldn't see it that way."

"Wilson, you'll be going—home—soon—to Denver—won't you?" she faltered.

"No," he replied, shortly.

"But what will you do? Surely you can't work—not so soon?"

"Columbine, I'll never—be able to ride again—like I used to," he said, tragically. "I'll ride, yes, but never the old way."

"Oh!" Columbine's tone, and the exquisite softness and tenderness with which she placed a hand on the rude crutch would have been enlightening to any one but these two absorbed in themselves. "I can't bear to believe that."

"I'm afraid it's true. Bad smash, Columbine! I just missed being club-footed."

"You should have care. You should have ... Wilson, do you intend to stay here with the Andrews?"

"Not much. They have troubles of their own. Columbine, I'm going to homestead one hundred and sixty acres."

"Homestead!" she exclaimed, in amaze. "Where?"

"Up there under Old White Slides. I've long intended to. You know that pretty little valley under the red bluff. There's a fine spring. You've been there with me. There by the old cabin built by prospectors?"

"Yes, I know. It's a pretty place—fine valley, but Wils, you can't *live* there," she expostulated.

"Why not, I'd like to know?"

"That little cubby-hole! It's only a tiny one-room cabin, roof all gone, chinks open, chimney crumbling. ...Wilson, you don't mean to tell me you want to live there alone?"

"Sure. What'd you think?" he replied, with sarcasm. "Expect me to *marry* some girl? Well, I wouldn't, even if any one would have a cripple."

"Who—who will take care of you?" she asked, blushing furiously.

"I'll take care of myself," he declared. "Good Lord! Columbine, I'm not an invalid yet. I've got a few friends who'll help me fix up the cabin. And that reminds me. There's a lot of my stuff up in the bunk-house at White Slides. I'm going to drive up soon to haul it away."

"Wilson Moore, do you mean it?" she asked, with grave wonder. "Are you going to homestead near White Slides Ranch—and *live* there—when—"

She could not finish. An overwhelming disaster, for which she had no name, seemed to be impending.

"Yes, I am," he replied. "Funny how things turn out, isn't it?"

"It's very—very funny," she said, dazedly, and she turned slowly away without another word.

"Good-by, Columbine," he called out after her, with farewell, indeed, in his voice.

All the way home Columbine was occupied with feelings that swayed her to the exclusion of rational consideration of the increasing perplexity of her situation. And to make matters worse, when she arrived at the ranch it was to meet Jack Belllounds with a face as black as a thunder-cloud.

"The old man wants to see you," he announced, with an accent that recalled his threat of a few hours back.

"Does he?" queried Columbine, loftily. "From the courteous way you speak I imagine it's important."

Belllounds did not deign to reply to this. He sat on the porch, where evidently he had awaited her return, and he looked anything but happy.

"Where is dad?" continued Columbine.

Jack motioned toward the second door, beyond which he sat, the one that opened into the room the rancher used as a kind of office and storeroom. As Columbine walked by Jack he grasped her skirt.

"Columbine! you're angry?" he said, appealingly.

"I reckon I am," replied Columbine.

"Don't go in to dad when you're that way," implored Jack. "He's angry, too—and—and—it'll only make matters worse."

From long experience Columbine could divine when Jack had done something in the interest of self and then had awakened to possible consequences. She pulled away from him without replying, and knocked on the office door.

"Come in," called the rancher.

Columbine went in. "Hello, dad! Do you want me?"

Belllounds sat at an old table, bending over a soiled ledger, with a stubby pencil in his huge hand. When he looked up Columbine gave a little start.

"Where've you been?" he asked, gruffly.

"I've been calling on Mrs. Andrews," replied Columbine.

"Did you go thar to see her?"

"Why—certainly!" answered Columbine, with a slow break in her speech.

"You didn't go to meet Wilson Moore?"

"No."

"An' I reckon you'll say you hadn't heerd he was there?"

"I had not," flashed Columbine.

"Wal, *did* you see him?"

"Yes, sir, I did, but quite by accident."

"Ahuh! Columbine, are you lyin' to me?"

The hot blood flooded to Columbine's cheeks, as if she had been struck a blow.

"*Dad!*" she cried, in hurt amaze.

Belllounds seemed thick, imponderable, as if something had forced a crisis in him and his brain was deeply involved. The habitual, cool, easy, bold, and frank attitude in the meeting of all situations seemed to have been encroached upon by a break, a bewilderment, a lessening of confidence.

"Wal, are you lyin'?" he repeated, either blind to or unaware of her distress.

"I could not—lie to you," she faltered, "even—if—I wanted to."

The heavy, shadowed gaze of his big eyes was bent upon her as if she had become a new and perplexing problem.

"But you seen Moore?"

"Yes—sir." Columbine's spirit rose.

"An' talked with him?"

"Of course."

"Lass, I ain't likin' thet, an' I ain't likin' the way you look an' speak."

"I am sorry. I can't help either."

"What'd this cowboy say to you?"

"We talked mostly about his injured foot."

"An' what else?" went on Belllounds, his voice rising.

"About—what he meant to do now."

"Ahuh! An' thet's homesteadin' the Sage Creek Valley?"

"Yes, sir."

"Did you want him to do thet?"

"I! Indeed I didn't."

"Columbine, not so long ago you told me this fellar wasn't sweet on you. An' do you still say that to me— are you still insistin' he ain't in love with you?"

"He never said so—I never believed it ... and now I'm sure—he isn't!"

"Ahuh! Wal, thet same day you was jest as sure you didn't care anythin' particular fer him. Are you thet sure now?"

"No!" whispered Columbine, very low. She trembled with a suggestion of unknown forces. Not to save a new and growing pride would she evade any question from this man upon whom she had no claim, to whom she owed her life and her bringing up. But something cold formed in her.

Belllounds, self-centered and serious as he strangely was, seemed to check his probing, either from fear of hearing more from her or from an awakening of former kindness. But her reply was a shock to him, and, throwing down his pencil with the gesture of a man upon whom decision was forced, he rose to tower over her.

"You've been like a daughter to me. I've done all I knowed how fer you. I've lived up to the best of my lights. An' I've loved you," he said, sonorously and pathetically. "You know what my hopes are—fer the boy—an' fer you....We needn't waste any more talk. From this minnit you're free to do as you like. Whatever you do won't make any change in my carin' fer you.... But you gotta decide. Will you marry Jack or not?"

"I promised you—I would. I'll keep my word," replied Columbine, steadily.

"So far so good," went on the rancher. "I'm respectin' you fer what you say....An' now, *when* will you marry him?"

The little room drifted around in Columbine's vague, blank sight. All seemed to be drifting. She had no solid anchor.

"Any—day you say—the sooner the—better," she whispered.

"Wal, lass, I'm thankin' you," he replied, with voice that sounded afar to her. "An' I swear, if I didn't believe it's best fer Jack an' you, why I'd never let you marry. ...So we'll set the day. October first! Thet's the day you was fetched to me a baby—more 'n seventeen years ago."

"October—first—then, dad," she said, brokenly, and she kissed him as if in token of what she knew she owed him. Then she went out, closing the door behind her.

Jack, upon seeing her, hastily got up, with more than concern in his pale face.

"Columbine!" he cried, hoarsely. "How you look! ...Tell me. What happened? Girl, don't tell me you've—you've—"

"Jack Belllounds," interrupted Columbine, in tragic amaze at this truth about to issue from her lips, "I've promised to marry you—on October first."

He let out a shout of boyish exultation and suddenly clasped her in his arms. But there was nothing boyish in the way he handled her, in the almost savage evidence of possession. "Collie, I'm mad about you," he began, ardently. "You never let me tell you. And I've grown worse and worse. To-day I—when I saw you going down there—where that Wilson Moore is—I got terribly jealous. I was sick. I'd been glad to kill him!... It made me see how I loved you. Oh, I didn't know. But now...Oh, I'm mad for you!" He crushed her to him, unmindful of her struggles; his face and neck were red; his eyes on fire. And he began trying to kiss her mouth, but failed, as she struggled desperately. His kisses fell upon cheek and ear and hair.

"Let me—go!" panted Columbine. "You've no— no—Oh, you might have waited." Breaking from him, she fled, and got inside her room with the door almost closed, when his foot intercepted it.

Belllounds was half laughing his exultation, half furious at her escape, and altogether beside himself.

"No," she replied, so violently that it appeared to awake him to the fact that there was someone besides himself to consider.

"Aw!" He heaved a deep sigh. "All right. I won't try to get in. Only listen.... Collie, don't mind my—my way of showing you how I felt. Fact is, I went plumb off my head. Is that any wonder, you—you darling—when I've been so scared you'd never have me? Collie, I've felt that you were the one thing in the world I wanted most and would never get. But now.... October first! Listen. I promise you I'll not drink any more—nor gamble—

nor nag dad for money. I don't like his way of running
the ranch, but I'll do it, as long as he lives. I'll even try
to tolerate that club-footed cowboy's brass in homesteading a ranch right under my nose. I'll—I'll do anything you ask of me."

"Then—please—go away!" cried Columbine, with
a sob.

When he was gone Columbine barred the door and
threw herself upon her bed to shut out the light and to
give vent to her surcharged emotions. She wept like a
girl whose youth was ending; and after the paroxysm
had passed, leaving her weak and strangely changed,
she tried to reason out what had happened to her. Over
and over again she named the appeal of the rancher,
the sense of her duty, the decision she had reached,
and the disgust and terror inspired in her by Jack Belllounds's reception of her promise. These were facts of
the day and they had made of her a palpitating, unhappy
creature, who nevertheless had been brave to face the
rancher and confess that which she had scarce confessed to herself. But now she trembled and cringed on
the verge of a catastrophe that withheld its whole truth.

"I begin to see now," she whispered, after the
thought had come and gone and returned to change
again. "If Wilson had—cared for me I—I might have—
cared, too.... But I do—care—something. I couldn't lie
to dad. Only I'm not sure—how much. I never dreamed
of—of *loving* him, or any one. It's so strange. All at once
I feel old. And I can't understand these—these feelings
that shake me."

So Columbine brooded over the trouble that had
come to her, never regretting her promise to the old

rancher, but growing keener in the realization of a complexity in her nature that sooner or later would separate the life of her duty from the life of her desire. She seemed all alone, and when this feeling possessed her a strange reminder of the hunter Wade flashed up. She stifled another impulse to confide in him. Wade had the softness of a woman, and his face was a record of the trials and travails through which he had come unhardened, unembittered. Yet how could she tell her troubles to him? A stranger, a rough man of the wilds, whose name had preceded him, notorious and deadly, with that vital tang of the West in its meaning! Nevertheless, Wade drew her, and she thought of him until the recurring memory of Jack Belllounds's rude clasp again crept over her with an augmenting disgust and fear. Must she submit to that? Had she promised that? And then Columbine felt the dawning of realities.

COLUMBINE was awakened in the gray dawn by the barking of coyotes. She dreaded the daylight thus heralded. Never before in her life had she hated the rising of the sun. Resolutely she put the past behind her and faced the future, believing now that with the great decision made she needed only to keep her mind off what might have been, and to attend to her duty.

At breakfast she found the rancher in better spirits than he had been for weeks. He informed her that Jack had ridden off early for Kremmling, there to make arrangements for the wedding on October first.

"Jack's out of his head," said Belllounds. "Wal, thet comes only onct in a man's life. I remember...Jack's goin' to drive you to Kremmlin' an' ther take stage fer Denver. I allow you'd better put in your best licks on fixin' up an' packin' the clothes you'll need. Women-folk naturally want to look smart on weddin'-trips."

"Dad!" exclaimed Columbine, in dismay. "I never thought of clothes. And I don't want to leave White Slides."

"But, lass, you're goin' to be married!" expostulated Belllounds.

"Didn't it occur to Jack to take me to Kremmling? I can't make new dresses out of old ones."

"Wal, I reckon neither of us thought of thet. But you can buy what you like in Denver."

Columbine resigned herself. After all, what did it matter to her? The vague, haunting dreams of girlhood would never come true. So she went to her wardrobe and laid out all her wearing apparel. Taking stock of it this way caused her further dismay, for she had nothing fit to wear in which either to be married or to take a trip to Denver. There appeared to be nothing to do but take the rancher's advice, and Columbine set about refurbishing her meager wardrobe. She sewed all day.

What with self-control and work and the passing of hours, Columbine began to make some approach to tranquillity. In her simplicity she even began to hope that being good and steadfast and dutiful would earn her a little meed of happiness. Some haunting doubt of this flashed over her mind like a swift shadow of a black wing, but she dispelled that as she had dispelled the fear and disgust which often rose up in her mind.

To Columbine's surprise and to the rancher's concern the prospective bridegroom did not return from Kremmling on the second day. When night came Bell-lounds reluctantly gave up looking for him.

Jack's non-appearance suited Columbine, and she would have been glad to be let alone until October first, which date now seemed appallingly close. On the afternoon of Jack's third day of absence from the ranch Columbine rode out for some needed exercise. Pronto not being available, she rode another mustang and one that kept her busy. On the way back to the ranch she avoided the customary trail which led by the cabins of Wade and the cowboys. Columbine had not seen one of her friends since the unfortunate visit to the Andrews ranch. She particularly shrank from meeting Wade, which feeling was in strange contrast to her former impulses.

As she rode around the house she encountered Wilson Moore seated in a light wagon. Her mustang reared, almost unseating her. But she handled him roughly, being suddenly surprised and angry at this unexpected meeting with the cowboy.

"Howdy, Columbine!" greeted Wilson, as she brought the mustang to his feet. "You're sure learning to handle a horse—since I left this here ranch. Wonder who's teaching you! I never could get you to rake even a bronc!"

The cowboy had drawled out his admiring speech, half amused and half satiric.

"I'm—mad!" declared Columbine. "That's why."

"What're you mad at?" queried Wilson.

She did not reply, but kept on gazing steadily at him. Moore still looked pale and drawn, but he had improved since last she saw him.

"Aren't you going to speak to a fellow?" he went on.

"How are you, Wils?" she asked.

"Pretty good for a club-footed has-been cow puncher."

"I wish you wouldn't call yourself such names," rejoined Columbine, peevishly. "You're not a club-foot. I hate that word!"

"Me, too. Well, joking aside, I'm better. My foot is fine. Now, if I don't hurt it again I'll sure never be a club-foot."

"You must be careful," she said, earnestly.

"Sure. But it's hard for me to be idle. Think of me lying still all day with nothing to do but read! That's what knocked me out. I wouldn't have minded the pain if I could have gotten about.... Columbine, I've moved in!"

"What! Moved in?" she queried, blankly.

"Sure. I'm in my cabin on the hill. It's plumb great. Tom Andrews and Bert and your hunter Wade fixed up the cabin for me. That Wade is sure a good fellow. And say! what he can do with his hands! He's been kind to me. Took an interest in me, and between you and me he sort of cheered me up."

"Cheered you up! Wils, were you unhappy?" she asked, directly.

"Well, rather. What'd you expect of a cowboy who'd crippled himself—and lost his girl?"

Columbine felt the smart of tingling blood in her face, and she looked from Wilson to the wagon. It contained saddles, blankets, and other cowboy accoutrements for which he had evidently come.

"That's a double misfortune," she replied, evenly. "It's too bad both came at once. It seems to me if I were a cowboy and—and felt so toward a girl, I'd have let her know."

"This girl I mean knew, all right," he said, nodding his head.

"She didn't—she didn't!" cried Columbine.

"How do *you* know?" he queried, with feigned surprise. He was bent upon torturing her.

"You meant me. I'm the girl you lost!"

"Yes, you are—God help me!" replied Moore, with genuine emotion.

"But you—you never told me—you never told me," faltered Columbine, in distress.

"Never told you what? That you were my girl?"

"No—no. But that you—you cared—"

"Columbine Belllounds, I told you—let you see— in every way under the sun," he flashed at her.

"Let me see—what?" faltered Columbine, feeling as if the world were about to end.

"That I loved you."

"Oh!...Wilson!" whispered Columbine, wildly.

"Yes—loved you. Could you have been so inno- cent—so blind you never knew? I can't believe it."

"But I never dreamed you—you—" She broke off dazedly, overwhelmed by a tragic, glorious truth.

"Collie!...Would it have made any difference?"

"Oh, all the difference in the world!" she wailed.

"What difference?" he asked, passionately.

Columbine gazed wide-eyed and helpless at the young man. She did not know how to tell him what all the difference in the world really was.

Suddenly Wilson turned away from her to listen. Then she heard rapid beating of hoofs on the road.

"That's Buster Jack," said the cowboy. "Just my luck! There wasn't any one here when I arrived. Reckon I oughtn't have stayed. Columbine, you look pretty much upset."

"What do I care how I look!" she exclaimed, with a sharp resentment attending this abrupt and painful break in her agitation.

Next moment Jack Belllounds galloped a foam-lashed horse into the courtyard and hauled up short with a recklessness he was noted for. He swung down hard and violently cast the reins from him.

"Ahuh! I gambled on just this," he declared, harshly.

Columbine's heart sank. His gaze was fixed on her face, with its telltale evidences of agitation.

"What've you been crying about?" he demanded.

"I haven't been," she retorted.

His bold and glaring eyes, hot with sudden temper, passed slowly from her to the cowboy. Columbine became aware then that Jack was under the influence of liquor. His heated red face grew darker with a sneering contempt.

"Where's dad?" he asked, wheeling toward her.

"I don't know. He's not here," replied Columbine, dismounting. The leap of thought and blood to Jack's face gave her a further sinking of the heart. The situation unnerved her.

Wilson Moore had grown a shade paler. He gathered up his reins, ready to drive off.

"Belllounds, I came up after my things I'd left in the bunk," he said, coolly. "Happened to meet Columbine and stopped to chat a minute."

"That's what *you* say," sneered Belllounds. "You

were making love to Columbine. I saw that in her face. You know it—and she knows it—and I know it.... You're a liar!"

"Belllounds, I reckon I am," replied Moore, turning white. "I did tell Columbine what I thought she knew— what I ought to have told long ago."

"Ahuh! Well, I don't want to hear it. But I'm going to search that wagon."

"What!" ejaculated the cowboy, dropping his reins as if they stung him.

"You just hold on till I see what you've got in there," went on Belllounds, and he reached over into the wagon and pulled at a saddle.

"Say, do you mean anything? ... This stuff's mine, every strap of it. Take your hands off."

Belllounds leaned on the wagon and looked up with insolent, dark intent.

"Moore, I wouldn't trust you. I think you'd steal anything you got your hands on."

Columbine uttered a passionate little cry of shame and protest.

"Jack, how dare you!"

"You shut up! Go in the house!" he ordered.

"You insult me," she replied, in bitter humiliation.

"Will you go in?" he shouted.

"No, I won't."

"All right, look on, then. I'd just as lief have you." Then he turned to the cowboy. "Moore, show up that wagon-load of stuff unless you want me to throw it out in the road."

"Belllounds, you know I can't do that," replied Moore, coldly. "And I'll give you a hunch. You'd better shut up yourself and let me drive on.... If not for her sake, then for your own."

Belllounds grasped the reins, and with a sudden jerk pulled them out of the cowboy's hands.

"You damn club-foot! Your gift of gab doesn't go with me," yelled Belllounds, as he swung up on the hub of the wheel. But it was manifest that his desire to search the wagon was only a pretense, for while he pulled at this and that his evil gaze was on the cowboy, keen to meet any move that might give excuse for violence. Moore evidently read this, for, gazing at Columbine, he shook his head, as if to acquaint her with a situation impossible to help.

"Columbine, please hand me up the reins," he said. "I'm lame, you know. Then I'll be going."

Columbine stepped forward to comply, when Belllounds, leaping down from the wheel, pushed her back with masterful hand. Opposition to him was like waving a red flag in the face of a bull. Columbine recoiled from his look as well as touch.

"You keep out of this or I'll teach you who's boss here," he said, stridently.

"You're going too far!" burst out Columbine.

Meanwhile Wilson had laboriously climbed down out of the wagon, and, utilizing his crutch, he hobbled to where Belllounds had thrown the reins, and stooped to pick them up. Belllounds shoved Columbine farther back, and then he leaped to confront the cowboy.

"I've got you now, Moore," he said, hoarse and low. Stripped of all pretense, he showed the ungovernable nature of his temper. His face grew corded and black. The hand he thrust out shook like a leaf. "You smooth-

tongued liar! I'm on to your game. I know you'd put her
against me. I know you'd try to win her—less than a
week before her wedding-day....But it's not for that I'm
going to beat hell out of you! It's because I hate you!
Ever since I can remember my father held *you* up to
me! And he sent me to—to—he sent me away because
of you. By God! that's why I hate you!"

All that was primitive and violent and base came
out with strange frankness in Belllounds's tirade. Only
when calm could his mind be capable of hidden cal-
culation. The devil that was in him now seemed ram-
pant.

"Belllounds, you're mighty brave to stack up this
way against a one-legged man," declared the cowboy,
with biting sarcasm.

"If you had two club-feet I'd only be the gladder,"
yelled Belllounds, and, swinging his arm, he slapped
Moore so that it nearly toppled him over. Only the injured foot, coming down hard, saved him.

When Columbine saw that, and then how Wilson
winced and grew deathly pale, she uttered a low cry,
and she seemed suddenly rooted to the spot, weak,
terrified at what was now inevitable, and growing sick
and cold and faint.

"It's a damn lucky thing for you I'm not packing a
gun," said Moore, grimly. "But you knew—or you'd
never hit me—you coward."

"I'll make you swallow that," snarled Belllounds,
and this time he swung his fist, aiming a heavy blow at
Moore.

Then the cowboy whirled aloft the heavy crutch.
"If you hit at me again I'll let out what little brains you've

got. God knows that's little enough!...Belllounds, I'm going to call you to your face—before this girl your bat-eyed old man means to give you. You're not drunk. You're only ugly—mean. You've got a chance now to lick me because I'm crippled. And you're going to make the most of it. Why, you cur, I could come near licking you with only one leg. But if you touch me again I'll brain you!...You never were any good. You're no good now. You never will be anything but Buster Jack—half dotty, selfish as hell, bull-headed and mean!...And that's the last word I'll ever waste on you."

"I'll kill you!" bawled Belllounds, black with fury.

Moore wielded the crutch menacingly, but as he was not steady on his feet he was at the disadvantage his adversary had calculated upon. Belllounds ran around the cowboy, and suddenly plunged in to grapple with him. The crutch descended, but to little purpose. Belllounds's heavy onslaught threw Moore to the ground. Before he could rise Belllounds pounced upon him.

Columbine saw all this dazedly. As Wilson fell she closed her eyes, fighting a faintness that almost overcame her. She heard wrestling, threshing sounds, and sodden thumps, and a scattering of gravel. These noises seemed at first distant, then grew closer. As she gazed again with keener perception, Moore's horse plunged away from the fiercely struggling forms that had rolled almost under his feet. During the ensuing moments it was an equal battle so far as Columbine could tell. Repelled, yet fascinated, she watched. They beat each other, grappled and rolled over, first one on top, then the other. But the advantage of being uppermost presently was Belllounds's. Moore was weakening. That became noticeable more and more after each time he had wrestled and rolled about. Then Belllounds, getting this position, lay with his weight upon Moore, holding him down, and at the same time kicking with all his might. He was aiming to disable the cowboy by kicking the injured foot. And he was succeeding. Moore let out a strangled cry, and struggled desperately. But he was held and weighted down. Belllounds raised up now and, looking backward, he deliberately and furiously kicked Moore's bandaged foot; once, twice, again and again, until the straining form under him grew limp. Columbine, slowly freezing with horror, saw all this. She could not move. She could not scream. She wanted to rush in and drag Jack off of Wilson, to hurt him, to kill him, but her muscles were paralyzed. In her agony she could not even look away. Belllounds got up astride his prostrate adversary and began to beat him brutally, swinging heavy, sodden blows. His face then was terrible to see. He meant murder.

Columbine heard approaching voices and the thumping of hasty feet. That unclamped her cloven tongue. Wildly she screamed. Old Bill Belllounds appeared, striding off the porch. And the hunter Wade came running down the path.

"Dad! he's killing Wilson!" cried Columbine.

"Hyar, you devil!" roared the rancher.

Jack Belllounds got up. Panting, disheveled, with hair ruffled and face distorted, he was not a pleasant sight for even the father. Moore lay unconscious, with ghastly, bloody features, and his bandaged foot showed great splotches of red.

"My Gawd, son!" gasped Old Bill. "You didn't pick on this hyar crippled boy?"

The evidence was plain, in Moore's quiet, pathetic form, in the panting, purple-faced son. Jack Belllounds did not answer. He was in the grip of a passion that had at last been wholly unleashed and was still unsatisfied. Yet a malignant and exultant gratification showed in his face.

"That—evens us—up, Moore," he panted, and stalked away.

By this time Wade reached the cowboy and knelt beside him. Columbine came running to fall on her knees. The old rancher seemed stricken.

"Oh—Oh! it was terrible—" cried Columbine. "Oh—he's so white—and the blood—"

"Now, lass, that's no way for a woman," said Wade, and there was something in his kind tone, in his look, in his presence, that calmed Columbine. "I'll look after Moore. You go get some water an' a towel."

Columbine rose to totter into the house. She saw a red stain on the hand she had laid upon the cowboy's face, and with a strange, hot, bursting sensation, strong and thrilling, she put that red place to her lips. Running out with the things required by Wade, she was in time to hear the rancher say, "Looks hurt bad, to me."

"Yes, I reckon," replied Wade.

While Columbine held Moore's head upon her lap the hunter bathed the bloody face. It was battered and bruised and cut, and in some places, as fast as Wade washed away the red, it welled out again.

Columbine watched that quiet face, while her heart throbbed and swelled with emotions wholly beyond her control and understanding. When at last Wilson opened his eyes, fluttering at first, and then wide, she felt a surge that shook her whole body. He smiled wanly at her, and at Wade, and then his gaze lifted to Belllounds.

"I guess—he licked me," he said, in weak voice. "He kept kicking my sore foot—till I fainted. But he licked me—all right."

"Wils, mebbe he did lick you," replied the old rancher, brokenly, "but I reckon he's damn little to be proud of—lickin' a crippled man—thet way."

"Boss, Jack'd been drinking," said Moore, weakly. "And he sure had—some excuse for going off his head. He caught me—talking sweet to Columbine...and then—I called him all the names—I could lay my tongue to."

"Ahuh!" The old man seemed at a loss for words, and presently he turned away, sagging in the shoulders, and plodded into the house.

The cowboy, supported by Wade on one side, with Columbine on the other, was helped to an upright position, and with considerable difficulty was gotten into the wagon. He tried to sit up, but made a sorry showing of it.

"I'll drive him home an' look after him," said Wade. "Now, Miss Collie, you're upset, which ain't no wonder. But now you brace. It might have been worse. Just you go to your room till you're sure of yourself again."

Moore smiled another wan smile at her. "I'm sorry," he said.

"What for? Me?" she asked.

"I mean I'm sorry I was so infernal unlucky—running into you—and bringing all this distress—to you.

It was my fault. If I'd only kept—my mouth shut!"

"You need not be sorry you met me," she said, with her eyes straight upon his. "I'm glad.... But oh! if your foot is badly hurt I'll never—never—"

"Don't say it," interrupted Wilson.

"Lass, you're bent on doin' somethin'," said Wade, in his gentle voice.

"Bent?" she echoed, with something deep and rich in her voice. "Yes, I'm bent—*bent* like your name—to speak my mind!"

Then she ran toward the house and up on the porch, to enter the living-room with heaving breast and flashing eyes. Manifestly the rancher was berating his son. The former gaped at sight of her and the latter shrank.

"Jack Belllounds," she cried, "you're not half a man. ...You're a coward and a brute!"

One tense moment she stood there, lightning scorn and passion in her gaze, and then she rushed out, impetuously, as she had come.

*C*OLUMBINE did not leave her room any more that day. What she suffered there she did not want any one to know. What it cost her to conquer herself again she had only a faint conception of. She did conquer, however, and that night made up the sleep she had lost the night before.

Strangely enough, she did not feel afraid to face the rancher and his son. Recent happenings had not only changed her, but had seemed to give her strength. When she presented herself at the breakfast-table Jack was absent. The old rancher greeted her with more than usual solicitude.

"Jack's sick," he remarked, presently.

"Indeed," replied Columbine.

"Yes. He said it was the drinkin' he's not accustomed to. Wal, I reckon it was what you called him. He didn't take much store on what you called him. He didn't take much store on what I called him, which was wuss. ...I tell you, lass, Jack's set his heart so hard on you thet it's turrible."

"Queer way he has of showing the—the affections of his heart," replied Columbine, shortly.

"Thet was the drink," remonstrated the old man, pathetic and earnest in his motive to smooth over the quarrel.

"But he promised me he would not drink any more."

Belllounds shook his gray old head sadly.

"Ahuh! Jack fires up an' promises anythin'. He means it at the time. But the next hankerin' thet comes over him wipes out the promise. I know....But he's had good excuse fer this break. The boys in town began celebratin' fer October first. Great wonder Jack didn't come home clean drunk."

"Dad, you're as good as gold," said Columbine, softening. How could she feel hard toward him?

"Collie, then you're not agoin' back on the ole man?"

"No."

"I was afeared you'd change your mind about marryin' Jack."

"When I promised I meant it. I didn't make it on conditions."

"But, lass, promises can be broke," he said, with the sonorous roll in his voice.

"I never yet broke one of mine."

"Wal, I hev. Not often, mebbe, but I hev....An', lass, it's reasonable. Thar's times when a man jest can't live up to what he swore by. An' fer a girl—why, I can see how easy she'd change an' grow overnight. It's only fair fer me to say that no matter what you think you owe me you couldn't be blamed now fer dislikin' Jack."

"Dad, if by marrying Jack I can help him to be a better son to you, and more of a man, I'll be glad," she replied.

"Lass, I'm beginnin' to see how big an' fine you are," replied Belllounds, with strong feeling. "An' it's worryin' me.... My neighbors hev always accused me of seein' only my son. Only Buster Jack! I was blind an' deaf as to him!... Wal, I'm not so damn blind as I used to be. The scales are droppin' off my ole eyes.... But I've got one hope left as far as Jack's concerned. Thet's marryin' him to you. An' I'm stickin' to it."

"So will I stick to it, dad," she replied. "I'll go through with October first!"

Columbine broke off, vouchsafing no more, and soon left the breakfast-table, to take up the work she had laid out to do. And she accomplished it, though many times her hands dropped idle and her eyes peered out of her window at the drab slides of the old mountain.

Later, when she went out to ride, she saw the cowboy Lem working in the blacksmith shop.

"Wal, Miss Collie, air you-all still hangin' round this hyar ranch?" he asked, with welcoming smile.

"Lem, I'm almost ashamed now to face my good friends, I've neglected them so long," she replied.

"Aw, now, what're friends fer but to go to? ... You're lookin' pale, I reckon. More like thet thar flower I see so much on the hills."

"Lem, I want to ride Pronto. Do you think he's all right, now?"

"I reckon some movin' round will do Pronto good. He's eatin' his haid off."

The cowboy went with her to the pasture gate and whistled Pronto up. The mustang came trotting, evidently none the worse for his injuries, and eager to resume the old climbs with his mistress. Lem saddled him, paying particular attention to the cinch.

"Reckon we'd better not cinch him tight," said Lem. "You jest be careful an' remember your saddle's loose."

"All right, Lem," replied Columbine, as she mounted. "Where are the boys this morning?"

"Blud an' Jim air repairin' fence up the crick."

"And where's Ben?"

"Ben? Oh, you mean Wade. Wal, I 'ain't seen him since yestidday. He was skinnin' a lion then, over hyar on the ridge. Thet was in the mawnin'. I reckon he's around, fer I seen some of the hounds."

"Then, Lem—you haven't heard about the fight yesterday between Jack and Wilson Moore?"

Lem straightened up quickly. "Nope, I 'ain't heerd a word."

"Well, they fought, all right," said Columbine, hurriedly. "I saw it. I was the only one there. Wilson was badly used up before dad and Ben got there. Ben drove off with him."

"But, Miss Collie, how'd it come off? I seen Wils the other day. Was up to his homestead. An' the boy jest manages to rustle round on a crutch. He couldn't fight."

"That was just it. Jack saw his opportunity, and he

forced Wilson to fight—accused him of stealing. Wils tried to avoid trouble. Then Jack jumped him. Wilson fought and held his own until Jack began to kick his injured foot. Then Wilson fainted and—and Jack beat him."

Lem dropped his head, evidently to hide his expression. "Wal, dog-gone me!" he ejaculated. "Thet's too bad."

Columbine left the cowboy and rode up the lane toward Wade's cabin. She did not analyze her deliberate desire to tell the truth about that fight, but she would have liked to proclaim it to the whole range and to the world. Once clear of the house she felt free, unburdened, and to talk, seemed to relieve some congestion of her thoughts.

The hounds heralded Columbine's approach with a deep and booming chorus. Sampson and Jim lay upon the porch, unleashed. The other hounds were chained separately in the aspen grove a few rods distant. Sampson thumped the boards with his big tail, but he did not get up, which laziness attested to the fact that there had been a lion chase the day before and he was weary and stiff. If Wade had been at home he would have come out to see what had occasioned the clamor. As Columbine rode by she saw another fresh lion-pelt pegged upon the wall of the cabin.

She followed the brook. It had cleared since the rains and was shining and sparkling in the rough, swift places, and limpid and green in the eddies. She passed the dam made by the solitary beaver that inhabited the valley. Freshly cut willows showed how the beaver was preparing for the long winter ahead. Columbine remembered then how greatly pleased Wade had been to learn about this old beaver; and more than once Wade had talked about trapping some younger beavers and bringing them there to make company for the old fellow.

The trail led across the brook at a wide, shallow place, where the splashing made by Pronto sent the trout scurrying for deeper water. Columbine kept to that trail, knowing that it led up into Sage Valley, where Wilson Moore had taken up the homestead property. Fresh horse tracks told her that Wade had ridden along there some time earlier. Pronto shied at the whirring of sage-hens. Presently Columbine ascertained they were flushed by the hound Kane, that had broken loose and followed her. He had done so before, and the fact had not displeased her.

"Kane! Kane! come here!" she called. He came readily, but halted a rod or so away, and made an attempt at wagging his tail, a function evidently somewhat difficult for him. When she resumed trotting he followed her.

Old White Slides had lost all but the drabs and dull yellows and greens, and of course those pale, light slopes that had given the mountain its name. Sage Valley was only one of the valleys at its base. It opened out half a mile wide, dominated by the looming peak, and bordered on the far side by an aspen-thicketed slope. The brook babbled along under the edge of this thicket. Cattle and horses grazed here and there on the rich, grassy levels. Columbine was surprised to see so many cattle and wondered to whom they belonged. All of Belllounds's stock had been driven lower down for the winter. There among the several horses that whistled at her approach she espied the white mustang Bell-lounds had given to Moore. It thrilled her to see him. And next, she suffered a pang to think that perhaps his owner might never ride him again. But Columbine held her emotions in abeyance.

The cabin stood high upon a level terrace, with clusters of aspens behind it, and was sheltered from winter blasts by a gray cliff, picturesque and crumbling, with its face overgrown by creeping vines and colorful shrubs. Wilson Moore could not have chosen a more secluded and beautiful valley for his homesteading adventure. The little gray cabin, with smoke curling from the stone chimney, had lost its look of dilapidation and disuse, yet there was nothing new that Columbine could see. The last quarter of the ascent of the slope, and the few rods across the level terrace, seemed extraordinarily long to Columbine. As she dismounted and tied Pronto her heart was beating and her breath was coming fast.

The door of the cabin was open. Kane trotted past the hesitating Columbine and went in.

"You son-of-a-hound-dog!" came to Columbine's listening ears in Wade's well-known voice. "I'll have to beat you—sure as you're born."

"I heard a horse," came in a lower voice, that was Wilson's.

"Darn me if I'm not gettin' deafer every day," was the reply.

Then Wade appeared in the doorway.

"It's nobody but Miss Collie," he announced, as he made way for her to enter.

"Good morning!" said Columbine, in a voice that

had more than cheerfulness in it.

"*Collie!* ... Did you come to see me?"

She heard this incredulous query just an instant before she saw Wilson at the far end of the room, lying under the light of a window. The inside of the cabin seemed vague and unfamiliar.

"I surely did," she replied, advancing. "How are you?"

"Oh, I'm all right. Tickled to death, right now.... Only, I hate to have you see this battered mug of mine."

"You needn't—care," said Columbine, unsteadily. And indeed, in that first glance she did not see him clearly. A mist blurred her sight and there was a lump in her throat. Then, to recover herself, she looked around the cabin.

"Well—Wils Moore—if this isn't fine!" she ejaculated, in amaze and delight. Columbine sustained an absolute surprise. A magic hand had transformed the interior of that rude old prospector's abode. A carpenter and a mason and a decorator had been wonderfully at work. From one end to the other Columbine gazed; from the big window under which Wilson lay on a blanketed couch to the open fireplace where Wade grinned she looked and looked and then up to the clean, aspen-poled roof and down to the floor, carpeted with deer hides. The chinks between the logs of the walls were plastered with red clay; the dust and dirt were gone; the place smelled like sage and wood-smoke and fragrant, frying meat. Indeed, there were a glowing bed of embers and a steaming kettle and a smoking pot; and the way the smoke and steam curled up into the gray old chimney attested to its splendid draught. In each corner hung a deer-head, from the antlers of which depended accoutrements of a cowboy—spurs, ropes, belts, scarfs, guns. One corner contained a cupboard, ceiling high, with new, clean doors of wood, neatly made; and next to it stood a table, just as new. On the blank wall beyond that were pegs holding saddles, bridles, blankets, clothes.

"He did it—all this inside," burst out Moore, delighted with her delight. "Quicker than a flash! Collie, isn't this great? I don't mind being down on my back. ...And he says they call him Hell-Bent Wade. I call him Heaven-Sent Wade!"

When Columbine turned to the hunter, bursting with her pleasure and gratitude, he suddenly dropped the forked stick he used as a lift, and she saw his hand shake when he stooped to recover it. How strangely that struck her!

"Ben, it's perfectly possible that you've been sent by Heaven," she remarked, with a humor which still held gravity in it.

"Me! A good angel? That'd be a new job for Bent Wade," he replied, with a queer laugh. "But I reckon I'd try to live up to it."

There were small sprigs of golden aspen leaves and crimson oak leaves on the wall above the foot of Wilson's bed. Beneath them, on pegs, hung a rifle. And on the window-sill stood a glass jar containing columbines. They were fresh. They had just been picked. They waved gently in the breeze, sweetly white and blue, strangely significant to the girl.

Moore laughed defiantly.

"Wade thought to fetch these flowers in," he explained. "They're his favorites as well as mine. It won't be long now till the frost kills them . . . and I want to be happy while I may!"

Again Columbine felt that deep surge within her, beyond her control, beyond her understanding, but now gathering and swelling, soon to be reckoned with. She did not look at Wilson's face then. Her downcast gaze saw that his right hand was bandaged, and she touched it with an unconscious tenderness.

"Your hand! Why is it all wrapped up?"

The cowboy laughed with grim humor.

"Have you seen Jack this morning?"

"No," she replied, shortly.

"Well, if you had, you'd know what happened to my fist."

"Did you hurt it on him?" she asked, with a queer little shudder that was not unpleasant.

"Collie, I busted that fist on his handsome face."

"Oh, it was dreadful!" she murmured. "Wilson, he meant to kill you."

"Sure. And I'd cheerfully have killed him."

"You two must never meet again," she went on.

"I hope to Heaven we never do," replied Moore, with a dark earnestness that meant more than his actual words.

"Wilson, will you avoid him—for my sake?" implored Columbine, unconsciously clasping the bandaged hand.

"I will. I'll take the back trails. I'll sneak like a coyote. I'll hide and I'll watch. . . . But, Columbine Bell-lounds, if he ever corners me again—"

"Why, you'll leave him to Hell-Bent Wade," interrupted the hunter, and he looked up from where he knelt, fixing those great, inscrutable eyes upon the cowboy. Columbine saw something beyond his face, deeper than the gloom, a passion and a spirit that drew her like a magnet. "An' now, Miss Collie," he went on, "I reckon you'll want to wait on our invalid. He's got to be fed."

"I surely will," replied Columbine, gladly, and she sat down on the edge of the bed. "Ben, you fetch that box and put his dinner on it."

While Wade complied, Columbine, shyly aware of her nearness to the cowboy, sought to keep up conversation.

"Couldn't you help yourself with your left hand?" she inquired.

"That's one worse," he answered, taking it from under the blanket, where it had been concealed.

"Oh!" cried Columbine, in dismay.

"Broke two bones in this one," said Wilson, with animation. "Say, Collie, our friend Wade is a doctor, too. Never saw his beat!"

"And a cook, too, for here's your dinner. You must sit up," ordered Columbine.

"Fold that blanket and help me up on it," replied Moore.

How strange and disturbing for Columbine to bend over him, to slip her arms under him and lift him! It recalled a long-forgotten motherliness of her doll-playing days. And her face flushed hot.

"Can't you move?" she asked, suddenly becoming aware of how dead a weight the cowboy appeared.

"Not—very much," he replied. Drops of sweat appeared on his bruised brow. It must have hurt him to move.

"You said your foot was all right."

"It is," he returned. "It's still on my leg, as I know darned well."

"Oh!" exclaimed Columbine, dubiously. Without further comment she began to feed him.

"It's worth getting licked to have this treat," he said.

"Nonsense!" she rejoined.

"I'd stand it again—to have you come here and feed me....But not from *him*."

"Wilson, I never knew you to be facetious before. Here, take this."

Apparently he did not see her outstretched hand.

"Collie, you've changed. You're older. You're a woman, now—and the prettiest—"

"Are you going to eat?" demanded Columbine.

"Huh!" exclaimed the cowboy, blankly. "Eat? Oh yes, sure. I'm powerful hungry. And maybe Heaven-Sent Wade can't cook!"

But Columbine had trouble in feeding him. What with his helplessness, and his propensity to watch her face instead of her hands, and her own mounting sensations of a sweet, natural joy and fitness in her proximity to him, she was hard put to it to show some dexterity as a nurse. And all the time she was aware of Wade, with his quiet, forceful presence, hovering near. Could he not see her hands trembling? And would he not think that weakness strange? Then driftingly came the thought that she would not shrink from Wade's reading her mind. Perhaps even now he understood her better than she understood herself.

"I can't—eat any more," declared Moore, at last.

"You've done very well for an invalid," observed Columbine. Then, changing the subject, she asked, "Wilson, you're going to stay here—winter here, dad would call it?"

"Yes."

"Are those your cattle down in the valley?"

"Sure. I've got near a hundred head. I saved my money and bought cattle."

"That's a good start for you. I'm glad. But who's going to take care of you and your stock until you can work again?"

"Why, my friend there, Heaven-Sent Wade," replied Moore, indicating the little man busy with the utensils on the table, and apparently hearing nothing.

"Can I fetch you anything to eat—or read?" she inquired.

"Fetch yourself," he replied, softly.

"But, boy, how could I fetch you anything without fetching myself?"

"Sure, that's right. Then fetch me some jam and a book—to-morrow. Will you?"

"I surely will."

"That's a promise. I know your promises of old."

"Then good-by till to-morrow. I must go. I hope you'll be better."

"I'll stay sick in bed till you stop coming."

Columbine left rather precipitously, and when she got outdoors it seemed that the hills had never been so softly, dreamily gray, nor their loneliness so sweet, nor the sky so richly and deeply blue. As she untied Pronto the hunter came out with Kane at his heels.

"Miss Collie, if you'll go easy I'll ketch my horse an' ride down with you," he said.

She mounted, and walked Pronto out to the trail, and slowly faced the gradual descent. It was really higher up there than she had surmised. And the view was beautiful. The gray, rolling foothills, so exquisitely colored at that hour, and the black-fringed ranges, one above the other, and the distant peaks, sunset-flushed across the purple, all rose open and clear to her sight, so wildly and splendidly expressive of the Colorado she loved.

At the foot of the slope Wade joined her.

"Lass, I'm askin' you not to tell Belllounds that I'm carin' for Wils," he said, in his gentle, persuasive way.

"I won't. But why not tell dad? He wouldn't mind. He'd do that sort of thing himself."

"Reckon he would. But this deal's out of the ordinary. An' Wils's not in as good shape as he thinks. I'm not takin' any chances. I don't want to lose my job, an' I don't want to be hindered from attendin' to this boy."

They had ridden as far as the first aspen grove when Wade concluded this remark. Columbine halted her horse, causing her companion to do likewise. Her former misgivings were augmented by the intelligence of Wade's sad, lined face.

"Ben, tell me," she whispered, with a hand going to his arm.

"Miss Collie, I'm a sort of doctor in my way. I studied some medicine an' surgery. An' I know. I wouldn't tell you this if it wasn't that I've got to rely on you to help me."

"I will—but go on—tell me," interposed Columbine trying to fortify herself.

"Wils's foot is all messed up. Buster Jack kicked it all out of shape. An' it's a hundred times worse than ever. I'm afraid of blood-poisonin' an' gangrene. You know gangrene is a dyin' an' rottin' of the flesh. . . . I told the boy straight out that he'd better let me cut his foot off. An' he swore he'd keep his foot or die! . . . Well, if gangrene does set in we can't save his leg, an' maybe not his life."

"Oh, it can't be as bad as all that!" cried Columbine. "Oh, I knew—I knew there was something. . . . Ben, you mean even at best now—he'll be a—" She broke off, unable to finish.

"Miss Collie, in any case Wils 'll never ride again—not like a cowboy."

That for Columbine seemed the worst and the last straw. Hot tears blinded her, hot blood gushed over her, hot heart-beats throbbed in her throat.

"Poor boy! That'll—ruin him," she cried. "He loved—a horse. He loved to ride. He was the—best rider of them all. And now he's ruined! He'll be lame—a cripple—club footed! . . . All because of that Jack Belllounds! The brute—the coward! I hate him! Oh, I *hate* him! . . . And I've got to marry him—on October first! Oh, God pity me!"

Blindly Columbine reeled out of her saddle and slowly dropped to the grass, where she burst into a violent storm of sobs and tears. It shook her every fiber. It was hopeless, terrible grief. The dry grass received her flood of tears and her incoherent words.

Wade dismounted and, kneeling beside her, placed

a gentle hand upon her heaving shoulder, but he spoke no word. By and by, when the storm had begun to subside, he raised her head.

"Lass, nothin' is ever so bad as it seems," he said, softly. "Come, sit up. Let me talk to you."

"Oh, Ben, something terrible *has* happened," she cried. "It's in *me!* I don't know what it is. But it'll kill me."

"I know," he replied, as her head fell upon his shoulder. "Miss Collie, I'm an old fellow that's had everythin' happen to him, an' I'm livin' yet, tryin' to help people along. No one dies so easy. Why, you're a fine, strong girl—an' somethin' tells me you was made for happiness. I know how things turn out. Listen—"

"But, Ben—you don't know—about me," she sobbed. "I've told you—I—hate Jack Belllounds. But I've—got to marry him!...His father raised me—from a baby. He brought me up. I owe him—my life....I've no relation—no mother—no father! No one loves me—for myself!"

"Nobody loves you!" echoed Wade, with an exquisite tone of repudiation. "Strange how people fool themselves! Lass, you're huggin' your troubles too hard. An' you're wrong. Why, everybody loves you! Lem an' Jim—why you just brighten the hard world they live in. An' that poor, hot-headed Jack—he loves you as well as he can love anythin'. An' the old man—no daughter could be loved more....An' I—I love you, lass, just like—as if you—might have been my own. I'm goin' to be the friend—the brother you need. An' I reckon I can come somewheres near bein' a mother, if you'll let me."

Something, some subtle power or charm, stole over

Columbine, assuaging her terrible sense of loss, of grief. There was tenderness in this man's hands, in his voice, and through them throbbed strong and passionate life and spirit.

"Do you really love me—*love* me?" she whispered, somehow comforted, somehow feeling that what he offered was what she had missed as a child. "And you want to be all that for me?"

"Yes, lass, an' I reckon you'd better try me."

"Oh, how good you are! I felt that—the very first time I was with you. I've wanted to come to you—to tell you my troubles. I love dad and he loves me, but he doesn't understand. Dad is wrapped up in his son. I've had no one. I never had any one."

"You have some one now," returned Wade, with a rich, deep mellowness in his voice that soothed Columbine and made her wonder. "An' because I've been through so much I can tell you what'll help you....Lass, if a woman isn't big an' brave, how will a man ever be? There's more in women than in men. Life has given you a hard knock, placin' you here—no real parents—an' makin' you responsible to a man whose only fault is blinded love for his son. Well, you've got to meet it, face it, with what a woman has more of than any man. Courage! Suppose you do hate this Buster Jack. Suppose you do love this poor, crippled Wilson Moore....Lass, don't look like that! Don't deny. You do love that boy. ...Well, it's hell. But you can never tell what'll happen when you're honest and square. If you feel it your duty to pay your debt to the old man you call dad—to pay it by marryin' his son, why do it, an' be a woman. There's nothin' as great as a woman can be. There's happiness that comes in strange, unheard-of ways. There's more in this life than what you want most. *You* didn't place yourself in this fix. So if you meet it with courage an' faithfulness to yourself, why, it'll not turn out as you dread....Some day, if you ever think you're broken-hearted, I'll tell you my story. An' then you'll not think your lot so hard. For I've had a broken heart an' ruined life, an' yet I've lived on an' on, findin' happiness I never dreamed would come, fightin' or workin'. An' how I found the world beautiful, an' how I love the flowers an' hills an' wild things so well—that, just that would be enough to live for!...An' think, lass, of what a wonderful happiness will come to me in showin' all this to you. That'll be the crownin' glory. An' if it's that much to me, then you be sure there's nothin' on earth I won't do for you."

Columbine lifted her tear-stained face with a light of inspiration.

"Oh, Wilson was right!" she murmured. "You are Heaven-sent! And I'm going to love you!"

A NEW spirit, or a liberation of her own, had fired Columbine, and was now burning within her, unquenchable and unutterable. Some divine spark had penetrated into that mysterious depth of her, to inflame and to illumine, so that when she arose from this hour of calamity she felt that to the tenderness and sorrow and fidelity in her soul had been added the lightning flash of passion.

"Oh, Ben—shall I be able to hold on to this?" she cried, flinging wide her arms, as if to embrace the winds of heaven.

"This what, lass?" he asked.

"This—this *woman!*" she answered, passionately, with her hands sweeping back to press her breast.

"No woman who wakes ever goes back to a girl again," he said, sadly.

"I wanted to die—and now I want to live—to fight. ...Ben, you've uplifted me. I was little, weak, miserable. ...But in my dreams, or in some state I can't remember or understand, I've waited for your very words. I was ready. It's as if I knew you in some other world, before I was born on this earth; and when you spoke to me here, so wonderfully—as my mother might have spoken—my heart leaped up in recognition of you and your call to my womanhood!...Oh, how strange and beautiful!"

"Miss Collie," he replied, slowly, as he bent to his saddle-straps, "you're young, an' you've no understandin' of what's strange an' terrible in life. An' beautiful, too, as you say....Who knows? Maybe in some former state I was somethin' to you. I believe in that. Reckon I can't say how or what. Maybe we were flowers or birds. I've a weakness for that idea."

"Birds! I like the thought, too," replied Columbine. "I love most birds. But there are hawks, crows, buzzards!"

"I reckon. Lass, there's got to be balance in nature. If it weren't for the ugly an' the evil, we wouldn't know the beautiful an' good....An' now let's ride home. It's gettin' late."

"Ben, ought I not go back to Wilson right now?" she asked, slowly.

"What for?"

"To tell him—something—and why I can't come tomorrow, or ever afterward," she replied, low and tremulously.

Wade pondered over her words. It seemed to Columbine that her sharpened faculties sensed something of hostility, of opposition in him.

"Reckon to-morrow would be better," he said, presently. "Wilson's had enough excitement for one day."

"Then I'll go to-morrow," she returned.

In the gathering, cold twilight they rode down the trail in silence.

"Good night, lass," said Wade, as he reached his cabin. "An' remember you're not alone any more."

"Good night, my friend," she replied, and rode on.

Columbine encountered Jim Montana at the corrals, and it was not too dark for her to see his foam-lashed horse. Jim appeared noncommittal, almost surly. But Columbine guessed that he had ridden to Kremmling and back in one day, on some order of Jack's.

"Miss Collie, I'll tend to Pronto," he offered. "An' yore supper'll be waitin'."

A bright fire blazed on the living-room hearth. The rancher was reading by its light.

"Hello, rosy-cheeks!" greeted the rancher, with unusual amiability. "Been ridin' ag'in' the wind, hey? Wal, if you ain't pretty, then my eyes are pore!"

"It's cold, dad," she replied, "and the wind stings. But I didn't ride fast nor far. . . . I've been up to see Wilson Moore."

"Ahuh! Wal, how's the boy?" asked Belllounds, gruffly.

"He said he was all right, but—but I guess that's not so," responded Columbine.

"Any friends lookin' after him?"

"Oh yes—he must have friends—the Andrewses and others. I'm glad to say his cabin is comfortable. He'll be looked after."

"Wal, I'm glad to hear thet. I'll send Lem or Wade up thar an' see if we can do anythin' fer the boy."

"Dad—that's just like you," replied Columbine, with her hand seeking his broad shoulder.

"Ahuh! Say, Collie, hyar's letters from 'most everybody in Kremmlin' wantin' to be invited up fer October first. How about askin' 'em?"

"The more the merrier," replied Columbine.

"Wal, I reckon I'll not ask anybody."

"Why not, dad?"

"No one can gamble on thet son of mine, even on his weddin'-day," replied Belllounds, gloomily.

"Dad, what'd Jack do to-day?"

"I'm not sayin' he did anythin'," answered the rancher.

"Dad, you can gamble on me."

"Wal, I should smile," he said, putting his big arm around her. "I wish you was Jack an' Jack was you."

At that moment the young man spoken of slouched into the room, with his head bandaged, and took a seat at the supper-table.

"Wal, Collie, let's go an' get it," said the rancher, cheerily. "I can always eat, anyhow."

"I'm hungry as a bear," rejoined Columbine, as she took her seat, which was opposite Jack.

"Where've you been?" he asked, curiously.

"Why, good evening, Jack! Did you finally notice me? . . . I've been riding Pronto, the first time since he was hurt. Had a lovely ride—up through Sage Valley."

Jack glowered at her with the one unbandaged eye, and growled something under his breath, and then began to stab meat and potatoes with his fork.

"What's the matter, Jack? Aren't you well?" asked Columbine, with a solicitude just a little too sweet to be genuine.

"Yes, I'm well," snapped Jack.

"But you look sick. That is, what I can see of your face looks sick. Your mouth droops at the corners. You're very pale—and red in spots. And your one eye glows with unearthly woe, as if you were not long for this world!"

The amazing nature of this speech, coming from the girl who had always been so sweet and quiet and backward, was attested to by the consternation of Jack and the mirth of his father.

"Are you making fun of me?" demanded Jack.

"Why, Jack! Do you think I would make fun of you? I only wanted to say how queer you look....Are you going to be married with one eye?"

Jack collapsed at that, and the old man, after a long stare of open-mouthed wonder, broke out: "Haw! Haw! Haw!...By Golly! lass—I'd never believed thet was in you....Jack, be game an' take your medicine....An' both of you forgive an' forget. Thar'll be quarrels enough, mebbe, without rakin' over the past."

When alone again Columbine reverted to a mood vastly removed from her apparent levity with the rancher and his son. A grave and inward-searching thought possessed her, and it had to do with the uplift, the spiritual advance, the rise above mere personal welfare, that had strangely come to her through Bent Wade. From their first meeting he had possessed a singular attraction for her that now, in the light of the meaning of his life, seemed to Columbine to be the man's nobility and wisdom, arising out of his travail, out of the terrible years that had left their record upon his face.

And so Columbine strove to bind forever in her soul the spirit which had arisen in her, interpreting from Wade's rude words of philosophy that which she needed for her own light and strength.

She appreciated her duty toward the man who had been a father to her. Whatever he asked that would she do. And as for the son she must live with the rest of her life, her duty there was to be a good wife, to bear with his faults, to strive always to help him by kindness, patience, loyalty, and such affection as was possible to her. Hate had to be reckoned with, and hate, she knew, had no place in a good woman's heart. It must be expelled, if that were humanly possible. All this was hard, would grow harder, but she accepted it, and knew her mind.

Her soul was her own, unchangeable through any adversity. She could be with that alone always, aloof from the petty cares and troubles common to people. Wade's words had thrilled her with their secret, with their limitless hope of an unknown world of thought and feeling. Happiness, in the ordinary sense, might never be hers. Alas for her dreams! But there had been given her a glimpse of something higher than pleasure and contentment. Dreams were but dreams. But she could still dream of what had been, of what might have been, of the beauty and mystery of life, of something in nature that called sweetly and irresistibly to her. Who could rob her of the rolling, gray, velvety hills, and the purple peaks and the black ranges, among which she had been found a waif, a little lost creature, born like a columbine under the spruces?

Love, sudden-dawning, inexplicable love, was her secret, still tremulously new, and perilous in its sweetness. That only did she fear to realize and to face, because it was an unknown factor, a threatening flame. Her sudden knowledge of it seemed inextricably merged with the mounting, strong, and steadfast stream of her spirit.

"I'll go to him. I'll tell him," she murmured. "He shall have *that!* . . . Then I must bid him—good-by—forever!"

To tell Wilson would be sweet; to leave him would be bitter. Vague possibilities haunted her. What might come of the telling? How dark loomed the bitterness! She could not know what hid in either of these acts until they were fulfilled. And the hours became long, and sleep far off, and the quietness of the house a torment, and the melancholy wail of coyotes a reminder of happy girlhood, never to return.

When next day the long-deferred hour came Columbine selected a horse that she could run, and she rode up the winding valley swift as the wind. But at the aspen grove, where Wade's keen, gentle voice had given her secret life, she suffered a reaction that made her halt and ascend the slope very slowly and with many stops.

Sight of Wade's horse haltered near the cabin relieved Columbine somewhat of a gathering might of emotion. The hunter would be inside and so she would not be compelled at once to confess her secret. This expectancy gave impetus to her lagging steps. Before she reached the open door she called out.

"Collie, you're late," answered Wilson, with both joy and reproach, as she entered. The cowboy lay upon his bed, and he was alone in the room.

"Oh! . . . Where is Ben?" exclaimed Columbine.

"He was here. He cooked my dinner. We waited, but you never came. The dinner got cold. I made sure you'd backed out—weren't coming at all—and I couldn't eat. . . . Wade said he knew you'd come. He went off with the hounds, somewhere . . . and oh, Collie, it's all right now!"

Columbine walked to his bedside and looked down upon him with a feeling as if some giant hand was tugging at her heart. He looked better. The swelling and redness of his face were less marked. And at that moment no pain shadowed his eyes. They were soft, dark, eloquent. If Columbine had not come with her avowed resolution and desire to unburden her heart she would have found that look in his eyes a desperately hard one to resist. Had it ever shone there before? Blind she had been.

"You're better," she said, happily.

"Sure—*now*. But I had a bad night. Didn't sleep till near daylight. Wade found me asleep. . . . Collie, it's good of you to come. You look so—so wonderful! I never saw your face glow like that. And your eyes—oh!"

"You think I'm pretty, then?" she asked, dreamily, not occupied at all with that thought.

He uttered a contemptuous laugh.

"Come closer," he said, reaching for her with a clumsy bandaged hand.

Down upon her knees Columbine fell. Both hands

flew to cover her face. And as she swayed forward she shook violently, and there escaped her lips a little, muffled sound.

"Why—Collie!" cried Moore, astounded. "Good Heavens! Don't cry! I—I didn't mean anything. I only wanted to feel you—touch your hand."

"Here," she answered, blindly holding out her hand, groping for his till she found it. Her other was still pressed to her eyes. One moment longer would Columbine keep her secret—hide her eyes—revel in the unutterable joy and sadness of this crisis that could come to a woman only once.

"What in the world?" ejaculated the cowboy, now bewildered. But he possessed himself of the trembling hand offered. "Collie, you act so strange.... You're *not* crying!...Am I only locoed, or flighty, or what? Dear, look at me."

Columbine swept her hand from her eyes with a gesture of utter surrender.

"Wilson, I'm ashamed—and sad—and gloriously happy," she said, with swift breathlessness.

"Why?" he asked.

"Because of—of something I have to tell you," she whispered.

"What is that?"

She bent over him.

"Can't you guess?"

He turned pale, and his eyes burned with intense fire.

"I won't guess...I daren't guess."

"It's something that's been true for years—forever,

it seems—something I never dreamed of till last night," she went on, softly.

"Collie!" he cried. "Don't torture me!"

"Do you remember long ago—when we quarreled so dreadfully—because you kissed me?" she asked.

"Do you think I could kiss *you*—and live to forget?"

"I love you!" she whispered, shyly, feeling the hot blood burn her.

That whisper transformed Wilson Moore. His arm flashed round her neck and pulled her face down to his, and, holding her in a close embrace, he kissed her lips and cheeks and wet eyes, and then again her lips, passionately and tenderly.

Then he pressed her head down upon his breast.

"My God! I can't believe! Say it again!" he cried, hoarsely.

Columbine buried her flaming face in the blanket covering him, and her hands clutched it tightly. The wildness of his joy, the strange strength and power of his kisses, utterly changed her. Upon his breast she lay, without desire to lift her face. All seemed different, wilder, as she responded to his appeal: "Yes, I love you! Oh, I love—love—love you!"

"Dearest! . . . Lift your face. . . . It's true now. I know. It's proved. But let me look at you."

Columbine lifted herself as best she could. But she was blinded by tears and choked with utterance that would not come, and in the grip of a shuddering emotion that was realization of loss in a moment when she learned the supreme and imperious sweetness of love.

"Kiss me, Columbine," he demanded.

Through blurred eyes she saw his face, white and

rapt, and she bent to it, meeting his lips with her first kiss, which was her last.

"Again, Collie—again!" he begged.

"No—no more," she whispered, very low, and encircling his neck with her arms she hid her face and held him convulsively, and stifled the sobs that shook her.

Then Moore was silent, holding her with his free hand, breathing hard, and slowly quieting down. Columbine felt then that he knew that there was something terribly wrong, and that perhaps he dared not voice his fear. At any rate, he silently held her, waiting. That silent wait grew unendurable for Columbine. She wanted to prolong this moment that was to be all she could ever surrender. But she dared not do so, for she knew if he ever kissed her again her duty to Belllounds would vanish like mist in the sun.

To release her hold upon him seemed like a tearing of her heartstrings. She sat up, she wiped the tears from her eyes, she rose to her feet, all the time striving for strength to face him again.

A loud voice, ringing from the cliffs outside, startled Columbine. It came from Wade calling the hounds. He had returned, and the fact stirred her.

"I'm to marry Jack Belllounds on October first."

The cowboy raised himself up as far as he was able. It was agonizing for Columbine to watch the changing and whitening of his face!

"No—no!" he gasped.

"Yes, it's true," she replied, hopelessly.

"*No!*" he exclaimed, hoarsely.

"But, Wilson, I tell you yes. I came to tell you. It's true—oh, it's true!"

"But, girl, you said you love me," he declared, transfixing her with dark, accusing eyes.

"That's just as terribly true."

He softened a little, and something of terror and horror took the place of anger.

Just then Wade entered the cabin with his soft tread, hesitated, and then came to Columbine's side. She could not unrivet her gaze from Moore to look at her friend, but she reached out with trembling hand to him. Wade clasped it in a horny palm.

Wilson fought for self-control in vain.

"Collie, if you love me, how can you marry Jack Belllounds?" he demanded.

"I must."

"Why must you?"

"I owe my life and my bringing up to his father. He wants me to do it. His heart is set upon my helping Jack to become a man. . . . Dad loves me, and I love him. I must stand by him. I must repay him. It is my duty."

"You've a duty to yourself—as a woman!" he rejoined, passionately. "Belllounds is wrapped up in his son. He's blind to the shame of such a marriage. But you're not."

"Shame?" faltered Columbine.

"Yes. The shame of marrying one man when you love another. You can't love two men. . . . You'll give yourself. You'll be his *wife!* Do you understand what that means?"

"I—I think—I do," replied Columbine, faintly. Where had vanished all her wonderful spirit? This fire-eyed boy was breaking her heart with his reproach.

"But you'll bear his children," cried Wilson. "Mother of—them—when you love me!...Didn't you think of that?"

"Oh no—I never did—I never did!" wailed Columbine.

"Then you'll think before it's too late?" he implored, wildly. "Dearest Collie, think! You won't ruin yourself! You won't? Say you won't!"

"But—Oh, Wilson, what *can* I say? I've got to marry him."

"Collie, I'll kill him before he gets you."

"You mustn't talk so. If you fought again—if anything terrible happened, it'd kill me."

"You'd be better off!" he flashed, white as a sheet.

Columbine leaned against Wade for support. She was fast weakening in strength, although her spirit held. She knew what was inevitable. But Wilson's agony was rending her.

"Listen," began the cowboy again. "It's your life— your happiness—your soul....Belllounds is crazy over that spoiled boy. He thinks the sun rises and sets in him....But Jack Belllounds is no good on this earth!... Collie dearest, don't think that's my jealousy. I am horribly jealous. But I know him. He's not worth *you!* No man is—and he the least. He'll break your heart, drag you down, ruin your health—kill you, as sure as you stand there. I want you to know I could prove to you what he is. But don't make me. Trust me, Collie. Believe me."

"Wilson, I do believe you," cried Columbine. "But

it doesn't make any difference. It only makes my duty harder."

"He'll treat you like he treats a horse or a dog. He'll beat you—"

"He never will! If he ever lays a hand on me—"

"If not that, he'll tire of you. Jack Belllounds never stuck to anything in his life, and never will. It's not in him. He wants what he can't have. If he gets it, then right off he doesn't want it. Oh, I've known him since he was a kid.... Columbine, you've a mistaken sense of duty. No girl need sacrifice her all because some man found her a lost baby and gave her a home. A woman owes more to herself than to any one."

"Oh, that's true, Wilson. I've thought it all.... But you're unjust—hard. You make no allowance for—for some possible good in every one. Dad swears I can reform Jack. Maybe I can. I'll pray for it."

"Reform Jack Belllounds! How can you save a bad egg? That damned coward! Didn't he prove to you what he was when he jumped on me and kicked my broken foot till I fainted? ... What do you want?"

"Don't say any more—please," cried Columbine. "Oh, I'm so sorry.... I oughtn't have come.... Ben, take me home."

"But, Collie, I love you," frantically urged Wilson. "And he—he may love you—but he's—Collie—he's been—"

Here Moore seemed to bite his tongue, to hold back speech, to fight something terrible and desperate and cowardly in himself.

Columbine heard only his impassioned declaration of love, and to that she vibrated.

"You speak as if this was one-sided," she burst out, as once more the gush of hot blood surged over her. "You don't love me any more than I love you. Not as much, for I'm a woman!...I love with all my heart and soul!"

Moore fell back upon the bed, spent and overcome.

"Wade, my friend, for God's sake do something," he whispered, appealing to the hunter as if in a last hope. "Tell Collie what it'll mean for her to marry Bell-lounds. If that doesn't change her, then tell her what it'll mean to me. I'll never go home. I'll never leave here. If she hadn't told me she loved me then, I might have stood anything. But now I can't. It'll kill me, Wade."

"Boy, you're talkin' flighty again," replied Wade. "This mornin' when I come you were dreamin' an' talkin'—clean out of your head.... Well, now, you an' Collie listen. You're right an' she's right. I reckon I never run across a deal with two people fixed just like you. But that doesn't hinder me from feelin' the same about it as I'd feel about somethin' I was used to."

He paused, and, gently releasing Columbine, he went to Moore, and retied his loosened bandage, and spread out the disarranged blankets. Then he sat down on the edge of the bed and bent over a little, running a roughened hand through the scant hair that had begun to silver upon his head. Presently he looked up, and from that sallow face, with its lines and furrows, and from the deep, inscrutable eyes, there fell a light which, however sad and wise in its infinite understanding of pain and strife, was still ruthless and unquenchable in its hope.

"Wade, for God's sake save Columbine!" impor- tuned Wilson.

"Oh, if you only could!" cried Columbine, impelled beyond her power to resist by that prayer.

"Lass, you stand by your convictions," he said, im- pressively. "An' Moore, you be a man an' don't make it so hard for her. Neither of you can do anythin'....Now there's old Belllounds—he'll never change. He might r'ar up for this or that, but he'll never change his cher- ished hopes for his son....But Jack might change! Lookin' back over all the years I remember many boys like this Buster Jack, an' I remember how in the nature of their doin's they just hanged themselves. I've a queer foresight about people whose trouble I've made my own. It's somethin' that never fails. When their trouble's goin' to turn out bad then I feel a terrible yearnin' to tell the story of Hell-Bent Wade. That foresight of trouble gave me my name....But it's not operatin' here....An' so, my young friends, you can believe me when I say some- thin' will happen. As far as October first is concerned, or any time near, Collie isn't goin' to marry Jack Bell- lounds."

CHAPTER
10

ONE day Wade remarked to Belllounds: "You can never tell what a dog is until you know him. Dogs are like men. Some of 'em look good, but they're really bad. An' that works the other way round. If a dog's born to run wild an' be a sheep-killer, that's what he'll be. I've known dogs that loved men as no humans could have loved them. It doesn't make any difference to a dog if his master is a worthless scamp."

"Wal, I reckon most of them hounds I bought had no good masters, judgin' from the way they act," replied the rancher.

"I'm developin' a first-rate pack," said Wade. "Jim hasn't any faults exceptin' he doesn't bay enough. Sampson's not as true-nosed as Jim, but he'll follow Jim, an' he has a deep, heavy bay you can hear for miles. So that makes up for Jim's one fault. These two hounds hang together, an' with them I'm developin' others. Denver will split off of bear or lion tracks when he jumps a deer. I reckon he's not young enough to be cured of that. Some of the younger hounds are comin' on fine. But there's two dogs in the bunch that beat me all hollow."

"Which ones?" asked Belllounds.

"There's that bloodhound, Kane," replied the hunter. "He's sure a queer dog. I can't win him. He minds me now because I licked him, an' once good an' hard when he bit me....But he doesn't cotton to me worth a damn. He's gettin' fond of Miss Columbine, an' I believe might make a good watch-dog for her. Where'd he come from, Belllounds?"

"Wal, if I don't disremember he was born in a prairie-schooner, comin' across the plains. His mother was a full-blood, an' come from Louisiana."

"That accounts for an instinct I see croppin' out in Kane," rejoined Wade. "He likes to trail a man. I've caught him doin' it. An' he doesn't take to huntin' lions or bear. Why, the other day, when the hounds treed a lion an' went howlin' wild, Kane came up, an' he looked disgusted an' went off by himself. He hunts by himself, anyhow. First off I thought he might be a sheep-killer. But I reckon not. He can trail men, an' that's about all the good he is. His mother must have been a slave-hunter, an' Kane inherits that trailin' instinct."

"Ahuh! Wal, train him on trailin' men, then. I've seen times when a dog like thet'd come handy. An' if he takes to Collie an' you approve of him, let her have him. She's been coaxin' me fer a dog."

"That isn't a bad idea. Miss Collie walks an' rides

alone a good deal, an' she never packs a gun."

"Funny about thet," said Belllounds. "Collie is game in most ways, but she'd never kill anythin'.... Wade, you ain't thinkin' she ought to stop them lonesome walks an' rides?"

"No, sure not, so long as she doesn't go too far away."

"Ahuh! Wal, supposin' she rode up out of the valley, west on the Black Range?"

"That won't do, Belllounds," replied Wade, seriously. "But Miss Collie's not goin' to, for I've cautioned her. Fact is I've run across some hard-lookin' men between here an' Buffalo Park. They're not hunters or prospectors or cattlemen or travelers."

"Wal, you don't say!" rejoined Belllounds. "Now, Wade, are you connectin' up them strangers with the stock I missed on this last round-up?"

"Reckon I can't go as far as that," returned Wade. "But I didn't like their looks."

"Thet comin' from you, Wade, is like the findin's of a jury.... It's gettin' along toward October. Snow'll be flyin' soon. You don't reckon them strangers will winter in the woods?"

"No, I don't. Neither does Lewis. You recollect him?"

"Yes, thet prospector who hangs out around Buffalo Park, lookin' fer gold. He's been hyar. Good fellar, but crazy on gold."

"I've met Lewis several times, one place and another. I lost the hounds day before yesterday. They treed a lion an' Lewis heard the racket, an' he stayed with them till I come up. Then he told me some interestin' news. You see he's been worryin' about this gang thet's rangin' around Buffalo Park, an' he's tried to get a line on them. Somebody took a shot at him in the woods. He couldn't swear it was one of that outfit, but he could swear he wasn't near shot by accident. Now Lewis says these men pack to an' fro from Elgeria, an' he has a hunch they're in cahoots with Smith, who runs a place there. You know Smith?"

"No, I don't, an' haven't any wish to," declared Bell-lounds, shortly. "He always looked shady to me. An' he's not been square with friends of mine in Elgeria. But no one ever proved him crooked, whatever was thought. Fer my part, I never missed a guess in my life. Men don't have scars on their face like his fer nothin'."

"Boss, I'm confidin' what I want kept under your hat," said Wade, quietly. "I knew Smith. He's as bad as the West makes them. I gave him that scar.... An' when he sees me he's goin' for his gun."

"Wal, I'll be darned! Doesn't surprise me. It's a small world.... Wade, I'll keep my mouth shut, sure. But what's your game?"

"Lewis an' I will find out if there is any connection between Smith an' this gang of strangers—an' the occasional loss of a few head of stock."

"Ahuh! Wal, you have my good will, you bet.... Sure thar's been some rustlin' of cattle. Not enough to make any rancher holler, an' I reckon there never will be any more of thet in Colorado. Still, if we get the drop on some outfit we sure ought to corral them."

"Boss, I'm tellin' you—"

"Wade, you ain't agoin' to start thet tellin' hell-bent

happenin's to come hyar at White Slides?" interrupted Belllounds, plaintively.

"No, I reckon I've no hunch like that now," responded Wade, seriously. "But I was about to say that if Smith is in on any rustlin' of cattle he'll be hard to catch, an' if he's caught there'll be shootin' to pay. He's cunnin' an' has had long experience. It's not likely he'd work openly, as he did years ago. If he's stealin' stock or buyin' an' sellin' stock that some one steals for him, it's only on a small scale, an' it'll be hard to trace."

"Wal, he might be deep," said Belllounds, reflectively. "But men like thet, no matter how deep or cunnin' they are, always come to a bad end. Jest works out natural. . . . Had you any grudge ag'in' Smith?"

"What I give him was for somebody else, an' was sure little enough. He's got the grudge against me."

"Ahuh! Wal, then, don't you go huntin' fer trouble. Try an' make White Slides one place thet'll disprove your name. All the same, don't shy at sight of anythin' suspicious round the ranch."

The old man plodded thoughtfully away, leaving the hunter likewise in a brown study.

"He's gettin' a hunch that I'll tell him of some shadow hoverin' black over White Slides," soliloquized Wade. "Maybe—maybe so. But I don't see any yet. . . . Strange how a man will say what he didn't start out to say. Now, I started to tell him about that amazin' dog Fox."

Fox was the great dog of the whole pack, and he had been absolutely overlooked, which fact Wade regarded with contempt for himself. Discovery of this particular dog came about by accident. Somewhere in the big corral there was a hole where the smaller dogs could escape, but Wade had been unable to find it. For that matter the corral was full of holes, not any of which, however, it appeared to Wade, would permit anything except a squirrel to pass in and out.

One day when the hunter, very much exasperated, was prowling around and around inside the corral, searching for this mysterious vent, a rather small dog, with short gray and brown woolly hair, and shaggy brows half hiding big, bright eyes, came up wagging his stump of a tail.

"Well, what do you know about it?" demanded Wade. Of course he had noticed this particular dog, but to no purpose. On this occasion the dog repeated so unmistakably former overtures of friendship that Wade gave him close scrutiny. He was neither young nor comely nor thoroughbred, but there was something in his intelligent eyes that struck the hunter significantly. "Say, maybe I overlooked somethin'? But there's been a heap of dogs round here an' you're no great shucks for looks. Now, if you're talkin' to me come an' find that hole."

Whereupon Wade began another search around the corral. It covered nearly an acre of ground, and in some places the fence-poles had been sunk near rocks. More than once Wade got down upon his hands and knees to see if he could find the hole. The dog went with him, watching with knowing eyes that the hunter imagined actually laughed at him. But they were glad eyes, which began to make an appeal. Presently, when Wade came to a rough place, the dog slipped under a shelving rock, and thence through a half-concealed hole in the fence;

and immediately came back through to wag his stump of a tail and look as if the finding of that hole was easy enough.

"You old fox," declared Wade, very much pleased, as he patted the dog. "You found it for me, didn't you? Good dog! Now I'll fix that hole, an' then you can come to the cabin with me. An' your name's Fox."

That was how Fox introduced himself to Wade, and found his opportunity. The fact that he was not a hound had operated against his being taken out hunting, and therefore little or no attention had been paid him. Very shortly Fox showed himself to be a dog of superior intelligence. The hunter had lived much with dogs and had come to learn that the longer he lived with them the more there was to marvel at and love.

Fox insisted so strongly on being taken out to hunt with the hounds that Wade, vowing not to be surprised at anything, let him go. It happened to be a particularly hard day on hounds because of old tracks and cross-tracks and difficult ground. Fox worked out a labyrinthine trail that Sampson gave up and Jim failed on. This delighted Wade, and that night he tried to find out from Andrews, who sold the dog to Belllounds, something about Fox. All the information obtainable was that Andrews suspected the fellow from whom he had gotten Fox had stolen him. Belllounds had never noticed him at all. Wade kept the possibilities of Fox to himself and reserved his judgment, and every day gave the dog another chance to show what he knew.

Long before the end of that week Wade loved Fox and decided that he was a wonderful animal. Fox liked to hunt, but it did not matter what he hunted. That depended upon the pleasure of his master. He would find hobbled horses that were hiding out and standing still to escape detection. He would trail cattle. He would tree squirrels and point grouse. Invariably he suited his mood to the kind of game he hunted. If put on an elk track, or that of deer, he would follow it, keeping well within sight of the hunter, and never uttering a single bark or yelp; and without any particular eagerness he would stick until he had found the game or until he was called off. Bear and cat tracks, however, roused the savage instinct in him, and transformed him. He yelped at every jump on a trail, and whenever his yelp became piercing and continuous Wade well knew the quarry was in sight. He fought bear like a wise old dog that knew when to rush in with a snap and when to keep away. When lions or wildcats were treed Fox lost much of his ferocity and interest. Then the matter of that particular quarry was ended. His most valuable characteristic, however, was his ability to stick on the track upon which he was put. Wade believed if he put Fox on the trail of a rabbit, and if a bear or lion were to cross that trail ahead of him, Fox would stick to the rabbit. Even more remarkable was it that Fox would not steal a piece of meat and that he would fight the other dogs for being thieves.

Fox and Kane, it seemed to the hunter in his reflective foreshadowing of events at White Slides, were destined to play most important parts.

Upon a certain morning, several days before October first—which date rankled in the mind of Wade—he left Moore's cabin, leading a pack-horse. The hounds he had left behind at the ranch, but Fox accompanied him.

"Wade, I want some elk steak," old Belllounds had said the day before. "Nothin' like a good rump steak! I was raised on elk meat. Now hyar, more'n a week ago I told you I wanted some. There's elk all around. I heerd a bull whistle at sunup to-day. Made me wish I was young ag'in!...You go pack in an elk."

"I haven't run across any bulls lately," Wade had replied, but he did not mention that he had avoided such a circumstance. The fact was Wade admired and loved the elk above all horned wild animals. So strange was his attitude toward elk that he had gone meat-hungry many a time with these great stags bugling near his camp.

As he climbed the yellow, grassy mountain-side, working round above the valley, his mind was not centered on the task at hand, but on Wilson Moore, who had come to rely on him with the unconscious tenacity of a son whose faith in his father was unshakable. The crippled cowboy kept his hope, kept his cheerful, grateful spirit, obeyed and suffered with a patience that was fine. There had been no improvement in his injured foot. Wade worried about that much more than Moore. The thing that mostly occupied the cowboy was the near approach of October first, with its terrible possibility for him. He did not talk about it, except when fever made him irrational, but it was plain to Wade how he prayed and hoped and waited in silence. Strange how he trusted Wade to avert catastrophe of Columbine's marriage! Yet such trust seemed familiar to Wade, as he reflected over past years. Had he not wanted such trust—had he not invited it?

For twenty years no happiness had come to Wade in any sense comparable to that now secretly his, as he lived near Columbine Belllounds, divining more and more each day how truly she was his own flesh and the image of the girl he had loved and married and wronged. Columbine was his daughter. He saw himself in her. And Columbine, from being strongly attracted to him and trusting in him and relying upon him, had come to love him. That was the most beautiful and terrible fact of his life—beautiful because it brought back the past, her babyhood, and his barren years, and gave him this sudden change, where he lived transported with the sense and the joy of his possession. It was terrible because she was unhappy, because she was chained to duty and honor, because ruin faced her, and lastly because Wade began to have the vague, gloomy intimations of distant tragedy. Far off, like a cloud on the horizon, but there! Long ago he had learned the uselessness of fighting his morbid visitations. But he clung to hope, to faith in life, to the victory of the virtuous, to the defeat of evil. A thousand proofs had strengthened him in that clinging.

There were personal dread and poignant pain for Wade in Columbine Belllounds's situation. After all, he had only his subtle and intuitive assurance that matters would turn out well for her in the end. To trust that now, when the shadow began to creep over his own daughter, seemed unwise—a juggling with chance.

"I'm beginnin' to feel that I couldn't let her marry that Buster Jack," soliloquized Wade, as he rode along the grassy trail. "Fust off, seein' how strong was her sense of duty an' loyalty, I wasn't so set against it. But somethin's growin' in me. Her love for that crippled boy, now, an' his for her! Lord! they're so young an' life must be so hot an' love so sweet! I reckon that's why I couldn't let her marry Jack....But, on the other hand, there's the old man's faith in his son, an' there's Collie's faith in herself an' in life. Now I believe in that. An' the years have proved to me there's hope for the worst of men....I haven't even had a talk with this Buster Jack. I don't know him, except by hearsay. An' I'm sure prejudiced, which's no wonder, considerin' where I saw him in Denver....I reckon, before I go any farther, I'd better meet this Belllounds boy an' see what's in him."

It was characteristic of Wade that this soliloquy abruptly ended his thoughtful considerations for the time being. This was owing to the fact that he rested upon a decision, and also because it was time he began to attend to the object of his climb.

Bench after bench he had ascended, and the higher he got the denser and more numerous became the aspen thickets and the more luxuriant the grass. Presently the long black slope of spruce confronted him, with its edge like a dark wall. He entered the fragrant forest, where not a twig stirred nor a sound pervaded the silence. Upon the soft, matted earth the hoofs of the horses made no impression and scarcely a perceptible thud.

Wade headed to the left, avoiding rough, rocky defiles of weathered cliff and wind-fallen trees, and aimed to find easy going up to the summit of the mountain bluff far above. This was new forest to him, consisting of moderate-sized spruce-trees growing so closely together that he had to go carefully to keep from snapping dead twigs. Fox trotted on in the lead, now and then pausing to look up at his master, as if for instructions.

A brightening of the dark-green gloom ahead showed the hunter that he was approaching a large glade or open patch, where the sunlight fell strongly. It turned out to be a swale, or swampy place, some few acres in extent, and directly at the foot of a last steep, wooded slope. Here Fox put his nose into the air and halted.

"What're you scentin', Fox, old boy?" asked Wade, with low voice, as he peered ahead. The wind was in the wrong direction for him to approach close to game without being detected. Fox wagged his stumpy tail and looked up with knowing eyes. Wade proceeded cautiously. The swamp was a rank growth of long, weedy grasses and ferns, with here and there a green-mossed bog half hidden and a number of dwarf oak-trees. Wade's horse sank up to his knees in the mire. On the other side showed fresh tracks along the wet margin of the swale.

"It's elk, all right," said Wade, as he dismounted. "Heard us comin'. Now, Fox, stick your nose in that track. An' go slow."

With rifle ready Wade began the ascent of the slope on foot, leading his horse. An old elk trail showed a fresh track. Fox accommodated his pace to that of the toiling hunter. The ascent was steep and led up through dense forest. At intervals, when Wade halted to catch his breath and listen, he heard faint snapping of dead ɔranches far above. At length he reached the top of the mountain, to find a wide, open space, with heavy forest in front, and a bare, ghastly, burned-over district to his right. Fox growled, and appeared about to dash forward. Then, in an opening through the forest, Wade espied a large bull elk, standing at gaze, evidently watching him. He was a gray old bull, with broken antlers. Wade made no move to shoot, and presently the elk walked out of sight.

"Too old an' tough, Fox," explained the hunter to the anxious dog. But perhaps that was not all Wade's motive in sparing him.

Once more mounted, Wade turned his attention to the burned district. It was a dreary, hideous splotch, a blackened slash in the green cover of the mountain. It sloped down into a wide hollow and up another bare slope. The ground was littered with bleached logs, trees that had been killed first by fire and then felled by wind. Here and there a lofty, spectral trunk still withstood the blasts. Across the hollow sloped a considerable area where all trees were dead and still standing—a melancholy sight. Beyond, and far round and down to the left, opened up a slope of spruce and bare ridge, where a few cedars showed dark, and then came black, spear-tipped forest again, leading the eye to the magnificent panorama of endless range on range, purple in the distance.

Wade found patches of grass where beds had been recently occupied.

"Mountain-sheep, by cracky!" exclaimed the hunter. "An' fresh tracks, too!...Now I wonder if it wouldn't do to kill a sheep an' tell Belllounds I couldn't find any elk."

The hunter had no qualms about killing mountain-sheep, but he loved the lordly stags and would have lied to spare them. He rode on, with keen gaze shifting everywhere to catch a movement of something in this wilderness before him. If there was any living animal in sight it did not move. Wade crossed the hollow, wended a circuitous route through the upstanding forest of dead timber, and entered a thick woods that skirted the rim of the mountain. Presently he came out upon the open rim, from which the depths of green and gray yawned mightily. Far across, Old White Slides loomed up, higher now, with a dignity and majesty unheralded from below.

Wade found fresh sheep tracks in the yellow clay of the rim, small as little deer tracks, showing that they had just been made by ewes and lambs. Not a ram track in the group!

"Well, that lets me out," said Wade, as he peered under the bluff for sight of the sheep. They had gone over the steep rim as if they had wings. "Beats hell how sheep can go down without fallin'! An' how they can hide!"

He knew they were near at hand and he wasted time peering to spy them out. Nevertheless, he could not locate them. Fox waited impatiently for the word to let him prove how easily he could rout them out, but this permission was not forthcoming.

"We're huntin' elk, you Jack-of-all-dogs," reprovingly spoke the hunter to Fox.

So they went on around the rim, and after a couple of miles of travel came to the forest, and then open heads of hollows that widened and deepened down. Here was excellent pasture and cover for elk. Wade left the rim to ride down these slow-descending half-open ridges, where cedars grew and jack-pines stood in clumps, and little grassy-bordered brooks babbled between. He saw tracks where a big buck deer had crossed ahead of him, and then he flushed a covey of grouse that scared the horses, and then he saw where a bear had pulled a rotten log to pieces. Fox did not show any interest in these things.

By and by Wade descended to the junction of these hollows, where three tiny brooklets united to form a stream of pure, swift, clear water, perhaps a foot deep and several yards wide.

"I reckon this's the head of the Troublesome," said Wade. "Whoever named this brook had no sense. . . . Yet here, at its source, it's gatherin' trouble for itself. That's the way of youth."

The grass grew thickly and luxuriantly and showed signs of recent grazing. Elk had been along the brook that morning. There were many tracks, like cow tracks, only smaller, deeper, and more oval; and there were beds where elk had lain, and torn-up places where bulls had plowed and stamped with heavy hoofs.

Fox trailed the herd to higher ground, where evidently they had entered the woods. Here Wade tied his horses, and, whispering to Fox, he proceeded stealthily through this strip of spruce. He came out to an open point, taking care, however, to keep well screened, from which he had a glimpse of a parklike hollow, grassy and watered. Working round to better vantage, he soon espied what had made Fox stand so stiff and bristling. A herd of elk were trooping up the opposite slope, scarcely a hundred yards distant. They had heard or scented him, but did not appear alarmed. They halted to look back. The hunter's quick estimate credited nearly two dozen to the herd, mostly cows. A magnificent bull, with wide-spreading antlers, and black head and shoulders and gray hind quarters, stalked out from the herd, and stood an instant, head aloft, splendidly significant of the wild. Then he trotted into the woods, his antlers noiselessly spreading the green. Others trotted off likewise. Wade raised his rifle and looked through the sight at the bull, and let him pass. Then he saw another over his rifle, and another. Reluctant and forced, he at last aimed and pulled trigger. The heavy Henry boomed out in the stillness. Fox dashed down with eager barks. When the smoke cleared away Wade saw the opposite slope bare except for one fallen elk.

Then he returned to his horses, and brought them back to where Fox perched beside the dead quarry.

"Well, Fox, that stag'll never bugle any more of a sunrise," said Wade. "Strange how we're made so we have to eat meat! I'd 'a' liked it otherwise."

He cut up the elk, and packed all the meat the horse could carry, and hung the best of what was left out of the reach of coyotes. Mounting once more, he ascended to the rim and found a slope leading down to the west. Over the basin country below he had hunted several days. This way back to the ranch was longer, he calculated, but less arduous for man and beast. His pack-horse would have hard enough going in any event. From time to time Wade halted to rest the burdened pack-animal. At length he came to a trail he had himself made, which he now proceeded to follow. It led out of the basin, through burned and boggy ground and down upon the forest slope, thence to the grassy and aspened uplands. One aspen grove, where he had rested before, faced the west, and, for reasons hard to guess, had suffered little from frost. All the leaves were intact, some still green, but most of them a glorious gold against the blue. It was a large grove, sloping gently, carpeted with yellow grass and such a profusion of purple asters as Wade had never seen in his flower-loving life. Here he dismounted and sat against an aspen-tree. His horses ruthlessly cropped the purple blossoms.

Nature in her strong prodigality had outdone herself here. Pale white the aspen-trees shone, and above was the fluttering, quivering canopy of gold tinged with green, and below clustered the asters, thick as stars in the sky, waving, nodding, swaying gracefully to each little autumn breeze, lilac-hued and lavender and pale violet, and all the shades of exquisite purple.

Wade lingered, his senses predominating. This was one of those moments that colored his lonely wanderings. Only to see was enough. He would have shut out the encroaching thoughts of self, of others, of life, had that been wholly possible. But here, after the first few moments of exquisite riot of his senses, where fragrance of grass and blossom filled the air, and blaze of gold canopied the purple, he began to think how beautiful the earth was, how Nature hid her rarest gifts for those who loved her most, how good it was to live, if only for these blessings. And sadness crept into his meditations because all this beauty was ephemeral, all the gold would soon be gone, and the asters, so pale and pure and purple, would soon be like the glory of a dream that had passed.

Yet still followed the saving thought that frost and winter must again yield to sun, and spring, summer, autumn would return with the flowers of their season, in that perennial birth so gracious and promising. The aspen leaves would quiver and slowly gild, the grass would wave in the wind, the asters would bloom, lifting star-pale faces to the sky. Next autumn, and every year, and forever, as long as the sun warmed the earth!

It was only man who would not always return to the haunts he loved.

CHAPTER

11

WHEN Bent Wade desired opportunities they seemed to gravitate to him.

Upon riding into the yard of White Slides Ranch he espied Jack Belllounds sitting in idle, moping posture on the porch. Something in his dejected appearance roused Wade's pity. No one else was in sight, so the hunter took advantage of the moment.

"Hey, Belllounds, will you give me a lift with this meat?" called Wade.

"Sure," replied Jack, readily enough, and he got up.

Wade led the pack-horse to the door of the store-cabin, which stood back of the kitchen and was joined to it by a roof. There, with Jack's assistance, he unloaded the meat and hung it up on pegs. This done, Wade set to work with knife in hand.

"I reckon a little trimmin' will improve the looks

of this carcass," observed Wade.

"Wade, we never had any one round except dad who could cut up a steer or elk," said Jack. "But you've got him beat."

"I'm pretty handy at most things."

"Handy!...I wish I could do just one thing as well as you. I can ride, but that's all. No one ever taught me anything."

"You're a young fellow yet, an' you've time, if you only take kindly to learnin'. I was past your age when I learned most I know."

The hunter's voice and his look, and that fascination which subtly hid in his presence, for the first time seemed to find the response of interest in young Belllounds.

"I can't stick, dad says, and he swears at me," replied Belllounds. "But I'll bet I could learn from you."

"Reckon you could. Why can't you stick to anythin'?"

"I don't know. I've been as enthusiastic over work as over riding mustangs. To ride came natural, but in work, when I do it wrong, then I hate it."

"Ahuh! That's too bad. You oughtn't to hate work. Hard work makes for what I reckon you like in a man, but don't understand. As I look back over my life—an' let me say, young fellar, it's been a tough one—what I remember most an' feel best over are the hardest jobs I ever did, an' those that cost the most sweat an' blood."

As Wade warmed to his subject, hoping to sow a good seed in Belllounds's mind, he saw that he was wasting his earnestness. Belllounds did not keep to the train of thought. His mind wandered, and now he was examining Wade's rifle.

"Old Henry forty-four," he said. "Dad has one. Also an old needle-gun. Say, can I go hunting with you?"

"Glad to have you. How do you handle a rifle?"

"I used to shoot pretty well before I went to Denver," he replied. "Haven't tried since I've been home.... Suppose you let me take a shot at that post?" And from where he stood in the door he pointed to a big hitching post near the corral gate.

The corral contained horses, and in the pasture beyond were cattle, any of which might be endangered by such a shot. Wade saw that the young man was in earnest, that he wanted to respond to the suggestion in his mind. Consequences of any kind did not awaken after the suggestion.

"Sure. Go ahead. Shoot low, now, a little below where you want to hit," said Wade.

Belllounds took aim and fired. A thundering report shook the cabin. Dust and splinters flew from the post.

"I hit it!" he exclaimed, in delight. "I was sure I wouldn't, because I aimed 'way under."

"Reckon you did. It was a good shot."

Then a door slammed and Old Bill Belllounds appeared, his hair upstanding, his look and gait proclaiming him on the rampage.

"Jack! What 'n hell are you doin'?" he roared, and he stamped up to the door to see his son standing there with the rifle in his hands. "By Heaven! If it ain't one thing it's another!"

"Boss, don't jump over the traces," said Wade. "I'll allow if I'd known the gun would let out a bellar like that I'd not have told Jack to shoot. Reckon it's because we're under the open roof that it made the racket. I'm wantin' to clean the gun while it's hot."

"Ahuh! Wal, I was scared fust, harkin' back to Indian days, an' then I was mad because I figgered Jack was up to mischief. . . . Did you fetch in the meat?"

"You bet. An' I'd like a piece for myself," replied Wade.

"Help yourself, man. An' say, come down an' eat with us fer supper."

"Much obliged, boss. I sure will."

Then the old rancher trudged back to the house.

"Wade, it was bully of you!" exclaimed Jack, gratefully. "You see how quick dad's ready to jump me? I'll bet he thought I'd picked a shooting-scrape with one of the cowboys."

"Well, he's gettin' old an' testy," replied Wade. "You ought to humor him. He'll not be here always."

Belllounds answered to that suggestion with a shadowing of eyes and look of realization, affection, remorse. Feelings seemed to have a quick rise and play in him, but were not lasting. Wade casually studied him, weighing his impressions, holding them in abeyance for a sum of judgment.

"Belllounds, has anybody told you about Wils Moore bein' bad hurt?" abruptly asked the hunter.

"He is, is he?" replied Jack, and to his voice and face came sudden change. "How bad?"

"I reckon he'll be a cripple for life," answered Wade, seriously, and now he stopped in his work to peer at Belllounds. The next moment might be critical for that young man.

"Club-footed!...He won't lord it over the cowboys any more—or ride that white mustang!" The softer, weaker expression of his face, that which gave him some title to good looks, changed to an ugliness hard for Wade to define, since it was neither glee, nor joy, nor gratification over his rival's misfortune. It was rush of blood to eyes and skin, a heated change that somehow to Wade suggested an anxious, selfish hunger. Belllounds lacked something, that seemed certain. But it remained to be proved how deserving he was of Wade's pity.

"Belllounds, it was a dirty trick—your jumpin' Moore," declared Wade, with deliberation.

"The hell you say!" Belllounds flared up, with scarlet in his face, with sneer of amaze, with promise of bursting rage. He slammed down the gun.

"Yes, the hell I say," returned the hunter. "They call me Hell-Bent Wade!"

"Are you friends with Moore?" asked Belllounds, beginning to shake.

"Yes, I'm that with every one. I'd like to be friends with you."

"I don't want you. And I'm giving you notice—you won't last long at White Slides."

"Neither will you!"

Belllounds turned dead white, not apparently from fury or fear, but from a shock that had its birth within the deep, mysterious, emotional reachings of his mind. He was utterly astounded, as if confronting a vague, terrible premonition of the future. Wade's swift words, like the ring of bells, had not been menacing, but prophetic.

"Young fellar, you need to be talked to, so if you've got any sense at all it'll get a wedge in your brain," went on Wade. "I'm a stranger here. But I happen to be a man who sees through things, an' I see how your dad handles you wrong. You don't know who I am an' you don't care. But if you'll listen you'll learn what might help you.... No boy can answer to all his wild impulses without ruinin' himself. It's not natural. There are other people—people who have wills an' desires, same as you have. You've got to live with people. Here's your dad an' Miss Columbine, an' the cowboys, an' me, an' all the ranchers, so down to Kremmlin' an' other places. These are the people you've got to live with. You can't go on as you've begun, without ruinin' yourself an' your dad an' the—the girl.... It's never too late to begin to be better. I know that. But it gets too late, sometimes, to save the happiness of others. Now I see where you're headin' as clear as if I had pictures of the future. I've got a gift that way.... An', Belllounds, you'll not last. Unless you begin to control your temper, to forget yourself, to kill your wild impulses, to be kind, to learn what love is—you'll never last! ... In the very nature of things, one comin' after another like your fights with Moore, an' your scarin' of Pronto, an' your drinkin' at Kremmlin', an' just now your r'arin' at me—it's in the very nature of life that goin' on so you'll sooner or later meet with hell! You've got to change, Belllounds. No half-way, spoiled-boy changin', but the straight right-about-face of a man! ... It means you must see you're no good an' have a change of heart. Men have revolutions like that. I was no good. I did worse than you'll ever do, because you're not big enough to be really bad, an' yet I've turned out worth livin'. . . . There, I'm through, an' I'm offerin' to be your friend an' to help you."

Belllounds stood with arms spread outside the door, still astounded, still pale; but as the long admonition and appeal ended he exploded stridently. "Who the hell are *you?* . . . If I hadn't been so surprised—if I'd had a chance to get a word in—I'd shut your trap! Are you a preacher masquerading here as hunter? Let me tell you, I won't be talked to like that—not by any man. Keep your advice an' friendship to yourself."

"You don't want me, then?"

"No," Belllounds snapped.

"Reckon you don't need either advice or friend, hey?"

"No, you owl-eyed, soft-voiced fool!" yelled Belllounds.

It was then Wade felt a singular and familiar sensation, a cold, creeping thing, physical and elemental, that had not visited him since he had been at White Slides.

"I reckoned so," he said, with low and gloomy voice, and he knew, if Belllounds did not know, that he was not acquiescing with the other's harsh epithet, but only greeting the advent of something in himself.

Belllounds shrugged his burly shoulders and slouched away.

Wade finished his dressing of the meat. Then he rode up to spend an hour with Moore. When he returned to his cabin he proceeded to change his hunter garb for the best he owned. It was a proof of his unusual preoccupation that he did this before he fed the hounds. It was sunset when he left his cabin. Montana Jim and

Lem hailed as he went by. Wade paused to listen to their good-natured raillery.

"See hyar, Bent, this ain't Sunday," said Lem.

"You're spruced up powerful fine. What's it fer?" added Montana.

"Boss asked me down to supper."

"Wal, you lucky son-of-a-gun! An' hyar we've no invite," returned Lem. "Say, Wade, I heerd Buster Jack roarin' at you. I was ridin' in by the storehouse.... 'Who the hell are you?' was what collared my attention, an' I had to laugh. An' I listened to all he said. So you was offerin' him advice an' friendship?"

"I reckon."

"Wal, all I say is thet you was wastin' yore breath," declared Lem. "You're a queer fellar, Wade."

"Queer? Aw, Lem, he ain't queer," said Montana. "He's jest white. Wade, I feel the same as you. I'd like to do somethin' fer thet locoed Buster Jack."

"Montana, you're the locoed one," rejoined Lem. "Buster Jack knows what he's doin'. He can play a slicker hand of poker than you."

"Wal, mebbe. Wade, do you play poker?"

"I'd hate to take your money," replied Wade.

"You needn't be so all-fired kind about thet. Come over to-night an' take some of it. Buster Jack invited himself up to our bunk. He's itchin' fer cards. So we says shore. Blud's goin' to sit in. Now you come an' make it five-handed."

"Wouldn't young Belllounds object to me?"

"What? Buster Jack shy at gamblin' with you? Not much. He's a born gambler. He'd bet with his grandmother an' he'd cheat the coppers off a dead nigger's eyes."

"Slick with cards, eh?" inquired Wade.

"Naw, Jack's not slick. But he tries to be. An' we jest go him one slicker."

"Wouldn't Old Bill object to this card-playin'?"

"He'd be ory-eyed. But, by Golly! we're not leadin' Jack astray. An' we ain't hankerin' to play with him. All the same a little game is welcome enough."

"I'll come over," replied Wade, and thoughtfully turned away.

When he presented himself at the ranch-house it was Columbine who let him in. She was prettily dressed, in a way he had never seen her before, and his heart throbbed. Her smile, her voice added to her nameless charm, that seemed to come from the past. Her look was eager and longing, as if his presence might bring something welcome to her.

Then the rancher stalked in. "Hullo, Wade! Supper's 'most ready. What's this trouble you had with Jack? He says he won't eat with you."

"I was offerin' him advice," replied Wade.

"What on?"

"Reckon on general principles."

"Humph! Wal, he told me you harangued him till you was black in the face, an'—"

"Jack had it wrong. He got black in the face," interrupted Wade.

"Did you say he was a spoiled boy an' thet he was no good an' was headin' plumb fer hell?"

"That was a little of what I said," returned Wade, gently.

"Ahuh! How'd thet come about?" queried Belllounds, gruffly. A slight stiffening and darkening overcast his face.

Wade then recalled and recounted the remarks that had passed between him and Jack; and he did not think he missed them very far. He had a great curiosity to see how Belllounds would take them, and especially the young man's scornful rejection of a sincerely offered friendship. All the time Wade was talking he was aware of Columbine watching him, and when he finished it was sweet to look at her.

"Wade, wasn't you takin' a lot on yourself?" queried the rancher, plainly displeased.

"Reckon I was. But my conscience is beholden to no man. If Jack had met me half-way that would have been better for him. An' for me, because I get good out of helpin' any one."

His reply silenced Belllounds. No more was said before supper was announced, and then the rancher seemed taciturn. Columbine did the serving, and most all of the talking. Wade felt strangely at ease. Some subtle difference was at work in him, transforming him, but the moment had not yet come for him to question himself. He enjoyed the supper. And when he ventured to look up at Columbine, to see her strong, capable hands and her warm, blue glance, glad for his presence, sweetly expressive of their common secret and darker with a shadow of meaning beyond her power to guess, then Wade felt havoc within him, the strife and pain and joy of the truth he never could reveal. For he could never reveal his identity to her without betraying his baseness to her mother. Otherwise, to hear her call him father would have been earning that happiness with a lie. Besides, she loved Belllounds as her father, and were this trouble of the present removed she would grow still closer to the old man in his declining days. Wade accepted the inevitable. She must never know. If she might love him it must be as the stranger who came to her gates, it must be through the mysterious affinity between them and through the service he meant to render.

Wade did not linger after the meal was ended despite the fact that Belllounds recovered his cordiality. It was dark when he went out. Columbine followed him, talking cheerfully. Once outside she squeezed his hand and whispered, "How's Wilson?"

The hunter nodded his reply, and, pausing at the porch step, he pressed her hand to make his assurance stronger. His reward was instant. In the bright starlight she stood white and eloquent, staring down at him with dark, wide eyes.

Presently she whispered: "Oh, my friend! It wants only three days till October first!"

"Lass, it might be a thousand years for all you need worry," he replied, his voice low and full. Then it seemed, as she flung up her arms, that she was about to embrace him. But her gesture was an appeal to the stars, to Heaven above, for something she did not speak.

Wade bade her good night and went his way.

The cowboys and the rancher's son were about to engage in a game of poker when Wade entered the dimly lighted, smoke-hazed room. Montana Jim was sticking tallow candles in the middle of a rude table; Lem was

searching his clothes, manifestly for money; Bludsoe
shuffled a greasy deck of cards, and Jack Belllounds was
filling his pipe before a fire of blazing logs on the hearth.

"Dog-gone it! I hed more money'n thet," complained Lem. "Jim, you rode to Kremmlin' last. Did you
take my money?"

"Wal, come to think of it, I reckon I did," replied
Jim, in surprise at the recollection.

"An' whar's it now?"

"Pard, I 'ain't no idee. I reckon it's still in Kremmlin'.
But I'll pay you back."

"I should smile you will. Pony up now."

"Bent Wade, did you come over calkilated to git
skinned?" queried Bludsoe.

"Boys, I was playin' poker tolerable well in Missouri
when you all was nursin'," replied Wade, imperturbably.

"I heerd he was a card-sharp," said Jim. "Wal, grab
a box or a chair to set on an' let's start. Come along,
Jack; you don't look as keen to play as usual."

Belllounds stood with his back to the fire and his
manner did not compare favorably with that of the genial cowboys.

"I prefer to play four-handed," he said.

This declaration caused a little check in the conversation and put an end to the amiability. The cowboys
looked at one another, not embarrassed, but just a little
taken aback, as if they had forgotten something that
they should have remembered.

"You object to my playin'?" asked Wade, quietly.

"I certainly do," replied Belllounds.

"Why, may I ask?"

"For all I know, what Montana said about you may

be true," returned Belllounds, insolently.

Such a remark flung in the face of a Westerner was an insult. The cowboys suddenly grew stiff, with steady eyes on Wade. He, however, did not change in the slightest.

"I might be a card-sharp at that," he replied, coolly. "You fellows play without me. I'm not carin' about poker any more. I'll look on."

Thus he carried over the moment that might have been dangerous. Lem gaped at him; Montana kicked a box forward to sit upon, and his action was expressive; Bludsoe slammed the cards down on the table and favored Wade with a comprehending look. Belllounds pulled a chair up to the table.

"What'll we make the limit?" asked Jim.

"Two bits," replied Lem, quickly.

Then began an argument. Belllounds was for a dollar limit. The cowboys objected.

"Why, Jack, if the ole man got on to us playin' a dollar limit he'd fire the outfit," protested Bludsoe.

This reasonable objection in no wise influenced the old man's son. He overruled the good arguments, and then hinted at the cowboys' lack of nerve. The fun faded out of their faces. Lem, in fact, grew red.

"Wal, if we're agoin' to *gamble*, thet's different," he said, with a cold ring in his voice, as he straddled a box and sat down. "Wade, lemme some money."

Wade slipped his hand into his pocket and drew forth a goodly handful of gold, which he handed to the cowboy. Not improbably, if this large amount had been shown earlier, before the change in the sentiment, Lem would have looked aghast and begged for mercy. As it

was, he accepted it as if he were accustomed to bor-
rowing that much every day. Belllounds had rendered
futile the easy-going, friendly advances of the cowboys,
as he had made it impossible to play a jolly little game
for fun.

The game began, with Wade standing up, looking
on. These boys did not know what a vast store of poker
knowledge lay back of Wade's inscrutable eyes. As a
boy he had learned the intricacies of poker in the country where it originated; and as a man he had played it
with piles of yellow coins and guns on the table. His
eagerness to look on here, as far as the cowboys were
concerned, was mere pretense. In Belllounds's case,
however, he had a profound interest. Rumors had
drifted to him from time to time, since his advent at
White Slides, regarding Belllounds's weakness for gambling. It might have been cowboy gossip. Wade held
that there was nothing in the West as well calculated
to test a boy, to prove his real character, as a game of
poker.

Belllounds was a feverish better, an exultant win-
ner, a poor loser. His understanding of the game was
rudimentary. With him, the strong feeling beginning to
be manifested to Wade was not the fun of matching wits
and luck with his antagonists, nor a desire to accu-
mulate money—for his recklessness disproved that—
but the liberation of the gambling passion. Wade recognized that when he met it. And Jack Belllounds was
not in any sense big. He was selfish and grasping in the
numberless little ways common to the game, and positive about his own rights, while doubtful of the claims
of others. His cheating was clumsy and crude. He held

out cards, hiding them in his palm, he shuffled the deck so he left aces at the bottom, and these he would slip to himself, and he was so blind that he could not detect his fellow-player in tricks as transparent as his own. Wade was amazed and disgusted. The pity he had felt for Belllounds shifted to the old father, who believed in his son with stubborn and unquenchable faith.

"Haven't you got something to drink?" Jack asked of his companions.

"Nope. Whar'd we git it?" replied Jim.

Belllounds evidently forgot, for presently he repeated the query. The cowboys shook their heads. Wade knew they were lying, for they did have liquor in the cabin. It occurred to him, then, to offer to go to his own cabin for some, just to see what this young man would say. But he refrained.

The luck went against Belllounds and so did the gambling. He was not a lamb among wolves, by any means, but the fleecing he got suggested that. According to Wade he was getting what he deserved. No cowboys, even such good-natured and fine fellows as these, could be expected to be subjects for Belllounds's cupidity. And they won all he had.

"I'll borrow," he said, with feverish impatience. His face was pale, clammy, yet heated, especially round the swollen bruises; his eyes stood out, bold, dark, rolling and glaring, full of sullen fire. But more than anything else his mouth betrayed the weakling, the born gambler, the self-centered, spoiled, intolerant youth. It was here his bad blood showed.

"Wal, I ain't lendin' money," replied Lem, as he

assorted his winnings. "Wade, here's what you staked me, an' much obliged."

"I'm out, an' I can't lend you any," said Jim.

Bludsoe had a good share of the profits of that quick game, but he made no move to lend any of it. Belllounds glared impatiently at them.

"Hell! you took my money. I'll have satisfaction," he broke out, almost shouting.

"We won it, didn't we?" rejoined Lem, cool and easy. "An' you can have all the satisfaction you want, right now or any time."

Wade held out a handful of money to Belllounds.

"Here," he said, with his deep eyes gleaming in the dim room. Wade had made a gamble with himself, and it was that Belllounds would not even hesitate to take money.

"Come on, you stingy cowpunchers," he called out, snatching the money from Wade. His action then, violent and vivid as it was, did not reveal any more than his face.

But the cowboys showed amaze, and something more. They fell straightway to gambling, sharper and fiercer than before, actuated now by the flaming spirit of this son of Belllounds. Luck, misleading and alluring, favored Jack for a while, transforming him until he was radiant, boastful, exultant. Then it changed, as did his expression. His face grew dark.

"I tell you I want drink," he suddenly demanded. "I know damn well you cowpunchers have some here, for I smelled it when I came in."

"Jack, we drank the last drop," replied Jim, who seemed less stiff than his two bunk-mates.

"I've some very old rye," interposed Wade, looking at Jim, but apparently addressing all. "Fine stuff, but awful strong an' hot!...Makes a fellow's blood dance."

"Go get it!" Belllounds's utterance was thick and full, as if he had something in his mouth.

Wade looked down into the heated face, into the burning eyes; and through the darkness of passion that brooked no interference with its fruition he saw this youth's stark and naked soul. Wade had seen into the depths of many such abysses.

"See hyar, Wade," broke in Jim, with his quiet force, "never mind fetchin' thet red-hot rye to-night. Some other time, mebbe, when Jack wants more satisfaction. Reckon we've got a drop or so left."

"All right, boys," replied Wade, "I'll be sayin' good night."

He left them playing and strode out to return to his cabin. The night was still, cold, starlit, and black in the shadows. A lonesome coyote barked, to be answered by a wakeful hound. Wade halted at his porch, and lingered there a moment, peering up at the gray old peak, bare and star-crowned.

"I'm sorry for the old man," muttered the hunter, "but I'd see Jack Belllounds in hell before I'd let Columbine marry him."

October first was a holiday at White Slides Ranch. It happened to be a glorious autumn day, with the sunlight streaming gold and amber over the grassy slopes. Far off the purple ranges loomed hauntingly. Wade had come down from Wilson Moore's cabin, his ears ringing with the crippled boy's words of poignant fear.

Fox favored his master with unusually knowing gaze. There was not going to be any lion-chasing or elk-hunting this day. Something was in the wind. And Fox, as a privileged dog, manifested his interest and wonder.

Before noon a buckboard with team of sweating horses halted in the yard of the ranch-house. Besides the driver it contained two women whom Belllounds greeted as relatives, and a stranger, a pale man whose dark garb proclaimed him a minister.

"Come right in, folks," welcomed Belllounds, with hearty excitement.

It was Wade who showed the driver where to put the horses. Strangely, not a cowboy was in sight, an omission of duty the rancher had noted. Wade might have informed him where they were.

The door of the big living-room stood open, and from it came the sound of laughter and voices. Wade, who had returned to his seat on the end of the porch, listened to them, while his keen gaze seemed fixed down the lane toward the cabins. How intent must he have been not to hear Columbine's step behind him!

"Good morning, Ben," she said.

Wade wheeled as if internal violence had ordered his movement.

"Lass, good mornin'," he replied. "You sure look sweet this October first—like the flower for which you're named."

"My friend, it *is* October first—my marriage day!" murmured Columbine.

Wade felt her intensity, and he thrilled to the brave,

sweet resignation of her face. Hope and faith were unquenchable in her, yet she had fortified herself to the wreck of dreams and love.

"I'd seen you before now, but I had some job with Wils, persuadin' him that we'd not have to offer you congratulations yet awhile," replied Wade, in his slow, gentle voice.

"*Oh!*" breathed Columbine.

Wade saw her full breast swell and the leaping blood wave over her pale face. She bent to him to see his eyes. And for Wade, when she peered with straining heart and soul, all at once to become transfigured, that instant was a sweet and all-fulfilling reward for his years of pain.

"You drive me mad!" she whispered.

The heavy tread of the rancher, like the last of successive steps of fate in Wade's tragic expectancy, sounded on the porch.

"Wal, lass, hyar you are," he said, with a gladness deep in his voice. "Now, whar's the boy?"

"Dad—I've not—seen Jack since breakfast," replied Columbine, tremulously.

"Sort of a laggard in love on his weddin'-day," rejoined the rancher. His gladness and forgetfulness were as big as his heart. "Wade, have you seen Jack?"

"No—I haven't," replied the hunter, with slow, long-drawn utterance. "But—I see—him now."

Wade pointed to the figure of Jack Belllounds approaching from the direction of the cabins. He was not walking straight.

Old man Belllounds shot out his gray head like a striking eagle.

"What the hell?" he muttered, as if bewildered at this strange, uneven gait of his son. "Wade, what's the matter with Jack?"

Wade did not reply. That moment had its sorrow for him as well as understanding of the wonder expressed by Columbine's cold little hand trembling in his.

The rancher suddenly recoiled.

"So help me Gawd—he's drunk!" he gasped, in a distress that unmanned him.

Then the parson and the invited relatives came out upon the porch, with gay voices and laughter that suddenly stilled when old Belllounds cried, brokenly: "Lass—go—in—the house."

But Columbine did not move, and Wade felt her shaking as she leaned against him.

The bridegroom approached. Drunk indeed he was; not hilariously, as one who celebrated his good fortune, but sullenly, tragically, hideously drunk.

Old Belllounds leaped off the porch. His gray hair stood up like the mane of a lion. Like a giant's were his strides. With a lunge he met his reeling son, swinging a huge fist into the sodden red face. Limply Jack fell to the ground.

"Lay there, you damned prodigal!" he roared, terrible in his rage. "You disgrace me—an' you disgrace the girl who's been a daughter to me! . . . If you ever have another weddin'-day it'll not be me who sets it!"

12

*N*OVEMBER was well advanced before there came indications that winter was near at hand.

One morning, when Wade rode up to Moore's cabin, the whole world seemed obscured in a dense gray fog, through which he could not see a rod ahead of him. Later, as he left, the fog had lifted shoulder-high to the mountains, and was breaking to let the blue sky show. Another morning it was worse, and apparently thicker and grayer. As Wade climbed the trail up toward the mountain-basin, where he hunted most these days, he expected the fog to lift. But it did not. The trail under the hoofs of the horse was scarcely perceptible to him, and he seemed lost in a dense, gray, soundless obscurity.

Suddenly Wade emerged from out the fog into brilliant sunshine. In amaze he halted. This phenomenon was new to him. He was high up on the mountain-side, the summit of which rose clear-cut and bold into the sky. Below him spread what resembled a white sea. It was an immense cloud-bank, filling all the valleys as if with creamy foam or snow, soft, thick, motionless, contrasting vividly with the blue sky above. Old White Slides stood out, gray and bleak and brilliant, as if it were an island rock in a rolling sea of fleece. Far across this strange, level cloud-floor rose the black line of the range. Wade watched the scene with a kind of rapture. He was alone on the heights. There was not a sound. The winds were stilled. But there seemed a mighty being awake all around him, in the presence of which Wade felt how little were his sorrows and hopes.

Another day brought dull-gray scudding clouds, and gusts of wind and squalls of rain, and a wailing through the bare aspens. It grew colder and bleaker and darker. Rain changed to sleet and sleet to snow. That night brought winter.

Next morning, when Wade plodded up to Moore's cabin, it was through two feet of snow. A beautiful glistening white mantle covered valley and slope and mountain, transforming all into a world too dazzlingly brilliant for the unprotected gaze of man.

When Wade pushed open the door of the cabin and entered he awakened the cowboy.

"Mornin', Wils," drawled Wade, as he slapped the snow from boots and legs. "Summer has gone, winter has come, an' the flowers lay in their graves! How are you, boy?"

Moore had grown paler and thinner during his long confinement in bed. A weary shade shone in his face and a shadow of pain in his eyes. But the spirit of his smile was the same as always.

"Hello, Bent, old pard!" replied Moore. "I guess I'm fine. Nearly froze last night. Didn't sleep much."

"Well, I was worried about that," said the hunter. "We've got to arrange things somehow."

"I heard it snowing. Gee! how the wind howled! And I'm snowed in?"

"Sure are. Two feet on a level. It's good I snaked down a lot of fire-wood. Now I'll set to work an' cut it up an' stack it round the cabin. Reckon I'd better sleep up here with you, Wils."

"Won't Old Bill make a kick?"

"Let him kick. But I reckon he doesn't need to know anythin' about it. It is cold in here. Well, I'll soon warm it up.... Here's some letters Lem got at Kremmlin' the other day. You read while I rustle some grub for you."

Moore scanned the addresses on the several envelopes and sighed.

"From home! I hate to read them."

"Why?" queried Wade.

"Oh, because when I wrote I didn't tell them I was hurt. I feel like a liar."

"It's just as well, Wils, because you swear you'll not go home."

"Me? I should smile not.... Bent—I—I—hoped Collie might answer the note you took her from me."

"Not yet. Wils, give the lass time."

"Time? Heavens! it's three weeks and more."

"Go ahead an' read your letters or I'll knock you on the head with one of these chunks," ordered Wade, mildly.

The hunter soon had the room warm and cheerful, with steaming breakfast on the red-hot coals. Presently, when he made ready to serve Moore, he was surprised to find the boy crying over one of the letters.

"Wils, what's the trouble?" he asked.

"Oh, nothing. I—I—just feel bad, that's all," replied Moore.

"Ahuh! So it seems. Well, tell me about it?"

"Pard, my father—has forgiven me."

"The old son-of-a-gun! Good! What for? You never told me you'd done anythin'."

"I know—but I did—do a lot. I was sixteen then. We quarreled. And I ran off up here to punch cows. But after a while I wrote home to mother and my sister. Since then they've tried to coax me to come home. This letter's from the old man himself. Gee! . . . Well, he says he's had to knuckle. That he's ready to forgive me. But I must come home and take charge of his ranch. Isn't that great? . . . Only I can't go. And I couldn't—I couldn't ever ride a horse again—if I did go."

"Who says you couldn't?" queried Wade. "*I* never said so. I only said you'd never be a bronco-bustin' cowboy again. Well, suppose you're not? You'll be able to ride a little, if I can save that leg. . . . Boy, your letter is damn good news. I'm sure glad. That will make Collie happy."

The cowboy had a better appetite that morning, which fact mitigated somewhat the burden of Wade's worry. There was burden enough, however, and Wade had set this day to make important decisions about Moore's injured foot. He had dreaded to remove the last dressing because conditions at that time had been unimproved. He had done all he could to ward off the threatened gangrene.

"Wils, I'm goin' to look at your foot an' tell you things," declared Wade, when the dreaded time could be put off no longer.

"Go ahead....And, pard, if you say my leg has to be cut off—why just pass me my gun!"

The cowboy's voice was gay and bantering, but his eyes were alight with a spirit that frightened the hunter.

"Ahuh!...I know how you feel. But, boy, I'd rather live with one leg an' be loved by Collie Belllounds than have nine legs for some other lass."

Wilson Moore groaned his helplessness.

"Damn you, Bent Wade! You always say what kills me!...Of course I would!"

"Well, lie quiet now, an' let me look at this poor, messed-up foot."

Wade's deft fingers did not work with the usual precision and speed natural to them. But at last Moore's injured member lay bare, discolored and misshapen. The first glance made the hunter quicker in his movements, closer in his scrutiny. Then he yelled his joy.

"Boy, it's better! No sign of gangrene! We'll save your leg!"

"Pard, I never feared I'd lose that. All I've feared was that I'd be club-footed....Let me look," replied the cowboy, and he raised himself on his elbow. Wade lifted the unsightly foot.

"My God, it's crooked!" cried Moore, passionately. "Wade, it's healed. It'll stay that way always! I can't move it!...Oh, but Buster Jack's ruined me!"

The hunter pushed him back with gentle hands.

"Wils, it might have been worse."

"But I never gave up hope," replied Moore, in poignant grief. "I couldn't. But *now!*...How can you look at that—that club-foot, and not swear?"

"Well, well, boy, cussin' won't do any good. Now lay still an' let me work. You've had lots of good news this mornin'. So I think you can stand to hear a little bad news."

"What! Bad news?" queried Moore, with a start.

"I reckon. Now listen....The reason Collie hasn't answered your note is because she's been sick in bed for three weeks."

"Oh no!" exclaimed the cowboy, in amaze and distress.

"Yes, an' I'm her doctor," replied Wade, with pride. "First off they had Mrs. Andrews. An' Collie kept askin' for me. She was out of her head, you know. An' soon as I took charge she got better."

"Heavens! Collie ill and you never told me!" cried Moore. "I can't believe it. She's so healthy and strong. What ailed her, Bent?"

"Well, Mrs. Andrews said it was nervous breakdown. An' Old Bill was afraid of consumption. An' Jack Belllounds swore she was only shammin'."

The cowboy cursed violently.

"Here—I won't tell you any more if you're goin' to cuss that way an' jerk around," protested Wade.

"I—I'll shut up," appealed Moore.

"Well, that puddin'-head Jack is more 'n you called him, if you care to hear my opinion....Now, Wils, the fact is that none of them know what ails Collie. But I know. She'd been under a high strain leadin' up to October first. An' the way that weddin'-day turned out—with Old Bill layin' Jack cold, an' with no marriage at all—why, Collie had a shock. An' after that she seemed pale an' tired all the time an' she didn't eat right. Well, when Buster Jack got over that awful punch he'd got from the old man he made up to Collie harder than ever. She didn't tell me then, but I saw it. An' she couldn't avoid him, except by stayin' in her room, which she did a good deal. Then Jack showed a streak of bein' decent. He surprised everybody, even Collie. He delighted Old Bill. But he didn't pull the wool over my eyes. He was like a boy spoilin' for a new toy, an' he got crazy over Collie. He's sure terribly in love with her, an' for days he behaved himself in a way calculated to make up for his drinkin' too much. It shows he can behave himself when he wants to. I mean he can control his temper an' impulse. Anyway, he made himself so good that Old Bill changed his mind, after what he swore that day, an' set another day for the weddin'. Right off, then, Collie goes down on her back.... They didn't send for me very soon. But when I did get to see her, an' felt the way she grabbed me—as if she was drownin'—then I knew what ailed her. It was love."

"Love!" gasped Moore, breathlessly.

"Sure. Jest love for a dog-gone lucky cowboy named Wils Moore!...Her heart was breakin', an' she'd have died but for me! Don't imagine, Wils, that people can't die of broken hearts. They do. I know. Well, all Collie needed was me, an' I cured her ravin' and made her eat, an' now she's comin' along fine."

"Wade, I've believed in Heaven since you came down to White Slides," burst out Moore, with shining eyes. "But tell me—what did you tell her?"

"Well, my particular medicine first off was to whisper in her ear that she'd never have to marry Jack Belllounds. An' after that I gave her daily doses of talk about you."

"Pard! She loves me—still?" he whispered.

"Wils, hers is the kind that grows stronger with time. I know."

Moore strained in his intensity of emotion, and he clenched his fists and gritted his teeth.

"Oh God! this's hard on me!" he cried. "I'm a man. I love that girl more than life. And to know she's suffering for love of me—for fear of that marriage being forced upon her—to know that while I lie here a helpless cripple—it's almost unbearable."

"Boy, you've got to mend now. We've the best of hope now—for you—for her—for everythin'."

"Wade, I think I love you, too," said the cowboy. "You're saving me from madness. Somehow I have faith in you—to do whatever you want. But how could you tell Collie she'd never have to marry Buster Jack?"

"Because I know she never will," replied Wade, with his slow, gentle smile.

"You *know* that?"

"Sure."

"How on earth can you prevent it? Belllounds will never give up planning that marriage for his son. Jack will nag Collie till she can't call her soul her own. Between them they will wear her down. My friend, *how* can you prevent it?"

"Wils, fact is, I haven't reckoned out how I'm goin' to save Collie. But that's no matter. Sufficient unto the day is the evil thereof. I will do it. You can gamble on me, Wils. You must use that hope an' faith to help you get well. For we mustn't forget that you're in more danger than Collie."

"I *will* gamble on you—my life—my very soul," replied Moore, fervently. "By Heaven! I'll be the man I might have been. I'll rise out of despair. I'll even reconcile myself to being a cripple."

"An', Wils, will you rise above hate?" asked Wade, softly.

"Hate! Hate of whom?"

"Jack Belllounds."

The cowboy stared, and his lean, pale face contracted.

"Pard, you wouldn't—you couldn't expect me to—to forgive him?"

"No. I reckon not. But you needn't hate him. I don't. An' I reckon I've some reason, more than you could guess.... Wils, hate is a poison in the blood. It's worse for him who feels it than for him against whom it rages. I know.... Well, if you put thought of Jack out of your mind—quit broodin' over what he did to you—an' realize that he's not to blame, you'll overcome your hate. For the son of Old Bill is to be pitied. Yes, Jack Belllounds needs pity. He was ruined before he was born. He never should have been born. An' I want you to understand that, an' stop hatin' him. Will you try?"

"Wade, you're afraid I'll kill him?" whispered Moore.

"Sure. That's it. I'm afraid you might. An' consider how hard that would be for Columbine. She an' Jack were raised sister an' brother, almost. It would be hard

on her. You see, Collie has a strange an' powerful sense
of duty to Old Bill. If you killed Jack it would likely kill
the old man, an' Collie would suffer all her life. You
couldn't cure her of that. You want her to be happy."

"I do—I do. Wade, I swear I'll never kill Buster Jack.
And for Collie's sake I'll try not to hate him."

"Well, that's fine. I'm sure glad to hear you promise
that. Now I'll go out an' chop some wood. We mustn't
let the fire go out any more."

"Pard, I'll write another note—a letter to Collie.
Hand me the blank-book there. And my pencil....And
don't hurry with the wood."

Wade went outdoors with his two-bladed ax and
shovel. The wood-pile was a great mound of snow. He
cleaned a wide space and a path to the side of the cabin.
Working in snow was not unpleasant for him. He liked
the cleanness, the whiteness, the absolute purity of new-
fallen snow. The air was crisp and nipping, the frost
crackled under his feet, the smoke from his pipe seemed
no thicker than the steam from his breath, the ax rang
on the hard aspens. Wade swung this implement like a
born woodsman. The chips flew and the dead wood
smelled sweet. Some logs he chopped into three-foot
pieces; others he chopped and split. When he tired a
little of swinging the ax he carried the cut pieces to the
cabin and stacked them near the door. Now and then
he would halt a moment to gaze away across the whitened slopes and rolling hills. The sense of his physical
power matched something within, and his heart warmed
with more than the vigorous exercise.

When he had worked thus for about two hours and
had stacked a pile of wood almost as large as the cabin

he considered it sufficient for the day. So he went indoors. Moore was so busily and earnestly writing that he did not hear Wade come in. His face wore an eloquent glow.

"Say, Wils, are you writin' a book?" he inquired.

"Hello! Sure I am. But I'm 'most done now. . . . If Columbine doesn't answer *this* . . ."

"By the way, I'll have two letters to give her, then—for I never gave her the first one," replied Wade.

"You son-of-a-gun!"

"Well, hurry along, boy. I'll be goin' now. Here's a pole I've fetched in. You keep it there, where you can reach it, an' when the fire needs more wood you roll one of these logs on. I'll be up to-night before dark, an' if I don't fetch you a letter it'll be because I can't persuade Collie to write."

"Pard, if you bring me a letter I'll obey you—I'll lie still—I'll sleep—I'll stand anything."

"Ahuh! Then I'll fetch one," replied Wade, as he took the little book and deposited it in his pocket. "Good-by, now, an' think of your good news that come with the snow."

"Good-by, Heaven-Sent Hell-Bent Wade!" called Moore. "It's no joke of a name any more. It's a fact."

Wade plodded down through the deep snow, stepping in his old tracks, and as he toiled on his thoughts were deep and comforting. He was thinking that if he had his life to live over again he would begin at once to find happiness in other people's happiness. Upon arriving at his cabin he set to work cleaning a path to the dog corral. The snow had drifted there and he had no easy task. It was well that he had built an inclosed house for the hounds to winter in. Such a heavy snow as this one would put an end to hunting for the time being. The ranch had an ample supply of deer, bear, and elk meat, all solidly frozen this morning, that would surely keep well until used. Wade reflected that his tasks round the ranch would be feeding hounds and stock, chopping wood, and doing such chores as came along in winter-time. The pack of hounds, which he had thinned out to a smaller number, would be a care on his hands. Kane had become a much-prized possession of Columbine's and lived at the house, where he had things his own way, and always greeted Wade with a look of disdain and distrust. Kane would never forgive the hand that had hurt him. Sampson and Jim and Fox, of course, shared Wade's cabin, and vociferously announced his return.

Early in the afternoon Wade went down to the ranch-house. The snow was not so deep there, having blown considerably in the open places. Some one was pounding iron in the blacksmith shop; horses were cavorting in the corrals; cattle were bawling round the hay-ricks in the barn-yard.

The hunter knocked on Columbine's door.

"Come in," she called.

Wade entered, to find her alone. She was sitting up in bed, propped up with pillows, and she wore a warm, woolly jacket or dressing-gown. Her paleness was now marked, and the shadows under her eyes made them appear large and mournful.

"Ben Wade, you don't care for me any more!" she exclaimed, reproachfully.

"Why not, lass?" he asked.

"You were so long in coming," she replied, now with petulance. "I guess now I don't want you at all."

"Ahuh! That's the reward of people who worry an' work for others. Well, then, I reckon I'll go back an' not give you what I brought."

He made a pretense of leaving, and he put a hand to his pocket as if to insure the safety of some article. Columbine blushed. She held out her hands. She was repentant of her words and curious as to his.

"Why, Ben Wade, I count the minutes before you come," she said. "What'd you bring me?"

"Who's been in here?" he asked, going forward. "That's a poor fire. I'll have to fix it."

"Mrs. Andrews just left. It was good of her to drive up. She came in the sled, she said. Oh, Ben, it's winter. There was snow on my bed when I woke up. I think I am better to-day. Jack hasn't been in here yet!"

At this Wade laughed, and Columbine followed suit.

"Well, you look a little sassy to-day, which I take is a good sign," said Wade. "I've got some news that will come near to makin' you well."

"Oh, tell it quick!" she cried.

"Wils won't lose his leg. It's gettin' well. An' there was a letter from his father, forgivin' him for somethin' he never told me."

"My prayers were answered!" whispered Columbine, and she closed her eyes tight.

"An' his father wants him to come home to run the ranch," went on Wade.

"Oh!" Her eyes popped open with sudden fright. "But he can't—he won't go?"

"I reckon not. He wouldn't if he could. But some

day he will, an' take you home with him."

Columbine covered her face with her hands, and was silent a moment.

"Such prophecies! They—they—" She could not conclude.

"Ahuh! I know. The strange fact is, lass, that they all come true. I wish I had all happy ones, instead of them black, croakin' ones that come like ravens. . . . Well, you're better to-day?"

"Yes. Oh yes. Ben, what have you got for me?"

"You're in an awful hurry. I want to talk to you, an' if I show what I've got then there will be no talkin'. You say Jack hasn't been in to-day?"

"Not yet, thank goodness."

"How about Old Bill?"

"Ben, you never call him my dad. I wish you would. When you *don't* it always reminds me that he's really *not* my dad."

"Ahuh! Well, well!" replied Wade, with his head bowed. "It is just queer I can never remember. . . . An' how was he to-day?"

"For a wonder he didn't mention poor me. He was full of talk about going to Kremmling. Means to take Jack along. Do you know, Ben, dad can't fool me. He's afraid to leave Jack here alone with me. So dad talked a lot about selling stock an' buying supplies, and how he needed Jack to go, and so forth. I'm mighty glad he means to take him. But my! won't Jack be sore."

"I reckon. It's time he broke out."

"And now, dear Ben—what have you got for me? I know it's from Wilson," she coaxed.

"Lass, would you give much for a little note from

Wils?" asked Wade, teasingly.

"Would I? When I've been hoping and praying for just that!"

"Well, if you'd give so much for a note, how much would you give me for a whole bookful that took Wils two hours to write?"

"Ben! Oh, I'd—I'd give—" she cried, wild with delight. "I'd *kiss* you!"

"You mean it?" he queried, waving the book aloft.

"Mean it? Come here!"

There was fun in this for Wade, but also a deep and beautiful emotion that quivered through him. Bending over her, he placed the little book in her hand. He did not see clearly, then, as she pulled him lower and kissed him on the cheek, generously, with sweet, frank gratitude and affection.

Moments strong and all-satisfying had been multiplying for Bent Wade of late. But this one magnified all. As he sat back upon the chair he seemed a little husky of voice.

"Well, well, an' so you kissed ugly old Bent Wade?"

"Yes, and I've wanted to do it before," she retorted. The dark excitation in her eyes, the flush of her pale cheeks, made her beautiful then.

"Lass, now you read your letter an' answer it. You can tear out the pages. I'll sit here an' be makin' out to be readin' aloud out of this book here, if any one happens in sudden-like!"

"Oh, how you think of everything!"

The hunter sat beside her pretending to be occupied with the book he had taken from the table when really he was stealing glances at her face. Indeed, she was more than pretty then. Illness and pain had enhanced the sweetness of her expression. As she read on it was manifest that she had forgotten the hunter's presence. She grew pink, rosy, scarlet, radiant. And Wade thrilled with her as she thrilled, loved her more and more as she loved. Moore must have written words of enchantment. Wade's hungry heart suffered a pang of jealousy, but would not harbor it. He read in her perusal of that letter what no other dreamed of, not even the girl herself; and it was certitude of tragic and brief life for her if she could not live for Wilson Moore. Those moments of watching her were unutterably precious to Wade. He saw how some divine guidance had directed his footsteps to this home. How many years had it taken him to get there! Columbine read and read and reread—a girl with her first love-letter. And for Wade, with his keen eyes that seemed to see the senses and the soul, there shone something infinite through her rapture. Never until that unguarded moment had he divined her innocence, nor had any conception been given him of the exquisite torture of her maiden fears or the havoc of love fighting for itself. He learned then much of the mystery and meaning of a woman's heart.

EAR WILSON, —The note and letter from you have taken my breath away. I couldn't tell—I wouldn't dare tell, how they made me feel.

"Your good news fills me with joy. And when Ben told me you wouldn't lose your leg—that you would get well— then my eyes filled and my heart choked me, and I thanked God, who'd answered my prayers. After all the heartache and dread, it's so wonderful to find things not so terrible as they seemed. Oh, I am thankful! You have only to take care of yourself now, to lie patiently and wait, and obey Ben, and soon the time will have flown by and you will be well again. Maybe, after all, your foot will not be so bad. Maybe you can ride again, if not so wonderfully as before, then well enough to ride on your father's range and look after his stock. For, Wilson, dear, you'll have to go home. It's your duty. Your father must be getting old now. He needs you. He has forgiven you—you bad boy! And you are very lucky. It almost kills me to think of your leaving White Slides. But that is selfish. I'm going to learn to be like Ben Wade. He never thinks of himself.

"Rest assured, Wilson, that I will never marry Jack Belllounds. It seems years since that awful October first. I gave my word then, and I would have lived up to it. But I've changed. I'm older. I see things differently. I love dad as well. I feel as sorry for Jack Belllounds. I still think I might help him. I still believe in my duty to his father. But I can't marry him. It would be a sin. I have no right to marry a man whom I do not love. When it comes to thought of his touching me, then I hate him. Duty toward dad is one thing, and I hold it high, but that is not reason enough for a woman to give herself. Some duty to myself is higher than that. It's hard for me to tell you—for me to understand. Love of you has opened my eyes. Still I don't think it's love of you that makes me selfish. I'm true to something in me that I never knew before. I could marry Jack, loving you, and utterly sacrifice myself, if it were right. But it would be wrong. I never realized this until you kissed me. Since then the thought of anything that approaches personal relations—any hint of intimacy with Jack fills me with disgust.

"So I'm not engaged to Jack Belllounds, and I'm never going to be. There will be trouble here. I feel it. I see it coming. Dad keeps at me persistently. He grows older. I don't think he's failing, but then there's a loss of memory, and an almost childish obsession in regard to the marriage he has set his heart on. Then his passion for Jack seems greater as he learns little by little that Jack is not all he might be. Wilson, I give you my word; I believe if dad ever really sees Jack as I see him or you see him, then something dreadful will happen. In spite of everything dad still believes in Jack. It's beautiful and terrible. That's one reason why I've wanted to help Jack. Well, it's not to be. Every day, every hour, Jack Belllounds grows farther from me. He and his father will try to persuade me to consent to this marriage. They may even try to force me. But in that way I'll be as hard and as cold as Old White Slides. No! Never! For the rest, I'll do my duty to dad. I'll stick to him. I could not engage myself to you, no matter how much I love you. And that's more every minute! . . . So don't mention taking me to your home—don't ask me again. Please, Wilson; your asking shook my very soul! Oh, how sweet that would be— your wife! . . . But if dad turns me away—I don't think he would. Yet he's so strange and like iron for all concerning Jack. If ever he turned me out I'd have no home. I'm a waif, you know. Then—then, Wilson . . . Oh, it's horrible to be in the position I'm in. I won't say any more. You'll understand, dear.

"It's your love that awoke me, and it's Ben Wade who has saved me. Wilson, I love him almost as I do dad, only strangely. Do you know I believe he had something to do with Jack getting drunk that awful October first. I don't mean Ben would stoop to get Jack drunk. But he might have cunningly put that opportunity in Jack's way. Drink is Jack's weakness, as gambling is his passion. Well, I know that the liquor was some fine old stuff which Ben gave to the cowboys. And it's significant now how Jack avoids Ben. He hates him. He's afraid of him. He's jealous because Ben is so much with me. I've heard Jack rave to dad about this. But dad is just to others, if he can't be to his son.

"And so I want you to know that it's Ben Wade who has saved me. Since I've been sick I've learned more of Ben. He's like a woman. He understands. I never have to tell him anything. You, Wilson, were sometimes stupid or stubborn (forgive me) about little things that girls feel but can't explain. Ben knows. I tell you this because I want you to understand how and why I love him. I think I love him most for his goodness to you. Dear boy, if I hadn't loved you before Ben Wade came I'd have fallen in love with you since, just listening to his talk of you. But this will make you conceited. So I'll go on about Ben. He's our friend. Why, Wilson, that sweetness, softness, gentleness about him, the heart that makes him love us, that must be only the woman in him. I don't know what a mother would feel like, but I do know that I seem strangely happier since I've confessed my troubles to this man. It was Lem who told me how Ben offered to be a friend to Jack. And Jack flouted him. I've a queer notion that the moment Jack did this he turned his back on a better life.

"To repeat, then, Ben Wade is our friend, and to me something more that I've tried to explain. Maybe telling you this will make you think more of him and listen to his advice. I hope so. Did any boy and girl ever before so need a friend? I need that something he instils in me. If I lost it I'd be miserable. And, Wilson, I'm such a coward. I'm so weak. I have such sinkings and burnings and tossings. Oh, I'm only a woman! But I'll die fighting. That is what Ben Wade instils into me. While there was life this strange little man would never give up hope. He makes me feel that he knows more than he tells.

Through him I shall get the strength to live up to my convictions, to be true to myself, to be faithful to you.

"With love,

"COLUMBINE."

"December 3d.

"DEAREST COLLIE,—Your last was only a note, and I told Wade if he didn't fetch more than a note next time there would be trouble round this bunk-house. And then he brought your letter!

"I'm feeling exuberant (I think it's that) to-day. First time I've been up. Collie, I'm able to get up! WHOOPEE! I walk with a crutch, and don't dare put my foot down. Not that it hurts, but that my boss would have a fit! I'm glad you've stopped heaping praise upon our friend Ben. Because now I can get over my jealousy and be half decent. He's the whitest man I ever knew.

"Now listen, Collie. I've had ideas lately. I've begun to eat and get stronger and to feel good. The pain is gone. And to think I swore to Wade I'd forgive Jack Belllounds and never hate him—or kill him! ... There, that's letting the cat out of the bag, and it's done now. But no matter. The truth is, though, that I never could stop hating Jack while the pain lasted. Now I could shake hands with him and smile at him.

"Well, as I said, I've ideas. They're great. Grab hold of the pommel now so you won't get thrown! I'm going to pitch! ... When I get well—able to ride and go about, which Ben says will be in the spring—I'll send for my father to come to White Slides. He'll come. Then I'll tell him everything, and if Ben and I can't win him to our side then *you* can. Father never could resist you. When he has fallen in love with you, which won't take long, then we'll go to old Bill Belllounds and lay the case before him. Are you still in the saddle, Collie?

"Well, if you are, be sure to get a better hold, for I'm going to run some next. Ben Wade approved of my plan. He says Belllounds can be brought to reason. He says he can *make* him see the ruin for everybody were you forced to marry Jack. Strange, Collie, how Wade included himself with you, me, Jack, and the old man, in the foreshadowed ruin! Wade is as deep as the cañon there. Sometimes when he's thoughtful he gives me a creepy feeling. At others, when he comes out with one of his easy, cool assurances that we are all right— that we will get each other—why, then something grim takes possession of me. I believe him, I'm happy, but there crosses my mind a fleeting realization—not of what our friend is now, but what he has been. And it disturbs me, chills me. I don't understand it. For, Collie, though I understand your feeling of what he is, I don't understand mine. You see, I'm a man. I've been a cowboy for ten years and more. I've seen some hard experiences and worked with a good many rough boys and men. Cowboys, Indians, Mexicans, miners, prospectors, ranchers, hunters—some of whom were bad medicine. So I've come to see men as you couldn't see them. And Bent Wade has been everything a man could be. He seems all men in one. And despite all his kindness and goodness and hopefulness, there is the sense I have of something deadly and terrible and inevitable in him.

"It makes my heart almost stop beating to know I have this man on my side. Because I sense in him the man element, the physical—oh, I can't put it in words, but I mean something great in him that can't be beaten. What he says *must* come true!...And so I've already begun to dream and to think of you as my wife. If you ever are—no! *when* you are, then I will owe it to Bent Wade. No man ever owed another for so precious a gift. But, Collie, I can't help a little vague dread—of what, I don't know, unless it's a sense of the possibilities of Hell-Bent Wade....Dearest, I don't want to worry you or frighten you, and I can't follow out my own gloomy fancies. Don't you mind too much what I think. Only you must realize that Wade is the greatest factor in our hopes of the future. My faith in him is so unshakable that it's foolish. Next to you I love him best. He seems even dearer to me than my own people. He has made me look at life differently. Likewise he has inspired you. But you, dearest Columbine, are only a sensitive, delicate girl, a frail and tender thing like the columbine flowers of the hills. And for you own sake you must not be blind to what Wade is capable of. If you keep on loving him and idealizing him, blind to what has made him great, that is, blind to the tragic side of him, then if he did something terrible here for you and for me the shock would be bad for you. Lord knows I have no suspicions of Wade. I have no clear ideas at all. But I do know that for you he would not stop at anything. He loves you as much as I do, only differently. Such power a pale, sweet-faced girl has over the lives of men!

"Good-by for this time.

"Faithfully,

"WILSON."

"January 10th.

"DEAR WILSON,—In every letter I tell you I'm better! Why, pretty soon there'll be nothing left to say about my health. I've been up and around now for days, but only lately have I begun to gain. Since Jack has been away I'm getting fat. I eat, and that's one reason I suppose. Then I move around more.

"You ask me to tell you all I do. Goodness! I couldn't and I wouldn't. You are getting mighty bossy since you're able to hobble around, as you call it. But you can't boss *me*! However, I'll be nice and tell you a little. I don't work very much. I've helped dad with his accounts, and all so hopelessly muddled since he let Jack keep the books. I read a good deal. Your letters are worn out! Then, when it snows, I sit by the window and watch. I love to see the snowflakes fall, so fleecy and white and soft! But I don't like the snowy world after the storm has passed. I shiver and hug the fire. I must have Indian in me. On moonlit nights to look out at Old White Slides, so cold and icy and grand, and over the white hills and ranges, makes me shudder. I don't know why. It's all beautiful. But it seems to me like death.... Well, I sit idly a lot and think of you and how terribly big my love has grown, and ... but that's all about that!

"As you know, Jack has been gone since before New Year's Day. He said he was going to Kremmling. But dad heard he went to Elgeria. Well, I didn't tell you that dad and Jack quarreled over money. Jack kept up his good behavior for so long that I actually believed he'd changed for the better. He kept at me, not so much on the marriage question, but to love him. Wilson, he nearly drove me frantic with his lovemaking. Finally I got mad and I pitched into him. Oh, I convinced him! Then he came back to his own self again. Like a flash he was Buster Jack once more. "You can go to hell!" he yelled at me. And such a look! . . . Well, he went out, and that's when he quarreled with dad. It was about money. I couldn't help but hear some of it. I don't know whether or not dad gave Jack money, but I think he didn't. Anyway, Jack went.

"Dad was all right for a few days. Really, he seemed nicer and kinder for Jack's absence. Then all at once he sank into the glooms. I couldn't cheer him up. When Ben Wade came in after supper dad always got him to tell some of those terrible stories. You know what perfectly terrible stories Ben can tell. Well, dad had to hear the worst ones. And poor me, I didn't want to listen, but I couldn't resist. Ben *can* tell stories. And oh, what he's lived through!

"I got the idea it wasn't Jack's absence so much that made dad sit by the hour before the fire, staring at the coals, sighing, and looking so God-forsaken. My heart just aches for dad. He broods and broods. He'll break out some day, and then I don't want to be here. There doesn't seem to be any idea when Jack will come home. He might never come. But Ben says he will. He says Jack hates work and that he couldn't be gambler enough or wicked enough to support himself without working. Can't you hear Ben Wade say that? 'I'll tell you,' he begins, and then comes a prophecy of trouble or evil. And, on the other hand, think how he used to say: 'Wait! Don't give up! Nothin' is ever so bad as it seems at first! Be true to what your heart says is right! It's never too late! Love is the only good in life! Love each other and wait and trust! It'll all come right in the end!' . . . And, Wilson, I'm bound to confess that both his sense of calamity and his hope of good seem infallible. Ben Wade is supernatural. Sometimes, just for a moment, I dare to let myself believe in what he says—that our dream will come true and I'll be yours. Then oh! oh! oh! joy and stars and bells and heaven! I—I . . . But what *am* I writing? Wilson Moore, this is quite enough for to-day. Take care you don't believe I'm so—so *very* much in love.

"Ever,

"COLUMBINE."

"*February*—.

"DEAREST COLLIE,—I don't know the date, but spring's coming. To-day I kicked Bent Wade with my once sore foot. It didn't hurt me, but hurt Wade's feelings. He says there'll be no holding me soon. I should say not. I'll eat you up. I'm as hungry as the mountain-lion that's been prowling round my cabin of nights. He's sure starved. Wade tracked him to a hole in the cliff.

"Collie, I can get around first rate. Don't need my crutch any more. I can make a fire and cook a meal. Wade doesn't think so, but I do. He says if I want to hold your affection, not to let you eat anything I cook. I can rustle around, too. Haven't been far yet. My stock has wintered fairly well. This valley is sheltered, you know. Snow hasn't been too deep. Then I bought hay from Andrews. I'm hoping for spring now, and the good old sunshine on the gray sage hills. And summer, with its columbines! Wade has gone back to his own cabin to sleep. I miss him. But I'm glad to have the nights alone once more. I've got a future to plan! Read that over, Collie.

"To-day, when Wade came with your letter, he asked me, sort of queer, 'Say, Wils, do you know how many letters I've fetched you from Collie?' I said, 'Lord, no, I don't, but they're a lot.' Then he said there were just forty-seven letters. Forty-seven! I couldn't believe it, and told him he was crazy. I never had such good fortune. Well, he made me count them, and, dog-gone it, he was right. Forty-seven wonderful love-letters from the sweetest girl on earth! But think of Wade remembering every one! It beats me. He's beyond understanding.

"So Jack Belllounds still stays away from White Slides. Collie, I'm sure sorry for his father. What it would be to have a son like Buster Jack! My God! But for your sake I go around yelling and singing like a locoed Indian. Pretty soon spring will come. Then, you wild-flower of the hills, you girl with the sweet mouth and the sad eyes—then I'm coming after you! And all the king's horses and all the king's men can never take you away from me again!

"Your faithful

"WILSON."

"March 19th.

"DEAREST WILSON,—Your last letters have been read and reread, and kept under my pillow, and have been both my help and my weakness during these trying days since Jack's return.

"It has not been that I was afraid to write—though, Heaven knows, if this letter should fall into the hands of dad it would mean trouble for me, and if Jack read it—I *am* afraid to think of that! I just have not had the heart to write you. But all the time I knew I must write and that I would. Only, now, what to say tortures me. I am certain that confiding in you relieves me. That's why I've told you so much. But of late I find it harder to tell what I know about Jack Belllounds. I'm in a queer state of mind, Wilson dear. And you'll wonder, and you'll be sorry to know I haven't seen much of Ben lately— that is, not to talk to. It seems I can't *bear* his faith in me, his hope, his love—when lately matters have driven me into torturing doubt.

"But lest you might misunderstand, I'm going to try to tell you something of what is on my mind, and I want you to read it to Ben. He has been hurt by my strange reluctance to be with him.

"Jack came home on the night of March second. You'll remember that day, so gloomy and dark and dreary. It snowed and sleeted and rained. I remember how the rain roared on the roof. It roared so loud we didn't hear the horse. But we heard heavy boots on the porch outside the living-room, and the swish of a slicker thrown to the floor. There was a bright fire. Dad looked up with a wild joy. All of a sudden he changed. He blazed. He recognized the heavy tread of his son. If I ever pitied and loved him it was then. I thought of the return of the Prodigal Son!...There came a knock on the door. Then dad recovered. He threw it open wide. The streaming light fell upon Jack Belllounds, indeed, but not as I knew him. He entered. It was the first time I ever saw Jack look in the least like a man. He was pale, haggard, much older, sullen, and bold. He strode in with a 'Howdy, folks,' and threw his wet hat on the floor, and walked to the fire. His boots were soaked with water and mud. His clothes began to steam.

"When I looked at dad I was surprised. He seemed cool and bright, with the self-contained force usual for him when something critical is about to happen.

"'Ahuh! So you come back,' he said.

"'Yes, I'm home,' replied Jack.

"'Wal, it took you quite a spell to get hyar.'

"'Do you want me to stay?'

"This question from Jack seemed to stump dad. He stared. Jack had appeared suddenly, and his manner was different from that with which he used to face dad. He had something up his sleeve, as the cowboys say. He wore an air of defiance and indifference.

"'I reckon I do,' replied dad, deliberately. 'What do you mean by askin' me thet?'

"'I'm of age, long ago. You can't make me stay home. I can do as I like.'

" 'Ahuh! I reckon you think you can. But not hyar at White Slides. If you ever expect to get this property you'll not do as you like.'

" 'To hell with that. I don't care whether I ever get it or not.'

"Dad's face went as white as a sheet. He seemed shocked. After a moment he told me I'd better go to my room. I was about to go when Jack said: 'No, let her stay. She'd best hear now what I've got to say. It concerns her.'

" 'So ho! Then you've got a heap to say?' exclaimed dad, queerly. 'All right, you have your say first.'

"Jack then began to talk in a level and monotonous voice, so unlike him that I sat there amazed. He told how early in the winter, before he left the ranch, he had found out that he was honestly in love with me. That it had changed him— made him see he had never been any good—and inflamed him with the resolve to be better. He had tried. He had succeeded. For six weeks he had been all that could have been asked of any young man. I am bound to confess that he was! …Well, he went on to say how he had fought it out with himself until he absolutely *knew* he could control himself. The courage and inspiration had come from his love for me. That was the only good thing he'd ever felt. He wanted dad and he wanted me to understand absolutely, without any doubt, that he had found a way to hold on to his good intentions and good feelings. And that was for *me!* …I was struck all a-tremble at the truth. It was true! Well, then, he forced me to a decision. Forced me, without ever hinting of this change, this possibility in him. I had told him I *couldn't* love him. Never! Then he said I could go to hell and he gave up. Failing to get money from dad he stole it, without compunction and without regret! He had gone to Kremmling, then to Elgeria.

" 'I let myself go,' he said, without shame, 'and I drank

and gambled. When I was drunk I didn't remember Collie. But when I was sober I did. And she haunted me. That grew worse all the time. So I drank to forget her.... The money lasted a great deal longer than I expected. But that was because I won as much as I lost, until lately. Then I borrowed a good deal from those men I gambled with, but mostly from ranchers who knew my father would be responsible.... I had a shooting-scrape with a man named Elbert, in Smith's place at Elgeria. We quarreled over cards. He cheated. And when I hit him he drew on me. But he missed. Then I shot him.... He lived three days—and died. That sobered me. And once more there came to me truth of what I might have been. I went back to Kremm-ling. And I tried myself out again. I worked awhile for Judson, who was the rancher I had borrowed most from. At night I went into town and to the saloons, where I met my gambling cronies. I put myself in the atmosphere of drink and cards. And I resisted both. I could make myself indifferent to both. As soon as I was sure of myself I decided to come home. And here I am.'

"This long speech of Jack's had a terrible effect upon me. I was stunned and sick. But if it did that to me *what* did it do to dad? Heaven knows, I can't tell you. Dad gave a lurch, and a great heave, as if at the removal of a rope that had all but strangled him.

"'Ahuh-huh!' he groaned. 'An' now you're hyar—what's thet mean?'

"'It means that it's not yet too late,' replied Jack. 'Don't misunderstand me. I'm not repenting with that side of me which is bad. But I've sobered up. I've had a shock. I see my ruin. I still love you, dad, despite—the cruel thing you did to me. I'm your son and I'd like to make up to you for all my shortcomings. And so help me Heaven! I can do that, and will do it, if Collie will marry me. Not only marry me—that's not be enough—but love me—I'm crazy for her love. It's terrible.'

" 'You spoiled weaklin'!' thundered dad. 'How 'n hell can I believe you?'

" 'Because I know it,' declared Jack, standing right up to his father, white and unflinching.

"Then dad broke out in such a rage that I sat there scared so stiff I could not move. My heart beat thick and heavy. Dad got livid of face, his hair stood up, his eyes rolled. He called Jack every name I ever heard any one call him, and then a thousand more. Then he cursed him. Such dreadful curses! Oh, how sad and terrible to hear dad!

" 'Right you are!' cried Jack, bitter and hard and ringing of voice. 'Right, by God! But am I all to blame? Did I bring myself here on this earth! . . . There's something wrong in me that's not all my fault. . . . You can't shame me or scare me or hurt me. I could fling in your face those damned three years of hell you sent me to! But what's the use for you to roar at me or for me to reproach you? I'm ruined unless you give me Collie—make her love me. That will save me. And I want it for your sake and hers—not for my own. Even if I do love her madly I'm not wanting her for that. I'm no good. I'm not fit to touch her. . . . I've just come to tell you the truth. I feel for Collie—I'd do for Collie—as you did for my mother! Can't you understand? I'm your son. I've some of you in me. And I've found out what it is. Do you and Collie want to take me at my word?'

"I think it took dad longer to read something strange and convincing in Jack than it took me. Anyway, dad got the stunning consciousness that Jack *knew* by some divine or intuitive power that his reformation was inevitable, if I loved him. Never have I had such a distressing and terrible moment as that revelation brought to me! I felt the truth. I could save Jack Belllounds. No woman is ever fooled at such critical moments of life. Ben Wade once said that I could have reformed Jack were it possible to love him. Now the truth of that came home to me, and somehow it was overwhelming.

"Dad received this truth—and it was beyond me to realize what it meant to him. He must have seen all his earlier hopes fulfilled, his pride vindicated, his shame forgotten, his love rewarded. Yet he must have seen all that, as would a man leaning with one foot over a bottomless abyss. He looked transfigured, yet conscious of terrible peril. His great heart seemed to leap to meet this last opportunity, with all forgiveness, with all gratitude; but his will yielded with a final and irrevocable resolve. A resolve dark and sinister!

"He raised his huge fists higher and higher, and all his body lifted and strained, towering and trembling, while his face was that of a righteous and angry god.

" 'My son, I take your word!' he rolled out, his voice filling the room and reverberating through the house. 'I give you Collie!...She will be yours!...But, by the love I bore your mother—I swear—if you ever steal again—I'll kill you!'

"I can't say any more—

"COLUMBINE."

SPRING came early that year at White Slides Ranch.

The snow melted off the valleys, and the wild flowers peeped from the greening grass while yet the mountain domes were white. The long stone slides were glistening wet, and the brooks ran full-banked, noisy and turbulent and roily.

Soft and fresh of color the gray old sage slopes came out from under their winter mantle; the bleached tufts of grass waved in the wind and showed tiny blades of green at the roots; the aspens and oaks, and the vines on fences and cliffs, and the round-clumped, brook-bordering willows took on a hue of spring.

The mustangs and colts in the pastures snorted and ran and kicked and cavorted; and on the hillsides the cows began to climb higher, searching for the tender greens, bawling for the new-born calves. Eagles shrieked the release of the snow-bound peaks, and the elks bugled their piercing calls. The grouse-cocks spread their gorgeous brown plumage in parade before their twittering mates, and the jays screeched in the woods, and the sage-hens sailed along the bosom of the gray slopes.

Black bears, and browns, and grizzlies came out of their winter's sleep, and left huge, muddy tracks on the trails; the timber wolves at dusk mourned their hungry calls for life, for meat, for the wildness that was passing; the coyotes yelped at sunset, joyous and sharp and impudent.

But winter yielded reluctantly its hold on the mountains. The black, scudding clouds, and the squalls of rain and sleet and snow, whitening and melting and vanishing, and the cold, clear nights, with crackling frost, all retarded the work of the warming sun. The day came, however, when the greens held their own with the grays; and this was the assurance of nature that spring could not be denied, and that summer would follow.

Bent Wade was hiding in the willows along the trail that followed one of the brooks. Of late, on several mornings, he had skulked like an Indian under cover, watching for some one. On this morning, when Columbine Belllounds came riding along, he stepped out into the trail in front of her.

"Oh, Ben! you startled me!" she exclaimed, as she held hard on the frightened horse.

"Good mornin', Collie," replied Wade. "I'm sorry to

scare you, but I'm particular anxious to see you. An' considerin' how you avoid me these days, I had to waylay you in regular road-agent style."

Wade gazed up searchingly at her. It had been some time since he had been given the privilege and pleasure of seeing her close at hand. He needed only one look at her to confirm his fears. The pale, sweet, resolute face told him much.

"Well, now you've waylaid me, what do you want?" she queried, deliberately.

"I'm goin' to take you to see Wils Moore," replied Wade, watching her closely.

"No!" she cried, with the red staining her temples.

"Collie, see here. Did I ever oppose anythin' you wanted to do?"

"Not—yet," she said.

"I reckon you expect me to?"

She did not answer that. Her eyes drooped, and she nervously twisted the bridle reins.

"Do you doubt my—my good intentions toward you—my love for you?" he asked, in gentle and husky voice.

"Oh, Ben! No! No! It's that I'm afraid of your love for me! I can't bear—what I have to bear—if I see you, if I listen to you."

"Then you've weakened? You're no proud, high-strung, thoroughbred girl any more? You're showin' yellow?"

"Ben Wade, I deny that," she answered, spiritedly, with an uplift of her head. "It's not weakness, but strength I've found."

"Ahuh! Well, I reckon I understand. Collie, listen.

Wils let me read your last letter to him."

"I expected that. I think I told him to. Anyway, I wanted you to know—what—what ailed me."

"Lass, it was a fine, brave letter—written by a girl facin' an upheaval of conscience an' soul. But in your own trouble you forget the effect that letter might have on Wils Moore."

"Ben! . . . I—I've lain awake at night—Oh, was he hurt?"

"Collie, I reckon if you don't see Wils he'll kill himself or kill Buster Jack," replied Wade, gravely.

"I'll see—him!" she faltered. "But oh, Ben—you don't mean that Wilson would be so base—so cowardly?"

"Collie, you're a child. You don't realize the depths to which a man can sink. Wils has had a long, hard pull this winter. My nursin' an' your letters have saved his life. He's well, now, but that long, dark spell of mind left its shadow on him. He's morbid."

"What does he—want to see me—for?" asked Columbine, tremulously. There were tears in her eyes. "It'll only cause more pain—make matters worse."

"Reckon I don't agree with you. Wils just wants an' needs to *see* you. Why, he appreciated your position. I've heard him cry like a woman over it an' our helplessness. What ails him is lovesickness, the awful feelin' which comes to a man who believes he has lost his sweetheart's love."

"Poor boy! So he imagines I don't love him any more? Good Heavens! How stupid men are! . . . I'll see him, Ben. Take me to him."

For answer, Wade grasped the bridle of her horse

and, turning him, took a course leading away behind the hill that lay between them and the ranch-house. The trail was narrow and brushy, making it necessary for him to walk ahead of the horse. So the hunter did not speak to her or look at her for some time. He plodded on with his eyes downcast. Something tugged at Wade's mind, an old, familiar, beckoning thing, vague and mysterious and black, a presage of catastrophe. But it was only an opening wedge into his mind. It had not entered. Gravity and unhappiness occupied him. His senses, nevertheless, were alert. He heard the low roar of the flooded brook, the whir of rising grouse ahead, the hoofs of deer on stones, the song of spring birds. He had an eye also for the wan wild flowers in the shaded corners. Presently he led the horse out of the willows into the open and up a low-swelling, long slope of fragrant sage. Here he dropped back to Columbine's side and put his hand upon the pommel of her saddle. It was not long until her own hand softly fell upon his and clasped it. Wade thrilled under the warm touch. How well he knew her heart! When she ceased to love any one to whom she had given her love then she would have ceased to breathe.

"Lass, this isn't the first mornin' I've waited for you," he said, presently. "An' when I had to go back to Wils without you—well, it was hard."

"Then he wants to see me—so badly?" she asked.

"Reckon you've not thought much about him or me lately," said Wade.

"No. I've tried to put you out of my mind. I've had so much to think of—why, even the sleepless nights have flown!"

"Are you goin' to confide in me—as you used to?"

"Ben, there's nothing to confide. I'm just where I left off in that letter to Wilson. And the more I think the more muddled I get."

Wade greeted this reply with a long silence. It was enough to feel her hand upon his and to have the glad comfort and charm of her presence once more. He seemed to have grown older lately. The fragrant breath of the sage slopes came to him as something precious he must feel and love more. A haunting transience mocked him from these rolling gray hills. Old White Slides loomed gray and dark up into the blue, grim and stern reminder of age and of fleeting time. There was a cloud on Wade's horizon.

"Wils is waitin' down there," said Wade, pointing to a grove of aspens below. "Reckon it's pretty close to the house, an' a trail runs along there. But Wils can't ride very well yet, an' this appeared to be the best place."

"Ben, I don't care if dad or Jack knew I've met Wilson. I'll tell them," said Columbine.

"Ahuh! Well, if I were you I wouldn't," he replied.

They went down the slope and entered the grove. It was an open, pretty spot, with grass and wild flowers, and old, bleached logs, half sunny and half shady under the new-born, fluttering aspen leaves. Wade saw Moore sitting on his horse. And it struck the hunter significantly that the cowboy should be mounted when an hour back he had left him sitting disconsolately on a log. Moore wanted Columbine to see him first, after all these months of fear and dread, mounted upon his horse. Wade heard Columbine's glad little cry, but he did not turn to look at her then. But when they reached the spot where Moore stood Wade could not resist the desire to see the meeting between the lovers.

Columbine, being a woman, and therefore capable of hiding agitation, except in moments of stress, met that trying situation with more apparent composure than the cowboy. Moore's long, piercing gaze took the rose out of Columbine's cheeks.

"Oh, Wilson! I'm so happy to see you on your horse again!" she exclaimed. "It's too good to be true. I've prayed for that more than anything else. Can you get up into your saddle like you used to? Can you ride well again?...Let me see your foot."

Moore held out a bulky foot. He wore a shoe, and it was slashed.

"I can't wear a boot," he explained.

"Oh, I see!" exclaimed Columbine, slowly, with her glad smile fading. "You can't put that—that foot in a stirrup, can you?"

"No."

"But—it—it will—you'll be able to wear a boot soon," she implored.

"Never again, Collie," he said, sadly.

And then Wade perceived that, like a flash, the old spirit leaped up in Columbine. It was all he wanted to see.

"Now, folks," he said, "I reckon two's company an' three's a crowd. I'll go off a little ways an' keep watch."

"Ben, you stay here," replied Columbine, hurriedly.

"Why, Collie? Are you afraid—or ashamed to be with me alone?" asked Moore, bitterly.

Columbine's eyes flashed. It was seldom they lost

their sweet tranquillity. But now they had depth and fire.

"No, Wilson, I'm neither afraid nor ashamed to be with you alone," she declared. "But I can be as natural— as much myself with Ben here as I could be alone. Why can't you be? If dad and Jack heard of our meeting the fact of Ben's presence might make it look different to them. And why should I heap trouble upon my shoulders?"

"I beg pardon, Collie," said the cowboy. "I've just been afraid of—of things."

"My horse is restless," returned Columbine. "Let's get off and talk."

So they dismounted. It warmed Wade's gloomy heart to see the woman-look in Columbine's eyes as she watched the cowboy get off and walk. For a crippled man he did very well. But that moment was fraught with meaning for Wade. These unfortunate lovers, brave and fine in their suffering, did not realize the peril they invited by proximity. But Wade knew. He pitied them, he thrilled for them, he lived their torture with them.

"Tell me—everything," said Columbine, impulsively.

Moore, with dragging step, approached an aspen log that lay off the ground, propped by the stump, and here he leaned for support. Columbine laid her gloves on the log.

"There's nothing to tell that you don't know," replied Moore. "I wrote you all there was to write, except"—here he dropped his head—"except that the last three weeks have been hell."

"They've not been exactly heaven for me," replied

Columbine, with a little laugh that gave Wade a twinge.

Then the lovers began to talk about spring coming, about horses and cattle, and feed, about commonplace ranch matters not interesting to them, but which seemed to make conversation and hide their true thoughts. Wade listened, and it seemed to him that he could read their hearts.

"Lass, an' you, Wils—you're wastin' time an' gettin' nowhere," interposed Wade. "Now let me go, so's you'll be alone."

"You stay right there," ordered Moore.

"Why, Ben, I'm ashamed to say that I actually forgot you were here," said Columbine.

"Then I'll remind you," rejoined the hunter. "Collie, tell us about Old Bill an' Jack."

"Tell you? What?"

"Well, I've seen changes in both. So has Wils, though Wils hasn't seen as much as he's heard from Lem an' Montana an' the Andrews boys."

"Oh!..." Columbine choked a little over her exclamation of understanding. "Dad has gotten a new lease on life, I guess. He's happy, like a boy sometimes, an' good as gold.... It's all because of the change in Jack. That is remarkable. I've not been able to believe my own eyes. Since that night Jack came home and had the—understanding with dad he has been another person. He has left me alone. He treats me with deference, but not a familiar word or look. He's kind. He offers the little civilities that occur, you know. But he never intrudes upon me. Not one word of the past! It is as if he would earn my respect, and have that or nothing.... Then he works as he never worked before—on dad's books, in the shop, out on the range. He seems obsessed with some thought all the time. He talks little. All the old petulance, obstinacy, selfishness, and especially his sudden, queer impulses, and bull-headed tenacity—all gone! He has suffered physical distress, because he never was used to hard work. And more, he's suffered terribly for the want of liquor. I've heard him say to dad: 'It's hell—this burning thirst. I never knew I had it. I'll stand it, if it kills me.... But wouldn't it be easier on me to take a drink now and then, at these bad times?' ...And dad said: 'No, son. Break off fer keeps! This taperin' off is no good way to stop drinkin'. Stand the burnin'. An' when it's gone you'll be all the gladder an' I'll be all the prouder.'...I have not forgotten all Jack's former failings, but I am forgetting them, little by little. For dad's sake I'm overjoyed. For Jack's I am glad. I'm convinced now that he's had his lesson—that he's sowed his wild oats—that he has become a man."

Moore listened eagerly, and when she had concluded he thoughtfully bent his head and began to cut little chips out of the log with his knife.

"Collie, I've heard a good deal of the change in Jack," he said, earnestly. "Honest Injun, I'm glad—glad for his father's sake, for his own, and for yours. The boys think Jack's locoed. But his reformation is not strange to me. If I were no good—just like he was— well, I could change as greatly for—for you."

Columbine hastily averted her face. Wade's keen eyes, apparently hidden under his old hat, saw how wet her lashes were, how her lips trembled.

"Wilson, you think then—you believe Jack will

last—will stick to his new ways?" she queried, hurriedly.

"Yes, I do," he replied, nodding.

"How good of you! Oh! Wilson, it's like you to be noble—splendid. When you might have—when it'd have been so natural for you to doubt—to scorn him!"

"Collie, I'm honest about that. And now you be just as honest. Do you think Jack will stand to his colors? Never drink—never gamble—never fly off the handle again?"

"Yes, I honestly believe that—providing he gets—providing I—"

Her voice trailed off faintly.

Moore wheeled to address the hunter.

"Pard, what do you think? Tell me now. Tell us. It will help me, and Collie, too. I've asked you before, but you wouldn't— Tell us now, do you believe Buster Jack will live up to his new ideals?"

Wade had long parried that question, because the time to answer it had not come till this moment.

"No," he replied, gently.

Columbine uttered a little cry.

"Why not?" demanded Moore, his face darkening.

"Reckon there are reasons that you young folks wouldn't think of, an' couldn't know."

"Wade, it's not like you to be hopeless for any man," said Moore.

"Yes, I reckon it is, sometimes," replied Wade, wagging his head solemnly. "Young folks, I'm grantin' all you say as to Jack's reformation, except that it's permanent. I'm grantin' he's sincere—that he's not playin' a part—that his vicious instincts are smothered under

a noble impulse to be what he ought to be. It's no trick.
Buster Jack has all but done the impossible."

"Then why isn't his sincerity and good work to be
permanent?" asked Moore, impatiently, and his gesture
was violent.

"Wils, his change is not moral force. It's passion."

The cowboy paled. Columbine stood silent, with
intent eyes upon the hunter. Neither of them seemed
to understand him well enough to make reply.

"Love can work marvels in any man," went on
Wade. "But love can't change the fiber of a man's heart.
A man is born so an' so. He loves an' hates an' feels
accordin' to the nature. It'd be accordin' to nature for
Jack Belllounds to stay reformed if his love for Collie
lasted. An' that's the point. It can't last. Not in a man
of his stripe."

"Why not?" demanded Moore.

"Because Jack's love will never be returned—satisfied. It takes a man of different caliber to love a woman
who'll never love him. Jack's obsessed by passion now.
He'd perform miracles. But that's not possible. The miracle necessary here would be for him to change his
moral force, his blood, the habits of his mind. That's
beyond his power."

Columbine flung out an appealing hand.

"Ben, I could pretend to love him—I might *make*
myself love him, if that would give him the power."

"Lass, don't delude yourself. You can't do that,"
replied Wade.

"How do you know what I can do?" she queried,
struggling with her helplessness.

"Why, child, I know you better than you know your-self."

"Wilson, he's right, he's right!" she cried. "That's why it's so terrible for me now. He knows my very heart. He reads my soul....I can *never* love Jack Belllounds. Nor *ever* pretend love!"

"Collie, if Ben knows you so well, you ought to listen to him, as you used to," said Moore, touching her hand with infinite sympathy.

Wade watched them. His pity and affection did not obstruct the ruthless expression of his opinions or the direction of his intentions.

"Lass, an' you, Wils, listen," he said, with all his gentleness. "It's bad enough without you makin' it worse. Don't blind yourselves. That's the hell with so many people in trouble. It's hard to see clear when you're sufferin' and fightin'. But *I* see clear....Now with just a word I could fetch this new Jack Belllounds back to his Buster Jack tricks!"

"Oh, Ben! No! No! No!" cried Columbine, in a dis-tress that showed how his force dominated her.

Moore's face turned as white as ashes.

Wade divined then that Moore was aware of what he himself knew about Jack Belllounds. And to his love for Moore was added an infinite respect.

"I won't unless Collie forces me to," he said, sig-nificantly.

This was the critical moment, and suddenly Wade answered to it without restraint. He leaped up, startling Columbine.

"Wils, you call me pard, don't you? I reckon you never knew me. Why, the game's most played out, an'

I haven't showed my hand! . . . I'd see Jack Belllounds in hell before I'd let him have Collie. An' if she carried out her strange an' lofty idea of duty—an' married him right this afternoon—I could an' I would part them before night!"

He ended that speech in a voice neither had ever heard him use before. And the look of him must have been in harmony with it. Columbine, wide-eyed and gasping, seemed struck to the heart. Moore's white face showed awe and fear and irresponsible primitive joy. Wade turned away from them, the better to control the passion that had mastered him. And it did not subside in an instant. He paced to and fro, his head bowed. Presently, when he faced around, it was to see what he had expected to see.

Columbine was clasped in Moore's arms.

"Collie, you didn't—you haven't—promised to marry him—again!"

"No, oh—no! I haven't! I was only—only trying to—to make up my mind. Wilson, don't look at me so terribly!"

"You'll not agree again? You'll not set another day?" demanded Moore, passionately. He strained her to him, yet held her so he could see her face, thus dominating her with both strength and will. His face was corded now, and darkly flushed. His jaw quivered. "You'll never marry Jack Belllounds! You'll not let sudden impulse—sudden persuasion or force change you? Promise! Swear you'll never marry him. Swear!"

"Oh, Wilson, I promise—I swear!" she cried. "Never! I'm yours. It would be a sin. I've been mad to—to blind myself."

"You love me! You love me!" he cried, in a sudden transport.

"Oh, yes, yes! I do."

"Say it then! Say it—so I'll never doubt—never suffer again!"

"I love you, Wilson! I—I love you—unutterably," she whispered. "I love you—so—I'm broken-hearted now. I'll never live without you. I'll die—I love you so!"

"You—you flower—you angel!" he whispered in return. "You woman! You precious creature! I've been crazed at loss of you!"

Wade paced out of earshot, and this time he remained away for a considerable time. He lived again moments of his own past, unforgettable and sad. When at length he returned toward the young couple they were sitting apart, composed once more, talking earnestly. As he neared them Columbine rose to greet him with wonderful eyes, in which reproach blended with affection.

"Ben, so this is what you've done!" she exclaimed.

"Lass, I'm only a humble instrument, an' I believe God guides me right," replied the hunter.

"I love you more, it seems, for what you make me suffer," she said, and she kissed him with a serious sweetness. "I'm only a leaf in the storm. But—let what will come. . . . Take me home."

They said good-by to Wilson, who sat with head bowed upon his hands. His voice trembled as he answered them. Wade found the trail while Columbine mounted. As they went slowly down the gentle slope, stepping over the numerous logs fallen across the way. Wade caught out of the tail of his eye a moving object along the outer edge of the aspen grove above them. It was the figure of a man, skulking behind the trees. He disappeared. Wade casually remarked to Columbine that now she could spur the pony and hurry on home. But Columbine refused. When they got a little farther on, out of sight of Moore and somewhat around to the left, Wade espied the man again. He carried a rifle. Wade grew somewhat perturbed.

"Collie, you run on home," he said, sharply.

"Why? You've complained of not seeing me. Now that I want to be with you . . . Ben, you see someone!"

Columbine's keen faculties evidently sensed the change in Wade, and the direction of his uneasy glance convinced her.

"Oh, there's a man! . . . Ben, it is—yes, it's Jack," she exclaimed, excitedly.

"Reckon you'd have it better if you say Buster Jack," replied Wade, with his tragic smile.

"Ah!" whispered Columbine, as she gazed up at the aspen slope, with eyes lighting to battle.

"Run home, Collie, an' leave him to me," said Wade.

"Ben, you mean he—he saw us up there in the grove? Saw me in Wilson's arms—saw me kissing him?"

"Sure as you're born, Collie. He watched us. He saw all your love-makin'. I can tell that by the way he walks. It's Buster Jack again! Alas for the new an' noble Jack! I told you, Collie. Now you run on an' leave him to me."

Wade became aware that she turned at his last words and regarded him attentively. But his gaze was riveted on the striding form of Belllounds.

"Leave him to you? For what reason, my friend?" she asked.

"Buster Jack's on the rampage. Can't you see that? He'll insult you. He'll—"

"I will not go," interrupted Columbine, and, halting her pony, she deliberately dismounted.

Wade grew concerned with the appearance of young Belllounds, and it was with a melancholy reminder of the infallibility of his presentiments. As he and Columbine halted in the trail, Belllounds's hurried stride lengthened until he almost ran. He carried the rifle forward in a most significant manner. Black as a thunder-cloud was his face. Alas for the dignity and pain and resolve that had only recently showed there!

Belllounds reached them. He was frothing at the mouth. He cocked the rifle and thrust it toward Wade, holding low down.

"You—meddling sneak! If you open your trap I'll bore you!" he shouted, almost incoherently.

Wade knew when danger of life loomed imminent. He fixed his glance upon the glaring eyes of Belllounds.

"Jack, seein' I'm not packin' a gun, it'd look sorta natural, along with your other tricks, if you bored me."

His gentle voice, his cool mien, his satire, were as giant's arms to drag Belllounds back from murder. The rifle was raised, the hammer reset, the butt lowered to the ground, while Belllounds, snarling and choking, fought for speech.

"I'll get even—with you," he said, huskily. "I'm on to your game now. I'll fix you later. But—I'll do you harm now if you mix in with this!"

Then he wheeled to Columbine, and as if he had just recognized her, a change that was pitiful and shocking convulsed his face. He leaned toward her, pointing with shaking, accusing hand.

"I saw you—up there. I watched—you," he panted.

Columbine faced him, white and mute.

"It was you—wasn't it?" he yelled.

"Yes, of course it was."

She might have struck him, for the way he flinched.

"What was that—a trick—a game—a play all fixed up for my benefit?"

"I don't understand you," she replied.

"Bah! You—you white-faced cat! . . . I saw you! Saw you in Moore's arms! Saw him hug you—kiss you! . . . Then—I saw—you put up your arms—round his neck—kiss him—kiss him—kiss him! . . . I saw all that—didn't I?"

"You must have, since you say so," she returned, with perfect composure.

"But *did* you?" he almost shrieked, the blood cording and bulging red, as if about to burst the veins of temples and neck.

"Yes, I did," she flashed. There was primitive woman uppermost in her now, and a spirit no man might provoke with impunity.

"*You love him?*" he asked, very low, incredulously, with almost insane eagerness for denial in his query.

Then Wade saw the glory of her—saw her mother again in that proud, fierce uplift of face, that flamed red and then blazed white—saw hate and passion and love in all their primal nakedness.

"Love him! Love Wilson Moore? Yes, you fool! I love him! Yes! *Yes!* YES!"

That voice would have pierced the heart of a

wooden image, so Wade thought, as all his strung nerves quivered and thrilled.

Belllounds uttered a low cry of realization, and all his instinctive energy seemed on the verge of collapse. He grew limp, he sagged, he tottered. His sensorial perceptions seemed momentarily blunted.

Wade divined the tragedy, and a pang of great compassion overcame him. Whatever Jack Belllounds was in character, he had inherited his father's power to love, and he was human. Wade felt the death in that stricken soul, and it was the last flash of pity he ever had for Jack Belllounds.

"You—you—" muttered Belllounds, raising a hand that gathered speed and strength in the action. The moment of a great blow had passed, like a storm-blast through a leafless tree. Now the thousand devils of his nature leaped into ascendancy. "You!—" He could not articulate. Dark and terrible became his energy. It was like a resistless current forced through leaping thought and leaping muscle.

He struck her on the mouth, a cruel blow that would have felled her but for Wade; and then he lunged away, bowed and trembling, yet with fierce, instinctive motion, as if driven to run with the spirit of his rage.

CHAPTER 15

WADE noticed that after her trying experience with him and Wilson and Belllounds Columbine did not ride frequently.

He managed to get a word or two with her whenever he went to the ranch-house, and he needed only look at her to read her sensitive mind. All was well with Columbine, despite her trouble. She remained upheld in spirit, while yet she seemed to brood over an unsolvable problem. She had said, "But—let what will come!"—and she was waiting.

Wade hunted for more than lions and wolves these days. Like an Indian scout who scented peril or heard an unknown step upon his trail, Wade rode the hills, and spent long hours hidden on the lonely slopes, watching with somber, keen eyes. They were eyes that knew what they were looking for. They had marked the strange sight of the son of Bill Belllounds, gliding along that trail where Moore had met Columbine, sneaking and stooping, at last with many a covert glance about, to kneel in the trail and compare the horse tracks there with horseshoes he took from his pocket. That alone made Bent Wade eternally vigilant. He kept his counsel. He worked more swiftly, so that he might have leisure for his peculiar seeking. He spent an hour each night with the cowboys, listening to their recounting of the day and to their homely and shrewd opinions. He haunted the vicinity of the ranch-house at night, watching and listening for that moment which was to aid him in the crisis that was impending. Many a time he had been near when Columbine passed from the living-room to her corner of the house. He had heard her sigh and could almost have touched her.

Buster Jack had suffered a regurgitation of the old driving and insatiate temper, and there was gloom in the house of Belllounds. Trouble clouded the old man's eyes.

May came with the spring round-up. Wade was called to use a rope and brand calves under the order of Jack Belllounds, foreman of White Slides. That round-up showed a loss of one hundred head of stock, some branded steers, and yearlings, and many calves, in all a mixed herd. Belllounds received the amazing news with a roar. He had been ready for something to roar at. The cowboys gave as reasons winter-kill, and lions, and perhaps some head stolen since the thaw. Wade emphatically denied this. Very few cattle had fallen prey to the big cats, and none, so far as he could find, had been frozen or caught in drifts. It was the young foreman who stunned them all. "Rustled," he said, darkly. "There's too many loafers and homesteaders in these hills!" And he stalked out to leave his hearers food for reflection.

Jack Belllounds drank, but no one saw him drunk, and no one could tell where he got the liquor. He rode hard and fast; he drove the cowboys one way while he went another; he had grown shifty, cunning, more intolerant than ever. Some nights he rode to Kremmling, or said he had been there, when next day the cowboys found another spent and broken horse to turn out. On other nights he coaxed and bullied them into playing poker. They won more of his money than they cared to count.

Columbine confided to Wade, with mournful whisper, that Jack paid no attention to her whatever, and that the old rancher attributed this coldness, and Jack's backsliding, to her irresponsiveness and her tardiness in setting the wedding-day that must be set. To this Wade had whispered in reply, "Don't ever forget what I said to you an' Wils that day!"

So Wade upheld Columbine with his subtle dominance, and watched over her, as it were, from afar. No longer was he welcome in the big living-room. Belllounds reacted to his son's influence.

Twice in the early mornings Wade had surprised Jack Belllounds in the blacksmith shop. The meetings were accidental, yet Wade ever remembered how coincidence beckoned him thither and how circumstance magnified strange reflections. There was no reason why Jack should not be tinkering in the blacksmith shop early of a morning. But Wade followed an uncanny guidance. Like his hound Fox, he never split on trails. When opportunity afforded he went into the shop and looked it over with eyes as keen as the nose of his dog. And in the dust of the floor he had discovered little circles with dots in the middle, all uniform in size. Sight of them did not shock him until they recalled vividly the little circles with dots in the earthen floor of Wilson Moore's cabin. Little marks made by the end of Moore's crutch! Wade grinned then like a wolf showing his fangs. And the vitals of a wolf could no more strongly have felt the instinct to rend.

For Wade, the cloud on his horizon spread and darkened, gathered sinister shape of storm, harboring lightning and havoc. It was the cloud in his mind, the foreshadowing of his soul, the prophetic sense of like to like. Where he wandered there the blight fell!

Significant was the fact that Belllounds hired new men. Bludsoe had quit. Montana Jim grew surly these days and packed a gun. Lem Billings had threatened to leave. New and strange hands for Jack Belllounds to direct had a tendency to release a strain and tide things over.

Every time the old rancher saw Wade he rolled his eyes and wagged his head, as if combating superstition with an intelligent sense of justice. Wade knew what troubled Belllounds, and it strengthened the gloomy mood that, like a poison lichen, seemed finding root.

Every day Wade visited his friend Wilson Moore, and most of their conversation centered round that which had become a ruling passion for both. But the time came when Wade deviated from his gentleness of speech and leisure of action.

"Bent, you're not like you were," said Moore, once, in surprise at the discovery. "You're losing hope and confidence."

"No. I've only somethin' on my mind."

"What?"

"I reckon I'm not goin' to tell you now."

"You've got *hell* on your mind!" flashed the cowboy, in grim inspiration.

Wade ignored the insinuation and turned the conversation to another subject.

"Wils, you're buyin' stock right along?"

"Sure am. I saved some money, you know. And what's the use to hoard it? I'll buy cheap. In five years I'll have five hundred, maybe a thousand head. Wade, my old dad will be pleased to find out I've made the start I have."

"Well, it's a fine start, I'll allow. Have you picked up any unbranded stock?"

"Sure I have. Say, pard, are you worrying about this two-bit rustler work that's been going on?"

"Wils, it ain't two bits any more. I reckon it's gettin' into the four-bit class."

"I've been careful to have my business transactions all in writing," said Moore. "It makes these fellows sore, because some of them can't write. And they're not used to it. But I'm starting this game in my own way."

"Have you sold any stock?"

"Not yet. But the Andrews boys are driving some thirty-odd head to Kremmling for me to be sold."

"Ahuh! Well, I'll be goin'," Wade replied, and it was

significant of his state of mind that he left his young friend sorely puzzled. Not that Wade did not see Moore's anxiety! But the drift of events at White Slides had passed beyond the stage where sympathetic and inspiring hope might serve Wade's purpose. Besides, his mood was gradually changing as these events, like many fibers of a web, gradually closed in toward a culminating knot.

That night Wade lounged with the cowboys and new hands in front of the little storehouse where Belllounds kept supplies for all. He had lounged there before in the expectation of seeing the rancher's son. And this time anticipation was verified. Jack Belllounds swaggered over from the ranch-house. He met civility and obedience now where formerly he had earned but ridicule land opposition. So long as he worked hard himself the cowboys endured. The subtle change in him seemed of sterner stuff. The talk, as usual, centered round the stock subjects and the banter and gossip of ranch-hands. Wade selected an interval when there was a lull in the conversation, and with eyes that burned under the shadow of his broad-brimmed sombrero he watched the son of Belllounds.

"Say, boys, Wils Moore has begun sellin' cattle," remarked Wade, casually. "The Andrews brothers are drivin' for him."

"Wal, so Wils's spread-eaglin' into a real rancher!" ejaculated Lem Billings. "Mighty glad to hear it. Thet boy shore will git rich."

Wade's remark incited no further expressions of interest. But it was Jack Bellllounds's secret mind that Wade wished to pierce. He saw the leaping of a thought that was neither interest nor indifference nor contempt, but a creative thing which lent a fleeting flash to the face, a slight shock to the body. Then Jack Belllounds bent his head, lounged there for a little while longer, lost in absorption, and presently he strolled away.

Whatever that mounting thought of Jack Belllounds's was it brought instant decision to Wade. He went to the ranch-house and knocked upon the living-room door. There was a light within, sending rays out through the windows into the semi-darkness. Columbine opened the door and admitted Wade. A bright fire crackled in the hearth. Wade flashed a reassuring look at Columbine.

"Evenin', Miss Collie. Is your dad in?"

"Oh, it's you, Ben!" she replied, after her start. "Yes, dad's here."

The old rancher looked up from his reading. "Howdy, Wade! What can I do fer you?"

"Belllounds, I've cleaned out the cats an' most of the varmints on your range. An' my work, lately, has been all sorts, not leavin' me any time for little jobs of my own. An' I want to quit."

"Wade, you've clashed with Jack!" exclaimed the rancher, jerking erect.

"Nothin' of the kind. Jack an' me haven't had words for a good while. I'm not denyin' we might, an' probably would clash sooner or later. But that's not my reason for quittin'."

Manifestly this put an entirely different complexion upon the matter. Belllounds appeared immensely relieved.

"Wal, all right. I'll pay you at the end of the month. Let's see, thet's not long now. You can lay off tomorrow."

Wade thanked him and waited for further remarks. Columbine had fixed big, questioning eyes upon Wade, which he found hard to endure. Again he tried to flash her a message of reassurance. But Columbine did not lose her look of blank wonder and gravity.

"Ben! Oh, you're not going to leave White Slides?" she asked.

"Reckon I'll hang around yet awhile," he replied.

Belllounds was wagging his head regretfully and ponderingly.

"Wal, I remember the day when no man quit me. Wal, Wal!—times change. I'm an old man now. Mebbe, mebbe I'm testy. An' then thar's thet boy!"

With a shrug of his broad shoulders he dismissed what seemed an encroachment of pessimistic thought.

"Wade, you're packin' off, then, on the trail? Always on the go, eh?"

"No, I'm not hurryin' off," replied Wade.

"Wal, might I ask what you're figgerin' on?"

"Sure. I'm considerin' a cattle deal with Moore. He's a pretty keen boy an' his father has a big ranchin' interests. I've saved a little money an' I'm no spring chicken any more. Wils has begun to buy an' sell stock, so I reckon I'll go in with him."

"Ahuh!" Belllounds gave a grunt of comprehension. He frowned, and his big eyes set seriously upon the blazing fire. He grasped complications in this information.

"Wal, it's a free country," he said at length, and

evidently his personal anxieties were subjected to his sense of justice. "Owin' to the peculiar circumstances hyar at my range, I'd prefer thet Moore an' you began somewhar else. Thet's natural. But you've my good will to start on an' I hope I've yours."

"Belllounds, you've every man's good will," replied Wade. "I hope you won't take offense at my leavin'. You see I'm on Wils Moore's side in—in what you called these peculiar circumstances. He's got nobody else. An' I reckon you can look back an' remember how you've taken sides with some poor devil an' stuck to him. Can't you?"

"Wal, I reckon I can. An' I'm not thinkin' less of you fer speakin' out like thet."

"All right. Now about the dogs. I turn the pack over to you, an' it's a good one. I'd like to buy Fox."

"Buy nothin', man. You can have Fox, an' welcome."

"Much obliged," returned the hunter, as he turned to go. "Fox will sure be help for me. Belllounds, I'm goin' to round up this outfit that's rustlin' your cattle. They're gettin' sort of bold."

"Wade, you'll do thet on your own hook?" asked the rancher, in surprise.

"Sure. I like huntin' men more than other varmints. Then I've a personal interest. You know the hint about homesteaders hearabouts reflects some on Wils Moore."

"Stuff!" exploded the rancher, heartily. "Do you think any cattleman in these hills would believe Wils Moore a rustler?"

"The hunch has been whispered," said Wade. "An'

you know how all ranchers say they rustled a little on the start."

"Aw, hell! Thet's different. Every new rancher drives in a few unbranded calves an' keeps them. But stealin' stock—thet's different. An' I'd as soon suspect my own son of rustlin' as Wils Moore."

Belllounds spoke with a sincere and frank ardor of defense for a young man once employed by him and known to be honest. The significance of the comparison he used had not struck him. His was the epitome of a successful rancher, sure in his opinions, speaking proudly and unreflectingly of his own son, and being just to another man.

Wade bowed and backed out of the door. "Sure that's what I'd reckon you'd say, Belllounds....I'll drop in on you if I find any sign in the woods. Good night."

Columbine went with him to the end of the porch, as she had used to go before the shadow had settled over the lives of the Belllounds.

"Ben, you're up to something," she whispered, seizing him with hands that shook.

"Sure. But don't you worry," he whispered back.

"Do they hint that Wilson is a rustler?" she asked, intensely.

"Somebody did, Collie."

"How vile! Who? Who?" she demanded, and her face gleamed white.

"Hush, lass! You're all a-tremble," he returned, warily, and he held her hands.

"Ben, they're pressing me hard to set another wedding-day. Dad is angry with me now. Jack has begun again to demand. Oh, I'm afraid of him! He has no respect for me. He catches at me with hands like claws. I have to jerk away.... Oh, Ben, Ben! dear friend, what on earth shall I do?"

"Don't give in. Fight Jack! Tell the old man you must have time. Watch your chance when Jack is away an' ride up the Buffalo Park trail an' look for me."

Wade had to release his hands from her clasp and urge her gently back. How pale and tragic her face gleamed!

Wade took his horses, his outfit, and the dog Fox, and made his abode with Wilson Moore. The cowboy hailed Wade's coming with joy and pestered him with endless questions.

From that day Wade haunted the hills above White Slides, early and late, alone with his thoughts, his plans, more and more feeling the suspense of happenings to come. It was on a June day when Jack Belllounds rode to Kremmling that Wade met Columbine on the Buffalo Park trail. She needed to see him, to find comfort and strength. Wade far exceeded his own confidence in his effort to uphold her. Columbine was in a strange state, not of vacillation between two courses, but of a standstill, as if her will had become obstructed and waited for some force to upset the hindrance. She did not inquire as to the welfare of Wilson Moore, and Wade vouchsafed no word of him. But she importuned the hunter to see her every day or no more at all. And Wade answered her appeal and her need by assuring her that he would see her, come what might. So she was to risk more frequent rides.

During the second week of June Wade rode up to visit the prospector, Lewis, and learned that which complicated the matter of the rustlers. Lewis had been suspicious, and active on his own account. According to the best of his evidence and judgment there had been a gang of rough men come of late to Gore Peak, where they presumably were prospecting. This gang was composed of strangers to Lewis. They had ridden to his cabin, bought and borrowed of him, and, during his absence, had stolen from him. He believed they were in hiding, probably being guilty of some depredation in another locality. They gave both Kremmling and Elgeria a wide berth. On the other hand, the Smith gang from Elgeria rode to and fro, like ranchers searching for lost horses. There were only three in this gang, including Smith. Lewis had seen these men driving unbranded stock. And lastly, Lewis casually imparted the information, highly interesting to Wade, that he had seen Jack Belllounds riding through the forest. The prospector did not in the least, however, connect the appearance of the son of Belllounds with the other facts so peculiarly interesting to Wade. Cowboys and hunters rode trails across the range, and though they did so rather infrequently, there was nothing unusual about encountering them.

Wade remained all night with Lewis, and next morning rode six miles along the divide, and then down into a valley, where at length he found a cabin described by the prospector. It was well hidden in the edge of the forest, where a spring gushed from under a low cliff. But for water and horse tracks Wade would not have found it easily. Rifle in hand, and on foot, he slipped around in the woods, as a hunter might have, to stalk drinking deer. There were no smoke, no noise, no horses anywhere round the cabin, and after watching awhile Wade went forward to look at it. It was an old ramshackle hunter's or prospector's cabin, with dirt floor, a crumbling fireplace and chimney, and a bed platform made of boughs. Including the door, it had three apertures, and the two smaller ones, serving as windows, looked as if they had been intended for port-holes as well. The inside of the cabin was large and unusually well lighted, owing to the windows and to the open chinks between the logs. Wade saw a deck of cards lying bent and scattered in one corner, as if a violent hand had flung them against the wall. Strange that Wade's memory returned a vivid picture of Jack Belllounds in just that act of violence! The only other thing around the place which earned scrutiny from Wade was a number of horseshoe tracks outside, with the left front shoe track familiar to him. He examined the clearest imprints very carefully. If they had not been put there by Wilson Moore's white mustang, Spottie, then they had been made by a horse with a strangely similar hoof and shoe. Spottie had a hoof malformed, somewhat in the shape of a triangle, and the iron shoe to fit it always had to be bent, so that the curve was sharp and the ends closer together than those of his other shoes.

Wade rode down to White Slides that day, and at the evening meal he casually asked Moore if he had been riding Spottie of late.

"Sure. What other horse could I ride? Do you think

I'm up to trying one of those broncs?" asked Moore, in derision.

"Reckon you haven't been leavin' any tracks up Buffalo Park way?"

The cowboy slammed down his knife. "Say, Wade, are you growing dotty? Good Lord! if I'd ridden that far—if I was able to do it—wouldn't you hear me yell?"

"Reckon so, come to think of it. I just saw a track like Spottie's, made two days ago."

"Well, it wasn't his, you can gamble on that," returned the cowboy.

Wade spent four days hiding in an aspen grove, on top of one of the highest foothills above White Slides Ranch. There he lay at ease, like an Indian, calm and somber, watching the trails below, waiting for what he knew was to come.

On the fifth morning he was at his post at sunrise. A casual remark of one of the new cowboys the night before accounted for the early hour of Wade's reconnoiter. The dawn was fresh and cool, with sweet odor of sage on the air; the jays were squalling their annoyance at this early disturber of their grove; the east was rosy above the black range and soon glowed with gold and then changed to fire. The sun had risen. All the mountain world of black range and gray hill and green valley, with its shining stream, was transformed as if by magic color. Wade sat down with his back to an aspen-tree, his gaze down upon the ranch-house and the corrals. A lazy column of blue smoke curled up toward the sky, to be lost there. The burros were braying, the calves were bawling, the colts were whistling. One of the hounds bayed full and clear.

The scene was pastoral and beautiful. Wade saw it clearly and whole. Peace and plenty, a happy rancher's home, the joy of the dawn and the birth of summer, the rewards of toil—all seemed significant there. But Wade pondered on how pregnant with life that scene was— nature in its simplicity and freedom and hidden cruelty, and the existence of people, blindly hating, loving, sac- rificing, mostly serving some noble aim, and yet with baseness among them, the lees with the wine, evil in- termixed with good.

By and by the cowboys appeared on their spring mustangs, and in twos and threes they rode off in dif- ferent directions. But none rode Wade's way. The sun rose higher, and there was warmth in the air. Bees began to hum by Wade, and fluttering moths winged uncertain flight over him.

At the end of another hour Jack Belllounds came out of the house, gazed around him, and then stalked to the barn where he kept his horses. For a little while he was not in sight; then he reappeared, mounted on a white horse, and he rode into the pasture, and across that to the hay-field, and along the edge of this to the slope of the hill. Here he climbed to a small clump of aspens. This grove was not so far from Wilson Moore's cabin; in fact, it marked the boundary-line between the rancher's range and the acres that Moore had acquired. Jack vanished from sight here, but not before Wade had made sure he was dismounting.

"Reckon he kept to that grassy ground for a reason of his own—and plainer to me than any tracks," so- liloquized Wade, as he strained his eyes. At length

Belllounds came out of the grove, and led his horse round to where Wade knew there was a trail leading to and from Moore's cabin. At this point Jack mounted and rode west. Contrary to his usual custom, which was to ride hard and fast, he trotted the white horse as a cowboy might have done when going out on a day's work. Wade had to change his position to watch Belllounds, and his somber gaze followed him across the hill, down the slope, along the willow-bordered brook, and so on to the opposite side of the great valley, where Jack began to climb in the direction of Buffalo Park.

After Belllounds had disappeared and had been gone for an hour, Wade went down on the other side of the hill, found his horse where he had left him, in a thicket, and, mounting, he rode around to strike the trail upon which Belllounds had ridden. The imprint of fresh horse tracks showed clear in the soft dust. And the left front track had been made by a shoe crudely triangular in shape, identical with that peculiar to Wilson Moore's horse.

"Ahuh!" muttered Wade, in greeting to what he had expected to see. "Well, Buster Jack, it's a plain trail now—damn your crooked soul!"

The hunter took up that trail, and he followed it into the woods. There he hesitated. Men who left crooked trails frequently ambushed them, and Belllounds had made no effort to conceal his tracks. Indeed, he had chosen the soft, open ground, even after he had left the trail to take to the grassy, wooded benches. There were cattle here, but not as many as on the more open aspen slopes across the valley. After deliberating a moment, Wade decided that he must risk being caught trailing Belllounds. But he would go slowly, trusting to eye and ear, to outwit this strangely acting foreman of White Slides Ranch.

To that end he dismounted and took the trail. Wade had not followed it far before he became convinced that Belllounds had been looking in the thickets for cattle; and he had not climbed another mile through the aspens and spruce before he discovered that Belllounds was driving cattle. Thereafter Wade proceeded more cautiously. If the long grass had not been wet he would have encountered great difficulty in trailing Belllounds. Evidence was clear now that he was hiding the tracks of the cattle by keeping to the grassy levels and slopes which, after the sun had dried them, would not leave a trace. There were stretches where even the keen-eyed hunter had to work to find the direction taken by Belllounds. But here and there, in other localities, there showed faint signs of cattle and horse tracks.

The morning passed, with Wade slowly climbing to the edge of the black timber. Then, in a hollow where a spring gushed forth, he saw the tracks of a few cattle that had halted to drink, and on top of these the tracks of a horse with a crooked left front shoe. The rider of this horse had dismounted. There was an imprint of a cowboy's boot, and near it little sharp circles with dots in the center.

"Well, I'll be damned!" ejaculated Wade. "I call that mighty cunnin'. Here they are—proofs as plain as writin'—that Wils Moore rustled Old Bill's cattle! . . . Buster Jack, you're not such a fool as I thought. . . . He's made somethin' like the end of Wils's crutch. An' knowin' how Wils uses that every time he gets off his horse, why, the dirty pup carried his instrument with him an' made these tracks!"

Wade left the trail then, and, leading his horse to a covert of spruce, he sat down to rest and think. Was there any reason for following Belllounds farther? It did not seem needful to take the risk of being discovered. The forest above was open. No doubt Belllounds would drive the cattle somewhere and turn them over to his accomplishes.

"Buster Jack's outbusted himself this time, sure," soliloquized Wade. "He's double-crossin' his rustler friends, same as he is Moore. For he's goin' to blame this cattle-stealin' onto Wils. An' to do that he's layin' his tracks so he can follow them, or so any good trailer can. It doesn't concern me so much now who're his pards in this deal. Reckon it's Smith an' some of his gang."

Suddenly it dawned upon Wade that Jack Belllounds was stealing cattle from his father. "Whew!" he whistled softly. "Awful hard on the old man! Who's to tell him when all this comes out? Aw, I'd hate to do it. I wouldn't. There's some things even I'd not tell."

Straightway this strange aspect of the case confronted Wade and gripped his soul. He seemed to feel himself changing inwardly, as if a gray, gloomy, sodden hand, as intangible as a ghostly dream, had taken him bodily from himself and was now leading him into shadows, into dreary, lonely, dark solitude, where all was cold and bleak; and on and on over naked shingles that marked the world of tragedy. Here he must tell his tale, and as he plodded on his relentless leader forced him to tell his tale anew.

Wade recognized this as his black mood. It was a morbid dominance of the mind. He fought it as he would have fought a devil. And mastery still was his. But his brow was clammy and his heart was leaden when he had wrested that somber, mystic control from his will.

"Reckon I'd do well to take up this trail to-morrow an' see where it leads," he said, and as a gloomy man, burdened with thought, he retraced his way down the long slope, and over the benches, to the grassy slopes and aspen groves, and thus to the sage hills.

It was dark when he reached the cabin, and Moore had supper almost ready.

"Well, old-timer, you look fagged out," called out the cowboy, cheerily. "Throw off your boots, wash up, and come and get it!"

"Pard Wils, I'm not reboundin' as natural as I'd like. I reckon I've lived some years before I got here, an' a lifetime since."

"Wade, you have a queer look, lately," observed Moore, shaking his head solemnly. "Why, I've seen a dying man look just like you—now—round the mouth—but most in the eyes!"

"Maybe the end of the long trail is White Slides Ranch," replied Wade, sadly and dreamily, as if to himself.

"If Collie heard you say that!" exclaimed Moore, in anxious concern.

"Collie an' you will hear me say a lot before long," returned Wade. "But, as it's calculated to make you happy—why, all's well. I'm tired an' hungry."

Wade did not choose to sit round the fire that night, fearing to invite interrogation from his anxious friend, and for that matter from his other inquisitively morbid self.

Next morning, though Wade felt rested, and the sky was blue and full of fleecy clouds, and the melody of birds charmed his ear, and over all the June air seemed thick and beating with the invisible spirit he loved, he sensed the oppression, the nameless something that presaged catastrophe.

Therefore, when he looked out of the door to see Columbine swiftly riding up the trail, her fair hair flying and shining in the sunlight, he merely ejaculated, "Ahuh!"

"What's that?" queried Moore, sharp to catch the inflection.

"Look out," replied Wade, as he began to fill his pipe.

"Heavens! It's Collie! Look at her riding! Uphill, too!"

Wade followed him outdoors. Columbine was not long in arriving at the cabin, and she threw the bridle and swung off in the same motion, landing with a light thud. Then she faced them, pale, and resolute, stern, all the sweetness gone to bitter strength—another and a strange Columbine.

"I've not slept a wink!" she said. "And I came as soon as I could get away."

Moore had no word for her, not even a greeting. The look of her had stricken him. It could have only one meaning.

"Mornin', lass," said the hunter, and he took her

hand. "I couldn't tell you looked sleepy, for all you said. Let's go into the cabin."

So he led Columbine in, and Moore followed. The girl manifestly was in a high state of agitation, but she was neither trembling nor frightened nor sorrowful. Nor did she betray any lack of an unflinching and indomitable spirit. Wade read the truth of what she imagined was her doom in the white glow of her, in the matured lines of womanhood that had come since yesternight, in the sustained passion of her look.

"Ben! Wilson! The worst has come!" she announced.

Moore could not speak. Wade held Columbine's hand in both of his.

"Worst! Now, Collie, that's a terrible word. I've heard it many times. An' all my life the worst's been comin'. An' it hasn't come yet. You—only twenty years old—talkin' wild—the worst has come! . . . Tell me your trouble now an' I'll tell you where you're wrong."

"Jack's a thief—a cattle-thief!" rang Columbine's voice, high and clear.

"Ahuh! Well, go on," said Wade.

"Jack has taken money from rustlers—*for cattle stolen from his father!*"

Wade felt the lift of her passion, and he vibrated to it.

"Reckon that's no news to me," he replied.

Then she quivered up to a strong and passionate delivery of the thing that had transformed her.

"I'M GOING TO MARRY JACK BELLLOUNDS!"

Wilson Moore leaped toward her with a cry, to be held back by Wade's hand.

"Now, Collie," he soothed, "tell us all about it."

Columbine, still upheld by the strength of her spirit, related how she had ridden out the day before, early in the afternoon, in the hope of meeting Wade. She rode over the sage hills, along the edges of the aspen benches, everywhere that she might expect to meet or see the hunter, but as he did not appear, and as she was greatly desirous of talking with him, she went on up into the woods, following the line of the Buffalo Park trail, though keeping aside from it. She rode very slowly and cautiously, remembering Wade's instructions. In this way she ascended the aspen benches, and the spruce-bordered ridges, and then the first rise of the black forest. Finally she had gone farther than ever before and farther than was wise.

When she was about to turn back she heard the thud of hoofs ahead of her. Pronto shot up his ears. Alarmed and anxious, Columbine swiftly gazed about her. It would not do for her to be seen. Yet, on the other hand, the chances were that the approaching horse carried Wade. It was lucky that she was on Pronto, for he could be trusted to stand still and not neigh. Columbine rode into a thick clump of spruces that had long, shelving branches, reaching down. Here she hid, holding Pronto motionless.

Presently the sound of hoofs denoted the approach of several horses. That augmented Columbine's anxiety. Peering out of her covert, she espied three horsemen trotting along the trail, and one of them was Jack Bell-lounds. They appeared to be in strong argument, judging from gestures and emphatic movements of their heads. As chance would have it they halted their horses not half a dozen rods from Columbine's place of concealment. The two men with Belllounds were rough-looking, one of them, evidently a leader, having a dark face disfigured by a horrible scar.

Naturally they did not talk loud, and Columbine had to strain her eyes to catch anything. But a word distinguished here and there, and accompanying actions, made transparent the meaning of their presence and argument. The big man refused to ride any farther. Evidently he had come so far without realizing it. His importunities were for "more head of stock." His scorn was for a "measly little bunch not worth the risk." His anger was for Belllounds's foolhardiness in "leavin' a trail." Belllounds had little to say, and most of that was spoken in a tone too low to be heard. His manner seemed indifferent, even reckless. But he wanted "money." The scar-faced man's name was "Smith." Then Columbine gathered from Smith's dogged and forceful gestures, and his words, "no money" and "bigger bunch," that he was unwilling to pay what had been agreed upon unless Belllounds promised to bring a larger number of cattle. Here Belllounds roundly cursed the rustler, and apparently argued that course "next to impossible." Smith made a sweeping movement with his arm, pointing south, indicating some place afar, and part of his speech was "Gore Peak." The little man, companion of Smith, got into the argument, and, dismounting from his horse, he made marks upon the smooth earth of the trail. He was drawing a rude map showing direction and locality. At length, when Belllounds nodded as if convinced or now informed, this third member of the party remounted, and seemed to have no more to say. Belllounds pondered sullenly. He snatched a switch from off a bough overhead and flicked his boot and stirrup with it, an action that made his horse restive. Smith leered and spoke derisively, of which speech Columbine heard, "Aw hell!" and "yellow streak," and "no one'd ever," and "son of Bill Belllounds," and "rustlin' stock." Then this scar-faced man drew out a buckskin bag. Either the contempt or the gold, or both, overbalanced vacillation in the weak mind of Jack Belllounds, for he lifted his head, showing his face pale and malignant, and without trace of shame or compunction he snatched the bag of gold, shouted a hoarse, "All right, damn you!" and, wheeling the white mustang, he spurred away, quickly disappearing.

The rustlers sat their horses, gazing down the trail, and Smith wagged his dark head doubtfully. Then he spoke quite distinctly, "I ain't a-trustin' thet Belllounds pup!" and his comrade replied, "Boss, we ain't stealin' the stock, so what th' hell!" Then they turned their horses and trotted out of sight and hearing up the timbered slope.

Columbine was so stunned, and so frightened and horrified, that she remained hidden there for a long time before she ventured forth. Then, heading homeward, she skirted the trail and kept to the edge of the forest, making a wide detour over the hills, finally reaching the ranch at sunset. Jack did not appear at the evening meal. His father had one of his spells of depression and seemed not to have noticed her absence. She lay awake all night thinking and praying.

Columbine concluded her narrative there, and, panting from her agitation and hurry, she gazed at the bowed figure of Moore, and then at Wade.

"I *had* to tell you this shameful secret," she began again. "I'm forced. If you do not help me, if something is not done, there'll be a horrible—end to all!"

"We'll help you, but how?" asked Moore, raising a white face.

"I don't know yet. I only *feel*—I only *feel* what may happen, if I don't prevent it.... Wilson, you must go home—at least for a while."

"It'll not look right for Wils to leave White Slides now," interposed Wade, positively.

"But why? Oh, I fear—"

"Never mind now, lass. It's a good reason. An' you mustn't fear anythin'. I agree with you—we've got to prevent this—this that's goin' to happen."

"Oh, Ben, my dear friend, we must prevent it—you *must!*"

"Ahuh! ... So I was figurin'."

"Ben, you must go to Jack an' tell him—show him the peril—frighten him terribly—so that he will not do—do this shameful thing again."

"Lass, I reckon I could scare Jack out of his skin. But what good would that do?"

"It'll stop this—this madness.... Then I'll marry him—and keep him safe—after that!"

"Collie, do you think marryin' Buster Jack will stop his bustin' out?"

"Oh, I *know* it will. He had conquered over the evil in him. I saw that. I felt it. He conquered over his baser nature for love of me. Then—when he heard—from my own lips—that I loved Wilson—why, then he fell. He didn't care. He drank again. He let go. He sank. And now he'll ruin us all. Oh, it looks as if he meant it that way! ...But I can change him. I will marry him. I will love him—or I will *live a lie!* I will make him think I love him!"

Wilson Moore, deadly pale, faced her with flaming eyes.

"Collie, *why?* For God's sake, explain why you will shame your womanhood and ruin me—all for that coward—that thief?"

Columbine broke from Wade and ran to Wilson, as if to clasp him, but something halted her and she stood before him.

"Because dad will kill him!" she cried.

"My God! what are you saying?" exclaimed Moore, incredulously. "Old Bill would roar and rage, but hurt that boy of his—never!"

"Wils, I reckon Collie is right. You haven't got Old Bill figured. I know," interposed Wade, with one of his forceful gestures.

"Wilson, listen, and don't set your heart against me. For I *must* do this thing," pleaded Columbine. "I heard dad swear he'd kill Jack. Oh, I'll never forget! He was terrible! If he ever finds out that Jack stole from his own father—stole cattle like a common rustler, and sold them for gold to gamble and drink with—he will kill him!...That's as true as fate....Think how horrible that would be for me! Because I'm to blame here, mostly. I fell in love with *you*, Wilson Moore, otherwise I could have saved Jack already.

"But it's not that I think of myself. Dad has loved me. He has been as a father to me. You know he's not my real father. Oh, if I only had a real one!...And I owe him so much. But then it's not because I owe him or because I love him. It's because of his own soul! . . . That splendid, noble old man, who has been so good to every one—who had only one fault, and that love of his son—must he be let go in blinded and insane rage at the failure of his life, the ruin of his son—must he be allowed to kill his own flesh and blood? . . . It would be *murder!* It would damn dad's soul to everlasting torment. No! No! I'll not let that be!"

"Collie—how about—your own soul?" whispered Moore, lifting himself as if about to expend a tremendous breath.

"That doesn't matter," she replied.

"Collie—Collie—" he stammered, but could not go on.

Then it seemed to Wade that they both turned to him unconscious of the inevitableness of his relation to this catastrophe, yet looking to him for the spirit, the guidance that became habitual to them. It brought the warm blood back to Wade's cold heart. It was his great reward. How intensely and implacably did his soul mount to that crisis!

"Collie, I'll never fail you," he said, and his gentle voice was deep and full. "If Jack can be scared into haltin' in his mad ride to hell—then I'll do it. I'm not promisin' so much for him. But I'll swear to you that Old Bellllounds's hands will never be stained with his son's blood!"

"Oh, Ben! Ben!" she cried, in passionate gratitude. "I'll love you—bless you all my life!"

"Hush, lass! I'm not one to bless. . . . An' now you must do as I say. Go home an' tell them you'll marry

Jack in August. Say August thirteenth."

"So long! Oh, why put it off? Wouldn't it be better—safer, to settle it all—once and forever?"

"No man can tell everythin'. But that's my judgment."

"Why August thirteenth?" she queried, with strange curiosity. "An unlucky date!"

"Well, it just happened to come to my mind—that date," replied Wade, in his slow, soft voice of reminiscence. "I was married on August thirteenth—twenty-one years ago. . . . An', Collie, my wife looked somethin' like you. Isn't that strange, now? It's a little world. . . . An' she's been gone eighteen years!"

"Ben, I never dreamed you ever had a wife," said Columbine, softly, with her hands going to his shoulder. "You must tell me of her some day. . . . But now—if you want time—if you think it best—I'll not marry Jack till August thirteenth."

"That'll give me time," replied Wade. "I'm thinkin' Jack ought to be—reformed, let's call it—before you marry him. If all you say is true—why we can turn him round. Your promise will do most. . . . So, then, it's settled?"

"Yes—dear—friends," faltered the girl, tremulously, on the verge of a breakdown, now that the ordeal was past.

Wilson Moore stood gazing out of the door, his eyes far away on the gray slopes.

"Queer how things turn out," he said, dreamily. "August thirteenth! . . . That's about the time the columbines blow on the hills....And I always meant columbine-time—"

Here he sharply interrupted himself, and the dreamy musing gave way to passion. "But I mean it yet! I'll—I'll die before I give up hope of you!"

WADE, watching Columbine ride down the slope on her homeward way, did some of the hardest thinking he had yet been called upon to do. It was not necessary to acquaint Wilson Moore with the deeper and more subtle motives that had begun to actuate him. It would not utterly break the cowboy's spirit to live in suspense. Columbine was safe for the present. He had insured her against fatality. Time was all he needed. Possibility of an actual consummation of her marriage to Jack Belllounds did not lodge for an instant in Wade's consciousness. In Moore's case, however, the present moment seemed critical. What should he tell Moore—what should he conceal from him?

"Son, come in here," he called to the cowboy.

"Pard, it looks—bad!" said Moore, brokenly.

Wade looked at the tragic face and cursed under his breath.

"Buck up! It's never as bad as it looks. Anyway, we *know* now what to expect, an' that's well."

Moore shook his head. "Couldn't you see how like steel Collie was? . . . But I'm on to you, Wade. You think by persuading Collie to put that marriage off that we'll gain time. You're gambling with time. You swear Buster Jack will hang himself. You won't quit fighting this deal."

"Buster Jack has slung the noose over a tree, an' he's about ready to slip his head into it," replied Wade.

"Bah! . . . You drive me wild," cried Moore, passionately. "How can you? Where's all that feeling you seemed to have for me? You nursed me—you saved my leg—and my life. You must have cared about me. But now—you talk about that dolt—that spoiled old man's pet—that damned cur, as if you believed he'd ruin himself. No such luck! no such hope! . . . Every day things grow worse. Yet the worse they grow the stronger you seem! It's all out of proportion. It's dreams. Wade, I hate to say it, but I'm sure you're not always—just right in your mind."

"Wils, now ain't that queer?" replied Wade, sadly. "I'm agreein' with you."

"Aw!" Moore shook himself savagely and laid an affectionate and appealing arm on his friend's shoulder. "Forgive me, pard! . . . It's me who's out of his head. . . . But my heart's broken."

"That's what you think," rejoined Wade, stoutly. "But a man's heart can't break in a day. I know. . . . An' the God's truth is Buster Jack will hang himself!"

Moore raised his head sharply, flinging himself back

from his friend so as to scrutinize his face. Wade felt the piercing power of that gaze.

"Wade, what do you mean?"

"Collie told us some interestin' news about Jack, didn't she? Well, she didn't know what I know. Jack Belllounds had laid a cunnin' an' devilish trap to prove you guilty of rustlin' his father's cattle."

"Absurd!" ejaculated Moore, with white lips.

"I'd never given him credit for brains to hatch such a plot," went on Wade. "Now listen. Not long ago Buster Jack made a remark in front of the whole outfit, includin' his father, that the homesteaders on the range were rustlin' cattle. It fell sort of flat, that remark. But no one could calculate on his infernal cunnin'. I quit workin' for Belllounds that night, an' I've put my time in spyin' on the boy. In my day I've done a good deal of spyin', but I've never run across any one slicker than Buster Jack. To cut it short—he got himself a white-speckled mustang that's a dead ringer for Spottie. He measured the tracks of your horse's left front foot—the bad hoof, you know, an' he made a shoe exactly the same as Spottie wears. Also, he made some kind of a contraption that's like the end of your crutch. These he packs with him. I saw him ride across the pasture to hide his tracks, climb up the sage for the same reason, an' then hide in that grove of aspens over there near the trail you use. Here, you can bet, he changed shoes on the left front foot of his horse. Then he took to the trail, an' he left tracks for a while, an' then he was careful to hide them again. He stole his father's stock an' drove it up over the grassy benches where even you or I couldn't track him next day. But up on top, when it suited him, he left

some horse tracks, an' in the mud near a spring-hole
he gets off his horse, steppin' with one foot—an' makin'
little circles with dots like those made by the end of
your crutch. Then 'way over in the woods there's a cabin
where he meets his accomplices. Here he leaves the
same horse tracks an' crutch tracks.... Simple as a b c,
Wils, when you see how he did it. But I'll tell you
straight—if I hadn't been suspicious of Buster Jack—
that trick of his would have made you a rustler!"

"Damn him!" hissed the cowboy, in utter consternation and fury.

"Ahuh! That's my sentiment exactly."

"I swore to Collie I'd never kill him!"

"Sure you did, son. An' you've got to keep that
oath. I pin you down to it. You can't break faith with
Collie.... An' you don't want his bad blood on your
hands."

"No! No!" he replied, violently. "Of course I don't.
I won't. But God! how sweet it would be to tear out his
lying tongue—to—"

"I reckon it would. Only don't talk about that,"
interrupted Wade, bluntly. "You see, now, don't you,
how he's about hanged himself."

"No, pard, I don't. We can't squeal that on him, any
more than we can squeal what Collie told us."

"Son, you're young in dealin' with crooked men.
You don't get the drift of motives. Buster Jack is not
only robbin' his father an' hatchin' a dirty trap for you,
but he's double-crossin' the rustlers he's sellin' the cattle to. He's riskin' their necks. He's goin' to find *your*
tracks, showin' you dealt with them. Sure, he won't give
them away, an' he's figurin' on their gettin' out of it,

maybe by leavin' the range, or a shootin'-fray, or some way. The big thing with Jack is that he's goin' to accuse you of rustlin' an' show your tracks to his father. Well, that's a risk he's given the rustlers. It happens that I know this scar-face Smith. We've met before. Now it's easy to see from what Collie heard that Smith is not trustin' Buster Jack. So, all underneath this Jack Belllounds's game, there's forces workin' unbeknown to him, beyond his control, an' sure to ruin him."

"I see. I see. By Heaven! Wade, nothing else but ruin seems possible!...But suppose it works out his way!...What then? What of Collie?"

"Son, I've not got that far along in my reckonin'," replied Wade.

"But for my sake—think. If Buster Jack gets away with his trick—if he doesn't hang himself by some blunder or fit of temper or spree—what then of Collie?"

Wade could not answer this natural and inevitable query for the reason that he had found it impossible of consideration.

"Sufficient unto the day is the evil thereof," he replied.

"Wade, you've said that before. It helped me. But now I need more than a few words from the Bible. My faith is low. I...oh, I tried to pray because Collie told me she had prayed! But what are prayers? We're dealing with a stubborn, iron-willed old man who idolizes his son; we're dealing with crazy boy, absolutely self-centered, crafty, and vicious, who'll stop at nothing. And, lastly, we're dealing with a girl who's so noble and high-souled that she'll sacrifice her all—her life to pay her debt. If she were really Bill Belllounds's daughter she'd *never* marry Jack, saying, of course, that he was not her brother.... Do you know that it will *kill* her, if she marries him?"

"Ahuh! I reckon it would," replied Wade, with his head bowed. Moore roused his gloomy forebodings. He did not care to show this feeling or the effect the cowboy's pleading had upon him.

"Ah! so you admit it? Well, then, what of Collie?"

"*If* she marries him—she'll have to die, I suppose," replied Wade.

Then Wilson Moore leaped at his friend and with ungentle hands lifted him, pushed him erect.

"Damn you, Wade! You're not square with me! You don't tell me all!" he cried, hoarsely.

"Now, Wils, you're set up. I've told you all I know. I swear that."

"But you couldn't stand the thought of Collie dying for that brute! You couldn't! Oh, I know. I can feel some things that are hard to tell. So, you're either out of your head or you've something up your sleeve. It's hard to explain how you affect me. One minute I'm ready to choke you for that damned strangeness—whatever it is. The next minute I feel it—I trust it, myself.... Wade, you're not—you *can't* be infallible!"

"I'm only a man, Wils, an' your friend. I reckon you do find me queer. But that's no matter. Now let's look at this deal—each from his own side of the fence. An' each actin' up to his own lights! You do what your conscience dictates, always thinkin' of Collie—not of yourself! An' I'll live up to my principles. Can we do more?"

"No, indeed, Wade, we can't," replied Moore, eloquently.

"Well, then, here's my hand. I've talked too much, I reckon. An' the time for talkin' is past."

In silence Moore gripped the hand held out to him, trying to read Wade's mind, apparently once more uplifted and strengthened by that which he could not divine.

Wade's observations during the following week brought forth the fact that Jack Belllounds was not letting any grass grow under his feet. He endeavored to fulfill his agreement with Smith, and drove a number of cattle by moonlight. These were part of the stock that the rancher had sold to buyers at Kremmling, and which had been collected and held in the big, fenced pasture down the valley next to the Andrews ranch. The loss was not discovered until the cattle had been counted at Kremmling. Then they were credited to loss by straying. In driving a considerable herd of half-wild steers, with an inadequate force of cowboys, it was no unusual thing to lose a number.

Wade, however, was in possession of the facts not later than the day after this midnight steal in the moonlight. He was forced to acknowledge that no one would have believed it possible for Jack Belllounds to perform a feat which might well have been difficult for the best of cowboys. But Jack accomplished it and got back home before daylight. And Wade was bound to admit that circumstantial evidence against Wilson Moore, which, of course, Jack Belllounds would soon present, would be damning and apparently irrefutable.

Waiting for further developments, Wade closely watched the ranch-house, which duty interfered with his attention to the outlying trails. What he did not want to miss was being present when Jack Belllounds accused Wilson Moore of rustling cattle.

So it chanced that Wade was chatting with the cowboys one Sunday afternoon when Jack, accompanied by three strangers, all mounted on dusty, tired horses, rode up to the porch and dismounted.

Lem Billings manifested unusual excitement.

"Montana, ain't thet Sheriff Burley from Kremmlin'?" he queried.

"Shore looks like him.... Yep, thet's him. Now what's doin'?"

The cowboys exchanged curious glances, and then turned to Wade.

"Bent, what do you make of thet?" asked Lem, as he waved his hand toward the house. "Buster Jack ridin' up with Sheriff Burley."

The rancher, Belllounds, who was on the porch, greeted the visitors, and then they all went into the house.

"Boys, it's what I've been lookin' for," replied Wade.

"Shore. Reckon we all have idees. An' if my idee is correct I'm agoin' to git pretty damn sore pronto," declared Lem.

They were all silent for a few moments, meditating over this singular occurrence, and watching the house. Presently Old Bill Belllounds strode out upon the porch, and, walking out into the court, he peered around as if looking for some one. Then he espied the little group of cowboys.

"Hey!" he yelled. "One of you boys ride up an' fetch Wils Moore down hyar!"

"All right, boss," called Lem, in reply, as he got up and gave a hitch to his belt.

The rancher hurried back, head down, as if burdened.

"Wade, I reckon you want to go fetch Wils?" queried Lem.

"If it's all the same to you. I'd rather not," replied Wade.

"By Golly! I don't blame you. Boys, shore 'n hell, Burley's after Wils."

"Wal, suppos'n' he is," said Montana. "You can gamble Wils ain't agoin' to run. I'd jest like to see him face thet outfit. Burley's a pretty square fellar. An' he's no fool."

"It's as plain as your nose, Montana, an' thet's shore big enough," returned Lem, with a hard light in his eyes. "Buster Jack's busted out, an' he's figgered Wils in some deal thet's rung in the sheriff. Wal, I'll fetch Wils." And, growling to himself, the cowboy slouched off after his horse.

Wade got up, deliberate and thoughtful, and started away.

"Say, Bent, you're shore goin' to see what's up?" asked Montana, in surprise.

"I'll be around, Jim," replied Wade, and he strolled off to be alone. He wanted to think over this startling procedure of Jack Belllounds's. Wade was astonished. He had expected that an accusation would be made against Moore by Jack, and an exploitation of such proofs as had been craftily prepared, but he had never imagined Jack would be bold enough to carry matters so far. Sheriff Burley was a man of wide experience, keen, practical, shrewd. He was also one of the countless men Wade had rubbed elbows with in the eventful past. It had been Wade's idea that Jack would be satisfied to face his father with the accusation of Moore, and thus cover his tracks. Whatever Old Belllounds might have felt over the loss of a few cattle, he would never have hounded and arrested a cowboy who had done well by him. Burley, however, was a sheriff, and a conscientious one, and he happened to be particularly set against rustlers.

Here was a complication of circumstances. What would Jack Belllounds insist upon? How would Columbine take this plot against the honor and liberty of Wilson Moore? How would Moore himself react to it? Wade confessed that he was helpless to solve these queries, and there seemed to be a further one, insistent and gathering—what was to be his own attitude here? That could not be answered, either, because only a future moment, over which he had no control, and which must decide events, held that secret. Worry beset Wade, but he still found himself proof against the insidious gloom ever hovering near, like his shadow.

He waited near the trail to intercept Billings and Moore on their way to the ranch-house; and to his surprise they appeared sooner than it would have been reasonable to expect them. Wade stepped out of the willows and held up his hand. He did not see anything unusual in Moore's appearance.

"Wils, I reckon we'd do well to talk this over," said Wade.

"Talk what over?" queried the cowboy, sharply.

"Why, Old Bill's sendin' for you, an' the fact of Sheriff Burley bein' here."

"Talk nothing. Let's see what they want, and then talk. Pard, you remember the agreement we made not long ago?"

"Sure. But I'm sort of worried, an' maybe—"

"You needn't worry about me. Come on," interrupted Moore. "I'd like you to be there. And, Lem, fetch the boys."

"I shore will, an' if you need any backin' you'll git it."

When they reached the open Lem turned off toward the corrals, and Wade walked beside Moore's horse up to the house.

Belllounds appeared at the door, evidently having heard the sound of hoofs.

"Hello, Moore! Get down an' come in," he said, gruffly.

"Belllounds, if it's all the same to you I'll take mine in the open," replied the cowboy, coolly.

The rancher looked troubled. He did not have the ease and force habitual to him in big moments.

"Come out hyar, you men," he called in the door.

Voices, heavy footsteps, the clinking of spurs, preceded the appearance of the three strangers, followed by Jack Belllounds. The foremost was a tall man in black, sandy-haired and freckled, with clear gray eyes, and a drooping mustache that did not hide stern lips and rugged chin. He wore a silver star on his vest, packed a gun in a greasy holster worn low down on his right side, and under his left arm he carried a package.

It suited Wade, then, to step forward; and if he expected surprise and pleasure to break across the sheriff's stern face he certainly had not reckoned in vain.

"Wal, I'm a son-of-a-gun!" ejaculated Burley, bending low, with quick movement, to peer at Wade.

"Howdy, Jim. How's tricks?" said Wade, extending his hand, and the smile that came so seldom illumined his sallow face.

"Hell-Bent Wade, as I'm a born sinner!" shouted the sheriff, and his hand leaped out to grasp Wade's and grip it and wring it. His face worked. "My Gawd! I'm glad to see you, old-timer! Wal, you haven't changed at all! ... Ten years! How time flies! An' it's shore you?"

"Same, Jim, an' powerful glad to meet you," replied Wade.

"Shake hands with Bridges an' Lindsay," said Burley, indicating his two comrades. "Stockmen from Grand Lake.... Boys, you've heerd me talk about him. Wade an' I was both in the old fight at Blair's ranch on the Gunnison. An' I've shore reason to recollect him! ... Wade, what're you doin' up in these diggin's?"

"Drifted over last fall, Jim, an' have been huntin' varmints for Belllounds," replied Wade. "Cleaned the range up fair to middlin'. An' since I quit Belllounds I've been hangin' round with my young pard here, Wils Moore, an' interestin' myself in lookin' up cattle tracks."

Burley's back was toward Belllounds and his son, so it was impossible for them to see the sudden little curious light that gleamed in his eyes as he looked hard at Wade, and then at Moore.

"Wils Moore. How d'ye do? I reckon I remember

you, though I don't ride up this way much of late years."

The cowboy returned the greeting civilly enough, but with brevity.

Belllounds cleared his throat and stepped forward. His manner showed he had a distasteful business at hand.

"Moore, I sent for you on a serious matter, I'm sorry to say."

"Well, here I am. What is it?" returned the cowboy, with clear, hazel eyes, full of fire, steady on the old rancher's.

"Jack, you know, is foreman of White Slides now. An' he's made a charge against you."

"Then let him face me with it," snapped Moore.

Jack Belllounds came forward, hands in his pockets, self-possessed, even a little swaggering, and his pale face and bold eyes showed the gravity of the situation and his mastery over it.

Wade watched this meeting of the rivals and enemies with an attention powerfully stimulated by the penetrating scrutiny Burley laid upon them. Jack did not speak quickly. He looked hard into the tense face of Moore. Wade detected a vibration of Jack's frame and a gleam of eye that showed him not wholly in control of exultation and revenge. Fear had not struck him yet.

"Well, Buster Jack, what's the charge?" demanded Moore, impatiently.

The old name, sharply flung at Jack by this cowboy, seemed to sting and reveal and inflame. But he restrained himself as with roving glance he searched Moore's person for sight of a weapon. The cowboy was unarmed.

"I accuse you of stealing my father's cattle," declared Jack, in low, husky accents. After he got the speech out he swallowed hard.

Moore's face turned a dead white. For a fleeting instant a red and savage gleam flamed in his steady glance. Then it vanished.

The cowboys, who had come up, moved restlessly. Lem Billings dropped his head, muttering. Montana Jim froze in his tracks.

Moore's dark eyes, scornful and piercing, never moved from Jack's face. It seemed as if the cowboy would never speak again.

"You call me thief! *You?*" at length he exclaimed.

"Yes, I do," replied Belllounds, loudly.

"Before this sheriff and your father you accuse me of stealing cattle?"

"Yes."

"And you accuse me before this man who saved my life, who *knows* me—before Hell-Bent Wade?" demanded Moore, as he pointed to the hunter.

Mention of Wade in that significant tone of passion and wonder was not without effect upon Jack Belllounds.

"What in hell do I care for Wade?" he burst out, with the old intolerance. "Yes, I accuse you. Thief, rustler!...And for all I know your precious Hell-Bent Wade may be—"

He was interrupted by Burley's quick and authoritive interference.

"Hyar, young man, I'm allowin' for your natural feelin's," he said, dryly, "but I advise you to bite your tongue. I ain't acquainted with Mister Moore, but I happen to know Wade. Do you savvy? . . . Wal, then, if you've any more to say to Moore get it over."

"I've had my say," replied Belllounds, sullenly.

"On what grounds do you accuse me?" demanded Moore.

"I trailed you. I've got my proofs."

Burley stepped off the porch and carefully laid down his package.

"Moore, will you get off your hoss?" he asked. And when the cowboy had dismounted and limped aside the sheriff continued, "Is this the hoss you ride most?"

"He's the only one I have."

Burley sat down upon the edge of the porch and, carefully unwrapping the package, he disclosed some pieces of hard-baked yellow mud. The smaller ones bore the imprint of a circle with a dot in the center, very clearly defined. The larger piece bore the imperfect but reasonably clear track of a curiously shaped horseshoe, somewhat triangular. The sheriff placed these pieces upon the ground. Then he laid hold of Moore's crutch, which was carried like a rifle in a sheath hanging from the saddle, and, drawing it forth, he carefully studied the round cap on the end. Next he inserted this end into both the little circles on the pieces of mud. They fitted perfectly. The cowboys bent over to get a closer view, and Billings was wagging his head. Old Belllounds had an earnest eye for them, also. Burley's next move was to lift the left front foot of Moore's horse and expose the bottom to view. Evidently the white mustang did not like these proceedings, but he behaved himself. The iron shoe on this hoof was somewhat triangular in shape. When Burley held the larger piece of mud, with its imprint, close to the hoof, it was not possible to believe that this iron shoe had not made the triangular-shaped track.

Burley let go of the hoof and laid the pieces of mud down. Slowly the other men straightened up. Some one breathed hard.

"Moore, what do them tracks look like to you?" asked the sheriff.

"They look like mine," replied the cowboy.

"They are yours."

"I'm not denying that."

"I cut them pieces of mud from beside a water-hole over hyar under Gore Peak. We'd trailed the cattle Belllounds lost, an' then we kept on trailin' them, clear to the road that goes over the ridge to Elgeria....Now Bridges an' Lindsay hyar bought stock lately from strange cattlemen who didn't give no clear idee of their range. Jest buyin' an' sellin', they claimed....I reckon the extra hoss tracks we run across at Gore Peak connects up them buyers an' sellers with whoever drove Belllounds's cattle up thar....Have you anythin' more to say?"

"No. Not here," replied Moore, quietly.

"Then I'll have to arrest you an' take you to Kremmlin' fer trial."

"All right. I'll go."

The old rancher seemed genuinely shocked. Red tinged his cheek and a flame flared in his eyes.

"Wils, you done me dirt," he said, wrathfully. "An' I always swore by you....Make a clean breast of the whole damn bizness, if you want me to treat you white. You must have been locoed or drunk, to double-cross me thet way. Come on, out with it."

"I've nothing to say," replied Moore.

"You act amazin' strange fer a cowboy I've knowed to lean toward fightin' at the drop of a hat. I tell you, speak out an' I'll do right by you....I ain't forgettin' thet White Slides gave you a hard knock. An' I was young once an' had hot blood."

The old rancher's wrathful pathos stirred the cowboy to a straining-point of his unnatural, almost haughty composure. He seemed about to break into violent utterance. Grief and horror and anger seemed at the back of his trembling lips. The look he gave Belllounds was assuredly a strange one, to come from a cowboy who was supposed to have stolen his former employer's cattle. Whatever he might have replied was cut off by the sudden appearance of Columbine.

"Dad, I heard you!" she cried, as she swept upon them, fearful and wide-eyed. "What has Wilson Moore done—that you'll do right by him?"

"Collie, go back in the house," he ordered.

"No. There's something wrong here," she said, with mounting dread in the swift glance she shot from man to man. "Oh! You're—Sheriff Burley!" she gasped.

"I reckon I am, miss, an' if young Moore's a friend of yours I'm sorry I came," replied Burley.

Wade himself reacted subtly and thrillingly to the presence of the girl. She was alive, keen, strung, growing white, with darkening eyes of blue fire, beginning to grasp intuitively the meaning here.

"My friend! He *was* more than that—not long ago. ...What has he done? Why are you here?"

"Miss, I'm arrestin' him."

"Oh! . . . For what?"

"Rustlin' your father's cattle."

For a moment Columbine was speechless. Then she burst out, "Oh, there's a terrible mistake!"

"Miss Columbine, I shore hope so," replied Burley, much embarrassed and distressed. Like most men of his kind, he could not bear to hurt a woman. "But it looks bad fer Moore. . . . See hyar! There! Look at the tracks of his hoss—left front foot—shoe all crooked. Thet's his hoss's. He acknowledges thet. An', see hyar! Look at the little circles an' dots. . . . I found these 'way over at Gore Peak, with the tracks of the stolen cattle. An' no *other* tracks, Miss Columbine!"

"Who put you on that trail?" she asked, piercingly.

"Jack, hyar. He found it fust, an' rode to Kremmlin' fer me."

"Jack! Jack Belllounds!" she cried, bursting into wild and furious laughter. Like a tigress she leaped at Jack as if to tear him to pieces. "You put the sheriff on that trail! You accuse Wilson Moore of stealing dad's cattle!"

"Yes, and I proved it," replied Jack, hoarsely.

"You! *You* proved it? So that's your revenge? . . . But you're to reckon with me, Jack Belllounds! You villain! You devil! You—" Suddenly she shrank back with a strong shudder. She gasped. Her face grew ghastly white. "*Oh, my God!* . . . horrible—unspeakable!" . . . She covered her face with her hands, and every muscle of her seemed to contract until she was stiff. Then her hands shot out to Moore.

"Wilson Moore, what have *you* to say—to this sheriff—to Jack Belllounds—to *me?*"

Moore bent upon her a gaze that must have pierced her soul, so like it was to a lightning flash of love and meaning and eloquence.

"Collie, they've got the proof. I'll take my medicine. ...Your dad is good. He'll be easy on me!"

"You lie!" she whispered. "And I will tell why you lie!"

Moore did not show the shame and guilt that should have been natural with his confession. But he showed an agony of distress. His hand sought Wade and dragged at him.

It did not need this mute appeal to tell Wade that in another moment Columbine would have flung the shameful truth into the face of Jack Belllounds. She was rising to that. She was terrible and beautiful to see.

"Collie," said Wade, with that voice he knew had strange power over her, with a clasp of her outflung hand, "no more! This is a man's game. It's not for a woman to judge. Not here! It's Wils's game—an' it's *mine*. I'm his friend. Whatever his trouble or guilt, I take it on my shoulders. An' it will be as if it were not!"

Moaning and wringing her hands, Columbine staggered with the burden of the struggle in her.

"I'm quite—quite mad—or dreaming. Oh, Ben!" she cried.

"Brace up, Collie. It's sure hard. Wils, your friend and playmate so many years—it's hard to believe! We all understand, Collie. Now you go in, an' don't listen to any more or look any more."

He led her down the porch to the door of her room, and as he pushed it open he whispered, "I will save you, Collie, an' Wils, an' the old man you call dad!"

Then he returned to the silent group in the yard.

"Jim, if I answer fer Wils Moore bein' in Kremmlin' the day you say, will you leave him with me?"

"Wal, I shore will, Wade," replied Burley, heartily.

"I object to that," interposed Jack Belllounds, stridently. "He confessed. He's got to go to jail."

"Wal, my hot-tempered young fellar, thar ain't any jail nearer'n Denver. Did you know that?" returned Burley, with his dry, grim humor. "Moore's under arrest. An' he'll be as well off hyar with Wade as with me in Kremmlin', an' a damn sight happier."

The cowboy had mounted, and Wade walked beside him as he started homeward. They had not progressed far when Wade's keen ears caught the words, "Say, Belllounds, I got it figgered thet you an' your son don't savvy this fellar Wade."

"Wal, I reckon not," replied the old rancher.

And his son let out a peal of laughter, bitter and scornful and unsatisfied.

G ORE PEAK was the highest point of the black range that extended for miles westward from Buffalo Park. It was a rounded dome, covered with timber and visible as a landmark from the surrounding country. All along the eastern slope of that range an unbroken forest of spruce and pine spread down to the edge of the valley. This valley narrowed toward its source, which was Buffalo Park. A few well-beaten trails crossed that country, one following Red Brook down to Kremmling; another crossing from the Park to White Slides; and another going over the divide down to Elgeria. The only well-known trail leading to Gore Peak was a branch-off from the valley, and it went round to the south and more accessible side of the mountain.

All that immense slope of timbered ridges, benches,

ravines, and swales west of Buffalo Park was exceedingly wild and rough country. Here the buffalo took to cover from hunters, and were safe until they ventured forth into the parks again. Elk and deer and bear made this forest their home.

Bent Wade, hunter now for bigger game than wild beasts of the range, left his horse at Lewis's cabin and penetrated the dense forest alone, like a deer-stalker or an Indian in his movements. Lewis had acted as scout for Wade, and had ridden furiously down to Sage Valley with news of the rustlers. Wade had accompanied him back to Buffalo Park that night, riding in the dark. There were urgent reasons for speed. Jack Belllounds had ridden to Kremmling, and the hunter did not believe he would return by the road he had taken.

Fox, Wade's favorite dog, much to his disgust, was left behind with Lewis. The bloodhound, Kane, accompanied Wade. Kane had been ill-treated and then beaten by Jack Belllounds, and he had left White Slides to take up his home at Moore's cabin. And at last he had seemed to reconcile himself to the hunter, not with love, but without distrust. Kane never forgave; but he recognized his friend and master. Wade carried his rifle and a buckskin pouch containing meat and bread. His belt, heavily studded with shells, contained two guns, both now worn in plain sight, with the one on the right side hanging low. Wade's character seemed to have undergone some remarkable change, yet what he represented then was not unfamiliar.

He headed for the concealed cabin on the edge of the high valley, under the black brow of Gore Peak. It was early morning of a July day, with summer fresh and new to the forest. Along the park edges the birds and squirrels were holding carnival. The grass was crisp and bediamonded with sparkling frost. Tracks of game showed sharp in the white patches. Wade paused once, listening. Ah! That most beautiful of forest melodies for him—the bugle of an elk. Clear, resonant, penetrating, with these qualities held and blended by a note of wildness, it rang thrillingly through all Wade's being. The hound listened, but was not interested. He kept close beside the hunter or at his heels, a stealthily stepping, warily glancing hound, not scenting the four-footed denizens of the forest. He expected his master to put him on the trail of men.

The distance from the Park to Gore Peak, as a crow would have flown, was not great. But Wade progressed slowly; he kept to the dense parts of the forest; he avoided the open aisles, the swales, the glades, the high ridges, the rocky ground. When he came to the Elgeria trail he was not disappointed to find it smooth, untrodden by any recent travel. Half a mile farther on through the forest, however, he encountered tracks of three horses, made early the day before. Still farther on he found cattle and horse tracks, now growing old and dim. These tracks, pointed toward Elgeria, were like words of a printed page to Wade.

About noon he climbed a rocky eminence that jutted out from a slow-descending ridge, and from this vantage-point he saw down the wavering black and green bosom of the mountain slope. A narrow valley, almost hidden, gleamed yellow in the sunlight. At the edge of this valley a faint column of blue smoke curled upward.

"Ahuh!" muttered the hunter, as he looked. The hound whined and pushed a cool nose into Wade's hand.

Then Wade resumed his noiseless and stealthy course through the woods. He began a descent, leading off somewhat to the right of the point where the smoke had arisen. The presence of the rustlers in the cabin was of importance, yet not so paramount as another possibility. He expected Jack Belllounds to be with them or meet them there, and that was the thing he wanted to ascertain. When he got down below the little valley he swung around to the left to cross the trail that came up from the main valley, some miles still farther down. He found it, and was not surprised to see fresh horse tracks, made that morning. He recognized those tracks. Jack Belllounds was with the rustlers, come, no doubt, to receive his pay.

Then the change in Wade, and the actions of a trailer of men, became more singularly manifest. He reverted to some former habit of mind and body. He was as slow as a shadow, absolutely silent, and the gaze that roved ahead and all around must have taken note of every living thing, of every moving leaf or fern or bough. The hound, with hair curling up stiff on his back, stayed close to Wade, watching, listening, and stepping with him. Certainly Wade expected the rustlers to have some one of their number doing duty as an outlook. So he kept uphill, above the cabin, and made his careful way through the thicket coverts, which at that place were dense and matted clumps of jack-pine and spruce. At last he could see the cabin and the narrow, grassy valley just beyond. To his relief the horses were unsaddled and grazing. No man was in sight. But there might be a dog. The hunter, in his slow advance, used keen and unrelaxing vigilance, and at length he decided that if there had been a dog he would have been tied outside to give an alarm.

Wade had now reached his objective point. He was some eighty paces from the cabin, in line with an open aisle down which he could see into the cleared space before the door. On his left were thick, small spruces, with low-spreading branches, and they extended all the way to the cabin on that side, and in fact screened two walls of it. Wade knew exactly what he was going to do. No longer did he hesitate. Laying down his rifle, he tied the hound to a little spruce, patting him and whispering for him to stay there and be still.

Then Wade's action in looking to his belt-guns was that of a man who expected to have recourse to them speedily and by whom the necessity was neither regretted nor feared. Stooping low, he entered the thicket of spruces. The soft, spruce-matted ground, devoid of brush or twig, did not give forth the slightest sound of step, nor did the brushing of the branches against his body. In some cases he had to bend the boughs. Thus, swiftly and silently, with the gliding steps of an Indian, he approached the cabin till the brown-barked logs loomed before him, shutting off the clearer light.

He smelled a mingling of wood and tobacco smoke; he heard low, deep voices of men; the shuffling and patting of cards; the musical click of gold. Resting on his knees a moment the hunter deliberated. All was exactly as he had expected. Luck favored him. These gamblers would be absorbed in their game. The door of the cabin was just around the corner, and he could glide noiselessly to it or gain it in a few leaps. Either method would serve. But which he must try depended upon the position of the men inside and that of their weapons.

Rising silently, Wade stepped up to the wall and peeped through a chink between the logs. The sunshine streamed through windows and door. Jack Belllounds sat on the ground, full in its light, back to the wall. He was in his shirt-sleeves. The gambling fever and the grievous soreness of a loser shone upon his pale face. Smith sat with back to Wade, opposite Belllounds. The other men completed the square. All were close enough together to reach comfortably for the cards and gold before them. Wade's keen eyes took this in at a single glance, and then steadied searchingly for smaller features of the scene. Belllounds had no weapon. Smith's belt and gun lay in the sunlight on the hard, clay floor, out of reach except by violent effort. The other two rustlers both wore their weapons. Wade gave a long scrutiny to the faces of these comrades of Smith, and evidently satisfied himself as to what he had to expect from them.

Wade hesitated; then stooping low, he softly swept aside the intervening boughs of spruce, glided out of the thicket into the open. Two noiseless bounds! Another, and he was inside the door!

"Howdy, rustlers! Don't move!" he called.

The surprise of his appearance, or his voice, or both, stunned the four men. Belllounds dropped his cards, and his jaw dropped at the same instant. These were absolutely the only visible movements.

"I'm in talkin' humor, an' the longer you listen the longer you'll have to live," said Wade. "But don't move!"

"We ain't movin'," burst out Smith. "Who're you, an' what d'ye want?"

It was singular that the rustler leader had not had a look at Wade, whose movements had been swift and who now stood directly behind him. Also it was obvious that Smith was sitting very stiff-necked and straight. Not improbably he had encountered such situations before.

"Who're you?" he shouted, hoarsely.

"You ought to know me." The voice was Wade's, gentle, cold, with depth and ring in it.

"I've heerd your voice somewhars—I'll gamble on thet."

"Sure. You ought to recognize my voice, Cap," returned Wade.

The rustler gave a violent start—a start that he controlled instantly.

"Cap! You callin' me thet?"

"Sure. We're old friends—*Cap Folsom!*"

In the silence, then, the rustler's hard breathing could be heard; his neck bulged red; only the eyes of his two comrades moved; Belllounds began to recover somewhat from his consternation. Fear had clamped him also, but not fear of personal harm or peril. His mind had not yet awakened to that.

"You've got me pat! But who're you?" said Folsom, huskily.

Wade kept silent.

"Who 'n hell is thet man?" yelled the rustler. It was not a query to his comrades any more than to the four winds. It was a furious questioning of a memory that stirred and haunted, and as well a passionate and fearful denial.

"His name's Wade," put in Belllounds, harshly. "He's the friend of Wils Moore. He's the hunter I told you about—worked for my father last winter."

"Wade? . . . What? *Wade!* You never told me his name. It ain't—it ain't—"

"Yes, it is, Cap," interrupted Wade. "It's the old boy that spoiled your handsome mug—long ago."

"*Hell-Bent Wade!*" gasped Folsom, in terrible accents. He shook all over. An ashen paleness crept into his face. Instinctively his right hand jerked toward his gun; then, as in his former motion, froze in the very act.

"Careful, Cap!" warned Wade. "It'd be a shame not to hear me talk a little. . . . Turn around now an' greet an old pard of the Gunnison days."

Folsom turned as if a resistless, heavy force was revolving his head.

"By Gawd! . . . Wade!" he ejaculated. The tone of his voice, the light in his eyes, must have been a spiritual acceptance of a dreadful and irrefutable fact—perhaps the proximity of death. But he was no coward. Despite the hunter's order, given as he stood there, gun drawn and ready, Folsom wheeled back again, savagely to throw the deck of cards in Belllounds's face. He cursed horribly. . . . "You spoiled brat of a rich rancher! Why 'n hell didn't you tell me thet varmint-hunter was Wade."

"I did tell you," shouted Belllounds, flaming of face.

"You're a liar! You never said Wade—W-a-d-e, right out, so I'd hear it. An' I'd never passed by Hell-Bent Wade."

"Aw, that name made me tired," replied Belllounds, contemptuously.

"Haw! Haw! Haw!" bawled the rustler. "Made you tired, hey? Think you're funny? Wal, if you knowed how many men thet name's made tired—an' tired fer keeps—you'd not think it so damn funny."

"Say, what 're you giving me? That Sheriff Burley tried to tell me and dad a lot of rot about this Wade. Why, he's only a little, bow-legged, big-nosed meddler—a man with a woman's voice—a sneaking cook and camp-doctor and cow-milker, and God only knows what else."

"Boy, you're correct. God only knows what else! . . . It's the *else* you've got to learn. An' I'll gamble you'll learn it. . . . Wade, have you changed or grown old thet you let a pup like this yap such talk?"

"Well, Cap, he's very amusin' just now, an' I want you-all to enjoy him. Because, if you don't force my hand I'm goin' to tell you some interestin' stuff about this Buster Jack. . . . Now, will you be quiet an' listen—an' answer for your pards?"

"Wade, I answer fer no man. But, so far as I've noticed, my pards ain't hankerin' to make any loud noise," Folsom replied, indicating his comrades, with sarcasm.

The red-bearded one, a man of large frame and gaunt face, wicked and wild-looking, spoke out, "Say, Smith, or whatever the hell's yore right handle—is this hyar a game we're playin'?"

"I reckon. An' if you turn a trick you'll be damn lucky," growled Folsom.

The other rustler did not speak. He was small,

swarthy-faced, with sloe-black eyes and matted hair, evidently a white man with Mexican blood. Keen, strung, furtive, he kept motionless, awaiting events.

"Buster Jack, these new pards of yours are low-down rustlers, an' one of them's worse, as I could prove," said Wade, "but compared with you they're all gentlemen."

Belllounds leered. But he was losing his bravado. Something began to dawn upon his obtuse consciousness.

"What do I care for you or your gabby talk?" he flashed, sullenly.

"You'll care when I tell these rustlers how you double-crossed them."

Belllounds made a spring, like that of a wolf in a trap; but when half-way up he slipped. The rustler on his right kicked him, and he sprawled down again, back to the wall.

"Buster, look into this!" called Wade, and he leveled the gun that quivered momentarily, like a compass needle, and then crashed fire and smoke. The bullet spat into a log. But it had cut the lobe of Belllounds's ear, bringing blood. His face turned a ghastly, livid hue. All in a second terror possessed him—shuddering, primitive terror of death.

Folsom haw-hawed derisively and in crude delight. "Say, Buster Jack, don't get any idee thet my ole pard Wade was shootin' at your head. Aw, no!"

The other rustlers understood then, if Belllounds had not, that the situation was in control of a man not in any sense ordinary.

"Cap, did you know Buster Jack accused my friend,

Wils Moore, of stealin' these cattle you're sellin'?" asked Wade, deliberately.

"What cattle did you say?" asked the rustler, as if he had not heard aright.

"The cattle Buster Jack stole from his father an' sold to you."

"Wal, now! Bent Wade at his old tricks! I might have knowed it, once I seen you.... Naw, I'd no idee Belllounds blamed thet stealin' on to any one."

"He did."

"Ahuh! Wal, who's this Wils Moore?"

"He's a cowboy, as fine a youngster as ever straddled a horse. Buster Jack hates him. He licked Jack a couple of times an' won the love of a girl that Jack wants."

"Ho! Ho! Quite romantic, I declare.... Say, thar's some damn queer notions I'm gettin' about you, Buster Jack."

Belllounds lay propped against the wall, sagging there, laboring of chest, sweating of face. The boldness of brow held, because it was fixed, but that of his eyes had gone; and his mouth and chin showed craven weakness. He stared in dread suspense at Wade.

"Listen. An' all of you sit tight," went on Wade, swiftly. "Jack stole the cattle from his father. He's a thief at heart. But he had a double motive. He left a trail—he left tracks behind. He made a crooked horseshoe, like that Wils Moore's horse wears, an' he put that on his own horse. An' he made a contraption—a little iron ring with a dot in it, an' he left the crooked shoe tracks, an' he left the little ring tracks—"

"By Gawd! I seen them funny tracks!" ejaculated

Folsom. "At the water-hole an' right hyar in front of the cabin. I seen them. I knowed Jack made them, somehow, but I didn't think. His white hoss has a crooked left front shoe."

"Yes, he has, when Jack takes off the regular shoe an' nails on the crooked one....Men, I followed those tracks. They lead up here to your cabin. Belllounds made them with a purpose....An' he went to Kremmlin' to get Sheriff Burley. An' he put him wise to the rustlin' of cattle to Elgeria. An' he fetched him up to White Slides to accuse Wils Moore. An' he trailed his own tracks up here, showin' Burley the crooked horse track an' the little circle—that was supposed to be made by the end of Moore's crutch—an' he led Burley with his men right to this cabin an' to the trail where you drove the cattle over the divide....An' then he had Burley dig out some cakes of mud holdin' these tracks, an' they fetched them down to White Slides. Buster Jack blamed the stealin' on to Moore. An' Burley arrested Moore. The trial comes off next week at Kremmlin'."

"Damn me!" exclaimed Folsom, wonderingly. "A man's never too old to learn! I knowed this pup was stealin' from his own father, but I reckoned he was jest a natural-born, honest rustler, with a hunch fer drink an' cards."

"Well, he's double-crossed you, Cap. An' if I hadn't rounded you up your chances would have been good for swingin'."

"Ahuh! Wade, I'd sure preferred them chances of swingin' to your over-kind interferin' in my bizness. Allus interferin', Wade, thet's your weakness!...But gimme a gun!"

"I reckon not, Cap."

"Gimme a gun!" roared the rustler. "Lemme sit hyar an' shoot the eyes outen this—lyin' pup of a Belllounds! ... Wade, put a gun in my hand—a gun with two shells— or only one. You can stand with your gun at my head. ...Let me kill this skunk!"

For all Belllounds could tell, death was indeed close. No trace of a Belllounds was apparent about him then, and his face was a horrid spectacle for a man to be forced to see. A froth foamed over his hanging lower lip.

"Cap, I ain't trustin' you with a gun just this particular minute," said Wade.

Folsom then bawled his curses to his comrades.

"———! Kill him! Throw your guns an' bore him—right in them bulgin' eyes!...I'm tellin' you— we've gotta fight, anyhow. We're agoin' to cash right hyar. But kill him first!"

Neither of Folsom's lieutenants yielded to the fierce exhortation of their leader or to their own evilly expressed passions. It was Wade who dominated them. Then ensued a silence fraught with suspense, growing more charged every long instant. The balance here seemed about to be struck.

"Wade, I've been a gambler all my life, an' a damn smart one, if I do say it myself," declared the rustler leader, his voice inharmonious with the facetiousness of his words. "An' I'll make a last bet."

"Go ahead, Cap. What'll you bet?" answered the cold voice, still gentle, but different now in its inflection.

"By Gawd! I'll bet all the gold hyar that Hell-Bent Wade wouldn't shoot any man in the back!"

"You win!"

Slowly and stiffly the rustler rose to his feet. When he reached his height he deliberately swung his leg to kick Belllounds in the face.

"Thar! I'd like to have a reckonin' with you, Buster Jack," he said. "I ain't dealin' the cards hyar. But somethin' tells me thet, shaky as I am in my boots, I'd liefer be in mine than yours."

With that, and expelling a heavy breath, he wrestled around to confront the hunter.

"Wade. I've no hunch to your game, but it's slower 'n I recollect you."

"Why, Cap, I was in a talkin' humor," replied Wade.

"Hell! You're up to some dodge. What'd you care fer my learnin' thet pup had double-crossed me? You won't let me kill him."

"I reckon I wanted him to learn what real men thought of him."

"Ahuh! Wal, an' now I've onlightened him, what's the next deal?"

"You'll all go to Kremmlin' with me an' I'll turn you over to Sheriff Burley."

That was the gauntlet thrown down by Wade. It was not unexpected, and acceptance seemed a relief. Folsom's eyeballs became living fire with the desperate gleam of the reckless chances of life. Cutthroat he might have been, but he was brave, and he proved the significance of Wade's attitude.

"Pards, hyar's to luck!" he rang out, hoarsely, and with pantherish quickness he leaped for his gun.

A tense, surcharged instant—then all four men, as if released by some galvanized current of rapidity, flashed into action. Guns boomed in unison. Spurts of red, clouds of smoke, ringing reports, and hoarse cries filled the cabin. Wade had fired as he leaped. There was a thudding patter of lead upon the walls. The hunter flung himself prostrate behind the bough framework that had served as bedstead. It was made of spruce boughs, thick and substantial. Wade had not calculated falsely in estimating it as a bulwark of defense. Pulling his second gun, he peeped from behind the covert.

Smoke was lifting, and drifting out of door and windows. The atmosphere cleared. Belllounds sagged against the wall, pallid, with protruding eyes of horror on the scene before him. The dark-skinned little man lay writhing. All at once a tremor stilled his convulsions. His body relaxed limply. As if by magic his hand loosened on the smoking gun. Folsom was on his knees, reeling and swaying, waving his gun, peering like a drunken man for some lost object. His temple appeared half shot away, a bloody and horrible sight.

"Pards, I got him!" he said, in strange, half-strangled whisper. "I got him! . . . Hell-Bent Wade! My respects! I'll meet you—thar!"

His reeling motion brought his gaze in line with Belllounds. The violence of his start sent drops of blood flying from his gory temple.

"Ahuh! The cards run—my way. Belllounds, hyar's to your—lyin' eyes!"

The gun wavered and trembled and circled. Folsom strained in last terrible effort of will to aim it straight. He fired. The bullet tore hair from Belllounds's head, but missed him. Again the rustler aimed, and the gun wavered and shook. He pulled trigger. The hammer clicked upon an empty chamber. With low and gurgling cry of baffled rage Folsom dropped the gun and sank face forward, slowly stretching out.

The red-bearded rustler had leaped behind the stone chimney that all but hid his body. The position made it difficult for him to shoot because his gun-hand was on the inside, and he had to press his body tight to squeeze it behind the corner of ragged stone. Wade had the advantage. He was lying prone with his right hand round the corner of the framework. An overhang of the bough-ends above protected his head when he peeped out. While he watched for a chance to shoot he loaded his empty gun with his left hand. The rustler strained and writhed his body, twisting his neck, and suddenly darting out his head and arm, he shot. His bullet tore the overhang of boughs above Wade's face. And Wade's answering shot, just a second too late, chipped the stone corner where the rustler's face had flashed out. The bullet, glancing, hummed out of the window. It was a close shave. The rustler let out a hissing, inarticulate cry. He was trapped. In his effort to press in closer he projected his left elbow beyond the corner of the chimney. Wade's quick shot shattered his arm.

There was no asking or offering of quarter here. This was the old feud of the West—of the vicious and the righteous in strife—both reared in the same stern school. The rustler gave his body such contortion that he was twisted almost clear around, with his right hand over his left shoulder. He punched the muzzle of his gun into a crack between two stones, and he pried to open them. The dry clay cement crumbled, the crack widened. Sighting along the barrel he alined it with the narrow strip of Wade's shoulder that was visible above the framework. Then he shot and hit. Wade shrank flatter and closer, hiding himself to better advantage. The rustler made his great blunder then, for in that moment he might have rushed out and killed his adversary. But, instead, he shot again—another time—a third. And his heavy bullets tore and splintered the boughs dangerously close to the hunter's head. Then came an awkward, almost hopeless task for the rustler, in maintaining his position while reloading his gun. He did it, and his panting attested to the labor and pain it cost him.

So much, in fact, that he let his knee protrude. Wade fired, breaking that knee. The rustler sagged in his tracks, his hip stuck out to afford a target for the remorseless Wade. Still the doomed man did not cry out, though it was evident that he could not now keep his body from sagging into sight of the hunter. Then with a desperate courage worthy of a better cause, and with a spirit great in its defeat, the rustler plunged out from his hiding-place, gun extended. His red beard, his gaunt face, fierce and baleful, his wabbling plunge that was really a fall, made a sight which was terrible. He hopped out of that fall. His gun began to blaze. But it only matched the blazes of Wade's. And the rustler pitched headlong over the framework, falling heavily against the wall beyond.

Then there was silence for a long moment. Wade stirred, as if to look around. Belllounds also stirred, and gulped, as if to breathe. The three prostrate rustlers lay inert, their positions singularly tragic and settled. The smoke again began to lift, to float out of the door and windows. In another moment the big room seemed less hazy.

Wade rose, not without effort, and he had a gun in each hand. Those hands were bloody; there was blood on his face, and his left shoulder was red. He approached Belllounds.

Wade was terrible then—terrible with a ruthlessness that was no pretense. To Belllounds it must have represented death—a bloody death which he was not prepared to meet.

"Come out of your trance, you pup rustler!" yelled Wade.

"For God's sake, don't kill me!" implored Belllounds, stricken with terror.

"Why not? Look around! My busy day, Buster!... An' for that Cap Folsom it's been ten years comin'.... I'm goin' to shoot you in the belly an' watch you get sick to your stomach!"

Belllounds, with whisper, and hands, and face, begged for his life in an abjectness of sheer panic.

"What!" roared the hunter. "Didn't you know I come to kill you?"

"Yes—yes! I've seen—that. It's awful!...I never harmed you....Don't kill me! Let me live, Wade. I swear to God I'll—I'll never do it again....For dad's sake—for Collie's sake—don't kill me!"

"I'm Hell-Bent Wade!...You wouldn't listen to them—when they wanted to tell you who I am!"

Every word of Wade's drove home to this boy the primal meaning of sudden death. It inspired him with an unutterable fear. That was what clamped his brow in a sweaty band and upreared his hair and rolled his eyeballs. His magnified intelligence, almost ghastly, grasped a hope in Wade's apparent vacillation and in the utterance of the name of Columbine. Intuition, a subtle sense, inspired him to beg in that name.

"Swear you'll give up Collie!" demanded Wade, brandishing his guns with bloody hands.

"Yes—yes! My God, I'll do anything!" moaned Bell-lounds.

"Swear you'll tell your father you'd had a change of heart. You'll give Collie up!...Let Moore have her!"

"I swear!...But if you tell dad—I stole his cattle—he'll do for me!"

"We won't squeal that. I'll save you if you give up the girl. Once more, Buster Jack—try an' make me believe you'll square the deal."

Belllounds had lost his voice. But his mute, fluttering lips were infinite proof of the vow he could not speak. The boyishness, the stunted moral force, replaced the manhood in him then. He was only a factor in the lives of others, protected even from this Nemesis by the greatness of his father's love.

"Get up, an' take my scarf," said Wade, "an' bandage these bullet-holes I got."

CHAPTER

18

WADE'S wounds were not in any way serious, and with Belllounds's assistance he got to the cabin of Lewis, where weakness from loss of blood made it necessary that he remain. Belllounds went home.

The next day Wade sent Lewis with pack-horse down to the rustler's cabin, to bury the dead men and fetch back their effects. Lewis returned that night, accompanied by Sheriff Burley and two deputies, who had been busy on their own account. They had followed horse tracks from the water-hole under Gore Peak to the scene of the fight, and had arrived to find Lewis there. Burley had appropriated the considerable amount of gold, which he said could be identified by cattlemen who had bought the stolen cattle.

When opportunity afforded Burley took advantage

of it to speak to Wade when the others were out of earshot.

"Thar was another man in thet cabin when the fight come off," announced the sheriff. "An' he come up hyar with you."

"Jim, you're locoed," replied Wade.

The sheriff laughed, and his shrewd eyes had a kindly, curious gleam.

"Next you'll be givin' me a hunch thet you're in a fever an' out of your head."

"Jim, I'm not as clear-headed as I might be."

"Wal, tell me or not, jest as you like. I seen his tracks—follered them. An' Wade, old pard, I've reck-oned long ago thar's a nigger in the wood-pile."

"Sure. An' you know me. I'd take it friendly of you to put Moore's trial off fer a while—till I'm able to ride to Kremmlin'. Maybe then I can tell you a story."

Burley threw up his hands in genuine apprehen-sion. "Not much! You ain't agoin' to tell *me* no story! ...But I'll wait on you, an' welcome. Reckon I owe you a good deal on this rustler round-up. Wade, thet must have been a man-sized fight, even fer you. I picked up twenty-six empty shells. An' the little half-breed had one empty shell an' five loaded ones in his gun. You must have got him quick. Hey?"

"Jim, I'm observin' you're a heap more curious than ever, an' you always was an inquisitive cuss," com-plained Wade. "I don't recollect what happened."

"Wal, wal, have it your own way," replied Burley, with good nature. "Now, Wade, I'll pitch camp hyar in the park to-night, an' to-morrer I'll ride down to White

Slides on my way to Kremmlin'. What're you wantin' me to tell Belllounds?"

The hunter pondered a moment.

"Reckon it's just as well that you tell him somethin'.... You can say the rustlers are done for an' that he'll get his stock back. I'd like you to tell him that the rustlers were more to blame than Wils Moore. Just say that an' nothin' else about Wils. Don't mention about your suspectin' there was another man around when the fight come off.... Tell the cowboys that I'll be down in a few days. An' if you happen to get a chance for a word alone with Miss Collie, just say I'm not bad hurt an' that all will be well."

"Ahuh!" Burley grunted out the familiar exclamation. He did not say any more then, but he gazed thoughtfully down upon the pale hunter, as if that strange individual was one infinitely to respect, but never to comprehend.

Wade's wounds healed quickly; nevertheless, it was more than several days before he felt spirit enough to undertake the ride. He had to return to White Slides, but he was reluctant to do so. Memory of Jack Belllounds dragged at him, and when he drove it away it continually returned. This feeling was almost equivalent to an augmentation of his gloomy foreboding, which ever hovered on the fringe of his consciousness. But one morning he started early, and, riding very slowly, with many rests, he reached the Sage Valley cabin before sunset. Moore saw him coming, yelled his delight and concern, and almost lifted him off the horse. Wade was too tired to talk much, but he allowed himself to be fed and put to bed and worked over.

"Boot's on the other foot now, pard," said Moore, with delight at the prospect of returning service. "Say, you're all shot up! And it's I who'll be nurse!"

"Wils, I'll be around to-morrow," replied the hunter. "Have you heard any news from down below?"

"Sure. I've met Lem every night."

Then he related Burley's version of Wade's fight with the rustlers in the cabin. From the sheriff's lips the story gained much. Old Bill Belllounds had received the news in a singular mood; he offered no encomiums to the victor; contrary to his usual custom of lauding every achievement of labor or endurance, he now seemed almost to regret the affray. Jack Belllounds had returned from Kremmling and he was present when Burley brought news of the rustlers. What he thought none of the cowboys vouchsafed to say, but he was drunk the next day, and he lost a handful of gold to them. Never had he gambled so recklessly. Indeed, it was as if he hated the gold he lost. Little had been seen of Columbine, but little was sufficient to make the cowboys feel concern.

Wade made scarcely any comment upon this news from the ranch; next day, however, he was up, and caring for himself, and he told Moore about the fight and how he had terrorized Belllounds and exhorted the promises from him.

"Never in God's world will Buster Jack live up to those promises!" cried Moore, with absolute conviction. "I know him, Ben. He meant them when he made them. He'd swear his soul away—then next day he'd lie or forget or betray."

"I'm not believin' that till I know," replied the hunter, gloomily. "But I'm afraid of him.... I've known bad men to change. There's a grain of good in all men—somethin' divine. An' it comes out now an' then. Men rise on steppin'-stones of their dead selves to higher things!... This is Belllounds's chance for the good in him. If it's not there he will do as you say. If it is—that scare he had will be the turnin'-point in his life. I'm hopin', but I'm afraid."

"Ben, you wait and see," said Moore, earnestly. "Heaven knows I'm not one to lose hope for my fellow-men—hope for the higher things you've taught me.... But human nature is human nature. Jack *can't* give Collie up, just the same as I *can't*. That's self-preservation as well as love."

The day came when Wade walked down to White Slides. There seemed to be a fever in his blood, which he tried to convince himself was a result of his wounds instead of the condition of his mind. It was Sunday, a day of sunshine and squall, of azure-blue sky, and great, sailing, purple clouds. The sage of the hills glistened and there was a sweetness in the air.

The cowboys made much of Wade. But the old rancher, seeing him from the porch, abruptly went into the house. No one but Wade noticed this omission of courtesy. Directly, Columbine appeared, waving her hand, and running to meet him.

"Dad saw you. He told me to come out and excuse him.... Oh, Ben, I'm so happy to see you! You don't look hurt at all. What a fight you had!... Oh, I was sick! But let me forget that.... How are you? And how's Wils?"

Thus she babbled until out of breath.

"Collie, it's sure good to see you," said Wade, feeling the old, rich thrill at her presence. "I'm comin' on tolerable well. I wasn't bad hurt, but I bled a lot. An' I reckon I'm older 'n I was when packin' gun-shot holes was nothin'. Every year tells. Only a man doesn't know till after.... An' how are you, Collie?"

Her blue eyes clouded, and a tremor changed the expression of her sweet lips.

"I am unhappy, Ben," she said. "But what could we expect? It might be worse. For instance, you might have been killed. I've much to be thankful for."

"I reckon so. We all have.... I fetched a message from Wils, but I oughtn't tell it."

"Please do," she begged, wistfully.

"Well, Wils says, tell Collie I love her every day more an' more, an' that my love keeps up my courage an' my belief in God, an' if she ever marries Jack Bell-lounds she can come up to visit my grave among the columbines on the hill."

Strange how Wade experienced comfort in thus torturing her! She was rosy at the beginning of his speech and white at its close. "Oh, it's true! it's true!" she whispered. "It'll kill him, as it will me!"

"Cheer up, Columbine," said Wade. "It's a long time till August thirteenth.... An' now tell me, why did Old Bill run when he saw me comin'?"

"Ben, I suspect dad has the queerest notion you want to tell him some awful bloody story about the rustlers."

"Ahuh! Well, not yet.... An' how's Jack Belllounds actin' these days?"

Wade felt the momentousness of that query, but it seemed her face had been telltale enough, without confirmation of words.

"My friend, somehow I hate to tell you. You're always so hopeful, so ready to think good instead of evil. ...But Jack has been rough with me, almost brutal. He was drunk once. Every day he drinks, sometimes a little, sometimes more. But drink changes him. And it's dragging dad down. Dad doesn't say so, yet I feel he's afraid of what will come next....Jack has nagged me to marry him right off. He wanted to the day he came back from Kremmling. He's eager to leave White Slides. Dad knows that, also, and it worries him. But of course I refused."

The presence of Columbine, so vivid and sweet and stirring, and all about her the sunlight, the golden gleams on the sage hills, and Wade's heart and brain and spirit sustained a subtle transformation. It was as if what had been beautiful with light had suddenly, strangely darkened. Then Wade imagined he stood alone in a gloomy house, which was his own heart, and he was listening to the arrival of a tragic messenger whose foot sounded heavy on the stairs, whose hand turned slowly upon the knob, whose gray presence opened the door and crossed the threshold.

"Buster Jack didn't break off with you, Collie?" asked the hunter.

"Break off with me!...No, indeed! Whatever possessed you to say that?"

"An' he didn't offer to give you up to Wils Moore?"

"Ben, are you crazy?" cried Columbine.

"Collie, listen. I'll tell you." The old urge knocked at Wade's mind. "Buster Jack was in the cabin, gamblin'

with the rustlers, when I cornered them. You remember
I meant to scare Buster Jack within an inch of his life?
Well, I made use of my opportunity. I worked up the
rustlers. Then I told Jack I'd give away his secret. He
made to jump an' run, I reckon. But he hadn't the nerve.
I shot a piece out of his ear, just to begin the fun. An'
then I told the rustlers how Jack had double-crossed
them. Folsom, the boss rustler, roared like a mad steer.
He was wild to kill Jack. He begged for a gun to shoot
out Jack's eyes. An' so were the other rustlers burnin'
to kill him. Bad outfit. There was a fight, which, I'm
bound to confess, was not short an' sweet. There was
a lot of shootin'. An' in a cabin gunshots almost lift the
roof. Folsom was on his knees, dyin', wavin' his gun,
whisperin' in fiendish glee that he had done for me.
When he saw Jack an' remembered he shook so with
fury that he scattered blood all over. An' he took long
aim at Jack, tryin' to steady his gun. He couldn't, an' he
missed, an' then fell over dead with his head on Jack's
knees. That left the red-bearded rustler, who had hid
behind the chimney. Jack watched the rest of that fight,
an' for a youngster it must have been nerve-rackin'. I
broke the rustler's arm, an' then his knee, an' then I got
him in the hip two more times before he hobbled out
to his finish. He'd shot me up considerable, so that when
I braced Jack I must have been a hair-raisin' sight. I
made Jack believe I meant to murder him. He begged
an' cried, an' he got to prayin' for his life for your sake.
It was sickenin', but it was what I wanted. So then I
made him swear he'd free you an' give you up to Moore."

"Oh! Oh, Ben, how awful!" whispered Columbine,

shuddering. "How *could* you tell me such a horrible story?"

"Reckon I wanted you to know how Jack come to make the promises an' what they were."

"Promises! What are promises or oaths to Jack Belllounds?" she cried, in passionate contempt. "You wasted your breath. Coward—liar that he is!"

"Ahuh!" Wade looked straight ahead of him as if he saw some expected and unpleasant thing far in the distance. Then with irresistible steps, neither swift nor slow, but ponderous, he strode to the porch and mounted the steps.

"Why, Ben, where are you going?" called Columbine, in surprise, as she followed him.

He did not answer. He approached the closed door of the living-room.

"Ben!" cried Columbine, in alarm.

But he had no reply for her—indeed, no thought of her. Without knocking, he opened the door with rude and powerful hand, and, striding in, closed it after him.

Bill Belllounds was standing, back against the great stone chimney, arms folded, a stolid and grim figure, apparently fortified against an intrusion he had expected.

"Wal, what do you want?" he asked, gruffly. He had sensed catastrophe in the first sight of the hunter.

"Belllounds, I reckon I want a hell of a lot," replied Wade. "An' I'm askin' you to see we're not disturbed."

"Bar the door."

Wade dropped the bar in place, and then, removing his sombrero, he wiped his moist brow.

"Do you see an enemy in me?" he asked, curiously.

"Speakin' out fair, Wade, there ain't any reason I can see that you're an enemy to me," replied Belllounds. "But I feel somethin'. It ain't because I'm takin' my son's side. It's more than that. A queer feelin', an' one I never had before. I got it first when you told the story of the Gunnison feud."

"Belllounds, we can't escape our fates. An' it was written long ago I was to tell you a worse an' harder story than that."

"Wal, mebbe I'll listen an' mebbe I won't. I ain't promisin', these days."

"Are you goin' to make Collie marry Jack?" demanded the hunter.

"She's willin'."

"You know that's not true. Collie's willin' to sacrifice love, honor, an' life itself, to square her debt to you."

The old rancher flushed a burning red, and in his eyes flared a spirit of earlier years.

"Wade, you can go too far," he warned. "I'm appreciation' your good-heartedness. It sort of warms me toward you....But this is my business. You've no call to interfere. You've done that too much already. An' I'm reckonin' Collie would be married to Jack now if it hadn't been for you."

"Ahuh!...That's why I'm thankin' God I happened along to White Slides. Belllounds, your big mistake is thinkin' your son is good enough for this girl. An' you're makin' mistakes about me. I've interfered here, an' you may take my word for it I had the right."

"Strange talk, Wade, but I'll make allowances."

"You needn't. I'll back my talk....But, first, I'm

askin' you—an' if this talk hurts, I'm sorry—why don't you give some of your love for your no-good Buster Jack to Collie?"

Belllounds clenched his huge fists and glared. Anger leaped within him. He recognized in Wade an outspoken, bitter adversary to his cherished hopes for his son and his stubborn, precious pride.

"By Heaven! Wade, I'll—"

"Belllounds, I can make you swallow that kind of talk," interrupted Wade. "It's man to man now. An' I'm a match for you any day. Savvy?...Do you think I'm damn fool enough to come here an' brace you unless I knew that. Talk to me as you'd talk about some other man's son."

"It ain't possible," rejoined the rancher, stridently.

"Then listen to me first....Your son Jack, to say the least, will ruin Collie. Do you see that?"

"By Gawd! I'm afraid so," groaned Belllounds, big in his humiliation. "But it's my one last bet, an' I'm goin' to play it."

"Do you know marryin' him will *kill* her?"

"What!...You're overdoin' your fears, Wade. Women don't die so easy."

"Some of them die, an' Collie's one that will, *if* she ever marries Jack."

"*If!*...Wal, she's goin' to."

"We don't agree," said Wade, curtly.

"Are you runnin' my family?"

"No. But I'm runnin' a large-sized *if* in this game. You'll admit that presently....Belllounds, you make me mad. You don't meet me man to man. You're not the Bill Belllounds of old. Why, all over this state of Colorado you're known as the whitest of the white. Your name's a byword for all that's square an' big an' splendid. But you're so blinded by your worship of that wild boy that you're another man in all pertainin' to him. I don't want to harp on his shortcomin's. I'm for the girl. She doesn't love him. She can't. She will only drag herself down an' die of a broken heart. . . . Now, I'm askin' you, before it's too late—give up this marriage."

"Wade! I've shot men for less than you've said!" thundered the rancher, beside himself with rage and shame.

"Ahuh! I reckon you have. But not men like me. . . . I tell you, straight to your face, it's a fool deal you're workin'—a damn selfish one—a dirty job, to put on an innocent, sweet girl—an' as sure as you stand there, if you do it, you'll ruin four lives!"

"Four!" exclaimed Belllounds. But any word would have expressed his humiliation.

"I should have said three, leavin' Jack out. I meant Collie's an' yours an' Wils Moore's."

"Moore's is about ruined already, I've a hunch."

"You can get hunches you never dreamed of, Belllounds, old as you are. An' I'll give you one presently. . . . But we drift off. Can't you keep cool?"

"Cool! With you rantin' hell-bent for election? Haw! Haw! . . . Wade, you're locoed. You always struck me queer. . . . An' if you'll excuse me, I'm gettin' tired of this talk. We're as far apart as the poles. An' to save what good feelin's we both have, let's quit."

"You don't love Collie, then?" queried Wade, imperturbably.

"Yes, I do. That's a fool idee of yours. It puts me out of patience."

"Belllounds, you're not her real father."

The rancher gave a start, and he stared as he had stared before, fixedly and perplexedly at Wade.

"No, I'm not."

"If she *were* your real daughter—your own flesh an' blood—an' Jack Belllounds was *my* son, would you let her marry him?"

"Wal, Wade, I reckon I wouldn't."

"Then how can you expect my consent to her marriage with your son?"

"WHAT!" Belllounds lunged over to Wade, leaned down, shaken by overwhelming amaze.

"Collie is my daughter!"

A loud expulsion of breath escaped Belllounds. Lower he leaned, and looked with piercing gaze into the face and eyes that in this moment bore strange resemblance to Columbine.

"So help me Gawd! . . . That's the secret? . . . Hell-Bent Wade! An' you've been on my trail!"

He staggered to his big chair and fell into it. No trace of doubt showed in his face. The revelation had struck home because of its very greatness.

Wade took the chair opposite. His likeness to Columbine had faded now. It had been love, a spirit, a radiance, a glory. It was gone. And Wade's face became the emblem of tragedy.

"Listen, Belllounds. I'll tell you! . . . The ways of God are inscrutable I've been twenty years tryin' to atone for the wrong I did Collie's mother. I've been a prospector for the trouble of others. I've been a bearer of their burdens. An' if I can save Collie's happiness an' her soul, I reckon I won't be denied the peace of meetin' her mother in the other world. . . . I recognized Collie the moment I laid eyes on her. She favors her mother in looks, an' she has her mother's sensitiveness, her fire an' pride, an' she even has her voice. It's low an' sweet— alto, they used to call it. . . . But I'd recognized Collie as my own if I'd been blind an' deaf. . . . It's over eighteen years ago that we had the trouble. I was no boy, but I was terribly in love with Lucy. An' she loved me with a passion I never learned till too late. We came West from Missouri. She was born in Texas. I had a rovin' disposition an' didn't stick long at any kind of work. But I was lookin' for a ranch. My wife had some money an' I had high hopes. We spent our first year of married life travelin' through Kansas. At Dodge I got tied up for a while. You know, in them days Dodge was about the wildest camp on the plains. My wife's brother run a place there. He wasn't much good. But she thought he was perfect. Strange how blood-relations can't see the truth about their own people! Anyway, her brother Spencer had no use for me, because I could tell how slick he was with the cards an' beat him at his own game. Spencer had a gamblin' pard, a cowboy run out of Texas, one Cap Fol—But no matter about his name. One night they were fleecin' a stranger an' I broke into the game, winnin' all they had. The game ended in a fight, with bloodshed, but nobody killed. That set Spencer an' his pard Cap against me. The stranger was a planter from Louisiana. He'd been an officer in the rebel army. A high-strung, handsome Southerner, fond of wine an' cards an' women. Well, he got to payin' my wife a good deal of attention when I was away, which happened to be often. She never told me. I was jealous those days.

"My little girl you call Columbine was born there durin' a long absence of mine. When I got home Lucy an' the baby were gone. Also the Southerner!...Spencer an' his pard Cap, an' others they had in the deal, proved to me, so it seemed, that the little girl was not really mine!...An' so I set out on a hunt for my wife an' her lover. I found them. An' I killed him before her eyes. But she was innocent, an' so was he, as came out too late. He'd been, indeed, her friend. She scorned me. She told me how her brother Spencer an' his friends had established guilt of mine that had driven her from me.

"I went back to Dodge to have a little quiet smoke with these men who had ruined me. They were gone. The trail led to Colorado. Nearly a year later I rounded them all up in a big wagon-train post north of Denver. Another brother of my wife's, an' her father, had come West, an' by accident or fate we all met there. We had a family quarrel. My wife would not forgive me—would not speak to me, an' her people backed her up. I made the great mistake to take her father an' other brothers to belong to the same brand as Spencer. In this I wronged them an' her.

"What I did to them, Belllounds, is one story I'll never tell to any man who might live to repeat it. But it drove my wife near crazy. An' it made me Hell-Bent Wade!...She ran off from me there, an' I trailed her all over Colorado. An' the end of that trail was not a hundred miles from where we stand now. The last trace

I had was of the burnin' of a prairie-schooner by Arapahoes as they were goin' home from a foray on the Utes.... The little girl might have toddled off the trail. But I reckon she was hidden or dropped by her mother, or some one fleein' for life. Your men found her in the columbines."

Belllounds drew a long, deep breath.

"What a man never expects always comes true.... Wade, the lass is yours. I can see it in the way you look at me. I can feel it.... She's been like my own. I've done my best, accordin' to my conscience. An' I've loved her, for all they say I couldn't see aught but Jack.... You'll take her away from me?"

"No. Never," was the melancholy reply.

"What! Why not?"

"Because she loves you.... I could never reveal myself to Collie. I couldn't win her love with a lie. An' I'd have to lie, to be false as hell.... False to her mother an' to Collie an' to all I hold high! I'd have to tell Collie the truth—the wrong I did her mother—the *hell* I visited upon her mother's people.... She'd fear me."

"Ahuh!...An' you'll never change—I reckon that!" exclaimed Belllounds.

"No. I changed once, eighteen years ago. I can't go back.... I can't undo all I hoped was good."

"You think Collie 'd fear you?"

"She'd never *love* me as she does you, or as she loves me even now. That is my rock of refuge."

"She'd hate you, Wade."

"I reckon. An' so she must never know."

"Ahuh!...Wal, wal, life is a hell of a deal! Wade, if you could live yours over again, knowin' what you know

now, an' that you'd love an' suffer the same—would you want to do it?"

"Yes. I love life, with all it brings. I wouldn't have the joy without the pain. But I reckon only men who've come to our years would want it over again."

"Wal, I'm with you thar. I'd take what came. Rain an sun!...But all this you tell, an' the hell you hint at, ain't changin' this hyar deal of Jack's an' Collie's. Not one jot!...If she remains my adopted daughter she marries my son....Wade, I'm haltered like the north star in that."

"Belllounds, will you take a day to think it over?" appealed Wade.

"Ahuh! But that won't change me."

"Won't it change you to know that if you force this marriage you'll lose all?"

"All! Ain't that more queer talk?"

"I mean lose all—your son, your adopted daughter—his chance of reformin', her hope of happiness. These ought to be all in life left to you."

"Wal, they are. But I can't see your argument. You're beyond me, Wade. You're holdin' back, like you did with your hell-bent story."

Ponderously, as if the burden and the doom of the world weighed him down, the hunter got up and fronted Belllounds.

"When I'm driven to tell I'll come....But, once more, old man, choose between generosity an' selfishness. Between blood tie an' noble loyalty to your good deed in its beginnin'....Will you give up this marriage for your son—so that Collie can have the man she loves?"

"You mean your young pard an' two-bit of a rustler—Wils Moore?"

"Wils Moore, yes. My friend, an' a man, Belllounds, such as you or I never was."

"No!" thundered the rancher, purple in the face.

With bowed head and dragging step Wade left the room.

By slow degrees of plodding steps, and periods of abstracted lagging, the hunter made his way back to Moore's cabin. At his entrance the cowboy leaped up with a startled cry.

"Oh, Wade!... Is Collie dead?" he cried.

Such was the extent of calamity he imagined from the somber face of Wade.

"No. Collie's well."

"Then, man, what on earth's happened?"

"Nothin' yet....But somethin' is goin' on in my mind....Moore, I'd like you to let me alone."

At sunset Wade was pacing the aspen grove on the hill. There was sunlight and shade under the trees, a rosy gold on the sage slopes, a purple-and-violet veil between the black ranges and the sinking sun.

Twilight fell. The stars came out white and clear. Night cloaked the valley with dark shadows and the hills with its obscurity. The blue vault overhead deepened and darkened. The hunter patrolled his beat, and hours were moments to him. He heard the low hum of the insects, the murmur of running water, the rustle of the wind. A coyote cut the keen air with high-keyed, staccato cry. The owls hooted, with dismal and weird plaint, one to the other. Then a wolf mourned. But these sounds only accentuated the loneliness and wildness of the silent night.

Wade listened to them, to the silence. He felt the wildness and loneliness of the place, the breathing of nature; he peered aloft at the velvet blue of the mysterious sky with its deceiving stars. All that had been of help to him through days of trial was now as if it had never been. When he lifted his eyes to the great, dark peak, so bold and clear-cut against the sky, it was not to receive strength again. Nature in its cruelty mocked him. His struggle had to do with the most perfect of nature's works—man.

Wade was now in passionate strife with the encroaching mood that was a mocker of his idealism. Many times during the strange, long martyrdom of his penance had he faced this crisis, only to go down to defeat before elemental instincts. His soul was steeped in gloom, but his intelligence had not yet succumbed to passion. The beauty of Columbine's character and the nobility of Moore's were not illusions to Wade. They were true. These two were of the finest fiber of human nature. They loved. They represented youth and hope—a progress through the ages toward a better race. Wade believed in the good to be, in the future of men. Nevertheless, all that was fine and worthy in Columbine and Moore was to go unrewarded, unfulfilled, because of the selfish pride of an old man and the evil passion of the son. It was a conflict as old as life. Of what avail were Columbine's high sense of duty, Moore's fine manhood, the many victories they had won over the headlong and imperious desires of love?

What avail were Wade's good offices, his spiritual teaching, his eternal hope in the order of circumstances working out to good? These beautiful characteristics of virtue were not so strong as the unchangeable passion of old Belllounds and the vicious depravity of his son. Wade could not imagine himself a god, proving that the wages of sin was death. Yet in his life he had often been an impassive destiny, meting out terrible consequences. Here he was incalculably involved. This was the cumulative end of years of mounting plots, tangled and woven into the web of his pain and his remorse and his ideal. But hope was dying. That was his strife-realization against the morbid clairvoyance of his mind. He could not help Jack Belllounds to be a better man. He could not inspire the old rancher to a forgetfulness of selfish and blinded aims. He could not prove to Moore the truth of the reward that came from unflagging hope and unassailable virtue. He could not save Columbine with his ideals.

The night wore on, and Wade plodded under the rustling aspens. The insects ceased to hum, the owls to hoot, the wolves to mourn. The shadows of the long spruces gradually merged into the darkness of night. Above, infinitely high, burned the pale stars, wise and cold, aloof and indifferent, eyes of other worlds of mystery.

In those night hours something in Wade died, but his idealism, unquenchable and inexplicable, the very soul of the man, saw its justification and fulfillment in the distant future.

The gray of the dawn stole over the eastern range, and before its opaque gloom the blackness of night

retreated, until valley and slope and grove were
shrouded in spectral light, where all seemed unreal.

And with it the gray-gloomed giant of Wade's mind,
the morbid and brooding spell, had gained its long-
encroaching ascendancy. He had again found the man
to whom he must tell his story. Tragic and irrevocable
decree! It was his life that forced him, his crime, his
remorse, his agony, his endless striving. How true had
been his steps! They had led, by devious and tortuous
paths, to the home of his daughter.

Wade crouched under the aspens, accepting this
burden as a man being physically loaded with tremendous weights. His shoulders bent to them. His
breast was sunken and labored. All his muscles were
cramped. His blood flowed sluggishly. His heart beat
with slow, muffled throbs in his ears. There was a
creeping cold in his veins, ice in his marrow, and
death in his soul. The giant that had been shrouded
in gray threw off his cloak, to stand revealed, black
and terrible. And it was he who spoke to Wade, in
dreadful tones, like knells. Bent Wade—man of misery—who could find no peace on earth—whose presence unknit the tranquil lives of people and poisoned
their blood and marked them for doom! Wherever he
wandered there followed the curse! Always this had
been so. He was the harbinger of catastrophe. He who
preached wisdom and claimed to be taught by the
flowers, who loved life and hated injustice, who mingled with his kind, ever searching for that one who
needed him, he must become the woe and the bane
and curse of those he would only serve! Insupportable
and pitiful fate! The fiends of the past mocked him,

like wicked ghouls, voiceless and dim. The faces of the men he had killed were around him in the gray gloom, pale, drifting visages of distortion, accusing him, claiming him. Likewise, these gleams of faces were specters of his mind, a procession eternal, mournful, and silent, wending their way on and on through the regions of his thought. All were united, all drove him, all put him on the trail of catastrophe. They foreshadowed the future, they inclosed events, they lured him with his endless illusions. He was in the vortex of a vast whirlpool, not of water or of wind, but of life. Alas! he seemed indeed the very current of that whirlpool, a monstrous force, around which evil circled and lurked and conquered. Wade—who had the ill-omened croak of the raven—Wade—who bent his driven steps toward hell!

In the brilliant sunlight of the summer morning Wade bent his resistless steps down toward White Slides Ranch. The pendulum had swung. The hours were propitious. Seemingly, events that already cast their shadows waited for him. He saw Jack Belllounds going out on the fast and furious ride which had become his morning habit.

Columbine intercepted Wade. The shade of woe and tragedy in her face were the same as he had pictured there in his gloomy vigil of the night.

"My friend, I was coming to you. . . . Oh, I can bear no more!"

Her hair was disheveled, her dress disordered, the hands she tremblingly held out bore discolored marks. Wade led her into the seclusion of the willow trail.

"Oh, Ben!...He fought me—like—a beast!" she panted.

"Collie, you needn't tell me more," said Wade, gently. "Go up to Wils. Tell him."

"But I must tell you. I can bear—no more....He fought me—hurt me—and when dad heard us—and came—Jack lied....Oh, the dog!...Ben, his father believed—when Jack swore he was only mad—only trying to shake me—for my indifference and scorn....But, my God!—Jack meant..."

"Collie, go up to Wils," interposed the hunter.

"I want to see Wils. I need to—I must. But I'm afraid. ...Oh, it will make things worse!"

"Go!"

She turned away, actuated by more than her will.

"*Collie!*" came the call, piercingly and strangely after her. Bewildered, startled by the wildness of that cry, she wheeled. But Wade was gone. The shaking of the willows attested to his hurry.

Old Belllounds braced his huge shoulders against the wall in the attitude of a man driven to his last stand.

"Ahuh!" he rolled, sonorously. "So hyar you are again?...Wal, tell your worst, Hell-Bent Wade, an' let's have an end to your croakin'."

Belllounds had fortified himself, not with convictions or with illusions, but with the last desperate courage of a man true to himself.

"I'll tell you..." began the hunter.

And the rancher threw up his hands in a mockery that was furious, yet with outward shrinking.

"Just now, when Buster Jack fought with Collie, he meant bad by her!"

"Aw, no! . . . He was jest rude—tryin' to be masterful. . . . An' the lass's like a wild filly. She needs a tamin' down."

Wade stretched forth a lean and quivering hand that seemed the symbol of presaged and tragic truth.

"Listen, Belllounds, an' I'll tell you. . . . No use tryin' to hatch a rotten egg! There's no good in your son. His good intentions he paraded for virtues, believin' himself that he'd changed. But a flip of the wind made him Buster Jack again. . . . Collie would sacrifice her life for duty to you—whom she loves as her father. Wils Moore sacrificed his honor for Collie—rather than let you learn the truth. . . . But they call me Hell-Bent Wade, an' *I* will tell you!"

The straining hulk of Belllounds crouched lower, as if to gather impetus for a leap. Both huge hands were outspread as if to ward off attack from an unseen but long-dreaded foe. The great eyes rolled. And underneath the terror and certainty and tragedy of his appearance seemed to surge the resistless and rising swell of a dammed-up, terrible rage.

"I'll tell you . . ." went on the remorseless voice. "I watched your Buster Jack. I watched him gamble an' drink. I trailed him. I found the little circles an' the crooked horse tracks—made to trap Wils Moore. . . . A damned cunnin' trick! . . . Burley suspects a nigger in the wood-pile. Wils Moore knows the truth. He lied for Collie's sake an' yours. He'd have stood the trial—an' gone to jail to save Collie from what she dreaded. . . . Belllounds, your son was in the cabin gamblin' with the rustlers when I cornered them.... I offered to keep Jack's secret if he'd swear to give Collie up. He swore on his knees, beggin' in her name!...An' he comes back to bully her, an' worse....Buster Jack!... He's the thorn in your heart, Belllounds. He's the rustler who stole your cattle!...Your pet son—a sneakin' thief!"

J ACK BELLOUNDS came riding down the valley trail. His horse was in a lather of sweat. Both hair and blood showed on the long spurs this son of a great pioneer used in his pleasure rides. He had never loved a horse.

At a point where the trail met the brook there were thick willow patches, with open, grassy spots between. As Belllounds reached this place a man stepped out of the willows and laid hold of the bridle. The horse shied and tried to plunge, but an iron arm held him.

"Get down, Buster," ordered the man.

It was Wade.

Belllounds had given as sharp a start as his horse. He was sober, though the heated red tinge of his face gave indication of a recent use of the bottle. That color quickly receded. Events of the last month had left traces of the hardening and lowering of Jack Belllounds's nature.

"Wha-at? ...Let go that bridle!" he ejaculated.

Wade held it fast, while he gazed up into the prominent eyes, where fear shone and struggled with intolerance and arrogance and quickening gleams of thought.

"You an' I have somethin' to talk over," said the hunter.

Belllounds shrank from the low, cold, even voice, that evidently reminded him of the last time he had heard it.

"No, we haven't," he declared, quickly. He seemed to gather assurance with his spoken thought and conscious fear left him. "Wade, you took advantage of me that day—when you made me swear things. I've changed my mind....And as for that deal with the rustlers, I've got my story. It's as good as yours. I've been waiting for you to tell my father. You've got some reason for not telling him. I've a hunch it's Collie. I'm on to you, and I've got my nerve back. You can gamble I—"

He had grown excited when Wade interrupted him.

"Will you get off that horse?"

"No, I won't," replied Belllounds, bluntly.

With swift and powerful lunge Wade pulled Belllounds down, sliding him shoulders first into the grass. The released horse shied again and moved away. Buster Jack raised himself upon his elbow, pale with rage and alarm. Wade kicked him, not with any particular violence.

"Get up!" he ordered.

The kick had brought out the rage in Belllounds at

the expense of the amaze and alarm.

"Did you kick *me?*" he shouted.

"Buster, I was only handin' you a bunch of flowers—some columbines, as your taste runs," replied Wade, contemptuously.

"I'll—I'll—" returned Buster Jack, wildly, bursting for expression. His hand went to his gun.

"Go ahead, Buster. Throw your gun on me. That'll save maybe a hell of a lot of talk."

It was then Jack Belllounds's face turned livid. Comprehension had dawned upon him.

"You—you want me to fight you?" he queried, in hoarse accents.

"I reckon that's what I meant."

No affront, no insult, no blow could have affected Buster Jack as that sudden knowledge.

"Why—why—you're crazy! Me fight you—a gunman," he stammered. "No—no. It wouldn't be fair. Not an even break!...No, I'd have no chance on earth!"

"I'll give you first shot," went on Wade, in his strange, monotonous voice.

"Bah! You're lying to me," replied Belllounds, with pale grimace. "You just want me to get a gun in my hand—then you'll drop me, and claim an even break."

"No. I'm square. You saw me play square with your rustler pard. He was a lifelong enemy of mine. An' a gun-fighter to boot!...Pull your gun an' let drive. I'll take my chances."

Buster Jack's eyes dilated. He gasped huskily. He pulled his gun, but actually did not have strength or courage enough to raise it. His arm shook so that the gun rattled against his chaps.

"No nerve, hey? Not half a man!...Buster Jack, why don't you finish game? Make up for your low-down tricks. At the last try to be worthy of your dad. In his day he was a real man....Let him have the consolation that you faced Hell-Bent Wade an' died in your boots!"

"I—can't—fight you!" panted Belllounds. "I know now!...I saw you throw a gun! It wouldn't be fair!"

"But I'll make you fight me," returned Wade, in steely tones. "I'm givin' you a chance to dig up a little manhood. Askin' you to meet me man to man! Handin' you a little the best of it to make the odds even!...Once more, will you be game?"

"Wade, I'll not fight—I'm going—" replied Bell-lounds, and he moved as if to turn.

"Halt!..." Wade leaped at the white Belllounds. "If you run I'll break a leg for you—an' then I'll beat your miserable brains out!...Have you no sense? Can't you recognize what's comin'?...*I'm goin' to kill you, Buster Jack!*"

"My God!" whispered the other, understanding fully at last.

"Here's where you pay for your dirty work. The time comes to every man. You've a choice, not to live—for you'll never get away from Hell-Bent Wade—but to rise above yourself at last."

"But what for? Why do you want to kill me? I never harmed you."

"Columbine is my daughter!" replied the hunter.

"Ah!" breathed Belllounds.

"She loves Wils Moore, who's as white a man as you are black."

Across the pallid, convulsed face of Belllounds

spread a slow, dull crimson.

"Aha, Buster Jack! I struck home there," flashed Wade, his voice rising. "That gives your eyes the ugly look.... I hate them lyin', bulgin' eyes of yours. An' when my time comes to shoot I'm goin' to put them both out."

"By Heaven! Wade, you'll have to kill me if you ever expect that club-foot Moore to get Collie!"

"He'll get her," replied Wade, triumphantly. "Collie's with him now. I sent her. I told her to tell Wils how you tried to force her—"

Belllounds began to shake all over. A torture of jealous hate and deadly terror convulsed him.

"Buster, did you ever think you'd get her kisses—as Wils's gettin' right now?" queried the hunter. "Good Lord! the conceit of some men! . . . Why, you poor, weak-minded, cowardly pet of a blinded old man—you conceited ass—you selfish an' spoiled boy! . . . Collie never had any use for you. An' now she hates you."

"It was you who made her!" yelled Belllounds, foaming at the mouth.

"Sure," went on the deliberate voice, ringing with scorn. "An' only a little while ago she called you a dog. . . . I reckon she meant a different kind of a dog than the hounds over there. For to say they were like you would be an insult to them. . . . Sure she hates you, an' I'll gamble right now she's got her arms around Wils's neck!"

"———!" hissed Belllounds.

"Well, you've got a gun in your hand," went on the taunting voice. "Ahuh! . . . Have it your way. I'm warmin' up now, an' I'd like to tell you . . ."

"Shut up!" interrupted the other, frantically. The blood in him was rising to a fever heat. But fear still clamped him. He could not raise the gun and he seemed in agony.

"Your father knows you're a thief," declared Wade, with remorseless, deliberate intent. "I told him how I watched you—trailed you—an' learned the plot you hatched against Wils Moore.... Buster Jack busted himself at last, stealin' his own father's cattle.... I've seen some ragin' men in my day, but Old Bill had them beaten. You've disgraced him—broken his heart—embittered the end of his life.... An' he'd mean for you what I mean now!"

"He'd never—harm me!" gasped Buster Jack, shuddering.

"He'd kill you—you white-livered pup!" cried Wade, with terrible force. "Kill you before he'd let you go to worse dishonor!...An' I'm goin' to save him stainin' his hands."

"I'll kill *you!*" burst out Belllounds, ending in a shriek. But this was not the temper that always produced heedless action in him. It was hate. He could not raise the gun. His intelligence still dominated his will. Yet fury had mitigated his terror.

"You'll be doin' me a service, Buster.... But you're mighty slow at startin'. I reckon I'll have to play my last trump to make you fight. Oh, by God! I can tell you!... Belllounds, there're dead men callin' me now. Callin' me not to murder you in cold blood! I killed one man once—a man who wouldn't fight—an innocent man! I killed him with my bare hands, an' if I tell you my story— an' how I killed him—an' that I'll do the same for you. ...You'll save me that, Buster. No man with a gun in his hands could face what he knew....But save me more. Save me the tellin'!"

"No! No! I won't listen!"

"Maybe I won't have to," replied Wade, mournfully. He paused, breathing heavily. The sober calm was gone.

Belllounds lowered the half-raised gun, instantly answering to the strange break in Wade's strained dominance.

"Don't tell me—any more! I'll not listen!...I won't fight! Wade, you're crazy! Let me off an' I swear—"

"Buster, I told Collie you were three years in jail!" suddenly interrupted Wade.

A mortal blow dealt Belllounds would not have caused such a shock of amaze, of torture. The secret of the punishment meted out to him by his father! The hideous thing which, instead of reforming, had ruined him! All of hell was expressed in his burning eyes.

"Ahuh!...I've known it long!" cried Wade, tragically. "Buster Jack, you're the man who must hear my story....*I'll tell you....*"

In the aspen grove up the slope of Sage Valley Columbine and Wilson were sitting on a log. Whatever had been their discourse, it had left Moore with head bowed in his hands, and with Columbine staring with sad eyes that did not see what they looked at. Columbine's mind then seemed a dull blank. Suddenly she started.

"Wils!" she cried. "Did you hear—anything?"

"No," he replied, wearily raising his head.

"I thought I heard a shot," said Columbine. "It—it sort of made me jump. I'm nervous."

Scarcely had she finished speaking when two clear, deep detonations rang out. Gun-shots!

"There!...Oh, Wils! Did you hear?"

"Hear!" whispered Moore. He grew singularly white. "Yes—yes!...Collie—"

"Wils," she interrupted, wildly, as she began to shake. "Just a little bit ago—I saw Jack riding down the trail!"

"Collie!...Those two shots came from Wade's gun! I'd know it among a thousand!...Are you sure you heard a shot before?"

"Oh, something dreadful has happened! Yes, I'm sure. Perfectly sure. A shot not so loud or heavy."

"My God!" exclaimed Moore, staring aghast at Columbine. "Maybe that's what Wade meant. I never saw through him."

"Tell me. Oh, I don't understand!" wailed Columbine, wringing her hands.

Moore did not explain what he meant. For a crippled man, he made quick time in getting to his horse and mounting.

"Collie, I'll ride down there. I'm afraid something has happened....I never understood him!...I forgot he was Hell-Bent Wade! If there's been a—a fight or any trouble—I'll ride back and meet you."

Then he rode down the trail.

Columbine had come without her horse, and she started homeward on foot. Her steps dragged. She knew something dreadful had happened. Her heart beat slowly and painfully; there was an oppression upon her breast; her brain whirled with contending tides of thought. She remembered Wade's face. How blind she had been! It exhausted her to walk, though she went so slowly. There seemed to be a chill and a darkening in the atmosphere, an unreality in the familiar slopes and groves, a strangeness and shadow upon White Slides Valley.

Moore did not return to meet her. His white horse grazed in the pasture opposite the first clump of willows, where Sage Valley merged into the larger valley. Then she saw other horses, among them Lem Billings's bay mustang. Columbine faltered on, when suddenly she recognized the horse Jack had ridden—a sorrel, spent and foam-covered, standing saddled, with bridle down and riderless—then certainty of something awful clamped her with horror. Men's husky voices reached her throbbing ears. Some one was running. Footsteps thudded and died away. Then she saw Lem Billings come out of the willows, look her way, and hurry toward her. His awkward, cowboy gait seemed too slow for his earnestness. Columbine felt the piercing gaze of his eyes as her own became dim.

"Miss Collie, thar's been—turrible fight!" he panted.

"Oh, Lem! . . . I know. It was Ben—and Jack," she cried.

"Shore. Your hunch's correct. An' it couldn't be no wuss!"

Columbine tried to see his face, the meaning that must have accompanied his hoarse voice; but she seemed going blind.

"Then—then—" she whispered, reaching out for Lem.

"Hyar, Miss Collie," he said, in great concern, as

he took kind and gentle hold of her. "Reckon you'd better wait. Let me take you home."

"Yes. But tell—tell me first," she cried, frantically. She could not bear suspense, and she felt her senses slipping away from her.

"My Gawd! who'd ever have thought such hell would come to White Slides!" exclaimed Lem, with strong emotion. "Miss Collie, I'm powerful sorry fer you. But mebbe it's best so.... They're both dead!... Wade just died with his head on Wils's lap. But Jack never knowed what hit him. He was shot plumb center—both his eyes shot out!... Wade was shot low down.... Montana an' me agreed thet Jack throwed his gun first an' Wade killed him after bein' mortal shot himself."

Late that afternoon, as Columbine lay upon her bed, the strange stillness of the house was disturbed by a heavy tread. It passed out of the living-room and came down the porch toward her door. Then followed a knock.

"Dad!" she called, swiftly rising.

Belllounds entered, leaving the door ajar. The sunlight streamed in.

"Wal, Collie, I see you're bracin' up," he said.

"Oh yes, dad, I'm—I'm all right," she replied, eager to help or comfort him.

The old rancher seemed different from the man of the past months. The pallor of a great shock, the havoc of spent passion, the agony of terrible hours, showed in his face. But Old Bill Belllounds had come into his own again—back to the calm, iron pioneer who had lived all events, over whom storm of years had broken,

whose great spirit had accepted this crowning catastrophe as it had all the others, who saw his own life
clearly, now that its bitterest lesson was told.

"Are you strong enough to bear another shock, my
lass, an' bear it now—so to make an end—so to-morrer
we can begin anew?" he asked, with the voice she had
not heard for many a day. It was the voice that told of
consideration for her.

"Yes, dad," she replied, going to him.

"Wal, come with me. I want you to see Wade."

He led her out upon the porch, and thence into the
living-room, and from there into the room where lay
the two dead men, one on each side. Blankets covered
the prone, quiet forms.

Columbine had meant to beg to see Wade once
before he was laid away forever. She dreaded the ordeal,
yet strangely longed for it. And here she was self-
contained, ready for some nameless shock and uplift,
which she divined was coming as she had divined the
change in Belllounds.

Then he stripped back the blanket, disclosing
Wade's face. Columbine thrilled to the core of her heart.
Death was there, white and cold and merciless, but as
it had released the tragic soul, the instant of deliverance
had been stamped on the rugged, cadaverous visage,
by a beautiful light; not of peace, nor of joy, nor of grief,
but of hope! Hope had been the last emotion of Hell-
Bent Wade.

"Collie, listen," said the old rancher, in deep and
trembling tones. "When a man's dead, what he's been
comes to us with startlin' truth. Wade was the whitest
man I ever knew. He had a queer idee—a twist in his

mind—an' it was thet his steps were bent toward hell.
He imagined thet everywhere he traveled there he
fetched hell. But he was wrong. His own trouble led him
to the trouble of others. He saw through life. An' he was
as big in his hope fer the good as he was terrible in his
dealin' with the bad. I never saw his like. . . . He loved
you, Collie, better than you ever knew. Better than Jack,
or Wils, or me! You know what the Bible says about
him who gives his life fer his friend. Wal, Wade was my
friend, an' Jack's, only we never could see! . . . An' he
was Wils's friend. An' to you he must have been more
than words can tell. . . . We all know what child's play it
would have been fer Wade to kill Jack without bein'
hurt himself. But he wouldn't do it. So he spared me
an' Jack, an' I reckon himself. Somehow he made Jack
fight an' die like a man. God only knows how he did
that. But it saved me from—from hell—an' you an' Wils
from misery. . . . Wade could have taken you from me
an' Jack. He had only to tell you his secret, an' he
wouldn't. He saw how you loved me, as if you were my
real child. . . . But, Collie, lass, it was *he* who was your
father!"

With bursting heart Columbine fell upon her knees
beside that cold, still form.

Belllounds softly left the room and closed the door
behind him.

*N*ATURE was prodigal with her colors that autumn. The frosts came late, so that the leaves did not gradually change their green. One day, as if by magic, there was gold among the green, and in another there was purple and red. Then the hilltops blazed with their crowns of aspen groves; and the slopes of sage shone mellow gray in the sunlight; and the vines on the stone fences straggled away in lines of bronze; and the patches of ferns under the cliffs faded fast; and the great rock slides and black-timbered reaches stood out in their somber shades.

Columbines bloomed in all the dells among the spruces, beautiful stalks with heavy blossoms, the sweetest and palest of blue-white flowers. Motionless they lifted their faces to the light. Out in the aspen groves, where the grass was turning gold, the columbines blew gracefully in the wind, nodding and swaying. The most exquisite and finest of these columbines hid in the shaded nooks, starsweet in the silent gloom of the woods.

Wade's last few whispered words to Moore had been interpreted that the hunter desired to be buried among the columbines in the aspen grove on the slope above Sage Valley. Here, then, had been made his grave.

One day Belllounds sent Columbine to fetch Moore down to White Slides. It was a warm, Indian-summer afternoon, and the old rancher sat out on the porch in his shirt-sleeves. His hair was white now, but no other change was visible in him. No restraint attended his greeting to the cowboy.

"Wils, I reckon I'd be glad if you'd take your old job as foreman of White Slides," he said.

"Are you asking me?" queried Moore, eagerly.

"Wal, I reckon so."

"Yes, I'll come," replied the cowboy.

"What'll your dad say?"

"I don't know. That worries me. He's coming to visit me. I heard from him again lately, and he means to take stage for Kremmling soon."

"Wal, that's fine. I'll be glad to see him.... Wils, you're goin' to be a big cattleman before you know it. Hey, Collie?"

"If you say so, dad, it'll come true," replied Columbine, with her hand on his shoulder.

"Wils, you'll be runnin' White Slides Ranch before long, unless Collie runs you. Haw! Haw!"

Collie could not reply to this startling announcement from the old rancher, and Moore appeared distressed with embarrassment.

"Wal, I reckon you young folks had better ride down to Kremmlin' an' get married."

This kindly, matter-of-fact suggestion completely stunned the cowboy, and all Columbine could do was to gaze at the rancher.

"Say, I hope I ain't intrudin' my wishes on a young couple that's got over dyin' fer each other," dryly continued Belllounds, with his huge smile.

"Dad!" cried Columbine, and then she threw her arms around him and buried her head on his shoulder.

"Wal, wal, I reckon that answers that," he said, holding her close. "Moore, she's yours, with my blessin' an' all I have....An' you must understand I'm glad things have worked out to your good an' to Collie's happiness. ...Life's not over fer me yet. But I reckon the storms are past, thank God!...We learn as we live. I'd hold it unworthy not to look forward an' to hope. I'm wantin' peace an' quiet now, with grandchildren around me in my old age....So ride along to Kremmlin' an' hurry home."

The evening of the day Columbine came home to White Slides the bride of Wilson Moore she slipped away from the simple festivities in her honor and climbed to the aspen grove on the hill to spend a little while beside the grave of her father.

The afterglow of sunset burned dull gold and rose in the western sky, rendering glorious the veil of purple over the ranges. Down in the lowlands twilight had come, softly gray. The owls were hooting; a coyote barked; from far away floated the mourn of a wolf.

Under the aspens it was silent and lonely and sad. The leaves quivered without any sound of rustling. Columbine's heart was full of a happiness that she longed to express somehow, there beside this lonely grave. It was what she owed the strange man who slept here in the shadows. Grief abided with her, and always there would be an eternal remorse and regret. Yet she had loved him. She had been his, all unconsciously. His life had been terrible, but it had been great. As the hours of quiet thinking had multiplied, Columbine had grown in her divination of Wade's meaning. His had been the spirit of man lighting the dark places; his had been the ruthless hand against all evil, terrible to destroy.

Her father! After all, how closely was she linked to the past! How closely protected, even in the hours of most helpless despair! Thus she understood him. Love was the food of life, and hope was its spirituality, and beauty was its reward to the seeing eye. Wade had lived these great virtues, even while he had earned a tragic name.

"I will live them. I will have faith and hope and love, for I am his daughter," she said. A faint, cool breeze strayed through the aspens, rustling the leaves whisperingly, and the slender columbines, gleaming pale in the twilight, lifted their sweet faces.

Columbine Would Honor Her Promise to Marry Jack Belllounds But Her Heart Was With Another Man . . .

"Dad said you were willing to marry me. Is that so?"

Columbine dropped her head. His question, kindly put, did not affront her, for it had been expected. But his actual presence, the meaning of his words, stirred in her an unutterable spirit of protest. She had already in her will consented to the demand of the old man; she was learning, however, that she could not force her flesh to consent to a surrender it did not desire.

"Yes, I'm willing," she replied bravely.

HarperPaperbacks by Zane Grey

THE DUDE RANGER
THE LOST WAGON TRAIN
THE MAN OF THE FOREST
THE RAINBOW TRAIL
WILDFIRE
THE BORDER LEGION
SUNSET PASS
30,000 ON THE HOOF
WANDERER OF THE WASTELAND
TWIN SOMBREROS
BOULDER DAM
THE MYSTERIOUS RIDER
THE DEER STALKER
THE TRAIL DRIVER
THE DESERT OF WHEAT
THE U. P. TRAIL
TO THE LAST MAN
WESTERN UNION
THUNDER MOUNTAIN
CODE OF THE WEST
ARIZONA AMES
THE THUNDERING HERD
HORSE HEAVEN HILL
VALLEY OF WILD HORSES
ROGUE RIVER FEUD
WILDERNESS TREK
BLACK MESA
THE VANISHING AMERICAN
CAPTIVES OF THE DESERT
THE SPIRIT OF THE BORDER
ROBBERS' ROOST
UNDER THE TONTO RIM

WILD HORSE MESA
THE MAVERICK QUEEN
THE LIGHT OF WESTERN STARS
MAJESTY'S RANCHO
WYOMING
THE CALL OF THE CANYON
FORLORN RIVER
RAIDERS OF SPANISH PEAKS
THE DAY OF THE BEAST
THE REEF GIRL
THE SHEPHERD OF GUADALOUPE
LOST PUEBLO
STRANGER FROM THE TONTO
KNIGHTS OF THE RANGE
WEST OF THE PECOS
SHADOW ON THE TRAIL
RIDERS OF THE PURPLE SAGE
STAIRS OF SAND
BETTY ZANE
THE ARIZONA CLAN
THE HASH KNIFE OUTFIT
THE HERITAGE OF THE DESERT
THE DRIFT FENCE
FIGHTING CARAVANS
THE LONE STAR RANGER
TAPPAN'S BURRO
THE FUGITIVE TRAIL
THE RANGER AND OTHER STORIES
BLUE FEATHER AND OTHER
    STORIES
DESERT GOLD
NEVADA